PRAISE FOR SAVING THE MUSIC

"In Saving the Music, author Chip LoCoco writes of the efforts undertaken by common villagers, priests, and even a Pope to protect Jews from the Nazis. He vividly depicts the horrors faced by the Jews as they confront the Holocaust. Filled with real heroism and high drama, this book brings perspective and depth to its subject. It's an exciting read on an important topic, and I strongly recommend it."

-Ronald Rychlak, Author of *Hitler, the War, and the Pope*

"This is a well composed novel that captures key moments of the Holocaust as it relates to the Italian people. I highly recommend it."

-Professor Vincent Lapomarda, S.J., Author of *The Jesuits and the Third Reich*

"This is a well-researched novel and reflects the situation as it then existed, hopefully, never to return."

-Fr. Peter Gumpel, S.J., postulator of the cause of beautification for Pius XII

"Chip LoCoco's novel, Saving the Music, is a realistic fact-based story of pain, fear and true heroism. The premise is solidly grounded on documented facts of the actions of the Catholic Church under the Pontificate of Pope Pius XII down to priests and individual Catholics. Saving the Music is an exciting and engrossing read, which joins the list of wonderful truth-based books of late that is shedding light on the truth ending the worst character assassination of the 20th Century. Bravo."

-Gary L. Krupp, Author of *Pope Pius XII and World War II- The Documented Truth*

BOOKS BY VINCENT LOCOCO

Tempesta's Dream:

A Story of Love, Friendship and Opera

BELLAFORTUNA SERIES

A Song for Bellafortuna - Book 1

Saving the Music - Book 2

SAVING THE MUSIC

A NOVEL

VINCENT B. "CHIP" LOCOCO

Cefalutana Press

AMDG

FOR MY FATHER

VINCENT THEODORE LOCOCO
1934-2017

CONTENTS

Music, when soft voices die,
  vibrates in the memory.

— PERCY SHELLEY

SAVING THE MUSIC

PREFACE

Even in silence, there is music. Silence descends and cloaks like a fog; words, actions, even thoughts can be hidden within it. Silence can unwittingly appear when words fail, or it can intentionally be culled as a strategy. It may deceive in its purpose, perhaps to disguise actions for good or to conceal indifference, disdain, intolerance, or evil. Silence may lay to rest pain, angst, or troubling thoughts, as it has the capacity to soothe and give peace. And in that regard, silence closely mirrors music.

However, unlike silence, music never deceives as it is always honest, real and universal. Music is like a spirit that rises up within the silence, within memories, within hearts and touches our innermost being.

But it is when music and silence combine that a powerful means of expression is formed, brightening the soul the same way a full moon illuminates the dark sky on a clear night.

There was silence over Rome on that cloudless, cold December night while a full moon hung high above. For the Eternal City, it was a peaceful night during a very tumultuous time. War raged across Europe. Italy had forged an alliance with Adolf Hitler's Germany, sealed with a pact of steel, creating a vice grip of oppression and fear.

Italian fathers and sons were off fighting for the Axis in a war, which by late 1942, much of the population no longer supported. However, Fascism still ruled Italy under the tutelage of Benito Mussolini, who held Rome under his brutal, ruthless boot.

In the very heart of Fascist Rome sat Vatican City, the seat of the Vicar of Christ, which was now like a small island surrounded by the enemies of its moral stature in the world. The current successor to St. Peter was Pope Pius XII, who, as Eugenio Pacelli, had been born in the city of Rome over sixty-six years before his election as the Supreme Pontiff.

Sitting at his desk in his papal study late that December night, Pius, immaculately clothed in his cream-colored cassock, zucchetto and gold cross, stared at the two sheets of paper that were in front of him, which were densely covered with his writing from top to bottom. He picked up his pen, and closed his eyes briefly, contemplating a title for his work that he had just finished composing. When he opened his eyes, he brought the pen to the very top of the first page and wrote: A Papal Protest against the Gruesome Persecution of the Jews.

He put the pen down on his desk, removed his glasses, and slowly rubbed the bridge of his nose between his fingers. Placing his glasses back on his nose, he hovered over the pages, reading again carefully each paragraph he had painstakingly written.

When he was done, he leaned back in his chair deep in thought, before he picked up the pages, and once more read them, paragraph by paragraph, contemplating each and every word. When he reached the end, he placed the pages on the desk, leaned back in his chair again, and sighed deeply.

With both hands, he clasped the gold crucifix that hung down by his chest, as he nervously twirled his thumbs. He then picked up the pen once again and stared at the pages before him. He gripped the pen tight and said out loud, "I cannot," before he hurled the pen across the room. He placed his elbows on the desk and his head fell forward heavily into his hands. His eyes became moist with tears.

Gathering himself, he stood up and reverently made the sign of the cross. He then grabbed the pages from his desk and walked briskly out of the study.

He made his way down a long hallway in the Apostolic Palace until he came to the kitchen, which was deserted at this time of night. He made his way over to a small stove that sat off in the corner with an open flame.

He opened the cast iron door to the stove but then paused. He stared intently at the two pages in his hands, and his attention focused on the working title he had added at the top. He then peered into the fire. As he did so, he slowly crumbled the two pages in his hands and then threw those pages into the fire.

The Holy Father stood silently as he watched the flames ignite the two pages. He waited until both pages were completely burned before retiring to his study.

PART I

VATICAN CITY
December 1942

A PRIEST AND A DIPLOMAT

*M*ichelangelo's majestic dome of St. Peter's Basilica shimmered under the bright December moon. Deep inside the adjacent Apostolic Palace, Father Biaggio Antonio Sanguinetti, a young Vatican priest, sat quietly on a simple wooden chair outside the closed office door of Luigi Cardinal Maglione, the Vatican Secretary of State.

That night, Biaggio had the task of escorting Harold H. Tittmann, Jr., an American diplomat, to a secret meeting with Maglione, the highest-ranking Cardinal at the Vatican.

While waiting in the deserted corridor for Tittmann's lengthy, late-night meeting to end, Biaggio hiked his black Roman cassock high above his ankles and leaned the back of his chair against the wall, making the front legs of the chair rise off the ground. This bad habit Biaggio had developed dating back to when he was a child in school, and one for which his nun teachers had failed in breaking him from doing; but not by a lack of trying on their part.

With his highly polished black shoes dangling off the marbled floor, he wondered what was being discussed between Tittmann and Maglione, but unable to hear anything, he focused his attention to the window across the way from where he was seated.

Biaggio could see the full moon through the window. The beautiful sight made his thoughts drift back to his home - to his small, secluded hilltop village in Sicily, situated beautifully among the Sicilian hills - and to his parents whom he had not seen in quite a long time. He imagined his mother kneading out dough in the sun-soaked kitchen, her knuckles red with arthritis, and he felt the same stab of homesickness he'd felt when he left home to enter the seminary. He shook his head to dispel the feeling. After all, he was a priest of the Vatican.

Besides Biaggio's other work around the Vatican, which included reforms to liturgical music, he also accompanied, or watched depending on whom you asked, the Allied diplomats who had come to live at the Vatican during the war. For you see, when Italy foolishly joined the War on the side of the Axis, Pope Pius XII immediately offered sanctuary to the Allied diplomats then living in Rome and allowed these diplomates to move into a convent on the grounds of the Vatican, Santa Marta, which he had converted into apartments for them. Being able to live at the Vatican offered these diplomats and their families a place to reside in safety and without fear of reprisals from their own country's now declared enemy.

However, the Holy See did not allow these Allied

diplomats to have visitors; they could not discuss politics in public; their phone calls and mail were monitored; they were never allowed to leave the grounds of the Vatican; and, when outside the confines of Santa Marta, they were almost always accompanied by a Vatican priest. As it was for the Pope, the Vatican became the diplomats' safe haven, and at the same time, their prison.

Although Biaggio escorted several different diplomates around the Vatican, he was most often assigned to Tittmann. Over the past few months, Biaggio had become friendly with the little American and enjoyed spending time with him. Tittmann, an Episcopalian, had been a pilot in Eddie Rickenbacker's 94th Squadron during World War I until five German fighter planes shot him down over France. He survived, though he lost his right leg, one kidney, and half of a lung, and suffered severe damage to one arm and his other leg. When he came home, he returned not only as a war hero, but perhaps as one of the most severely injured American soldiers to survive 'the war to end all wars.' After many surgeries and years of rehabilitation, he'd recovered as best he could and entered the diplomatic service of the United States government.

Over the past few days, Biaggio had led Tittmann to many meetings with Vatican officials. The sudden, large uptick in the number of meetings did not go unnoticed by Biaggio. Something important was going on. He was certain of that. But what it was, he had no idea. He hated not knowing, as he felt more and more like nothing more than a glorified errand boy.

The excitement of coming to live and work in the Vatican had waned over the past months, as Biaggio began to question if his true calling to the priesthood was to serve in an administrative role, instead of a priestly life pastoring people.

As the night wore on, Biaggio's head began to bob up and down over his stiff white Roman collar as boredom took hold, and he fought his desire to fall asleep at the late hour. With his sleepy eyes half-closed, Biaggio's gaze bore even more pointedly at the full moon. The moon, that orb suspended in the clear, silent night sky, sat peacefully as always, far above the horizon, drawing the eye's gaze upward, in the same way that strains of music raise the soul's imagination aloft to higher levels of hope. His thoughts drifted once again to his village as memories of the music of his village poured over his heart, and he thought of his own participation as a violinist in concerts held in the main square of his tiny village, with his father lovingly conducting the village orchestra. Back then, life in the village was magical. A place of love, friendship, prosperity and peace. But those were just memories now. The consequences of war had come to his village, and he was fully aware that all of his fellow villagers, including his very own parents, were suffering as a result. Though he took great pride in being a Vatican priest and knew that he was blessed with the opportunity to serve his beloved pope, Pope Pius XII, a sense of guilt always lingered in Biaggio's soul as he often compared his villagers' plight to his own, residing in luxury at the Vatican.

Suddenly, the silence in the corridor was pierced by the raised voice of Harold Tittmann from behind the closed office door.

Biaggio's eyes flashed open wide, surprised as Tittmann rarely showed a lot of emotion, so whatever was going on behind that closed door certainly had stoked a passionate fire in the American. Biaggio gently put the front legs of his chair down on the floor as he eagerly leaned forward, straining to hear what was being said, but he could not make out the muffled words as Cardinal Maglione's volume soon matched Tittmann's in return. But just as quickly as it had started, the sound of the raised voices disappeared, as silence once again took hold in the corridor. Like before, Biaggio hiked his cassock above his ankles and leaned the back of his chair against the wall, as his feet dangled once again from the floor.

Just then, the door to Cardinal Maglione's office flew open, and Harold Tittmann, with a solemn expression on his face, lumbered out of the office alone.

Startled by the opening of the door, Biaggio's body jerked, causing his chair to rock forward quickly. The front legs of his chair came crashing down on the floor, making a sound that echoed loudly down the deserted hallway.

Tittmann's somber expression changed as he chuckled. "Padre Sanguinetti, with all of that racket, you will wake St. Peter from his slumber."

Biaggio, with his cheeks flushed from embarrassment, quickly stood up and rearranged his cassock. He slowly rubbed his knuckles on his right hand, as he remembered the whack they would receive from Sister Angelina back when he was in school after crashing his raised chair on the ground when he had fallen asleep in her class. He gathered himself and replied simply to Tittmann, "*Scusi.*"

"Let's go," replied Tittmann, as he leaned heavily on his cane with his good arm, supporting his burdensome prosthetic leg.

Not another word was spoken between the two, as

Biaggio sensed the American diplomat was lost in his thoughts from the meeting he had just left. They departed the Apostolic Palace and slowly proceeded across St. Peter's Square toward the Vatican Hospice of Santa Marta, which sat adjacent to the Basilica. They passed the Arch of Bells and approached the gate to the courtyard of Santa Marta. Tittmann stopped. Being a consummate and true diplomat, Tittmann never discussed his dealings with Vatican officials with anyone, including Biaggio. On this night, however, Tittmann could not contain his frustration.

He bore his stare right at Biaggio, before whispering, "How can the Vatican remain silent?"

Biaggio asked in his broken English, "What do you mean?"

"I approached Cardinal Maglione one last time to see if the Pope would join the United States, Great Britain, the Soviets, and other Allies in our declaration against the Nazi's persecution of the Jews."

Biaggio glanced around as he lowered his voice and asked, "Will he join in?"

Tittmann sighed. "Cardinal Maglione says that the Pope does not believe he can join in this declaration."

With a quizzical look, Biaggio asked, "What does the declaration say?"

"It states that the Nazis will pay for their crimes. Their crimes committed against humanity. Their crimes committed against the very heart of morality."

Biaggio noticed that Tittmann was gripping the top of his cane even tighter. The American diplomat paused and breathed deeply before continuing. "We know that the Nazis are transporting Jews in freight cars to labor camps in Eastern

Europe in conditions of appalling horror and brutality. Once at the camps, the able-bodied are slowly worked to death. For the infirm and the old, they are left to die of exposure and starvation or some are deliberately massacred in mass executions."

Biaggio could feel his stomach turn as he ran his right hand through his black hair. He responded in a hushed tone. "My God. The rumors are true?"

"Rumors? These are facts, not rumors. We believe the number of victims is somewhere in the many hundreds of thousands consisting of entirely innocent men, women and even children," continued Tittmann.

Biaggio sighed heavily as he repeated again, "My God."

"It's all true," replied Tittmann. "Yet, the Pope will not join in our declaration."

Biaggio put his head down in thought. He was fully aware of the talk among some who believed that Pope Pius XII was too diplomatic, too worried about protecting the institution of the Church, rather than speaking out loudly against the Nazis and Hitler, but Biaggio had always put such beliefs aside.

"I'm sure the Pontiff has his reasons," Biaggio stated. "These are difficult times, times that require prudence and prayer."

Tittmann shook his head. "I respectfully disagree. I believe these times require action. I too have tried to break that silence. This past summer, when *Il Messagero* published that photo of 50 Jews at forced labor digging ditches on the banks of the Tiber River, I brought my disgust to Monsignor Montini and asked that the Holy See make a public protest. The response I got was that the Pope was deeply troubled by the photo, and that an oral protest would be lodged, but that no public demonstration of his disapproval would be forthcoming."

Biaggio was silent as he nervously rubbed his temples.

Tittmann leaned in closer to Biaggio. "President Roosevelt's personal representative, Myron Taylor, believes that the Pope's silence is endangering his moral authority in the world. Minister Osborne has advised me that his British government is equally as frustrated."

Biaggio uncomfortably shifted his stance and silently folded his arms across his chest. He finally replied in a frustrated tone. "I am sure His Holiness is doing what he thinks is best."

Tittmann extended his hand. "I'm sorry for bringing this up to you at this late hour. Thanks for escorting me."

Biaggio shook Tittmann's hand. When they let go, Tittmann said, "I know you love the Pope, as do I. My boss, Myron Taylor, has great respect for him as well. We both know what he is facing in his position as head of the Church. But I do believe for his own good, he must speak out. He must break his silence."

Biaggio's eyes narrowed as he quickly replied, "I know he has spoken out many times about his disgust of Hitler and the Nazis and how he envisions a Germany free of Hitler and Nazism. Look, I believe Pope Pius is one of the holiest men I have ever met, and who constantly calls upon the faithful to offer charity to all. I am unaware of the silence you speak of and really don't know what else you want me to say."

Tittmann smiled at the young priest. "You can tell me to have a good night."

Biaggio chuckled. *"Buona notte, mio amico."*

"Buona notte, Padre."

Biaggio watched as Tittmann turned and plodded toward Santa Marta. Biaggio made his way back toward the Apostolic Palace. As he walked through St. Peter's Square, he passed the Basilica again. As he approached the Apostolic Palace, he took notice of a light in the window on the top right side of the building. He knew that was the bedroom of Pope Pius XII. Seeing the light on at this time of night was not surprising. The Pope slept little with all that was going on in the world.

Staring at the window, Biaggio pondered the questions raised by Harold Tittmann. Since coming to work at the Vatican, Biaggio grew to adore the Pope, his Pope. If Pius was indeed silent, surely there was a reason. There had to be. Yet, why would the Pope not join such a simple declaration? Biaggio had no answer.

Biaggio reached the door to the Palace. A Swiss Guardsman, his colorful uniform partially covered by a long, black cape, waved Biaggio in, and he made his way to his small bedroom inside.

A short time later, as he lay in bed, Biaggio's mind was filled with the image of a cattle car loaded with Jews. He tried to shake it away – tried to think again of his mother back home and the smell of baking bread permeating the entire home – but the image of the cattle car would not budge. Even with his thirty years on this earth, Biaggio could not comprehend how Hitler could be so cruel.

He also began to question for the first time if the Pope was being too prudent, too careful with his treatment toward the Nazis.

Biaggio again thought of his own life, living in the relative comfort of Vatican City, while people were suffering all over the world. He did not follow his vocation to be a babysitter to diplomats. He became a priest to help those in need. To help those suffering. But what could he do? He was nothing more than a simple priest working at the Vatican.

His mind became fixated on the railcars and the horrendous journey for the Jews. A journey to their death. It took a while, but Biaggio finally drifted asleep.

The Vatican was silent.

2

THE MUSICIANS

*F*or Heinrich Bergman, it wasn't the packed, cramped conditions on the train. It wasn't the bitter, biting cold. It wasn't the stench, the nauseating smell that constantly turned his stomach. It wasn't the fact that he could not sit or lie down. It wasn't even the realization that he had no idea where he was going. For Heinrich Bergman, it was the two buckets sitting close by his feet that garnered his full attention.

Earlier that morning, Heinrich, a twenty-six-year-old Viennese musician, had been herded onto the platform of the Aspang Rail Station along with the rest of the *Untermenschen* of Vienna. His two closest friends, Alfred Keller and Kurt Hofmann, were with him, but they had been shuffled into a different line, as they all waited to board the train with the rest of the so-called undesirables.

Heinrich stood silently in line. His dark wool flat cap was

pulled low over his chestnut curls. His espresso colored brown eyes only showed despair, not the yearning they once did. A long black coat, weathered and beaten, hung heavily on his thin body. On the front of his coat, he wore the yellow star, the emblem of his guilt of being an enemy of the Third Reich.

With his jaw clenched, Heinrich gripped the handle of his suitcase tight, which turned his knuckles white from the strain as he looked for his friends on the platform. His shoulders drooped when he could not see them among all the other Jews lined up to board the train.

On that crisp, frigid December morning, the cloudless Viennese sky was a deep, beautiful azure blue. Heinrich peered up at the stunning sky. He took in a deep breath, the cold air burning his throat. Upon exhaling, he sighed. He knew that the view did not match the gloom and sadness in his very heart and soul.

Waffen-SS soldiers, in their gray-green Nazi uniforms and highly polished black boots, stood all around the train platform with their machine guns at the ready, a strong reminder that resistance was futile. A few soldiers held tightly to German Shepherds. The dogs barked wildly and flashed their teeth. With each bark, Heinrich's heart skipped a beat.

Blood red Nazi flags, each punctuated with a stark black swastika, fluttered in the stiff breeze, casting elongated shifting shadows on the train platform. Even though Nazi flags since the Anschluss had come to dominate the entire landscape of Vienna, they still instilled fear. All around the platform hung travel posters showing images of beautiful locations outside of Vienna, keeping up the charade that the train was taking the Jews to a better place - a place far away from Nazi-dominated Vienna.

Standing in stark contrast to the serene pictures displayed on the posters were the freight cars lined up in front of the Jews. Heinrich stared at them in dazed disbelief as he quickly realized that this was his transportation out of Vienna. A freight car, as if he and his fellow Jews were nothing more than cattle. With his left hand, Heinrich rubbed the stubble on his face reminding him that he had not shaved nor bathed for days.

An elderly Jewish couple standing in front of Heinrich drew his attention as they gently and lovingly grasped their hands together. At that moment, Heinrich's thoughts drifted to his parents, and he quickly realized that he never felt so alone in his entire life.

"Leave your luggage on the platform," calmly ordered a young Nazi soldier to the Jews. "If you have not done so already, make sure you label it. Last name first. It will be put onto the next train," he lied.

Heinrich gingerly set down his luggage. His name, written in big red letters, was already emblazoned across the front in an attempt to protect the contents therein. While his luggage did contain a few pieces of clothing, most importantly, it held his memories, memories from a life in music.

As he glared down at his luggage, those memories came to the forefront of his mind, and like waves lapping over and over again along a pristine beach, they washed over his very soul. He hated to leave his memories behind on the platform.

But he was scared, exhausted and broken. Yet, the more he gazed at his luggage, the more he became aware of a stirring deep inside of him. Even in his despair, the faint fire of courage still smoldered. This was the same courage that for the past few months had allowed him to go into hiding in Vienna and kept him one step ahead of the Gestapo; that was until he, along with his friends, Alfred and Kurt, were all betrayed and rounded up for deportation.

Standing on the train platform, he became determined that his memories would not be left behind. His eyes darted to and fro, making sure he was not being watched before he unlatched his luggage and pulled out a dark, brown violin case.

The older Jewish man standing in front of him whispered with concern, "*Bist du verrückt?* (Are you nuts?) They will kill you if you try to get on the train with that."

Heinrich clutched the case close to his chest. "It's coming with me," he said, before turning and looking at the elderly man's wife. He then replied pointedly. "It's all I have left."

The older man nodded his head with understanding as he patted Heinrich on his shoulder.

That case held Heinrich's prized 18th century Stradivarius violin. He held it even tighter against his chest as he thought to himself that those Nazi bastards had not broken him completely just yet. He swiftly hid the case under his knee-length coat just as he and the other Jews were ordered to make their way to the railcars.

Heinrich boarded the last railcar, which was the first of the convoy of twenty to be loaded. He stood below the one small window, its opening covered with barbed wire. He leaned his violin case against the wall. A German soldier, standing outside the open door, yelled to the Jews already inside, "Raise your hands above your heads to make room for the others."

Heinrich pressed his leg against his violin case and followed the order. Ninety Jews were crammed into the railcar. Heinrich sighed with relief when he noticed Alfred Keller and Kurt Hofmann enter the car. The three friends all stood apart, but at least they were together.

The bond between the three friends went far beyond mere friendship. They all had been members of the prestigious Vienna Philharmonic Orchestra. That was until they were dismissed from the orchestra simply because they were Jews.

A tall German officer suddenly appeared in the doorway of the train. *Oberst* Friedrich Klotz, the Nazi train commander, was a physically imposing, giant of a man, whose athletic and toned physique filled his uniform to perfection. He stood silent, his hands clasped tightly behind him. From under his visor cap, his cold, lifeless slate eyes stared at the Jews inside the railcar. He removed his cap, exposing his stark bald head. His mouth slowly curled up at the edges in an almost cynical smile. He pointed to a young Jewish man, and then breaking his silence, he said in a brutal and robust tone, *"Sie sind verantwortlich für diese Viehwagen."* (You are in charge of this Cattle Wagon.)

The young man raised his hands to his chest as if seeking clarification, but did not dare respond. *Oberst* Klotz continued. "If anyone even tries to escape, you will be shot." He paused and looked at the other Jews inside the railcar. "For the escapee, you will die like the dog that you are."

He made a gesture with his left hand, and the soldiers nearby slide the door closed. With the clang of the lock, a shiver shot through Heinrich's entire body. He feared his fate was sealed with that locked door. People around Heinrich began crying, which made him believe they shared the same belief regarding their own destiny. A few people near him begin to repeat over and over again one of the most famous Jewish prayers: *"Sh'ma Yisrael, Adonai Eloheinu, Adonai Echad."* (Hear O Israel, the Lord is our God, the Lord is one.) Heinrich found himself mumbling the prayer as well.

Heinrich could hear the other cars being loaded. All the while, dogs could be heard barking up and down the platform as the Germans continued to yell orders to the Jews as the other railcars were filled.

Then there was profound silence. Not a peaceful one that brings serenity and calm, but instead the type of deep, dark silence that forces a person's mind to turn inward to confront the fears and anxieties buried deep within one's very own soul. Heinrich closed his eyes as he tried to overcome his personal inner struggle, a battle he quickly lost. He hoped the train would soon depart as he found the waiting unbearable. Yet, it remained motionless.

The day slowly turned to night, and still the train had not moved. The night was the worst. Even though there was a full moon high overhead, the one small window inside the railcar offered little illumination. Blackness surrounded Heinrich, while the temperature plummeted. With so many people squeezed together, the air inside was thick and suffocating.

Heinrich peered through the barbed wire covered window and noticed the bright full moon lingering in the sky above, as if it were the watchful eye of an old friend. Seeing the moon out of the railcar window made him think of the

Rathausplatzin, the moonlit splattered square in Vienna, where he and his friends would often go to drink beer, admire the pretty girls, and listen to the piazza orchestra playing the music of Vienna's own Mozart. The moon gazed silently over the tracks, the railcars, and the Jews within. Yet this very silence conjured for Heinrich the memories of the lilting notes of the haunting music of Vienna. Staring back at the moon in his own silence, his eyes welled with tears.

As the hours passed and the cold grew even deeper, Heinrich Bergman's attention turned completely to the two buckets at his feet. One bucket was empty. It had contained brown colored water, which the occupants of the railcar consumed within the first hour. The bucket remained empty although the occupants prayed that the door would be opened, and the bucket filled up once again.

The other bucket was the latrine. The passengers had shoved the bucket by foot to those passengers who needed it. But the bucket had quickly filled up and overflowed, and the contents covered the floor. Now people were forced to give up their dignity while they urinated and defecated in their clothes. The smell inside the cattle car soon became nauseating.

"Two buckets," Heinrich pondered. Why only two for ninety people? He was convinced it was the Nazi way of showing compassion for the *Untermenschen*. Two buckets. Somehow, being transfixed on those two buckets, he was able to keep his mind off the terrible situation in which he and his friends found themselves.

Heinrich had been on the train for more than sixteen hours when a prolonged whistle pierced the cold night air. He heard the sound of a German guard climb the ladder on the back of the railcar and take his position seated on top. Then the wheels started to grind slowly against the track before the car surged forward. The train finally began its journey. Heinrich and the rest of the *Untermenschen* were leaving Vienna.

3

THE COMPOSER

or a Jew, if there was one place you did not want to find yourself, Munich was it. But that was precisely where Ludwig Adler found himself.

Ludwig, a small, bespectacled man with a kind face and giant smile, was a gifted Jewish composer from Munich. His music had been performed all over Germany. That was until Joseph Goebbels, the Reich Minister of Propaganda, declared Ludwig's music as *Entartete Musik* (Degenerate Music), and his music was outlawed. Ludwig Adler and his music were soon forgotten.

Ludwig tried to scratch out a life as best he could for his family, all the while living among the dwindling population of Jews in Munich as each week more and more Jews were being rounded up and brought to camps on the outskirts of the city.

It was late one afternoon when Ludwig walked slowly down the streets of Munich. His head was bowed, and his heart heavy. He had tried to obtain a visa earlier that day so that he and his family could get out of Munich. But once again, he was denied.

He reached his home. Before opening the door, he took off his glasses and slowly cleaned them with his handkerchief. When he put them back on, he noticed a paper tacked to the door. He read the notice and proceeded to rub his temples furiously. He dreaded telling his wife what he had just read.

His eyes caught the *mezuzah* affixed to the doorframe. He remembered when he and Anikka placed it there after purchasing the home so many years ago. It was a much happier time back then. He raised his hand and gently touched the small wooden case, as his mind was flooded with memories of his youth, growing up in a very observant Jewish household. With his entry into the secular world of music, his religious observances had over time become lax, but his faith and attachment to his Jewish roots were still as strong as ever. He reached for the door handle and entered his home.

His wife met him in the foyer. She asked with hope, "Any luck? Did you get it?"

He frowned. "No, Anikka. They said no visas are being given to the Jews."

Anikka sighed. "Oh, Ludwig, what are we going to do? We need to get out of Munich. We need to move our family somewhere safe."

"I know, Anikka. I know. But we can't get out."

She pointed at his hand. "What's that?"

He took a deep breath. "This was on the door. It's a notice. Orders."

"Orders? Orders to do what?"

"The Gestapo says we must leave for the resettlement camp at Theresienstadt."

"Leave our house?" Anikka blubbered. "Is there nothing we can do?"

"Anikka, I have no answers. But I do know that we must go. We have no other option. I tried. Believe me, I tried. I even looked into going into hiding, but it's too dangerous, and I don't know who would take us in."

"When do we have to leave?"

Ludwig swallowed hard. "By the end of the day."

Anikka twirled her hands nervously in front of her and repeated, "By the end of the day." She slowly crumpled to her knees and then, looking up at Ludwig, choked with tears, she asked, "What will happen to us?"

Looking at the tears running down his wife's cheeks, his own eyes welled up. He reached down and offered his hand and pulled her up. "I don't know." He paced the wooden floor in front of her. We have no choice in this and will just have to make do. We must believe all will be well."

She rolled her eyes toward the ceiling. "All will be well? We have to abandon our house. What about Klaus and Nannerl? What are we supposed to tell our children? What about us? What about all of our friends and family who have gone to the camps at Milberthausen or Theresienstadt? They have just disappeared, without another word or trace. Is that our destiny?"

"I don't know what you expect me to do."

"Why, Ludwig? Why is this happening? They stopped us from going to restaurants, even taking walks in the park with our kids. They even stopped your music. And now this. Our home."

"I have tried to get us out. I'm sorry. I could not. I tried."

Anikka quickly extended her arms and hugged her husband. "I know, Ludwig. I know you did. I'm sorry. I'm just so scared."

He kissed her. "I will never let anything happen to you and the children. Nothing. If moving keeps us alive, then so be it. We still have each other. That is all that matters."

"I need to pack for the children and us."

As she turned to leave, Ludwig sighed. "The Gestapo says each family member is allowed to take only one suitcase."

His wife said not a word but left the room in tears to start packing.

WITHIN THREE HOURS, the Adlers were on the street walking to Gestapo headquarters, where transports would take them to the camp. Ludwig's suitcase was full of more musical scores than clothes. Annika's was filled with more items for the kids than for herself. While they walked along the Munich streets, they passed the physician's office of Dr. Phillipp Stolz located at *Brauhausstrasse 8*.

Phillipp and his wife, Inga, were huge patrons of the arts in Munich and had provided an enormous boon to Ludwig at the early stage of his career. They loved Ludwig's compositions and regularly invited the Adlers over to their home for dinner, along with other guests, who were also all heavily involved in the arts. After dinner, the Stolzes' home would be filled with the sounds of the piano as Ludwig played his newest compositions to the attendees, which consisted of impresarios, directors and conductors from all over Germany. Many doors were opened to Ludwig thanks to his friendship with the Stolzes; that was until his music was outlawed by the Nazis. The Stolzes' friends stopped coming to see Ludwig. Soon, the Stolzes reluctantly stopped having him over. Ludwig had not seen the Stolzes in quite some time.

Phillipp just so happened to look out his office window and saw his old friend and family walk by with their suitcases. Phillipp quickly ran out and caught up to Ludwig. Phillipp simply said, "*Mein Haus, jetzt.*" (My house, now.)

THE ADLERS immediately went into hiding at the Stolz home at *Plazi 46*, which was very close to Dr. Stolz's physician's office and near the famous *Marienplatz*. They lived in a tiny cellar hidden by a trap door in the kitchen. They spent every day and night in the cellar. The Stolzes provided them with clothes and food, but the food quantities were limited because the pantry at the Stolz home had to remain as if they were still only providing for two mouths. The Gestapo was known to look at the pantry on a raid, as a fully stocked pantry was a sure sign Jews were being hidden in the home. The Gestapo also watched the stores to see how much food a household purchased.

Ludwig and Anikka were prepared to flee the cellar with their children at a moment's notice. They lived out of their suitcases and kept the cellar neat. They slept on bedrolls that could easily be put away because cots would alert the Nazis that people were sleeping down there.

The Adlers were well aware of the danger they were in

and of the sacrifice the Stolzes were making. If it were ever discovered that they were hiding Jews, Phillipp and Inga would be shot, and the Adlers immediately would be sent to a labor camp.

Sunday night was the only time the Adler family came out of the cellar. The family would sit in the parlor with the Stolzes, as Ludwig played his scores on the piano. Before calling it a night, the Stolzes would watch the children, as Ludwig and Annika retreated to the cellar, undressed, and made love, a momentary respite from the absolute hell they were living.

As THE DAYS and months passed, Ludwig and Anikka began learning from the Stolzes the rumors concerning the fate of the Jews of Munich whose homes had been confiscated after they were forced into the camp. The Jews were being deported away from Munich to bigger camps such as Dachau and Auschwitz. The Adlers knew they owed their lives to the courage of the Stolz family. As the Adlers grew more and more accustomed to their routine, they began to feel safe in the cellar. Because the Stolzes were a very well-respected Catholic Munich family with many connections, the Gestapo never considered checking their home for Jews.

One day in mid-December, while Phillipp was at work at the hospital, Inga was in the parlor knitting. The Adlers were down in the cellar. Anikka was working through math problems with the children while Ludwig laid on his bedroll, listening to his wife's teaching.

The Adlers noticed water dripping down into the cellar

through the floorboards in the kitchen. At the very same time, Inga walked into the kitchen and saw water pouring from the cabinet underneath the sink. She looked out the window above the sink and noticed her neighbor, Gunter Kaufmann. He did a lot of odd jobs in the neighborhood. Although the Stolzes had never used his services before, Inga knew her husband spoke to him regularly, and she always saw Gunter at Mass when they attended on Sundays. She opened the kitchen window and called to Gunter to come have a look at the sink.

As he made his way to their house, Inga stomped on the trapdoor with her foot, the signal for the Adlers to remain quiet. Gunter knocked on the door, and Inga let him in.

4

A LEAP OF FAITH

*T*he train engineer, Dieter Bertram, could not understand why the train had been so delayed in making the scheduled short trip to the camp at Mauthausen. He had been instructed by the commander at the Aspang Rail Station in Vienna to remain there for hours. No reason was given, which did not surprise him, particularly when dealing with the Nazis. Delays were almost always expected for the *Sonderzüge* (Special trains), which had low priority for movement, as the Nazis exhibited a complete indifference to the fate of their human cargo. Day had turned to night, and still the train sat.

Oberst Klotz, the train commander for this trip, at last, walked by the open window of the engine and gave a thumbs up to Dieter. Dieter pulled on the train whistle, giving three short bursts. He leaned his head out the window and saw *Oberst* Klotz climb on the railcar behind the engine. The train slowly began to pull away from the station.

Finally moving now, Dieter sped the train up. He was uncertain if the delay had changed the plan. He hoped not. He would soon find out.

HEINRICH BERGMAN STOOD SILENTLY inside the railcar. He wished he could speak with his friends. Although together in the same railcar, they were worlds apart, separated by darkness, strangers and death. Heinrich picked up his violin case and held it close to his chest as his thoughts drifted back to the concert hall, to a packed house and to tremendous ovations. He quickly got lost in his world of music, the music of Mozart, Beethoven, and Bach.

Heinrich's friend, Alfred Keller, stood by the door. A young pregnant mother and her six-year-old son were next to him. Alfred spoke at length to the young mother, Anna Klein, and had discovered that her husband had been killed by the Nazis weeks before. Alfred tried his best to give a little extra space for the pregnant Anna and her son, constantly asking others to make room. This small action provided Anna with some semblance of decency, something that had disappeared long ago in Vienna. Anna held tightly to her son, Josef, trying to keep him warm. Her hand nervously patted her son's chest, yet she spoke to the child with a calming, soothing voice, assuring her son that all would be well. The way Anna spoke to and comforted her son made Alfred think of his own parents and to his days growing up in Melk, a picturesque town located on the southern bank of the Danube River, not too far from Vienna, and known mostly for its massive hilltop abbey. He longed to see his own parents, but they had been sent to a labor camp in Poland a few months before. He was told the name of the camp – Auschwitz - but it meant nothing to Alfred. He wondered if his parents had endured the same horrific train ride.

Kurt Hofmann stood on the opposite side of the railcar from Heinrich. Kurt felt packed in the railcar like sardines in a tin. He just wanted off the train. At this point, he did not care where it was going. In the dark and cold, his thoughts drifted to Gina Schiff, the love of his life. Kurt loved three things in life – Vienna, music, and Gina Schiff. He slowly rubbed his temples as tears flowed down his cheeks. The three things he loved most in this world had all been taken away from him. He was forced out of Vienna just as he had been forced out of the Vienna Philharmonic. As for Gina, he had no idea where she was or if he would ever see her again.

ABOUT THREE MILES outside of the town of Melk, Dieter saw two red lights from a lantern, far down the tracks. A smile came across the train engineer's lips. The plan was still on. He began to slow the train down.

Oberst Klotz, the train commander for this trip, rode in the troop car directly behind the engine. He felt the train slow down and quickly made his way to the engineer.

"Why are we slowing?" he asked with authority as he entered the cabin, pulling on his black visor cap over his bald head.

"Danger lights," replied Dieter. "See those two red lights down the track. I must stop the train. We need to inspect the track."

"Damn. We are already so late. I will get the mechanic. We will all go inspect the track."

Jurgen Goss, Roland Dorn, and Petra Peiper lay close to the tracks alongside an embankment. The three young Austrians were part of the resistance movement. They had been helping Jews and secretly fighting the Germans for months now. But this day was an even bigger event. For the first time, they were going to attempt to free Jews from a train convoy. They knew it would be difficult, but having the engineer of the train sympathize with your cause could make it work. At least that was their hope. One of the leaders of the Resistance, Father Heinrich Maier, an energetic young Catholic priest, had assured them that the engineer was trustworthy.

Only a week ago, the three Austrians had met with Dieter at a Viennese bar to plan the attack. The others had let Petra do the talking that night. She was a beautiful woman. They figured the engineer would not say no to her. As predicted, Dieter was enraptured by her.

He agreed to help. He assured the trio that the other train personnel – the mechanic and coal assistants – would not interfere. On the other hand, the Nazi guards and the commander would present a problem but hopefully one that could be overcome.

Dieter informed them about a train scheduled to depart in a week headed to Mauthausen, which would provide the perfect opportunity to pull off their plan. As of late, the small number of trains moving the now dwindling population of Jews still being deported from Vienna usually went to camps in Germany or Poland. But due to overcrowding at those camps, the destination for this train and its occupants was Mauthausen. He pointed out that trains making the short trek to Mauthausen would be very lightly guarded. He also advised them of the location of the guards onboard the train. He assured them that for a train making the journey during the day, there would only be three guards and an *Oberst*. One guard always sat on the top of the last car, one always sat on the top of the car nearest the middle, and one guard rode with the *Oberst* in the troop car, which would be located behind the engine and coal car. For longer trips to the camps located in Poland and Germany, the last car was a caboose where the *Oberst* rode. With no caboose on this train, an attack on the last few cars was much more feasible. The engineer even picked the location for the attack. There was a spot, very isolated, just a few miles outside of Melk, very close to a forest. With the engineer on board, the plan went into action.

THE PLAN WAS to attack the train during the day when there would be fewer guards rather than a train running at night. Jurgen, Roland and Petra sat in the nearby woods watching the track, trying to stay warm. But the train never came that day. When night came, they moved closer to the track. They prayed if the train was coming tonight, that no more guards had been added to defend it. Their only supplies were pliers, a knife and one pistol with six bullets.

Well into the night, and just as they were about to give up on the train coming, they finally saw the light from the locomotive and moved into action. Petra ran down the tracks and placed the lantern and then returned to the two men. Jurgen handed her a pair of pliers while Roland readied his pistol.

As the train got closer to the lantern, Dieter leaned hard on the brakes and brought the train to a full and complete stop. He had hit his mark right on point. The three resistance fighters laid on the ground right next to the last railcar. Just as the engineer had advised, a guard was seated on the roof of the last car.

The poor passengers on the train had no idea where they were or why they were stopped. When the train came to a complete stop, Dieter blew the whistle. At the very same time, Roland took his shot. The train whistle blocked out the sound of the single gunshot. The guard on top of the last car took the bullet directly in his head and fell backward onto the top of the train, making not a sound.

Jurgen patted Roland on the head, congratulating him on his shot, and then the three of them quickly made their way to the railcars.

Meanwhile, Dieter climbed down from the engine. *Oberst* Klotz and the mechanic exited the coal car and met Dieter by the engine. The guard from the troop car ran up to meet them and was immediately met by *Oberst* Klotz barking orders. 'Take your position. The three of us are going to check the tracks. Wilhelm and Otto will be guarding the back part of the train." *Oberst* Klotz leaned in close and said, "Erik, shoot anything that moves."

Oberst Klotz, Dieter, and the mechanic then began walking in front of the engine to check the tracks. As instructed, Erik took his position outside the train, watching the first half of the convoy. The second guard, Wilhelm Kliest, came down from the top of the car in the middle of the convoy and took his position, machine gun at the ready, trained on the cars within his sight. Because of the darkness, he could not see the last three cars, but he knew Otto, from his position by the last car, could see those cars.

Jurgen reached the door of the last car and attacked the lock furiously with the pliers. Roland and Petra went to the second to last car and did the same.

All of the *Untermenschen* inside the last railcar could hear Jurgen working on the door lock. They had no idea what was going on, and their anxiety only grew with the uncertainty. Josef had awoken when the train stopped, and now with the commotion outside, he pressed tightly against his mother. Alfred, close to the door, shouted to the person outside the door, "Who are you?"

The railcar became silent.

"*Ich bin ein Freund,*" Jurgen replied from outside the door.

The Jews began murmuring among themselves, "He says he is a friend."

Jurgen added, "We are Austrians. We work with the Resistance. We will get you out."

Alfred turned to the others. "He is trying to help us. He is attempting to unlock the door."

Meanwhile, the guard situated in the middle of the convoy thought he heard a noise toward the back of the train. Wilhelm began to walk that way to see what it was and to speak with Otto, the guard in the back.

Alfred faced the door again. "Where are we?"

"On the outskirts of Melk," came the reply from Jurgen outside the door.

Alfred repeated out loud, "Melk," as he thought of his old home.

"I almost have it," Jurgen said.

The Jews grabbed hold of each other. Anxiety turned into excitement inside the railcar.

Petra and Roland were close to getting the lock undone on the second to last car. Jurgen's hands were cold, and it was tough to handle the pliers, but he knew he had to act fast.

Oberst Klotz, Dieter and the mechanic returned to the train after checking the tracks. *Oberst* Klotz was cursing the delay. "What a waste of time. Give the signal. Let's go," he huffed.

As Dieter climbed on board, he hoped that his Austrian collaborators had had enough time to get the doors open. He pulled the cord in the engine and gave three short whistle blows, the signal that the train was going to start and for the guards to take their positions back on the train.

As Wilhelm made his way to the back of the train, he heard the whistles announcing the train was about to move. He climbed a ladder on one of the cars, reached the top, and began walking on top of the train toward the back.

The train slowly started to move. Jurgen, Roland and Petra started walking with the train, desperately trying to get the doors open.

Suddenly, there was the sound of machine gunfire. Jurgen turned away from the lock on the last car and looked toward the front of the train. Just as he did so, he saw Petra by the second to last railcar take a bullet in the back, fall hard against the train and then spin around, before crumbling to the ground. Roland looked to the area where the shots were fired and saw the German guard two cars ahead. Roland lifted his pistol and returned fire.

Wilhelm heard the bullets whiz by before he fired again. His shots found their target as Roland took two rounds to the chest. He fell backward, dead before he even hit the ground.

The train picked up speed. Jurgen tried to keep up, passing the dead bodies of Roland and Petra. *Oberst* Klotz had heard the gunshots but did not know what was happening in the back of the train. Dieter slowed the train. That was all Jurgen needed. He took his pliers and hit the lock of the last car with full force. The lock finally broke open.

Wilhelm fired again, hitting Jurgen squarely in the right shoulder. In much pain and unable to move his shattered right arm, Jurgen took his left hand and reached for the lock and unlatched the door. "Got it!" he yelled to the inhabitants inside. With all of the muscle he could muster, he slid the door open a crack.

That was enough for Alfred to squeeze his hands through the crack and slide the door open, just as there was another burst of gunfire. As the door was opened, Alfred saw Jurgen take a bullet right in the forehead. He died instantly and fell to the ground.

Oberst Klotz, finally aware that the train had slowed down, said to the engineer, "Speed up, now."

Dieter did not follow the order.

Oberst Klotz then pulled out his Luger and placed it right against Dieter's right temple and said, "Speed up, or I swear, I will blow your fucking brains out."

Dieder reluctantly pressed the throttle.

"*Schneller du Bastard*. Faster. Get me to the station at Melk. Something has happened back there!" shouted *Oberst* Klotz.

The train surged forward, as the *Untermenschen* in the last railcar stood in shock as the forest passed in front of the open door. From his position, Wilhelm could now see Otto's dead body sprawled across the top of the last car. He could not tell that the door of the last car had been opened.

Alfred turned to everyone in the railcar. "Now is the time. We must go. You must jump from the train."

A woman standing close to the door yelled, "We are going too fast."

The young man who had been put in charge of the cattle car by *Oberst* Klotz back at the train station, yelled, "No one leaves the car. No one. Do you want to die? They will kill all of us."

The Jews moved further back in the railcar. This gave Heinrich on the right and Kurt on the left enough room to push past the others and reach Alfred.

Kurt spoke first. "Alfred. Heinrich. We need to go. If we stay, we die. I guess we are close to Melk."

Alfred turned to Anna and pleaded by saying, "Come with us."

"I cannot. I am pregnant. I will slow you down. They will catch you." Then in tears, she said, "Take Josef. Take him. Save him. Please."

Alfred picked up the young boy who was screaming for his mother. "Take him," she pressed. "Please take him."

"Come with us," Alfred begged.

Anna shook her head no, disappearing into the crowd to put distance between her and her son. Alfred's last memory of Josef's mother was the look of utter grief on her face.

Heinrich, with his violin case, Alfred, holding Josef tightly, and Kurt all stood in the doorway. Alfred turned one more time to the others in the railcar and said again, "You stay, you die." Then with emphasis, he said, "*Springen*. Jump, jump now."

The three friends looked at each other one last time and then leaped from the train. It was a leap of faith. It was a leap to freedom.

5

FATHER ALFRED DELP, S.J

The Adlers heard the noises coming from the kitchen as Gunter Kaufmann worked on the leak under the sink. In no time at all, the water that had been coming through the floorboards down into the cellar had ceased, a sure sign that the leak was repaired. The Adlers heard the man leave, and they went back to their daily, monotonous routine down in the cellar.

Before dinner that night, the Adlers heard the front door of the Stolz home open, and footsteps quickly moving toward the kitchen. The footsteps indicated the presence of three people. The trap door opened, and Phillipp, Inga and a priest came down the steps. Inga was in tears.

Ludwig Adler looked first at the priest and then at Inga, before asking Phillipp, "What is the matter, Phillipp?"

Inga spurted out, "I'm sorry. I'm so sorry."

Phillipp looked kindly at his wife and then turned to Ludwig, saying with haste, "There was a leak in the kitchen."

Anikka spoke up. "We know. The water was cascading down here."

Phillipp said, "My neighbor fixed it, but he noticed that the water was not pooling on the floor. He asked my wife what was under the floor, as he wanted to go clean up the mess. My wife said there was nothing under there. He grew suspicious and stated that the water was going down into a cellar. My wife denied its existence. When he left, she noticed him investigating the home from our backyard. He discovered the existence of the cellar and heard you down here." Phillipp bit his bottom lip as he looked directly at Ludwig and Anikka. "Within the last hour, we have received word from our friends that Gunter Kaufmann has betrayed us to the Nazis."

Anikka clung to her children and began to cry.

Inga, in a tearful voice, said, "I should never have let him in. Never."

Phillipp spoke with authority. "Listen, we have no time. The Gestapo is coming. This is Father Alfred Delp of the Society of Jesus."

The priest nodded, as Phillipp continued, "He will take you somewhere safe tonight."

With an unlit cigar dangling from his mouth, Father Delp said, "*Zusammenpacken*. Pack up everything. Leave nothing behind. Take your yellow star off and put it in your luggage. We need to go now. You will spend the night in the Church of St. Michael. We will discuss plans tomorrow to get you out of Munich immediately."

Anikka, with her voice breaking, said, "Where will we go?"

"We are making plans for you," Father Delp responded.

"The underground will assist. You will know more tomorrow. Let's go. We must leave now."

Ludwig asked, "Are the Stolzes coming with us?"

Phillipp responded, "No. Hurry. You must go. We will be okay. I am a physician for some of the Nazis. They won't find anything here, and they will leave us alone."

The Adlers quickly packed, and once all semblance of anyone living in the cellar was dealt with, they went up the stairs one by one. Little Nannerl was last.

She stopped on the stairs and ran back down to grab a doll she had left inside an old box in the corner. She grabbed the toy and then realized that she still was wearing her Jewish star. She removed the star and placed it on top of the small box in the corner of the cellar. She then joined the others as they made their way to the front door.

Father Delp stepped outside and checked the street. All was clear.

Ludwig hugged Phillipp. He did the same to Inga, who was still beside herself with grief. Anikka hugged them as well. The Stolzes then hugged the children.

"Go," said Phillipp to Ludwig.

Ludwig said, "We owe you and your wife our life."

"You don't owe us anything, Ludwig. Just save your family and continue to make music, my friend. We will miss all of you."

"*Auf Wiedersehen*, Phillipp."

"We will pray for you," said Phillipp.

"Likewise," replied Ludwig. They shook hands again.

Fr. Delp came back inside the doorway and said, "It's all clear. We need to go now. If we are stopped, let me do all the talking. Ready?"

Ludwig looked at his wife and his children, before responding, "Yes."

The Adlers and Father Delp departed.

THE CHURCH WAS ONLY a few blocks away. Led by Father Delp, they spoke not a word, walking among the shadows. As they crossed the Marienplatz, they walked close to the town hall, avoiding walking directly through the center of the square. The exquisite Glockenspiel set quietly high above. They continued onto Kaufingerstrasse and made it to the beautiful and dignified, Jesuit Renaissance church of St. Michael. Fr. Delp quickly ushered them into an old crypt below the altar, where the tomb of Bavaria's fairy-tale king, Ludwig II, was located among other ruling family members of the Wittelsbach dynasty.

Father Delp walked the Adlers over to a corner and pointed out blankets stacked on top of each other. "Sleep here," he said. "You will be safe. The Nazis will not come inside."

"*Danke*," said Ludwig.

"I will come by in the morning. Monsignor Hebert knows you are here. He is in the rectory. Under no circumstances should you leave the crypt tonight."

The Adlers, with fear embedded in their eyes, nodded in agreement. Father Delp laid his right hand on Ludwig's shoulder and, with a compassionate smile, said, "I promise, Ludwig, you and your family will be safe tonight. Get some rest." Father Delp bade the family a good night and then departed the crypt leaving the Adlers alone.

The numerous tombs filled up the entire dark, dank crypt. Ludwig and Anikka laid out the blankets. Anikka laid down between her two children, who both snuggled close to her, between the two tombs. She and the children quickly fell asleep, while Ludwig sat against the wall next to Mad King Ludwig's ornately decorated tomb. Ludwig would not sleep tonight, he told himself. His ears strained for the sounds of anything, anyone coming down to the crypt. The words of Father Delp, "You will be safe," provided little comfort.

His thoughts drifted to the last few months. He knew his wife looked to him to protect her and the children, but everything that was happening to them now seemed out of his control. As the night wore on, he began to gently hum the music from the *adagio* portion of his violin concerto, in hopes to make his mind forget, at least for tonight, all they had been through. He fought sleep. Suddenly, as he was nodding off, he thought he heard in the distance the sound of two gunshots. He had seen so much violence, too much violence. He longed for peace. He finally lost his battle, and he drifted off to sleep.

6

ON THE RUN

Forty of the ninety Jews in the last railcar jumped that night. From his position atop the railcar, Wilhelm mowed down ten of the escapees. The train continued to the station at Melk, where *Oberst* Klotz quickly let the Germans stationed there know what had happened. German soldiers from Melk, led by *Oberst* Klotz, would begin searching the woods at dawn. The Germans were not that concerned. They knew they would find the Jews.

HEINRICH, Kurt and Alfred trudged single file through the woods. Josef clung tightly to Alfred's neck as he rode on his back. They walked slowly as their legs felt heavy as logs to lift. The brisk wind made the frigid air seem even colder. Their breaths smoked as they made their way deep into the forest.

These were the same woods that, as a young boy, Alfred hunted with his father, but in the middle of the night, he was not quite sure where they were. The three friends kept pushing further into the forest. Slivers of moonlight through the dense tree canopy overhead provided just enough light to allow them to make their way through the woods.

Heinrich still carried his violin case, which was miraculously unharmed by his leap from the train. He had not played the violin in quite some time, and he was unsure if he would ever play it again. But holding it provided a memory. A memory of a time when music and art dominated Vienna and not the hate and violence that had taken over.

Alfred kept assuring Josef that he would see his mother again, soon. Of course, Alfred had no idea if that was true or not. Josef kept saying over and over again that he was hungry and cold, and that he wanted his mother.

They were all tired and cold but kept pushing themselves to continue. They had no plan about where to go or what to do. As the night wore on, each of the men came to the absolute belief that death was certain if they were caught. That thought kept them pushing on and on.

They scrambled down a steep green bank and plunged into an even denser set of trees. Hungry, tired, enveloped in darkness, and with no clear path to follow in the tangled undergrowth, their progress was greatly slowed.

They soon came upon a clump of thick bushes. Alfred stopped and turned to his friends. "The sun will be up soon. We should hide here among the bushes and take a quick break. Once the sun comes up, I will have a quick look around. With the sunlight, I should be able to figure out where we are. I grew up in these woods. I just need to get my bearings in the daylight."

The small, exhausted group crawled under and to the center of the thick set of bushes. They laid down and remained silent, straining to hear any sounds at all, but could only hear the howling wind through the trees. Alfred slowly rubbed his hand through Josef's hair, keeping the young boy quiet and holding him tight to keep him warm in the cold air.

As dawn began to break, the sun's morning rays came through the trees providing more and more light down in the forest. Underneath the bushes, however, darkness still prevailed.

Heinrich asked in a whisper, "Alfred, do you have any idea where we should go?"

"I will in a second. I will be right back. Josef, stay with them. Keep quiet."

Heinrich moved over next to the young boy and told Alfred, "He's fine. I will keep him warm."

Just as the early morning sunlight finally penetrated the thick bushes, Alfred said, "Ok. I will not be gone long. I will take a quick look around."

"Just be careful," Kurt whispered.

Alfred crawled out of the bushes.

When he had left, Kurt asked, "Heinrich, do you think the Nazis will be looking for us?"

"Yes."

"How many jumped with us? How many were killed?"

"I'm not sure. I know when I looked back, I saw two or three get hit."

"I saw an elderly couple, holding hands as they jumped,"

Kurt explained. "They were shot immediately when they hit the ground. They never had a chance."

Heinrich bowed his head and shut his eyes, and breathed deeply. As he reflected back to the train station, he wondered if that was the same elderly couple who Kurt had seen getting shot.

Kurt asked, "Heinrich, do you think anyone else made it?"

"I don't know. When I heard that machine gun, I took off into the woods with you and Alfred."

Kurt nodded his head in agreement. "I just put my head down and ran right into the forest. What will happen if we are caught?"

Heinrich suddenly sat up and pressed his finger to his lips. His face went ashen white as he heard far off in the distance the sound of barking dogs. "Kurt, do you hear that?"

"I hear it. German Shepherds. My God, the Nazis are coming for us. Alfred better come back quick."

"Shh. Listen. Quiet. I hear movement."

They both sat motionless, while Kurt held Josef tight. Just then, Alfred came crawling back under the bushes. Heinrich and Kurt sighed with relief. Alfred crawled close to them and, in a low voice, said, "I'm sure you heard it too. We cannot stay here. The dogs will find us."

"But the Nazis will see us moving in the daylight," Heinrich retorted.

"After walking about, I know exactly where we are. There is a farm not too far away. We can hide in the barn until tonight. There is a little creek. I know it will be freezing, but the dogs will lose our scent if we walk in the creek a little way."

Heinrich asked, "Then where? Where should we go after we leave the farm?"

"The Abbey," replied Alfred. "I used to study music with a monk who lives at the Abbey. He now runs the school there. Although I have not seen or spoken to him in many years, I know he will help us. We will make our way quickly to the barn, and then we will wait until tonight to go to the Abbey. There is a tunnel, hidden down in the forest that leads right to the Abbey. The monks use it all the time to get to the woods. My friends and I used to play inside it. I'm pretty sure I can find it. The monks will help us."

Kurt huffed. "Help us just like our 'friend' back in Vienna who betrayed us and turned us over to the Gestapo. I am putting my trust in no one, especially a non-Jew."

"The monks, I believe, are our only option at this point."

"I agree," Heinrich quickly replied. "We have no other option than to trust people. Those people who opened the railcar door died for us. They freed us and gave us a chance of life. So, we have a plan. Let's hurry to this farmhouse. I am exhausted and freezing to death."

As they scurried from under the bushes, suddenly, far off in the distance, the sound of a gunshot echoed through the forest. The three friends stood rooted in horror, as Josef began to cry. As Alfred tried to comfort him, Heinrich said, "We have to move quickly. Kurt, I think we found out the answer to your question. Others did make it into the woods. The Nazis must have found one of the escapees."

"Let's get to the creek," Alfred said. "Listen, the dogs are getting closer."

They spoke not another word to each other but quickly left the bushes and continued deeper into the woods. Still, the sound of the barking of the dogs pursued them. They followed Alfred and finally came to the creek. On either side of the deeply dug bed were muddy, steep banks. A dog would have a tough time trying to traverse the banks, or so they hoped.

They carefully made their way down the bank into the creek. They waded in the creek for quite a way until they climbed the bank and cut across an open field. At the end of the field sat an old, dilapidated barn. The doors were off of the small structure, and part of the roof was caved in.

Alfred looked dejectedly at the sight before him. "Sorry. It used to be in much better shape."

Kurt replied, "That's all right. Let's just get inside."

They made their way quickly and quietly to the barn and went inside. Alfred put Josef down and sat next to him. Their feet were frozen from walking in the creek. They removed their socks and shoes and placed them outside the barn in hopes that the sun would help dry them. They came back inside and looked around.

Alfred said, "I know the roof is caved in, but perhaps we should go up in the hayloft and seek shelter. At least, if the Nazis find the barn, they may just think no one would be up in the loft with only half a roof."

The three friends and Josef climbed up a ladder to the loft. They pulled the ladder up into the loft and then proceeded to sit down on top of clumps of hay. Alfred laid Josef down, using the hay as his blanket. Josef's eyes blinked over and over again as he fought back the urge to sleep. The three friends listened intently but heard no more barking dogs or gunshots.

Alfred told his two friends, "Sorry for the

accommodations. I thought we would be warmer. At least we are together."

"Your idea to come to the farm was a good one," Heinrich said. "Josef seems comfortable. And I agree, most importantly we are together. I prayed on that train platform earlier that the two of you would join me in the same railcar. I was thrilled when you did. There is no doubt in my mind that God wants us to be together, just as he kept us together in Vienna when we were hiding."

Kurt asked, "You think we did the right thing; I mean by jumping?"

Without hesitation, Alfred replied, "Yes."

Heinrich nodded. "Maybe that's why we were together in that railcar. It was meant to be. You have my word until this blasted war is over, I will never leave the two of you. I promise."

Both Alfred and Kurt replied, "Same here."

Heinrich pointed to Josef. "And the same for our little friend over there."

Alfred smiled. "Thank you."

Kurt asked, "Do you think they shot everyone left behind? The ones who didn't jump."

Heinrich nodded. "Kurt, you cannot dwell on it. It was a chance we had to take. We had to try to escape. Have no regrets. That door was opened for a reason. Now, get some sleep. We have a big night ahead of us."

"I will stay awake and will wake the two of you if I hear anything," Alfred said.

"I will take over in a few hours," Kurt replied. "Just wake me when you want to sleep."

Heinrich, using his violin case as his pillow, laid down. "If the two of you have the watch, I will go to sleep."

Kurt laughed. "Yes, old man, you need your sleep."

"Old man? I'm twenty-six and only a year older than the two of you."

"Yes, but we look younger."

They all laughed, as Heinrich said, "Wake me when it's time to go."

As they tried to get comfortable, Heinrich rolled over. In his mind, the faces of the other Jews in the railcar flashed before him. They did the right thing by jumping. He kept telling himself that over and over again, fighting through feelings of guilt that washed over him. He slowly drifted asleep.

Meanwhile, Kurt continued speaking with Alfred. Soon, Kurt turned his attention to his loved ones and asked Alfred, "Do you think we will ever see our families again? Do you think they are still alive?"

"They wanted us to survive. That is why they wanted us to go into hiding together so that we could live. And that is what we must do. And hopefully, when this is all over, we will all be reunited with our families. We have to believe that is exactly what will happen."

"God, I miss them so much. My Gina, and all of them."

Alfred responded with kindness. "I know, Kurt. I know. I miss my family as well, and I miss our music. These last few days, I have been reflecting back to our time in the Philharmonic. God, we were so blessed. A life dedicated to music in Vienna was a good life."

"A life that was taken away from us."

Alfred shrugged. "True, but they can never take away our memories. Never."

Kurt rubbed his chin with his hand. "I feel like we let our friends and family down. We hid while they suffered. Just like the train. We jumped from the train, while others remained."

Alfred stared directly ahead. "Kurt, we did the right thing. Try to sleep. We will need our strength tonight."

"Just give me three hours, then I will take over the watch."

"All right. I'll wake you in three hours."

Kurt tried to sleep, but his mind wandered to thoughts of Gina. He had met Gina when she was in school studying dance, while he studied voice for a career in opera. But with her support, he decided to become a cellist and pursue his goal of becoming a member of the Vienna Philharmonic. He planned to marry her once his career path had been secured. But things worked out much differently. Graduation for Gina would never come. She had been expelled from school for being Jewish. Then he was expelled from the Philharmonic. As time passed, Gina and Kurt still saw each other. That was until Gina, and her family, were deported to a labor camp six months ago. He had not seen nor heard from her since. Kurt finally drifted asleep.

Meanwhile, Alfred's thoughts drifted to Anna Klein. All she wanted, all she cared about was saving her son. He turned and looked at the now sleeping Josef, covered under the hay. He wondered what the future held for that little boy and what would become of Josef's mother. He also wondered what the future held for all of them.

Although the temperature inside the barn was below

freezing, it was better than being outside completely exposed to the elements. Alfred made his way over to Josef and laid next to him, holding the young boy tightly. Alfred tried to fight his urge to close his eyes. A battle he quickly lost, as he fell fast asleep.

The three friends and Josef slept so hard they did not hear the sound of the gunshot close by that echoed throughout the forest.

The Nazis had just discovered another escapee and stood him up in a clearing. With his back turned, he was shot and killed.

With that death, the Nazis had killed all of the Jews who had escaped from the train, except for three men and a young boy. The Nazis continued to search for them. Meanwhile, the roads to Melk were now being watched. *Oberst* Klotz believed the remaining Jews in the forest had nowhere to hide. He would find them. They would be killed before nightfall. After all, no one escapes from the trains.

THE THREE FRIENDS awoke early in the evening. Alfred apologized over and over again for falling asleep and not waking Kurt.

Kurt responded, "It's fine. We needed the rest. Now listen."

They sat quietly in the hayloft straining to hear any sounds but heard nothing. They were fully expecting the Nazis to walk into the barn at any moment.

They waited until well after midnight to begin their journey to the tunnel. Heinrich asked, "How far is it?"

"Not too far," advised Alfred. "But the Germans stationed in Melk would be able to see us making our way to the tunnel during the day. I was afraid it would be too dangerous. That's why I wanted to wait till night. I know this part of the forest like the back of my hand. I can get us there in the darkness."

They promised Josef food once they got to the Abbey. They left the barn, stopping momentarily to listen for the sound of dogs or the searchers. They heard nothing but the brisk wind through the trees. They put their damp shoes and socks back on and began making their way to the tunnel.

They trudged single file once again. The thicket was just as dense as before, but Alfred, familiar with the area, confidently lead them through it. They had gone a good distance when they thought they heard the sound of a dog.

7

SAFE PASSAGE

*F*ather Delp returned to the crypt first thing in the morning. He held identification papers in his hands. He woke up the Adler family.

"Munich is far too dangerous a place for you to stay. For that matter, all of Germany is not a welcome place for Jews. You must get out. There is no place safe to hide. There are too many betrayers looking to turn people in who are hiding Jews. These are your papers. The resistance worked on these last night when I left you. These papers will be your identity while you travel. You are citizens of Switzerland now, simply returning home."

Ludwig and Anikka stared at the photos of individuals who resembled both of them in passing.

Father Delp continued, "You are boarding a train that leaves at ten this morning."

Anikka asked, "Are you coming with us?"

"No. I will go with you to the station. Talk to no one. Just get on that train."

The Adlers gathered their belongings. As they did so, Father Delp pulled Ludwig off to the side. From his pocket, he pulled out a Jewish star. "Put this in your luggage, Ludwig. It's for one of your kids. You never know if they may need it."

"They have one already."

"One of them left their star in the cellar. The Gestapo discovered that star last night when they raided the Stolzes' home."

Ludwig closed his eyes and thought immediately about those gunshots he heard last night. With his eyes still closed, he asked, "Were they killed?"

Father Delp replied, "Yes."

Ludwig brought his hands up to his face as tears began pouring from his eyes. His heart ached, and grief covered him like a thick blanket as he thought about his friends. When he opened his eyes, he said, with his voice breaking through his sobs, "My God. Their own neighbor and friend turned them in. A person who they knew betrayed them. Why? My God, why?"

Father Delp shrugged. "Because he put himself before another."

"Don't tell my wife, Father."

"No. And never let your children know."

Father Delp walked back to Anikka and the children and said, "Everyone ready? We have a car coming in twenty minutes. We will be going straight to the station."

Anikka spoke up. "Father, you have been very kind. You and the Stolzes have been a Godsend."

"There are still good people in this world, *Frau Adler*. There are still good people."

Composing himself, Ludwig walked over to her. Anikka asked, "Father Delp, where is the train taking us?"

"You are going to Lucerne. There you will meet Father Michael Koch, another Jesuit like myself. He is a good man and will give you additional papers to get you and your family somewhere safe."

"Where?" questioned Anikka.

"Father Koch will be able to explain more. It's best for me not to know where you go. I hope you understand. Please tell no one about my help."

Anikka began to cry as the events of the past few hours and the impending journey washed over her. Ludwig tried to comfort her by holding her in his arms.

Ludwig then said, "Father Delp, my wife and I thank you for all of your help."

"Ludwig, I know you don't know me. But I know you through your music. I have heard your compositions on many occasions. I even attended one of the parties at the Stolzes' home. You are a gifted soul. You are an angel who was touched by God with a musical gift. Germany has killed too many of its angels."

"But why help us? Why risk your life for ours? You know what can happen, Father."

"Of course. But, if through my life, I am able to bring a little more love in the world, a little more kindness, if I can bring more light and truth into this world, then I would not have lived my life in vain. That is what God demands of me. I know you are not a believer in the Messiah, Ludwig. But I know you have a strong love of God."

"Father Delp, I am a religious person, not observant as I once was, but you are correct, my wife and I both have a strong love of God and are proud of our Jewish faith."

Father Delp said, "Rest assured, God is watching over you and your family. My sole purpose behind my vocation is to show the world the presence of God. He is the reason I am here. As for your family, your strong belief in your God, my God, will save you and your family. Trust Him. If by helping you and your family, I can show others God's work in this world, then so be it."

"Thank you, Father."

"We must go. The car should be here to take us to the train. You are now officially Marcel and Judith Kennel of Lucerne, Switzerland. I hope you have enjoyed your stay in Munich."

Ludwig and Anikka both laughed, unsure when or if they would ever laugh again.

8

THE ABBEY

*T*he town of Melk stands to the western end of the Wachau Valley, a wine-producing region in Lower Austria. It is a small, sleepy town, ever under the watchful eye of its massive Benedictine monastery that stands proudly on a rocky bluff high above the town and the Danube River below.

There was much excitement this morning inside the Abbey. Refugees had arrived through the tunnel during the night and were found by the monks out in the Abbey gardens. The Abbot was informed, and he ordered that they be fed a hearty breakfast and then sent to the foyer outside the library to await meeting with him.

Adso Eco was the Abbot of Melk. He was a man of fifty, tall and athletic-looking, with a dark complexion that complimented the black habit he wore. He made his way to the foyer by the library, where he found the three Jewish refugees and a young boy.

As he entered the foyer, Abbot Adso smiled broadly, and with his arms open wide, said, "My sons, welcome. Welcome to Melk Abbey. I am Abbott Adso Eco. I know you spoke with a few of our monks this morning. I know how you escaped the train."

Alfred spoke for the group, "Thank you, Abbott Adso. I am Alfred Keller. I was born in Melk, and although I did not attend school at *Stiftsgymnasium Melk* here in the Abbey, I did study music here almost every afternoon with Father Schier before my family moved to Vienna many, many years ago." He then pointed to his two friends and continued the introductions. "This is Heinrich Bergman and Kurt Hofmann, both of Vienna. And this is Josef Klein. His mother stayed on the train. She is waiting for him."

The Abbot placed his hands on the little boy's head. "Bless you, child. Your momma is well and can't wait to see you again." He then turned to Alfred. "Welcome back to Melk Abbey."

"I am here not as a visitor," Alfred said. "We would like to request sanctuary."

The Abbot smiled and nodded his head with understanding. "My monks would protect you till their death, which would happen if I allowed you to stay. Melk is far too dangerous for you to stay here. You need to move on."

"Abbott Adso, we are merely Jewish musicians, with an abandoned child from Vienna. We have nowhere else to go. Please allow us to stay here."

"My sons, even if I wanted to I could not. The Nazis are all over Melk."

Alfred asked, "Is Father Wilhelm Schier still here?"

"No, my son. He left a few years ago. Father Coelestin

Schoiko replaced him as head of the school. One of Schoiko's first actions was to close the school. Father Schoiko is close to the Nazis."

Alfred said, "Closed? It was one of the oldest schools in all of Austria."

"These are terrible times for our Abbey, for Melk and all of Austria. You must move on quickly. You cannot stay here."

The three dear friends anxiously looked at each other, before Abbott Adso said, "Besides, my monks are telling me that the Germans are searching the forest high and low for the three of you. You were wise to use the tunnel. The Nazis are watching all the roads leading into town. Eventually, the Germans will leave the forest and search Melk. They will make their way up here to see if we have seen you. You must leave here."

Heinrich said, "We have no place to go."

The Abbot turned to him. "Lucerne. A boat will leave in an hour down the Danube. We have papers for you to get to Lucerne. Father Michael Koch knows you are coming. He works with the resistance. We have been in contact with him. He will help. He is a good man, even though he is a Jesuit. He will find placement for you somewhere. Too many dangerous places now."

The three friends resolved themselves to placing their trust in Abbot Adso. Relieved that there was a plan, they smiled at each other. "Thank you, Abbott Adso," replied Alfred, Heinrich and Kurt.

Abbot Adso replied, "You must go down to the river. Brother John will lead you. You are all in my prayers." The Abbott clapped his hands, and a monk came and stood next to him.

"This is Brother John. He will take you first to clean up, shave, and put on monk habits and then will proceed to take you to the boat. Brother John also will take young Josef and leave him here with our monks. We will get a young mother from Melk to follow not far behind the three of you with Josef as if he was her own child. She will meet you with him at the boat. Then the three of you and Josef will depart for Lucerne. When you arrive in Lucerne, tell no one what occurred here. I beg you."

The Abbot then walked over to Josef. He picked him up into his arms. "How old are you, my son?"

"Six," the young boy timidly responded.

"You are a courageous young man." The Abbot placed his hand over Josef's heart. "May God travel with you now and for the rest of your life."

Josef smiled as the Abbot placed him down and said to all of them, "Now, go with Brother John. Godspeed, my children. We will pray for your safe journey."

PART II

CASTEL GANDOLFO
December 1942

9

CASTEL GANDOLFO

*E*arly one morning, Monsignor Celso Benigno Luigi
Costantini walked the precisely landscaped gardens
of Castel Gandolfo, the Pope's residence twenty miles
southwest of Rome. Dating back to 1678, popes had come to
this history-rich location in the Alban Hills as a means to
escape the stress of the Vatican; where popes could relax
while taking long strolls through the acres of exquisite
gardens that surround the 400-year-old papal palace, and
where, in the summer, they enjoyed the cool climate and mild
breezes, away from the stifling heat of Rome.

Since the outbreak of war, Pope Pius XII had not left the
confines and security of Vatican City, and he no longer visited
his beloved Castel Gandolfo. Any important matters to be
handled at Castel Gandolfo fell to Monsignor Costantini, who
didn't mind at all, as he loved getting away from the politics
of the Vatican and from his overworked position as secretary
of the *Sacra Congregazione di Propaganda Fide* (Congregation

for the Propagation of the Faith), handling all Catholic missionary communities throughout the world. Spending a few days at Castel Gandolfo afforded Monsignor Costantini the opportunity to take his long morning walks in the beautiful gardens, which were located below the Apostolic Palace.

The Apostolic Palace sat perched high on a rocky outcrop above Italy's Lake Albano. In addition to the Apostolic Palace, the grounds of Castel Gandolfo housed the Vatican Observatory, villas, two cloistered convents behind the papal enclosure, as well as a farm with chickens and cattle. And down in the gardens, one could find the ruins of the opulent residence of the First Century Roman Emperor, Domitian, and an imperial theater, both of which provided glimpses to the location's long historical importance.

Although the Apostolic Palace is beautiful in its intimacy, the gardens are what makes the location striking. There are three tiers known as the Barberini Gardens built on the same site as Domitian's ancient villa. Orchards of apricot, peach and olive trees are scattered throughout the grounds, as begonias, ageratum, pansies and other ornamental flowers add color, particularly in the spring when they are in full bloom. Shady holm oaks, towering cedars, stately cypresses, and sculptured hedges line secluded paths in the gardens that offer pleasant strolling areas, punctuated with statutes throughout. Monsignor Costantini favored the shady lanes of the part of the gardens called the *Giardino Della Madonnina*.

As he walked amid the beautiful gardens that brisk December morning, he was deep in thought. Three more refugees with a child in tow, all from Vienna, arrived last night at Castel Gandolfo. They had come from Lucerne.

Father Michael Koch had sent them. They joined the other Jews who were already hiding there. The Jews hiding at Castel Gandolfo were all musicians. Father Koch had sent all the other Jewish refugees under his protection to the priests at the Gregorian University in Rome, who would find placement for them or hide them at the Seminary itself.

The care of the Jewish musicians and their families at Castel Gandolfo fell to Monsignor Costantini. Italian born, he was highly intelligent with degrees in philosophy and theology. At sixty-six, he was the same age as Pope Pius XII and had been ordained to the priesthood the very same year as the Pontiff as well (1899). In his earlier years, Costantini was a beloved pastor in Concordia near Venice before being named as an Apostolic delegate to China, where for 19 years he lived and championed evangelization to the Chinese people. He was also a prolific writer, a lover of art, and a sculptor in his own right. Upon his return back to Italy, he became an outspoken critic of Italy aligning itself with Hitler and stated on many occasions that Italy would be following the Anti-Christ into war. He was the perfect choice in handling the refugees at Castel Gandolfo as he was a kind, caring soul, had a passing knowledge of the German language, and, most importantly, was a person whom the Pope trusted without question or concern.

The Jewish musicians and their families were all huddled in a small villa located on the grounds. Cots were set up to provide a place to rest and hopefully offer a feeling of safety that most had not felt for a very long time.

Monsignor Costantini had not met the latest additions, but he would soon. He needed to meditate in the gardens this morning. Shortly, he would be leaving for Rome to attend a highly secret, important meeting at the Vatican with the Pope, the Roman Curia, the administrative unit of the Holy See, and other leaders of the Church hierarchy, all who assisted the Pope in governing the Church.

Monsignor Costantini had been told of the arrival of the newest refugees late last night. He knew Sister Margerita Kirsch, the Pope's handpicked person in charge of Castel Gandolfo, would take good care of them.

WHEN THE THREE refugees from Vienna arrived at the Castel Gandolfo, Sister Margerita led them to the villa. She took the sleeping Josef from Alfred's arms and carried him to the building. Once inside, she showed them to the area where they could rest.

Kurt spoke for the group, as he knew Italian from his days studying opera. "*Grazie, Suor Margerita,*" he said.

"*Prego.* But please, you can speak German with me. I was born in Cologne and worked a short time with Pope Pius XII when he was Papal Nuncio in Munich. I know your travels have not been easy. But you are safe now. Get some rest. An excellent breakfast awaits you in the morning. Monsignor Costantini will talk with you tomorrow. Sleep."

She walked to a cot and put Josef down, covering the child with a warm blanket. She kissed him on his forehead and then bid everyone a good night.

Kurt and Alfred climbed into bed and quickly fell asleep. Heinrich Bergman was also exhausted. The past few days traveling from Lucerne and then to Rome were nerve-racking. He made his way to his cot, the violin case he had carried with him from Vienna still in hand. He opened the case and pulled out the violin to check on it.

The violin was dark in color but with a deep varnish of orange-brown undertones. The exquisite purfling and tracery around the sides and the scroll made it look more like a piece of art than a musical instrument. There was no doubt this violin had been crafted by a genius luthier. And it was, crafted in 1721 by none other than Antonio Stradivari in his workshop in his hometown of Cremona, Italy. Inside the violin, the paper label was still visible. Written in Latin, it read: *Antonius Stradivarius Cremonensis Faciebat Anno 1721.*

As Heinrich climbed into the cot, the gentlemen next to him sat up in his cot and asked, "Is that a Stradivarius?"

"It is. You must be a musician?"

"I am. My name is Ludwig Adler. I am from Munich."

"Not Ludwig Adler the composer?"

"Indeed."

"I have heard and played some of your compositions. It's an honor to meet you."

"It's an honor to have someone remember my music, especially now. What is your name?"

"I am Heinrich Bergman from Vienna."

"How in God's name do you have a Stradivarius?"

"It's known as the Vinterberg Stradivarius. It was a gift from my music teacher a long time ago. He had been a pupil of Karl Goldmark, who handed it down to him. Supposedly, this violin was originally owned by a musician at the Burgtheater, Karlheinz Vinterberg, who played at the premiere of Mozart's *Le Nozze di Figaro.*"

Ludwig said excitedly, "If only that violin could talk. And to think, Mozart heard it play."

"It has stayed with me all the way from Vienna. The Nazis never took it from me. Once they almost did, but the idiot guard thought it was a worthless Jewish fiddle."

Ludwig laughed before continuing. "Did you play in an orchestra?"

"I was in the Vienna Philharmonic before being dismissed."

"Really. I'm sure I heard you play. What a fabulous orchestra. You were dismissed for being a Jew?"

"Yes, there were thirteen of us altogether. My other two friends sleeping over there were members with me. We were treated as outcasts by the very people we worked, studied and drank with daily. We became nothing more than dirty Jews to them."

"Whose child is that?"

"We escaped from a Nazi train. The boy's mother asked my friend, Alfred, to take the child."

"You are the ones who escaped the train? A priest in Lucerne told us the story and said he was awaiting your arrival when we left."

"Father Koch?"

"Yes."

"He sent you here?" He sent us here as well."

"All of the Jews in this room are musicians from Germany and Austria," replied Ludwig. "I guess Father Koch was trying to keep us together. He advised us that he could not get us out of Switzerland as he has been doing, so he sent us to Rome. He must have done the same with you and the other musicians. My children will be thrilled to have that boy of yours to play with. They are very bored."

"That would be great. We constantly try to keep him from thinking about his mother."

"What happened to his mother?"

Heinrich frowned. "She stayed on the train."

"Get some rest. We will talk more tomorrow."

Heinrich rolled over and finally slept.

———————

MONSIGNOR COSTANTINI CONTINUED WALKING that morning amid the sculptured gardens, but he paid little attention to his surroundings. His mind was preparing for the meeting with the Pope. He looked at his watch and then began making his way to the villa to meet the new refugees before leaving for Rome.

POPE PIUS XII

*T*he *Sala Bologna* is located within the Northern wing of the Pope's private quarters, deep inside the Vatican Apostolic Palace. It is a long, rectangular room. On the lower walls, huge frescos, commissioned in 1575 by Pope Gregory XIII, provide differing bird's-eye views of the medieval city of Bologna. Intimate in their details, the images show the importance the city of Bologna once held in Italy, thanks in large part to the University of Bologna, the oldest university in the world. The stunning ceiling above, in exquisite colors, represents the celestial sphere. Directly below the celestial image sits the likenesses of ten ancient astronomers situated in ten individual colonnades.

Under the image of the heavens, a large table ran the length of the room. The Pope was seated in a high-backed chair at the head of the table. As usual, Monsignor Celso Costantini, who had arrived in Rome earlier that day from Castel Gandolfo, sat at his side. Also in attendance at the high-level meeting was his Secretary of State, Luigi Cardinal Maglione, the Pope's Jesuit priest secretary, Father Robert Lieber, members of the Roman Curia, as well as some of the most powerful Archbishops within the Church. The purpose of the meeting was to discuss the Jewish refugee problem.

Pope Pius XII was fully aware that Catholic priests all over Europe were already playing a huge role in rescuing Jews at great peril to themselves. He was also mindful of the fact that the Church was already involved in helping Jews emigrate out of Europe. This was perilous for the Church as it was facing persecution from Hitler's Germany.

Monsignor Costantini was the man who was most involved with the emigration plan. In his position as secretary for the *Propaganda Fide*, he was a member of the Curia, although he liked only a few of his fellow members, as he thought that most were providing a disservice to his beloved Pope. He knew the Pope better than most.

After Costantini returned home from China for health reasons, Pope Pius XI, at the behest of then-Cardinal Eugenio Pacelli, the future Pope Pius XII, offered Costantini the position he currently held with the *Propaganda Fide*. Pacelli and Costantini grew closer as the years passed, and when Pacelli became Pope, Costantini seemed to always be in attendance at high-level meetings. The Pontiff came to rely on Costantini for the handling of many matters, and their relationship was one of warmth and respect.

Publicly, Pope Pius XII put forth the persona of a solitary figure. Even though he often confided in Monsignor Costantini, Monsignor Maglione, Father Lieber, and Sister Pascalina Lehnert, who was his longtime housekeeper and confidant, none of them had a deep, personal friendship with a man who since adolescence had lived his life to be in the world but not of it, as dictated by his spiritual guide, *The Imitation of Christ* by Thomas à Kempis. Pius always ate alone, and his daily walk in the Vatican gardens or at Castel Gandolfo, when he used to go there, were ever solitary. But, Pius, through small conversations, relied heavily on the friendship of Monsignor Costantini.

Where Monsignor Costantini was noticeably open and engaging in dealing with others, Pius was quiet and somewhat of an introvert. Yet, Pius was a skilled orator and was able to speak in many different languages. All his life, and even more so as Pope, Pius was always guarded, restrained, formal, and measured in his speech. Every word spoken was well thought out and had a precise meaning. Critics said his style of speaking was too pontifical, to ponderous, and not direct enough, so no one knew exactly what he was trying to say. In contrast, supporters said his style was exactly what would be expected from a Pope, particularly from one so intelligent and reverent.

Pius had large dark, piercing eyes that punctuated his studious, serious look. His outside reputation was that of a man who was restrained and aloof. However, once people met him, their perception would change as a warm, boyish inviting smile overtook his usual stern look. People often were surprised by his animated style and welcoming way, which went against the descriptions of him in the press. His charisma was astonishing, and his presence radiated calm and holiness. However, there always was a distance due to his supreme calling and his intractable mission to maintain the dignity of his high office.

He was a very disciplined man, highly intelligent, and

punctual to a fault. Some even thought that he projected the aura of a mystic, detached from the cares of everyday life. Others viewed him as ascetic and as an intellectual. As for Monsignor Costantini, he viewed Eugenio Pacelli as a courageous, saintly man, and one of the greatest men he had ever met in his life.

Pius was tall and slender, with a face that was thin and pallid. He wore steel-rim glasses that set confidently on his rather prominent Roman nose. His hands were long and tapered and were always expressive when he spoke. His voice had a commanding but plaintive tone. At the meeting, he wore his usual cream-colored cassock and *zucchetto*. And as always, his gold crucifix dangled from a large gold chain around his neck.

Everyone in attendance sat around the table, while other staff members sat in chairs against the walls. The Pope asked Monsignor Costantini to discuss the Jewish situation in Italy as well as the current status of emigration.

Monsignor Costantini began by discussing the racial laws passed by Benito Mussolini in 1938, which were very harsh for the Jewish people living in Italy. They banned all Jews from banking, government and education positions. They disallowed Jewish children from attending school with non-Jews. They made marriage between a Jew and a non-Jew illegal. Jews' property was also subject to confiscation.

He then said with emphasis, "Keep in mind, when these laws were issued, they were not met with outrage by the Italian people but instead with indifference. Over time, though, these laws have become despised by many ordinary Italians, with some offering their support to the Jewish people at great peril to themselves. Some Italians have allowed Jews to transfer their businesses and property over to them for safekeeping during this very trying time. Enforcement of these laws by the Italian leadership has not always been aggressively enforced. There are a number of loopholes that were added into the laws that made it easier for government officials to make exceptions."

He pointed out that compared to other parts of Europe, they were not nearly carried out to the degree that they were in other Axis countries, which made the German leadership complain about Italy's lax attitude toward the Jews. "For whatever reason, the Fascists have never bought into the idea of sanctioned abuse," he said. "Furthermore, the Italian government has refused to permit deportations of the Jewish population living in Italy. However, because of the economic conditions and psychological insults suffered by the Jews, life is still hard for them. Imagine the pain they must feel when they were once welcomed into Italian life, and now are no longer even considered Italians." He paused and eyed everyone around the table, who sat quietly, absorbed by every word uttered so far. As he turned his head, he looked directly at Pope Pius XII, who gently nodded his head, urging him on.

Monsignor Costantini then turned his attention to the Jews streaming into Italy. "Italy has welcomed into its borders many foreign Jews fleeing persecution in other parts of Europe," he said. Monsignor Costantini pointed out that for the foreign Jews entering Italy, conditions were even tougher, with most being interred in camps, at the insistence of the Italian leadership. However, even these camps, for the most part, allowed families to live together, send their children to school, and allowed Jews to practice their faith. Monsignor

Costantini stated that the ultimate goal for Jews in Europe, including those in Italy, was emigration to Palestine or America, if they would allow it.

"As most of you know, Signor Valobra's DELASEM (Delegation for the Assistance of Jewish Emigrants) has been instrumental in helping Jews all across Italy in all sorts of ways," he said. "The Vatican, of course, has been involved with assisting the Jews as well. As most of you know, some of the Roman Jews who were forced from their jobs have secretly been employed here at the Vatican in various roles. We also have been providing large numbers of baptismal certificates, allowing Jews to leave areas of Europe where they are being persecuted, and seek a safer area to live. However, I am greatly concerned that it is becoming increasingly difficult to get the Jews out of Europe."

Monsignor Costantini then related story after story of Jews being unable to leave for various reasons and issues. "The Port of Genoa is becoming dangerous as the Germans and Blackshirts are much involved there. Switzerland is beginning to allow only women and children to emigrate there. We are running out of escape routes."

Cardinal Maglione stood and said, "We still continue to provide fake visas and baptismal certificates to many Jews, allowing them to pass as Christians. But, without a doubt, emigration will only get more and more problematic. Providing them with a fake Christian identity does allow them to live in Italian communities."

The Pope, who had been quiet during Costantini's discourse, replied, "As all of you know, a few churches and monasteries are already hiding Jews among the Italian people, passing them off as Catholics. But more can and must be done. While we continue to offer our assistance with emigration, we need to develop a plan and a way for more Jewish refugees to be hidden in Italy."

There was a deep murmur by the majority of those in attendance. The debate raged as some thought the Church should not get involved. They feared that Hitler would eventually try to destroy the Church if he ever discovered the level of the Vatican's involvement. Others disagreed. They believed that hiding some Jews in Italy offered the Jews the best chance to be saved.

Pedro Cardinal Segura y Saenz, who was the Archbishop of Seville and one of the few non-Italians at the meeting, said, "Why Italy? What will keep the Jews safe in Italy as opposed to other places?"

Monsignor Costantini turned to the Pope. "Your Holiness, may I respond?"

"Certainly," the Pope replied.

"Italy is where his Holiness's influence is strongest. Also, consider this. Even while under the control of Mussolini, the Italians are not an anti-Semitic people."

Alfredo Cardinal Ildefonso Schuster, the powerful and influential residential Archbishop of Milan, rose. "I think we are all missing the point. I believe that the Church has been silent for too long. Instead of talking about helping the Jews to get out of Europe or assisting the Jews in hiding, the Church, through you, your Holiness, should speak out much more aggressively against the atrocities. You should take on Hitler."

The debate grew even more heated. At one point, Cardinal Schuster said with emphasis, "Your Holiness, with all due respect, your silence threatens the very moral authority of our Church. You must speak out."

Monsignor Costantini responded, "The Vatican is surrounded by Fascist Rome. Yet, at the same time, the Vatican is dependent upon those very same enemies for all of its food, water, electrical supplies, and even its garbage disposal. The Vatican survives due to one factor and one factor alone. To all outsiders, including both the Fascists and the Nazis, the Vatican is an independent and neutral state. This designation is based on the Lateran Treaty of 1929, which not only recognized Vatican City as such, but also authorized papal governance of certain other extraterritorial properties such as the Basilica of St. John Lateran, the offices of the Propagation of the Faith, and Castel Gandolfo. In return, the Holy See had pledged itself to perpetual neutrality in all international relations. Thus, every action by the Holy See during the war has to be taken with careful consideration so as not to upset the appearance of neutrality."

While arguments raged on, the Pope sat with his head down, fingering the gold crucifix that sat close to his chest. Finally, the exhausted Pontiff had heard enough. He slowly rose from his chair. This brought an immediate silence to the room. "As you know, in all of my dealings with Germany, I have tried preserving Vatican neutrality. I believe that this is the best position for our Church. First, if we would speak aggressively against Hitler, I shudder to think what would happen to all of our brother and sister German Catholics. Hitler's retribution would be swift and strong. Secondly, Hitler would bring devastation to Rome, including Vatican City. We cannot allow either thing to happen. So, our public stance must remain neutral. But I do believe that by taking a neutral position, Vatican City may become a refuge for war victims one day. So, that is why I disagree that speaking out is the thing we should do, and why instead I believe we have to tread very carefully."

Cardinal Schuster spoke up again and forcefully said, "But the Jews all across Europe are being mistreated and persecuted. Surely you cannot remain silent about their suffering."

The Pope wasted no time with his response. He said, "As for the Jews, I have been greatly troubled over their sufferings. I believe it is my obligation to try to do whatever is in my power to make their fate easier. Yet, every word that we address, and every one of our public declarations must be seriously considered in the interest of the Jews to avoid unwittingly making their situation more difficult. My priests out there, the ones who are actually doing the work, constantly beg me not to make public protests. They say it only increases the persecution of the very people they are trying to help. I am also acutely aware that the Nazis are murdering my priests for this very work. They do this work even though they have the absolute knowledge they could be killed instantly. Their fear is not that they will be caught. They do not even fear death. Their only fear is that their work will be stopped, leaving them unable to assist the Jews they are trying to save. They truly believe, and I agree, that the longer they can continue their work, the more Jews will be saved. They are convinced that loud protests from me and the Vatican would result in the discontinuation of their work in German-controlled countries."

The Pope looked up and down the table, eyeing each person, before stating, "Need I remind you what happened to our Dutch sons and daughters. It was just last year the Bishops there took on the Nazis and spoke out against the seizure and deportation of Jews and the confiscation of their property in Holland. The Bishops had a pastoral letter read at all of the masses. Yes, Cardinal Schuster. Here is an example for you of what happens when the Church speaks up. As a result, within a week of that letter being read, the SS rounded up thousands and thousands of Catholics of Jewish descent, including every priest, monk and nun who had any Jewish blood whatsoever, and deported them to camps. Now tell me. What good did it do? Did it save a life?"

He paused a moment, as he thought of his own Papal protest that he had written and then burned in the kitchen stove. He then eyed them all again before returning his gaze directly to Cardinal Schuster. "I ask you if the words of the Dutch Bishops brought the persecution of thousands and thousands, how many would be persecuted because of my words; 100,000, 200,000, or more?"

Everyone around the table remained silent.

"And remember what Archbishop Andrea Cassulo, Papal Nuncio in Romania, told us at this same table when he spoke with us not too long ago. He said that he was fully aware that he had to proceed cautiously because his actions could hurt, instead of being useful to so many wretched persons whom he must often listen to and try to help. He understood, better than most of you, the horrible predicament that our Church is facing. We endeavor to speak the truth while at the same time protect the Church and its members, as well as the Jews. I pray to God that happiness will return to all the Jews. If I can assist them by speaking out cautiously, while at the same time working behind the scenes to save them and lessen their suffering, so be it. We will continue trying to help the Jews to get out of Europe. At the same time, you will get the word out to all of your religious brothers and sisters that we must act to save all human lives if at all possible, which may mean Jews being hidden within Catholic communities. As for my part, the Church will rely on ordinary Italians to save the Jews. It is my prayer that the Italians will welcome the refugees and protect them. *In nomine Patris, et Filii, et Spiritus Sancti.*"

The entire Curia and the Archbishops in attendance made the sign of the cross, as the lengthy meeting came to an end. The Pope walked away from the table and motioned Monsignor Costantini over. As the Pope exited the room, Monsignor Costantini walked at his side.

"The Curia has been won over," Monsignor Costantini stated.

The Pope laughed and said, "For now. That will change. Most have no backbone. The younger ones do. I like to refer to them as the '*Giovani Patrioti*' (Young Patriots). They are the ones who one day will save our Church. The others are too set in their ways. A few of them yell and scream that I should speak out more. Don't they realize that if I truly believed it would help, I would run out onto the balcony overlooking St. Peter's Square and shout at the top of my lungs against the atrocities? But I am certain the reverse would be the result."

The Pope became quiet. The duo walked down a long corridor, past the dining hall where the Pope's beloved canaries lived in cages, to the large library, dominated by floor to ceiling bookcases loaded with books. This was the Pope's sanctuary. They entered and sat down in chairs located in the middle of the room. Sister Pascalina Lehnert entered with two cups of tea and served them.

Sister Pascalina, a pretty, disarmingly petite nun from Southern Germany, for many years had acted as the Pope's housekeeper, part-time secretary, protector and friend, dating all the way back to when he was Papal Nuncio in Germany. Having followed him back to Rome when he became Vatican Secretary of State, Pacelli had asked her to remain once he was elected Pope. She was the first woman to ever live inside the Apostolic Palace at the Vatican, and her closeness and the power she wielded due to her friendship with the Pope was envied by some members of the Curia. Some clergy despairingly called her *La Popessa* (The Lady Pope) as they viewed her as the Pope's gatekeeper and the person through which you had to navigate to get an audience. She was devoted to the Pope, and considered herself nothing more than his humble servant.

"Thank you, Sister," said Monsignor Costantini, as middle-aged nun handed him his tea.

As she turned and handed the Pope his tea, the Pontiff, in a tired and frustrated tone, said to Costantini, "Back to when I first worked in Germany as Papal Nuncio, I fought against Nazism and anti-Semitism. I remember like it was yesterday when, as Cardinal Secretary of State, Pope Pius XI asked me to help draft his *Mit Brenneder Sorge* (With Burning Concern), his anti-Nazi encyclical, the only one written in German so there would be no doubt that his words would reach the intended ears of who it was written for, the German people."

Monsignor Costantini immediately quoted verbatim the words written by then-Cardinal Pacelli:

"Whoever exalts race, or the people, or the State, or a particular form of State, or the depositories of power, or any other fundamental value of the human community - however necessary and honorable be their function in worldly things - whoever raises these notions above their standard value and divinizes them to an idolatrous level, distorts and perverts an order of the world planned and created by God; he is far from the true faith in God and from the concept of life which that faith upholds."

The Pope smiled, much impressed that Monsignor Costantini knew the words so well. Sister Pascalina interjected slowly, "Hitler knew well who crafted those words."

Monsignor Costantini laughed. "That is correct, Sister. He was infuriated. And you, your Holiness, became and have remained his enemy."

Pius grabbed his gold crucifix dangling by his chest. "That encyclical showed what National Socialism truly is: an arrogant apostasy from Jesus Christ, the denial of his doctrine and of his work of redemption. National Socialism is not based on love, but instead, it is based on a cult of violence, the idolatry of race and blood. National Socialism's ultimate goal is the absolute overthrow of human liberty and dignity. The Pope's encyclical was smuggled into Germany, secretly printed by local German presses and on Palm Sunday 1937 heroically read from pulpits all across Germany. And the result, hundreds of arrests, including many of our clergy, and the closing of twelve printing presses. Persecutions against the German Catholic Church also intensified quickly. Yet, we continued to raise our voice against the Nazis. In my first encyclical as Pope, *Summi Pontificatus*, I offered the truism which I have lived my entire life – A world where there is no Gentile or Jew, but Christ is all and in all."

While grabbing his crucifix even tighter, he said, "From my time working in Germany, I saw first-hand that loud protests have no effect on Hitler; none, other than an increase in his desire for hatred and fear. Yet, I am told again and again by critics to speak out. And when I do, I am told that I did not go far enough, even by leaders who have done nothing to confront the issue or even raise a finger to draw attention to these tragedies. These critics of mine have no idea what we are doing in the shadows to assist the persecuted. But, in the shadows is where it is and where it must remain." The Pope was quiet momentarily before he said almost in a whisper, "*Ad majora mala vitanda.* (To avoid greater evils.) That is what I owe to the persecuted."

Sister Pascalina made the sign of the cross, and wishing the two friends a goodnight, she left to retire for the night.

Once she had left, Monsignor Costantini said, "I agree with everything you said tonight, your Holiness."

The Pope sighed. "I don't know if what we are doing is correct or not. I pray daily that the Holy Spirit directs my actions. I know for certain that the anti-Nazi resistance leaders in Germany want me to tread very carefully. They constantly ask me to not speak out or to limit what is said on Vatican Radio criticizing the regime."

Costantini nodded his head with understanding and replied, "I remember before the War when I heard you warn many leaders that 'Nothing is lost with peace, everything may be lost with war.' Yet, your words fell upon deaf ears as Italy foolhardily entered the war and sided with the devil."

"My words could not keep Italy out of this war, yet somehow it is believed my words would stop a madman."

Monsignor Costantini leaned forward in his chair and said, "With the War now raging, your attention turns to the persecuted and the oppressed and the best way to offer assistance to them."

The Pope responded, "I feel a deep obligation to the priests and Catholic laity all over Europe who at this very moment are protecting Jews and other oppressed persons. We need to do whatever we can to protect our sons and daughters and at the same time continue to save those who are persecuted. But what some members of the Curia do not understand is that publicly the Vatican must and shall remain neutral. After all, I will be the Holy Father to both the victors and the vanquished when this terrible war is over. It is my hope in remaining neutral that I may be able to broker a peace so that this terrible war will end. So, we must put forth the face of neutrality, Vatican neutrality. Just as we did when we worked in conjunction with the British in our endorsement of the attempt to assassinate Hitler, we must always act in secret, while in public we maintain, with conviction, that in every conflict the Vatican is and will remain impartial. While behind the scenes, we must do whatever we can to assist those in need."

Costantini raised his finger and asked, "Speaking about assisting those in need, can I speak to you about our issue at Castel Gandolfo?"

"I know about our issue. Music has always meant the world to me. When I was a young boy, I played the violin. I often wonder if I should have pursued a career as such. As a young priest, when I was overwhelmed with the stress of work, I would play my violin for hours; it brought me to a place of comfort. The music of Brahms, Bach, Mozart, Beethoven, and Mendelssohn has provided to me countless hours of joy. But more important than the joy that music can bring, music provides a way for our Lord to call us to the realm of higher things. Art, and music, in particular, is the noblest manifestation of human genius. Can you think of anything other than music whose sole purpose is to express in human works the absolute infinite divine beauty of God? What a gift musicians have been given. By using their talent, they can bring this music to us. What do you wish to do about our . . . issue?"

"I want to keep them together. All of them."

The Pope smiled. "If I can repay the debt that I owe to music by providing solace to the people who bring it forth, then so be it. Our issue at Castel Gandolfo makes my mind wander back to my days as Papal Nuncio in Bavaria and my good friend, Ossip Gabrilowitsch."

"The pianist?" asked Costantini.

"Yes. He was a very talented pianist as well as a composer. His wife, Clara Clemens, who was the daughter of Mark Twain, was a singer. Ossip was a Russian Jew. At the outbreak of the Great War, he was arrested for being Jewish. My friend, Bruno Walter, the conductor, had been trying to have Ossip freed for weeks. He asked me to assist. I was able to get Ossip freed and then shipped off to America where he lived out his days with Clara. His music flourished in America. After this terrible war is over, the world will need music. Come, walk with me to my private chapel and tell me what is your plan for saving the music."

11

GIOVANE PATRIOTA

 he next morning, Monsignor Celso Costantini was again walking in the gardens, but this time within the beautiful Vatican Gardens. He thought back to his meeting with Eugenio Pacelli late into the night at the Pope's private chapel. His dear friend, the Vicar of Christ, and the man who filled the shoes of St. Peter on earth as the 260th successor, had agreed to put the fate of a few Jewish musicians and their families housed at Castel Gandolfo on him. Monsignor Costantini knew he now had to find placement for the fifteen Jewish musicians and their families. He desired to keep them together, but to do so, he would have to hide them in an Italian city somewhere, as hiding them on Vatican property would be too dangerous. Costantini was fully aware that the Jews' fate rested with the decision he would make. Soon, he would be leaving to return to Castel Gandolfo, where he would meet with all of the refugees. What he would tell them and where they would be placed, he had no answer.

As he walked by the statue of St. Thérèse of Lisieux, the guardian of the gardens, his mind was so fixated on the matter at hand that he did not hear the sound of footsteps approaching. His thoughts were interrupted when Father Biaggio Sanguinetti came up to him. "*Scusi*, Monsignor Costantini."

"*Si*," Costantini replied as if waking up from a slumber. "Ah, Father Sanguinetti. How is Cardinal Alonzo?"

"He is doing well. We are hard at work on some recommendations for liturgical reforms to church music."

Costantini, thinking of the Jewish musicians, chuckled. "Music. I'm a little busy handling my own music issues. What can I do for you?"

"Nothing. I am here to help you, I think. The Pope came to me this morning and said to find you."

Somewhat surprised, Monsignor Costantini asked, "Find me? Why did he want you to find me?"

"I don't know. He simply said to find you and inform you that I am a *Giovane Patriota*."

Costantini smiled. "A *Giovane Patriota*, huh?"

"Why he wanted me to tell you that I have no idea."

Costantini laughed hard. "Is that all he wanted you to tell me?"

Biaggio chuckled as he said, "No. He said to seek you out and offer my services for an issue you are handling at Castel Gandolfo."

Monsignor Costantini jerked his head, momentarily caught off guard by the mention of Castel Gandolfo, as his face turned deeply serious. He bit his lip while pondering what to say. He stared at the young priest in front of him. All of his laughter had ended. He finally responded by asking a question. "My issue? Did His Holiness tell you what my issue is?"

"No."

Monsignor Costantini tuned his gaze briefly skyward before he bore his stare into Biaggio's eyes. "But His Holiness sent you to help me?"

"Yes."

"And to help me with my . . . issue?"

"Monsignor Costantini, if I may ask. What issue are you handling at Castel Gandolfo?"

Monsignor Costantini went silent. He quickly debated with himself what to say. Telling Biaggio what his issue was would certainly be a risk. Yet, the Pope had to have a reason why he sent Father Sanguinetti to him. Surely, in doing so, the Pope trusted the young priest. If the Pope trusted him, then he would also. He said matter-of-factly, "There are Jewish refugees hiding at Castel Gandolfo."

Biaggio's mouth opened in surprise. "Jewish refugees, your eminence?"

"Yes."

Biaggio looked quizzically at Monsignor Costantini and replied, "Now I really don't know why the Pope sent me to you. I'm just a simple Vatican priest. How could I possibly help?"

Monsignor Costantini shrugged his shoulders. "I'm not sure either." Then as an afterthought, Monsignor Costantini added, "The Jewish refugees are all musicians."

Somewhat surprised, Biaggio asked, "Musicians?"

"Yes. Fifteen musicians and their families from all over Europe are hiding at Castel Gandolfo. They are not all together there by chance."

Biaggio's mind flashed back to his conversation just a few nights ago with Harold Tittmann. Ever since that discussion, Biaggio had been pondering the Pope's alleged silence. Was the Vatican really involved in hiding Jews? What a dangerous proposition, but wonderful at that same time.

Biaggio shook his head. "I had no idea the Vatican was involved in hiding Jews."

"My son, the Pope is and has been doing all that he can to save Jews. He has spoken out on many occasions. And he is helping the Jews not just through words but also through actions. Through emigration, issuing fake baptismal certificates, bringing Jews to take positions inside the Vatican and the Palatine Guard, protests when he believes they may work, and by letting all of his religious brothers and sisters and Catholic laity know that they should open their hearts and souls to the Jews, and all persons being persecuted. But he acts prudently as he is fully aware of the terrible effects his words could bring upon the Jews as well as Catholics. He hears the criticism of others as to what they believe he should say. Just last week, the Allies issued a declaration condemning the Nazis and letting the world know that the Nazi's goal is the complete extermination of the Jews."

"Yes, I am aware of that document."

"I believe that the Allied declaration is a very powerful and emotionally worded document. Anyone who reads it cannot claim that they do not know what the Nazis are doing to the Jews. The Allies have stated in that document exactly what they desire, wish and expect the Pope to say publicly in condemning the Nazis. However, take my word, those words by the Allies will quickly pass away. Those words will not stop the killing. There also will be no race from the Allies to open their doors to rescue the Jews from their plight. After all, words are words. But actions are actions. Actions more than words. The Pope is in a very tough spot, and he is correct in acting with prudence, yet at the same time, trying to do what he can to save the persecuted, like my issue at Castel Gandolfo."

"What will happen to them?"

"I am burdened with the placement of these Jewish musicians. They must be hidden in Italy . . . somewhere. I want to keep them all together."

"But where Monsignor?"

"I am reminded of an old Chinese proverb from my time I spent in China. 'If your strength is small, don't carry heavy burdens.' This is a heavy burden. I know I need help with this decision. I need to hide them in a community where people will be willing to accept them, where people will protect them, and where people would be willing to perhaps face death for taking them in." Monsignor Costantini sighed. "I have absolutely no idea where to send these musicians."

Biaggio clasped his hands in front of his face before he smiled broadly. Weeks of leading diplomats to and fro, feelings that his vocation was languishing as the world suffered outside the walls of the Vatican, suddenly were an afterthought as he now saw the light as to how he could help. "Musicians," Biaggio repeated. "I think I know a place; a place that will take them in; a place that will hide them; a place that will protect them; and a place that would die for them, if necessary."

"Does such a place exist?"

"It does, Monsignor Costantini. I'm from that place. My mother and father still live there."

"And where is this place?"

"In Sicily. In the small, secluded, hilltop village of Bellafortuna. The villagers are God-loving people. They also have an immense passion for music. I know they will willingly accept these people. Monsignor Pietro Mancini is the man we need to speak with. He will help."

"Is he a good man?"

"He is beloved by every villager of Bellafortuna and would go to his grave to protect the people under his watch. He is a decent soul. He is the reason why I am a priest. He is also an excellent musician. He taught both my father and me how to play the violin."

"Summon him here immediately."

"I will do so."

Monsignor Costantini, with the look of someone who had just had a heavy burden lifted from their shoulders, extended his hand toward Biaggio and clasped it tightly. "*Grazie, Father Sanguinetti.*"

"*Prego.* Thank you for trusting me with this. I will not let you down. Let me go make contact with Monsignor Mancini and my father. I will tell them to come to Rome at once."

Monsignor Costantini bowed his head and clasped his hands in prayer as he chanted, "*Gloria Patri, et Filio, et Spiritui Sancto. Sicut erat in principio, et nunc, et semper, et in saecula saeculorum.*"

"Amen," replied Biaggio.

"Of course, tell no one. I don't need to tell you what

would happen if the Nazis found out what the Pope is doing."

"Of course. Not a word."

Biaggio turned and left the gardens, as Monsignor Costantini whispered under his breath, *"Giovane Patriota; Bellafortuna."*

12

A SUMMONS TO ROME

*T*hree days later, a train was on its way to Rome. Onboard were Monsignor Pietro Mancini and Giuseppe Sanguinetti, both from the small village of Bellafortuna, Sicily. The two dear friends sat next to each other, talking the whole time as the landscape of Italy passed outside the windows.

"It's a shame there will be no *La Bohème*," said Monsignor Mancini.

Giuseppe replied, "It was a tough decision to cancel the summer opera festival. But our hands were tied. We use so many additional musicians from Palermo and other parts of Sicily to supplement our *Opera Orchestra di Bellafortuna* for the festival, but they cannot join us this year because of the war. Times are tough right now and have forced the cancellation of the entire season."

"All of Sicily is suffering due to the Allied blockade."

"Agreed."

Monsignor Mancini said, "At least your wine store and the Boccale Winery are doing well."

"I would not be that enthusiastic. They are both surviving mostly because we export a lot of wine to Palermo. The Germans discovered our wine. They love *Vino di Bellafortuna* and drink a lot of it."

"Talking about exporting, it will be good to see your son in Rome. Why did Biaggio ask that you bring me? Did he say what we are meeting about?"

"No. He just said for me to drop everything and get you to Rome. We are supposed to meet Biaggio at the Vatican."

"I wonder what this is all about. Maybe Pius XII is abdicating, and I am being named as the new pope."

Giuseppe nodded. "*Si.* That's it. Sorry, but Biaggio told me not to tell you."

The two friends laughed heartily.

Monsignor Mancini then said, "I haven't been to Rome in a while or seen Biaggio in some time. It will be good to see him again."

"I can't wait to see my boy."

The train continued on the way to Naples and then made the short trek up to Rome.

ONCE AT THE VATICAN, the duo was rushed to the *Stanza della Segnatura* (Room of the Signatura) in the Papal Apartments. Four gorgeous frescos by Raphael dominated the room. In the middle of the room was a large table with four chairs.

The room once housed the library of Julius II. The themes

of wisdom and thought, perfectly suited for the history of the room, echoed throughout the vibrant colored frescos.

A priest showed Monsignor Mancini and Giuseppe Sanguinetti inside. He closed the door on his way out. While they waited, Giuseppe could not take his eyes off the fresco of Adam and Eve on the ceiling.

"God, this room is spectacular," he whispered.

Monsignor Mancini said, "The colors are incredible. Look at the wall over there. That is Raphael's *School of Athens*. It's probably his most famous."

The art class was interrupted when the door opened and in walked Father Biaggio Antonio Sanguinetti.

"Papa," the young priest exclaimed as he ran across the room.

Giuseppe stood up to receive his son in a huge embrace. After a few moments, Biaggio turned and hugged Monsignor Mancini. He asked, "Are you taking good care of my papa, Monsignor?"

"I try. He is always busy with the opera."

"Puccini's *La Bohème* this year," said Biaggio.

Giuseppe frowned. "No. Not this year. We had to cancel the festival. War is taking its toll at home and all of Sicily."

Biaggio sighed. "No opera. I do hate this war." He paused a moment. "How's mamma?"

"Misses you. She will ask me for full details on how you look."

"And what will you tell her?"

"If Mamma Lucia were still alive, she would have you eating *Spitzetedda* every night to gain more weight."

Biaggio laughed. "Papa, how is the wine store? I miss hanging out at old *Il Paradiso*."

"Business is slow, but we are surviving."

"And Santo. How's Santo?"

"Still running the winery, but selling *Vino di Bellafortuna* is tough going. But our Bellafortuna wine is still the best wine money can buy. Santo is working hard to keep the Boccale Winery running. He is one tough businessman."

Biaggio quickly replied, "Well, he is a Vasaio, and the son of Vitellio at that."

They all laughed.

Monsignor Mancini asked, "Biaggio, you told your father you wanted to see me. What is this all about?"

"It is not for me to say. But wait. Here is the man who can."

The door opened and a gentleman walked into the room. He wore a simple black cassock, with a wooden cross that fell to his mid-chest. His hair was grey, which made his piercing blue eyes, gleaming behind small round glasses, stand out even more. His mustache and goatee still retained a few streaks of black hair, given him a younger appearance. Although average of height, he carried himself in a manner that made him immediately command a room.

Biaggio said, "May I present Monsignor Celso Costantini." As Monsignor Costantini approached, Biaggio added, "Your Excellency, may I introduce Monsignor Pietro Mancini and my father, Giuseppe Sanguinetti. Both from the tiny Sicilian village of Bellafortuna."

Monsignor Costantini moved toward the two visitors. He reached Monsignor Mancini first and hugged him. He then turned to Giuseppe and hugged him as well. He said, "It is such a pleasure to meet the both of you. Father Sanguinetti has told me all about the both of you as well as your lovely village. And, as for papa Sanguinetti here, you should be very proud of your boy. He is doing wonderful work for us here at the Vatican. Thank you for supporting his vocation."

Giuseppe smiled large. "His mother and I are both very proud of him."

Monsignor Mancini asked, "Monsignor Costantini, what can we do for you?"

Costantini bore his stare directly at Monsignor Mancini. "Is it true you both love music?"

Monsignor Mancini tweaked his head sideward, slightly caught off guard by the question, before responding, "It is true. Signor Sanguinetti is in charge of the opera festival we hold every year in our village. As for myself, I have loved music all my life. When I was in the seminary, studying at the Gregorian University, I always tried to slip away to the Rome Opera whenever I could."

"You went to the Greg? As did our Pope. His Holiness and I would like for you to do something for us." He rubbed his right hand across his mouth, all the while studying the middle-aged priest before him. "You love music. You must have a . . . let's call it . . . a soft spot for musicians?"

"I do. God reveals Himself through music, and the musician is his instrument."

Costantini turned to Biaggio and smiled. He then turned back to Monsignor Mancini. "Let me tell you a story about some musicians."

13

THE PLAN IS REVEALED

t the very same time that Monsignor Costantini was meeting with Monsignor Mancini and Giuseppe Sanguinetti at the Vatican, Heinrich Bergman sat on his cot in the villa at Castel Gandolfo, reading through a musical score, while Ludwig Adler sat next to him on the floor with his back up against the wall. Next to Ludwig lay Heinrich's violin locked in its case. Ludwig Adler sat quietly, allowing Heinrich the opportunity to go through the composition the Munich composer had just completed, which he had been working on over the past few days. As Heinrich worked through Ludwig's score in his head, he could hear the pathos, suffering and pain in the music while the absolute beauty of the melody was evident throughout the work. He particularly was struck with the stunning beauty of the section of the score with violin solo.

Once he finished, he laid the score on his cot. Ludwig eagerly asked, "Well?"

"Spectacular. It takes your breath away. It's as if you have created a window into the human body, and one is peering directly at the human soul, a glimpse into a person's most intimate emotions, wants and desires. There is such sadness to this piece but with a hint of hope. Kurt will love the cello parts. But the violin solo is absolute perfection."

"I'm glad you like it. I used a portion of a violin concerto I was writing, but I don't think it will ever see the light of day. The feelings from that part of the concerto were a perfect fit for this piece, so I stole it."

"It is just such a moving piece. You are truly a talented composer. What will you call your new composition?"

"*Münchner Tränen*. (Munich's Tears)."

"Very appropriate. That is a perfect name. Mind if I let Alfred and Kurt take a look?" He paused to smile. "Alfred will be disappointed that there are no clarinet solos."

"Of course not. But you will have to get Alfred to stop playing hide and seek with my kids, Josef, and some of the other children."

"That might be tough."

Ludwig extended his hand out and touched the violin case. "Heinrich, would you play the violin solo for me?"

Heinrich looked down toward his violin, and with his eyes still lowered, said, "No."

"Why not? You have carried it all the way from Vienna, but it sits here untouched."

"I'm just not in the mood. Let me go relieve Alfred with the children. I want him to look at your score."

After Heinrich left to find Alfred, Kurt and Anikka came into the room. Anikka told Ludwig, "The children are having a splendid time with Alfred. Kurt and I went with Father

Dominic Ermanno, our tour guide, to see the Grotto and walk in the gardens. We saw Alfred down there playing hide and seek with all of them. This place is so beautiful and peaceful."

Kurt added, "Father Dominic was correct when he said on our tour that the gardens are a place where the splendor of art and the glory of nature co-exist."

Ludwig picked up his musical score. "It is also a place that provides inspiration. It's good to be writing again."

Anikka put her hand to her heart. "Is it finished?"

Ludwig replied, "Yes. Heinrich was just reading it." Ludwig turned to Kurt. "He left to find Alfred as he wants the two of you to look at it."

"I would be honored," replied Kurt.

Ludwig nodded. "The three of you have been so kind to my family."

Kurt replied, "To be around a family that shows how much they love each other lessons my pain. It provides memories of the people I was closest to who are now far away. I have no idea where they are and if they are even alive. But, when you see such love, memories of everything before this horrible war come flooding back."

"Very well stated," Ludwig said. "We all need something to ground us, to give us hope. For me, it's my music. For you, it's your memories. For others, it's a violin." At those words, he pointed to Heinrich's violin. "Why doesn't he play?"

"Tragedy. That's why he does not play."

"What happened?"

Kurt took a deep breath and sighed. "It's a sad, painful story, but I will tell it if you wish to hear it."

"I do."

"You see, we all began our careers as members of the

Wiener Staatsoper (Vienna State Opera). However, after a lengthy selection process, all three of us were allowed to join the *Wiener Philharmoniker* (Vienna Philharmonic Orchestra). Wilhelm Furtwängler, the famous conductor, eventually noticed our skills. We quickly moved up the ranks. Music consumed our entire life as we relished living in the magical, musical and artistic world of Vienna. At least that was until we, along with ten other members, were all dismissed from the orchestra because we were Jews. The remaining members of the Philharmonic abandoned us, mostly due to fear, or in some instances, a suddenly realized intense hatred for Jews."

"I know the feeling well," interjected Ludwig

"Dismissal was a bitter pill we struggled to swallow for all of us living in Vienna," Kurt continued. "Once it became illegal to hire Jews in Vienna, we could not find jobs. As the situation worsened, we all moved in together. We shared space with many relatives, including Heinrich's mother. His father had been arrested by the Gestapo months earlier and was shipped off to a camp somewhere in Germany. We still don't know where. Heinrich took it upon himself to watch over his mother. He loved that woman with his whole being. One day, Heinrich went into one of the bedrooms. He played his violin, working through some of Mendelssohn's violin music. He played Mendelssohn because the Nazis hated that music."

Ludwig and Anikka laughed as Kurt continued. "His mother was outside with the other relatives. My family and I were out there as well. Some Gestapo thugs came along and ordered a few of us to clean the street in front of the home with small brushes and a few pails of water. I guess Heinrich's uncle moved too slowly for their liking. They began to beat him. Heinrich's mother tried to intervene on behalf of her brother and she was immediately shot point-blank in the head. She died instantly."

Anikka covered her mouth with her hand as she gasped.

"They killed his uncle too," Kurt continued. "They made us clean up the mess on the ground before they left. Heinrich never heard the gunshots; he never heard the commotion. He was lost in his music. When the Gestapo departed, I ran to his room and told him what had just happened. He laid his violin down and ran outside. He has never played it since. He carries it with him, but never plays it."

The Adlers sat in complete silence, tears streaming down their faces. Finally, Anikka asked, "What happened after that? I mean how did all of you end up here?"

"Well, the Gestapo started to make life even harder as the goal of ridding Vienna of all the Jews began to take hold. Deportations were increased. Most of the Jews were sent to labor camps in other parts of Austria and sometimes to camps outside of the country.

"At the insistence of our families, the three of us soon went into hiding together as the forced deportations in Vienna picked up at a brisk pace. Our families were eventually deported to camps while we remained hidden. We stayed with non-Jewish friends, constantly moving from house to house, trying to stay one step ahead of the Gestapo. It was while staying at one such friend's home that a neighbor betrayed us. It was a man we trusted and confided in who betrayed us. The Gestapo came the next morning and arrested us. We were forced into a deportation center on the outskirts of Vienna, where we awaited our fate. Within a few days, we were herded with other Jews to Aspang Rail Station for deportation. And then, as you know, somehow, we were freed from the train, and here we are, all of us together, and now with Josef, along with that violin Heinrich carries."

Anikka, still with tears pouring from her eyes, said, "I am so sorry for what you have been through, all of you. But at least you are safe now."

Kurt replied, "Thank you. But all of us have been through it. Including your own family."

"God saved you from that train for a reason," Ludwig said. "You may not know why just yet. But there is a reason."

Just then, Alfred walked into the room. "Heinrich told me to come look at your score."

Ludwig handed it to him, as Alfred and Kurt sat on the cot and began looking at the composition together.

WHEN MONSIGNOR COSTANTINI finished relating the story of the Jewish musicians hiding at Castel Gandolfo to Monsignor Mancini and Giuseppe, the two friends from Bellafortuna sat quietly. Finally, Monsignor Mancini straightened in his chair and asked, "Monsignor Costantini, what is it that you want us to do?"

"Save these Jewish musicians."

"How?"

"Hide them in Bellafortuna."

Both Monsignor Mancini and Giuseppe glanced at each other. "In our village?" asked Monsignor Mancini.

Monsignor Costantini nodded.

Giuseppe spoke for the first time since the Monsignor spoke. "There is not one Jew in our entire village."

Monsignor Mancini added, "Giuseppe is correct. Not one. As a matter of fact, I have never even met a Jew. I am nothing more than a simple priest. Sicily is suffering. Bellafortuna has not been spared. Food is rationed. Our own villagers are struggling. It is a dark time for Sicily."

Monsignor Costantini said passionately, "*Lux in tenebris lucet.* (Light shines in the darkness.) Save them."

Monsignor Mancini asked, "How can we save these people?"

In a reassuring voice, Monsignor Costantini said, "I will assist you. I run the emigration section for the Jewish refugees. We will obtain false identities for these Jews. They will become Catholic villagers of Bellafortuna. We will give them identity cards. This will allow them to obtain ration cards to help them with food issues. With their assumed identities, they will be able to live openly in your village. The success or failure of this endeavor will ultimately fall on your flock."

Monsignor Mancini cocked his head to the right and lifted his brow. "And what am I to tell my flock?"

"Tell them they must organize themselves to help these Jewish musicians who are being persecuted by the Germans. This is what the Holy Father, Pope Pius XII, desires. Through your actions, over the furrow of misery and suffering brought on by this stupid war, passes the smile of God, which pours out the oil of fraternal love. Everything must be done with the greatest secrecy and prudence. One slip of the tongue will mean death for them and . . . perhaps even your flock."

Biaggio spoke directly to his father and Monsignor Mancini. "Bellafortuna is a special place. It's a place of decency where music and opera thrive. There is not a day that goes by that I do not reflect on that place and its people. With so much hate in the world, it stands in stark contrast with its good-heartedness, grace, decency and love. It is a place of light in the darkness. What better way for the world to see its spirit than for the entire village to save other souls." Biaggio eyed his father. "If Antonio were still alive, you know what he would do."

"My father would have put his life on the line to save these people without question."

Monsignor Mancini replied, "That is exactly what your father would have done, Giuseppe. And I know God would want me to do the same. Both the Jews and Catholics read the same passage in Genesis that we are all created in God's image. God is our father, and we are all his children." Monsignor Mancini stood and extended his hand toward Costantini. "Monsignor Costantini, Bellafortuna will accept them and protect them."

Monsignor Costantini smiled, stood, and warmly grabbed the hand offered to him. He said, "*Grazie.*" He then raised one finger and said quietly, "*Un'ultima cosa.* (One last thing.) No matter what happens, you must make sure the Holy See and the Pope himself are never implicated in having any role in the placement of these refugees. You must swear it."

Monsignor Mancini turned and looked at Giuseppe, who nodded in agreement. Monsignor Mancini quickly replied, "*Noi giuriamo.* (We swear it.) We will protect that secret . . . with our lives."

Biaggio proudly smiled as he stared at both his father and Monsignor Mancini, the men who had been his mentors from his younger years growing up in Bellafortuna.

Monsignor Costantini said, "Good. Then let us pray that it all goes well."

LATER THAT NIGHT, Biaggio sat in the parlor of the small guesthouse inside the Vatican where his father and Monsignor Mancini were staying. The duo from Bellafortuna sat across from him. Talk quickly turned to the events from earlier that day.

Monsignor Mancini said, "I can guarantee you, I never would have imagined that this is the reason why you summoned me to Rome."

Giuseppe and Biaggio laughed. "Absolutely," Giuseppe replied. "Hide Jews in Bellafortuna?" The muscles in his face tightened. "It does put Bellafortuna in a precarious spot, but one that I do believe our villagers will willingly accept."

Monsignor Mancini replied, "I have no doubt they will accept this mission, even though I do agree it is very dangerous for all of us."

Biaggio replied, "I guess in my rush to provide an answer to Monsignor Costantini's dilemma as to where to place his refugees, I did not fully think of the danger I would be putting the inhabitants of Bellafortuna in. For that, I am sorry."

Monsignor Mancini nodded in a comforting sort of way. "I know we are doing the right thing. This war has been terrible for Italy and all of Europe. The persecutions of the Jews have been an abomination. We must all do everything we can to stand up to Mussolini and Hitler."

Giuseppe stood. "And taking in these Jews is a great way to do so."

The trio continued speaking together late into the night.

LATER, Biaggio crawled into his bed in his small apartment inside the Vatican. It was so good spending time tonight with his father and Monsignor Mancini. He missed them, his mother, and all of his fellow villagers back in Bellafortuna.

His thoughts turned to the last few days. Why did the Pope select him to assist Monsignor Costantini? After all, he didn't think the Pope knew him that well. Yet, he had been selected to assist in the placing of the Jews. He knew his father and Mancini were right in taking the Jews in, yet it was something that Mancini said that Biaggio could not get out of his mind. *"We must all do everything we can to stand up to Mussolini and Hitler."*

Biaggio's thoughts turned to Pope Pius XII. He was in awe of the Pope and believed that he was one of the most intelligent and moral people he had ever met. Yet, on one side were the detractors who believed he should speak out forcefully against Hitler. This was contrasted against what Biaggio had learned Pius was doing behind the scenes to hide Jews. As he contemplated it all, the one conclusion Biaggio came to with absolute certainty and clarity was that through his own actions, he had put Bellafortuna directly in the crosshairs of the Fascists, and worse, potentially the Nazis.

He dropped to his knees at the side of his bed. He made the sign of the cross, clasped his hands together and closed his eyes. "Jesus, I know your hand guided the decision to get me involved in this matter. Please protect my villagers. They love you. They are good people. They are already suffering due to this war. Don't let more suffering or harm come to them. As for the Jewish musicians and their families, please protect them also. I am solely responsible for offering Bellafortuna as their hiding spot. Keep them safe. Allow my villagers to accept them and protect them. If danger does come upon them, please send my villagers your spirit of courage so that we can do what we have to do to keep them safe, perhaps with our own life if necessary."

He climbed back in bed but debated with himself for a long time if bringing the Jews to Bellafortuna was the right thing to do, both for the Jews and his villagers. His internal debate provided no answer.

THE TOMB OF THE FISHERMAN

*T*he sun rose over Rome the next day, Christmas Eve. Very early that morning, Biaggio and Monsignor Costantini huddled together in a small, secluded office in the Apostolic Palace as they hashed out the plan on transporting the Jews to Bellafortuna. Monsignor Giovanni Battista Montini, the Undersecretary of State, (and the future Pope Paul VI) joined the duo in their discussions as a plan was developed. Monsignor Montini was heavily involved in assisting Jews throughout Italy, and thus his experience in the matter was thought to be very beneficial.

When the meeting wrapped up, Biaggio walked with Costantini, who was on his way to pick up his bags before making his way back to Castel Gandolfo. As they walked down a long corridor, Biaggio said, "I think the plan we put in place for transportation is the best we could expect."

"I agree. The logistics of getting them there is a grave concern for us, but I am confident our plan will work. I will be returning this morning to Castel Gandolfo. Come there tomorrow as I plan to meet with the refugees and tell them of their impending move. You should be there with me."

"They will be upset."

"I know."

"And then once in Bellafortuna, it will fall upon my villagers to protect them."

"Yes. But with faith, we will prevail."

Biaggio bit his lip as he thought momentarily before responding, "Faith is easy when it concerns your life and decisions that involve only you. But when you have to rely on faith for decisions which will impact others and the trust that they put in you, then you would much rather have certainty than faith."

Costantini stopped and looked kindly at Biaggio. He then glanced at his watch and said, "I have time. Come follow me."

He led Biaggio through back passages inside the Apostolic Palace, which eventually led to an alcove inside St. Peter's Basilica. They came to a door between the statues of St. Andrew and St. Veronica. Costantini opened the door, which led to a tunnel and eventually to a heavily locked bronze door.

He pulled out a key and opened the door, and the duo walked down a metal staircase, which led down to the Vatican crypt. They walked a little way until they came to a tomb.

A pink, marble sarcophagus sat within a beautifully decorated arched recess. On top of the sarcophagus sat the sculptured serene figure of a man resting in full papal vestments. On the very front of the sarcophagus was a carved laurel wreath with the monogram of Christ in the center. On the very top ledge were the words:

PIVS XI PONT. MAX.

Costantini said, "Before Pope Pius XI died, then-Cardinal Pacelli was placed in charge of preparing this burial spot for his beloved friend. Pacelli wanted to put a chapel by the tomb, but the ceilings were too low so he had some work done to expand the area for the final resting place of the pope. While digging to expand the area, the floor gave way, and one of the workers fell through the hole. They discovered something."

"What did they discover?" asked Biaggio.

Costantini was quiet but led Biaggio down the hall a bit where there was a huge hole in the ground with ladders leading down. Biaggio peered over the edge and looked down. Beautiful murals of flowers, birds, and other wildlife could be seen on the walls."

Biaggio said, "It's beautiful."

Costantini replied, "The worker who fell found himself down there in a hidden, forgotten world. It was just the beginning of the adventure. He had discovered an ancient, pagan Roman mortuary. They dug deeper and found the richly adorned tomb of a Roman Consul's daughter. But it was when they continued digging that they found the most amazing find. They found the very simple tomb of a young Christian woman, with Christian inscriptions on her tomb. They knew the importance of finding a Christian tomb among pagan tombs. All worked stopped as Pacelli and other highest-ranking Vatican officials were called to see the find for their own eyes."

Biaggio, fully intrigued by the story being told, asked, "What was so important about finding that woman's tomb?"

"A Legend; the legend of the death and burial of St. Peter. As I know you are aware, sometime around 65 AD, St. Peter came to Rome where, during the Christian persecutions by Nero, he was crucified on Vatican Hill near the Circus of Nero, very close to where we are standing now. The crucifixion took place near an ancient Egyptian obelisk which sat in the middle of the Circus."

"Not the same obelisk that sits out front of the Basilica in St. Peter's Square?"

"Indeed. That same obelisk which witnessed his martyrdom was moved a few hundred yards centuries later where it sits today right in the middle of St. Peter's Square. As depicted in Michelangelo's fresco, St. Peter was hung on a cross upside down at his own request as a mark of humility, yet crucified none the less just like his Master before him. It was rumored among the faithful that his body was buried nearby in an outdoor necropolis somewhere near the spot where he was crucified. Early Christians, in the dead of night, would climb the hill and venerate the spot of his burial. Eventually, a small monument was built over his grave by these early faithful. Tradition and legend held that around the year 300, Emperor Constantine built a basilica dedicated to St. Peter over the burial spot. Much of the necropolis was leveled to support the structure. When the construction of the new St. Peter's Basilica began in the 1500s, they followed that tradition and kept the high altar directly over the supposed burial spot of St. Peter. And above the necropolis, the Vatican grottos were added where popes and kings alike were buried. During the 1600s, excavations were attempted to find the grave of the fisherman, but only pagan graves were found, and the necropolis was soon forgotten, probably by choice as the Vatican was horrified that based on their excavations to date the great seat of Christianity perhaps set not on the tombs of Saints, but on the graves of pagans.

"But now with the work being done down here, a Christian tomb had been found. Cardinal Pacelli wanted to continue to excavate deeper to look for the grave of St. Peter, but the dying pope was told by advisors that it was sacrilegious while others thought it could damage and weaken the very foundation of the basilica itself, and thus Pope Pius XI would not let the excavation move forward. But with Pope Pius XI's death, Pacelli, now as Pope, was then free to pursue the idea of digging deeper."

Biaggio asked, "Is that what they are doing down here?"

"Pope Pius loves science, particularly archeology, and believes science and religion can coexist. And being a Roman himself, he wanted to prove once and for all that Peter had come to Rome, and it was here in Rome that he met his death. Yet, he was faced with a great dilemma. He could proceed with the excavation, which could ultimately verify the tradition of St. Peter's burial. But on the flip side, if no bones were found, then it would allow those who argued Peter never came to Rome powerful support for that position, such as was held by German Protestants who Pacelli knew well from his time in Germany. And most importantly, failure to find St. Peter's tomb and bones would call into question the Vatican's status as the seat of the Papacy, right at a time when the Vatican is already surrounded by hate in the form of the

Nazis and the Fascists. It would prove that St. Peter's Basilica was built on a pagan foundation. Pope Pius decided to take the gamble and proceed with the excavation. He did so because of faith. Our Pope had absolute faith, that indeed he would discover the bones of St. Peter. That faith drove his decision to proceed, even against monumental results if his trust in faith turned out to be wrong."

Biaggio asked, "Has anything been found?"

"What I am about to tell you, of course, is of utmost secrecy, which only a handful of people know. Deep down there, they found votive offerings, murals and coins dating from the time of Peter. They also found the tombs of the very first popes who wanted to be buried next to their predecessor, the first pope." Monsignor Costantini paused and then said, "And just recently, they believe they have finally found the burial spot of St. Peter and have recovered his bones."

There was silence as Biaggio went to a knee and peered again down the hole. Still looking down inside the hole, he said in Latin and almost as if in prayer, *"Et ego tibi, quia tu es Petrus, et super hanc petram aedificábo Ecclésiam meam, et portae inferi non praevalébunt advérsus eam."* (And I say to you: That you are Peter, and upon this rock I will build my church, and the gates of hell will not overpower it.)

Costantini put his hand on Biaggio's shoulder as he said, "Of course, this is all highly secret, as the Pope is not even using Vatican money to pay for the work, but instead an American oilman from Texas, George Strake."

"Why have they not released this information?"

"They still need to verify and test what they found, which will take time, but they truly believe they have found the tomb of the fisherman. I tell you all of this for one reason. I know what I am asking of you and your villagers is difficult and hard, and that my request puts the village of Bellafortuna directly against and opposed to the doctrine of hate imbued by the Nazis and Fascists. Yet, after meeting your father and Monsignor Mancini, and hearing them speak of your village, as well as your own testimony, I know God was the inspiration for the Pope bringing you to me and that your village is the right choice."

Biaggio stood up and asked. "Why did he ask me? Why did he choose me?"

"I can't answer that. Other than to say, your love of music must have played a part and the fact that he must have seen something in your character which he knew he could trust, just like me showing you this highly secret endeavor down here. Earlier, you said you wished for certainty instead of faith. Keep this in mind. Faith is the root. Certainty is the tree. Your faith will save the Jews."

Biaggio smiled before saying, "No, Monsignor, my villagers, because of my faith, will save them."

Costantini reached his hand out and shook hands with Biaggio, before glancing once again at his watch. He said, "I must get back to Castel Gandolfo."

"Thank you for taking me down here," replied Biaggio.

Costantini outstretched his hands and pointed his fingers in both directions toward the corridors leading to all of the other tombs down in the Vatican crypt. He said, "All of these people buried down here served the Lord. Love them or hate them, agree or disagree with them, but respect that they all held steadfast to a belief that the most important thing they could do with their life was to serve others in the name of Jesus Christ. Father Biaggio Sanguinetti, you have answered that same call. Don't thank me for taking you down here, thank the Holy Spirit. That same spirit which led me to tell you about this secret project down here is the same spirit that led me to entrust the Jewish musicians to you. I am greatly concerned for these people. Do what you must to protect them at all costs."

Biaggio turned away from Costantini and closed his eyes, as the full weight of the undertaking in front of him took over every fiber of his being. He opened his eyes and turned back to him before replying, "You put all of your trust in me. I will not let you down."

"I know. Now, let me get back."

As they began to leave, Biaggio turned one last time and looked at the hole in the ground. An ancient story he was told as child by Monsignor Mancini came flooding to his head. The story went that as Nero's persecutions took hold, St. Peter fled Rome to avoid capture and death. Along the Appian Way, St. Peter encountered Christ. Peter asked him, *"Quo Vadis, Domine?"* (Where are you going, Lord?) The Lord replied, *"Romam vado iterum crucifigi."* (To Rome, to be crucified again). Peter, ashamed that the Lord was taking his place, joyfully returned to Rome ready to meet his fate and be martyred for his faith.

Biaggio did not know if the *Quo Vadis* legend was true or not, but recalling that story while staring at the hole that led to the Fisherman's tomb made him understand completely that for him and his village there was no turning back now.

15

VATICAN RADIO

*P*ope Pius XI and now his successor, Pope Pius XII, had used Vatican Radio to spread the word to all the faithful across the entire world. Vatican Radio had been set up by the father of the radio, Guglielmo Marconi, and was run by the Jesuit Order.

With the outbreak of war, instead of just using the radio to spread the gospel across the world, Pope Pius XII began to use the radio to alert his audience about Catholic oppression in Poland as well as the roundup of the Jewish population and their forced confinement to ghettos.

As the war progressed, Vatican Radio quickly became a disguised propaganda tool of the Vatican, calling upon all Catholics, the majority of whom were under Nazi rule, to spiritually stand up to the Nazi and Fascist ideology. Needless to say, Vatican Radio was soon banned in Germany. Yet, many Germans, including the Nazi leadership, were still listening.

Such was the case later that afternoon on Christmas Eve. The Jewish refugees were in a parlor inside the Apostolic Palace at Castel Gandolfo huddled around a radio so they could listen to Pope Pius XII's annual Christmas Address on Vatican Radio. A table was in the middle of the room.

Ludwig and Anikka were seated on either side of Monsignor Costantini, who was at the head of the table and who had just returned back from Rome. Heinrich, Alfred and Kurt were at the opposite end. Some of the other Jews stood around the table while a few others were seated at the table and in other chairs inside the parlor. The radio sat against a wall close to a fireplace.

The Jews were talking amongst themselves when the Pope's voice crackled across the airwaves. Ludwig asked for quiet, which was granted immediately by his fellow Jews, as the Pope began his address.

"Miei cari figli del mondo intero."

The Jews turned to Monsignor Costantini, who translated the Italian words into German for the group. *"My dear children of the whole world."*

Anikka grabbed Monsignor Costantini's sleeve. "He is addressing not just the Christian world, but everyone. Monsignor Costantini, with his other hand, tapped Anikka's hand and smiled at her, before continuing translating the Pope's address.

"As the Holy Christmas season comes around each year, the message of Jesus, who is light in the midst of darkness, echoes once more from the Crib of Bethlehem in the ears of Christians and re-echoes in their hearts with an ever-new freshness of joy and piety. It promises mercy, love, peace to the countless hosts of those in suffering and tribulation who see their happiness shattered and

their efforts broken in the tempestuous strife and hate of our stormy days."

After his words of introduction, the address moved to the Church's role in society.

"The Church would be untrue to herself, ceasing to be a mother, if she turned a deaf ear to her children's anguished cries, which reach her from every class of the human family. She does not intend to take sides for any of the particular forms in which the several peoples and States strive to solve the gigantic problems of domestic order or international collaboration, as long as these forms conform to the law of God."

The Pope then turned his attention to human rights and the role a civil society plays in defending those rights. In particular, the Pope tried to show the connection between human rights and democracy. He defended the dignity of the human person and acknowledged the existence of certain fundamental personal rights.

The Jews listened intently while Monsignor Costantini tried to keep up with the translation. It was impossible for him to translate every word, but he did his best to let his listeners get a feel for what was being said.

"In any case, whatever be the change or transformation, the scope of every social life remains identical, sacred, obligatory; it is the development of the personal values of man as the image of God; and the obligation remains with every member of the human family to realize his unchangeable destiny, whosoever be the legislator and the authority whom he obeys. In consequence, there always remains, too, his inalienable right, which no opposition can nullify—a right which must be respected by friend and foe—to a legal order and practice which appreciate and understand that it is their essential duty to serve the common good."

The pope then turned his attention to the War and called for a renewal of society across all nations.

"And who can see the end of this progressive demoralization of the people, who can wish to watch helplessly this disastrous progress? Should they not rather, over the ruins of a social order which has given such tragic proof of its ineptitude as a factor for the good of the people, gather together the hearts of all those who are magnanimous and upright, in the solemn vow not to rest until in all peoples and all nations of the earth a vast legion shall be formed of those handfuls of men who, bent on bringing back society to its center of gravity, which is the law of God, aspire to the service of the human person and of his common life ennobled in God.

"Mankind owes that vow to the countless dead who lie buried on the field of battle: The sacrifice of their lives in the fulfillment of their duty is a holocaust offered for a new and better social order. Mankind owes that vow to the innumerable sorrowing host of mothers, widows, and orphans who have seen the light, the solace and the support of their lives wrenched from them. Mankind owes that vow to those numberless exiles whom the hurricane of war has torn from their native land and scattered in the land of the stranger; who can make their own the lament of the Prophet: "Our inheritance is turned to aliens; our house to strangers."

The Pope then paused, before saying with deep emotion. *"Questor voto l'umanità lo deve alle centinaia di migliaia di persone, le quali, senza veruna colpa propria, talora solo per ragione di nazionalità o di stirpe, sono destinate alla morte o ad un progressivo deperimento."*

Ludwig Adler quickly sat upright in his chair and asked Monsignor Costantini, "What did he just say?"

Monsignor Costantini replied. *"Humanity owes this vow to those hundreds of thousands who, without any fault on their part, sometimes only because of their nationality or race, have been marked down for death or gradual extinction."*

Ludwig stood up. All the Jews stared at him. "My God!" he exclaimed. "He has just spoken out against the Nazis." The Jews did not hear the rest of the speech as they savored the words of the Pope. Anikka made her way over to Ludwig, and with tears in her eyes, she fell into his embrace. Heinrich, Alfred and Kurt had their arms around each other's shoulders, with each of their faces in a huge grin.

With the commotion going inside the parlor, Monsignor Costantini stopped translating as no one was paying attention anymore. He looked around at the joyous faces of the Jews in the room. Slowly, however, the smile on his face changed to a frown as his mind quickly turned to a meeting set for tomorrow, a meeting when the Jews would be told about their impending move to Bellafortuna.

He was brought out of his thoughts when he felt a tug around his shoulder and realized Ludwig was pulling him out of the chair. Once standing, Ludwig offered his hand. Monsignor Costantini grasped it tightly. His frown turned back into a smile.

"*Grazie*, Monsignor Costantini. *Grazie*. We are so happy here . . . and now this. What a joyous day," Ludwig said emphatically.

Monsignor Costantini bowed his head, closed his eyes, and nodded slowly. His smile disappeared once again, while the Jews in the room continued the celebration.

16

THE DEPARTURE

*T*he next day, Christmas, Biaggio woke up early, read from his Breviary, and, before leaving Vatican City for Castel Gandolfo, he drank a cup of black coffee while reading the newspaper. He stumbled across an article that greatly interested him. It quoted a New York Times editorial concerning the Pope's Christmas radio address. The article stated:

"No Christmas sermon reaches a larger congregation than the message Pope Pius XII addresses to a war-torn world at this season. This Christmas more than ever he is a lonely voice crying out of the silence of a continent. The Pulpit from whence he speaks is more than ever like the Rock on which the Church was founded, a tiny island lashed and surrounded by a sea of war. In these circumstances, in any circumstances, indeed, no one would expect the Pope to speak as a political leader, or a war leader, or in any other

*role than that of a preacher ordained to stand above the
battle, tied impartially, as he says, to all people and willing
to collaborate in any new order which will bring a just
peace."*

A smile came across Biaggio's face. For weeks he had
debated in his own mind what the critics had said about the
Pope, but ultimately, he came to the conclusion that the Pope
was doing what he thought was best. Perhaps others were
now coming to the same conclusion.

As he folded the newspaper his thoughts drifted to his
meeting with the Jewish refugees later that day. His stomach
turned as he anticipated what their reaction to the news of
their impending move would be once they were told. He
finished his coffee, got dressed, and departed for Castel
Gandolfo.

BIAGGIO MET Monsignor Costantini in the private chapel at
Castel Gandolfo for a very intimate Christmas Mass for the
staff who lived there. During the Mass, Biaggio's thoughts
turned to Bellafortuna as he reminisced about Christmas in
his tiny village, and the splendid mass always presided over
by Monsignor Mancini in the beautiful little church right in
the heart of his village, the *Chiesa della Madonna*. As he did so,
he prayed hard for the protection of his fellow villagers for
what was soon to be required of them.

After mass, Monsignor Costantini and Biaggio walked
together as they made their way to the villa where the Jewish
refugees were located.

"Monsignor, how are our friends this morning?"

"They are still excited by the Pope's words from yesterday."

"It was a great statement," Biaggio said. "Have you seen the New York Times editorial?"

"Yes. On top of that, the reports we received are that the Nazis are enraged by the address and called the Pontiff a 'Jew lover' and a 'mouthpiece of the Jewish war criminals', among other things. They certainly know who their enemy is and when he speaks, that he is speaking directly against them. Now, let's go meet with our friends."

They reached the door to the villa, where the meeting was to take place. The Jews were already inside, waiting while the nuns on staff watched all the children, including young Josef, in another part of the villa.

The Jewish refugees stood in the middle of the room listening intently as Monsignor Costantini, in his best German, advised them of their impending move to Bellafortuna. Their joy of yesterday during the Pope's radio address was quickly transformed into sadness and fear. The refugees became aware that the respite Castel Gandolfo had provided was soon coming to an end.

Biaggio stood off to the side of Monsignor Costantini, taking in quietly the scene unfolding in front of him. He scanned the families standing together in the room. They were all dressed simply, with sweaters and jackets provided to them by some of the staff at Castel Gandolfo. Many of the couples stood holding hands, as they listened to what Costantini was telling them. Tears were in most of their eyes. Biaggio took particular notice of a gentleman and lady standing close to him. The husband enveloped his wife in a tight, warm embrace as she silently cried uncontrollably.

Costantini then introduced the group to Biaggio, explaining who he was and how it was his idea to move them to Bellafortuna.

Biaggio began speaking to the group, with Monsignor Costantini translating his words. "You will love Bellafortuna. The people are good, decent and kind. Monsignor Pietro Mancini and my father, Giuseppe Sanguinetti, are already making plans. They will leave from Rome for Bellafortuna tomorrow to prepare for your arrival. I know the villagers of Bellafortuna will take you in and protect you."

Ludwig, the gentleman who was standing next to Biaggio with his wife, was the first of the Jews to ask a question. "Will we have to hide? I don't know if my family can do that again." All of the Jews voiced their agreement.

Monsignor Costantini replied, "From what Giuseppe Sanguinetti and Monsignor Mancini told us when we met in Rome, the Germans are nowhere near Bellafortuna. It is a small, secluded village. We believe you will be able to assume your new life in the village, living with and among the villagers."

Kurt asked, "What do you mean 'assume your new life?'"

Monsignor Costantini said to the entire group, "We have birth certificates and baptismal certificates along with new identity cards. You will all become 'Catholic' residents of Bellafortuna, Sicily. This will allow you to live among the other villagers as one of them. You must forget your Jewish identity for now. You cannot be heard or seen saying Jewish prayers. All of you must pretend to be Italian Catholics."

The refugees all looked at each other in utter disbelief.

A musician from Hamburg asked, "How will this work? We will be captured again."

"By the grace of God, this will work," replied Monsignor Costantini. "You and your families will leave in three days to travel to the small village, under the guise of pilgrims returning home after a religious trip to Rome. Bellafortuna has no political, industrial or military significance. Nazi or Italian guards will not be interested in pilgrims from Bellafortuna."

Ezra Berkowitz, a refugee from Bamberg, Germany, said, "But very few of us speak Italian."

Ludwig raised his hand. "I do a little. I picked it up studying music all these years. But I agree, not many others do."

Monsignor Costantini answered, "Neither do most of the Germans. Some of our priests who live here will come work with all of you on the Italian language over the next few days. They will give you a very quick lesson on Italian phrases to get you through a brief conversation with a German guard. Father Sanguinetti and Father Dominic will accompany you during your travels. Father Dominic speaks Italian, but he also speaks perfect German from the time he spent working in Germany with the Pope. Hopefully, he can speak for the group, particularly if an Italian stops you."

Anikka, still in tears, spoke up. "Monsignor Costantini, you and everyone here has been so kind. We have had a moment to forget our troubles. Why can't we just stay here?"

Monsignor Costantini shook his head negatively. "Although Italy bears no ill will toward the Jews, the city of Rome is becoming dangerous. The Germans have a presence in Rome. That is why we can't keep you here. It does not provide a safe haven. And, if discovered here, it would be dangerous for the Vatican, the Pope, and the Church. We need to find out if hiding Jews in Italy works."

Hans Voelker, a Jew from Berlin, stood and bellowed, "So are we are nothing but guinea pigs? If it all fails, we are the ones who will be killed. Not you."

All of the refugees began speaking at once, arguing different points. Heinrich, Alfred and Kurt thought back to the neighbor who had betrayed them. Now they were being asked to put their trust, not in just a few individuals, but an entire village.

As the debate reached a fever pitch, Ludwig shouted. "*Schweigen.*" The room quickly grew silent as a tomb. He said, "Listen to yourselves. Father Sanguinetti told us the villagers of Bellafortuna are willing to take us in. My God, we should be on our knees, thanking him on behalf of his people. He must surely know that it would mean certain death for his people if they are caught helping us. Don't you all see that this is our only chance for life?"

Kurt said, "With all due respect to Father Biaggio and Monsignor Costantini, we are being asked to put our faith and trust in people whom we do not know. Most of us know what happens by putting our trust in others."

Most of the refugees nodded.

Ludwig replied, "I understand your fear. I understand your wariness to trust others. But here, just like Abraham, we must put our trust in God. And that is what we are really being asked to do. In so doing, we will pray that His goodness will surround these villagers, and the Lord will work through them, and they, in turn, will protect us. Putting our trust in the Lord is all we can do."

Heinrich spoke up. "Ludwig is correct. We go to Bellafortuna, and, placing our trust in God, we will put our lives in the hands of the villagers." The other Jews, one by one, slowly begin to all nod in agreement, bobbing their heads to and fro as they became resolved to their fate. Fear was, however, evident in their eyes.

Biaggio, fully aware that Ludwig's actions had turned the tide of the meeting, quickly turned toward Ludwig and extended his hand. Ludwig grabbed it firmly, as Biaggio whispered a simple, "*Grazie.*"

Ludwig whispered back, "I just hope you are correct about your village."

Biaggio simply replied, "I am."

Meanwhile, Monsignor Costantini walked over to where Heinrich stood and handed him his new birth certificate. The forged document had been made to look many years older. "It is a pleasure to meet you, *Signor Matteo Gagliano*, a Catholic pilgrim visiting Rome from Bellafortuna, Sicily. Merry Christmas."

Heinrich smiled. "No. Not Merry Christmas. *Buon Natale*, your Excellency."

Monsignor Costantini chuckled. "*Buon Natale, Matteo.*" He turned to the rest of the Jews and said, "Please step forward to receive your new names. Afterward, you will begin learning some Italian phrases. There is little time. You leave for Bellafortuna in three days."

Heinrich made his way over to Kurt and Alfred. Kurt, with sadness evident in his eyes, dejectedly said, "Dismissed once again."

With kindness, Heinrich looked at his two friends and

replied, "Not this time. This move, I truly believe, is an attempt to save us."

"I hope you are right. I surely do," replied Kurt.

Heinrich said, "Good, then let's go learn some Italian."

The Jews began to depart the villa. As they did so, Biaggio bore his stare toward Ludwig, who was walking hand in hand with his wife. Ludwig looked toward Biaggio. The young priest gently bowed his head toward him.

Ludwig nodded back and departed the villa.

TWO DAYS LATER, Biaggio, who had returned to Rome to prepare for his trip back home to Sicily, was summoned to escort Harold Tittmann to an audience with the Pontiff himself. When the meeting was concluded, Biaggio walked Tittmann back to his residence. Along the way, Tittmann turned to his friend. "There is something I want to discuss with you. I want to tell you about my meeting with the Pope this morning. I owe it to you."

"You don't owe me anything."

"Well, I believe I do. The purpose of my meeting with him was to voice the opinion of some in the American government that his Christmas message did not go far enough in calling out the atrocities of the Nazis."

Biaggio frowned. "But I have heard nothing but glowing reviews of it, except of course from the Nazis, as it should be."

"I'm not done. I also reiterated our frustration at his refusal to join the Allied Declaration Against German Atrocities."

Biaggio breathed deeply. "I don't really want to go through all of this again."

"Please let me finish. The Pope provided to me his reasons with regard to both of my issues I presented to him. As for his Christmas message, he believes that he had spoken clearly and that it was obvious to whom he was referring. He also referenced some other speeches he gave, as well as some Vatican Radio broadcasts. He hopes the American people will agree. I promised to let the State Department know his feelings."

"What did he say about the declaration?"

"The Pope felt that he could not speak out against German atrocities without mentioning the serious and brutal atrocities being committed by the Soviets. He did not want to join in a declaration that included the Soviets calling out atrocities for which they themselves are guilty. I will say I came to understand his arguments, particularly because of the way he laid them out. I am sure there will be many in my country who still disagree with his approach. But I wanted to let you know that I have come to understand his decision making on the matter."

Biaggio smiled. "I put my trust in the Pope, as he is privy to much more information than me."

"Fair enough. The Pope is quite concerned that Rome will be bombed. He has instructed me to reach out to Myron Taylor and Minister Osborne to make sure that it does not happen. The British are much more in favor of bringing the war to Rome as Italian planes flew bombing missions over London. I will be meeting with Cardinal Maglione next week to discuss those issues. I want you to be there for that meeting."

"I'm leaving in a few days to return home to Sicily for a bit."

"That's wonderful. What's the reason for the trip?"

Biaggio was silent for a moment. He finally replied, "Just taking some pilgrims who visited Rome back to my village."

"Have a safe trip."

"I hope so. Take care of yourself."

They slowly continued walking as their conversation turned to American sports, and baseball in particular.

SINCE THEIR MEETING with Biaggio and Costantini, the Jewish refugees worked hard on their Italian lessons. They learned key Italian phrases. They hoped it would be just enough to get them through a checkpoint. They all dreaded leaving the comfort and peace of Castel Gandolfo.

For Kurt, the Italian lessons brought back memories of the Italian language courses he took while studying opera. Those early lessons made it possible for him to assist some of the other Jews in learning the phrases.

Finally, the day arrived when the group of fifteen Jewish musicians and their families prepared to embark on their long journey to Sicily with Biaggio and Father Dominic.

Before they left Castel Gandolfo, they huddled together, and encouraged by Monsignor Costantini, were offered the opportunity to recite together an old Jewish prayer. They looked at each other, unsure what to say, as they all had not prayed publicly in quite some time.

Finally, Ludwig Adler stepped forward. He lowered his head as his mind rushed back to his days when daily prayer was a fixture in his life. He missed those days. He lifted his head and began to intone an ancient Jewish prayer, a traveler's prayer.

As he did so, the others bowed their heads. A few, who knew the words, tried to intone the prayer with Ludwig.

> *"And Jacob went on his way, and the angels of God met him. And when Jacob saw them, he said this is a camp of God, and he called the name of that place Mahanaim. Behold, I send an angel before you to keep you by the way, and bring you into the place for which I have prepared. May the Lord bless you, and keep you. May the Lord make his face to shine upon you, and be gracious to you. May the Lord turn his face to you, and give you peace."*

At the conclusion of the prayer, all of the Jewish musicians said, "Amen." Monsignor Costantini walked over and hugged Ludwig, telling him in Hebrew, *"Kein Yehi Ratzon."* (May this be God's will.) Ludwig smiled.

As for the Jewish musicians and their families, they did not know when or if they would ever recite or hear a Jewish prayer again.

PART III

BELLAFORTUNA
December 1942

17

THE PREPARATION

*W*hen Monsignor Mancini and Giuseppe Sanguinetti arrived back in the beautiful but secluded hilltop village of Bellafortuna, they immediately called for a meeting with the governing body of the village, the *Società della Libertà per Bellafortuna*.

The *Società* consisted of ten members. Giuseppe Sanguinetti, Monsignor Mancini and Santo Vasaio were among them. The other seven members all worked either in the valley or the village. Of those six, one was a female, as the membership had always consisted of at least one woman since its inception.

Dating back to the early 1900s, when Antonio Sanguinetti, Giuseppe's father, established the *Società*, this group of village leaders had always been the voice of the people. The members of this select group were entrusted with the responsibility to do whatever was necessary to protect the community and to allow the village to continue to thrive.

With the coming of the war to Sicily, their duties were put to the test. However, through a well-developed plan, they succeeded as best they could.

Over the past few years, the *Società* had been instrumental in keeping the *Camicie Nere* (Blackshirts), the supporters of Fascism, out of Bellafortuna. They met with the *Camicie Nere*, lied about their allegiance, and, as a result, were left alone, in particular by the *Organizzazione per la Vigilanza e la Repressione dell'Antifascismo* (*OVRA*), Benito Mussolini's feared secret police. The added benefit of befriending the *Camicie Nere* was that the Nazis on the island left Bellafortuna unmolested since it was under the supposed control of the Fascists.

The *Società* also assisted with helping their fellow villagers as the war made life increasingly difficult in Bellafortuna. A large number of the male villagers between the ages of 18-25 were off fighting for Italy in a war they did not believe in. The villagers, for their part, had quickly become disillusioned with *Il Duce* and disliked the Nazis even more. They grew weary of war and hoped that the rumors of a pending Allied invasion of Sicily were true. There was much talk amongst the villagers as they prayed that the Allies would invade Sicily and Italy would join the Allies. Yet, at the same time, the villagers of Bellafortuna were very concerned that Bellafortuna could suffer significant damage from any Allied bombing. The villagers prayed that tragedy would not visit their beloved village while they waited for the safe return of their sons. All the while, they put their trust in the *Società* to lead and protect them.

The hastily called meeting was held as usual in the dining room of the *Albergo di Bellafortuna,* the only hotel in the village. The massive, two-story building was located in the main square of Bellafortuna, the *Piazza Santa Croce*. Looking at the building, the nature and purpose of the structure were hidden, as it resembled a huge home instead of a hotel. The lack of a sign anywhere on the outside identifying it as a hotel only added to the building's mystery.

The building had once been the home of the powerful Vasaio family. A few years after his father's death, Santo Vasaio sold the *Palazzo Vasaio* to the village, and he moved to the valley where he lived in and ran the Boccale Winery and olive presses. Eventually, the *Palazzo Vasaio* was converted into a hotel capable of housing visitors from other parts of Sicily and Italy attending the annual summer opera festival held at the *Anfiteatro di Bellafortuna*, an old Greek amphitheater down in the valley that had been redesigned to hold concerts and opera. Lately, though, because of the war, the hotel rarely had any visitors, but the villagers still utilized the building for meetings.

A large solid mahogany table sat in the middle of the dining room, with a fireplace located against the far wall. Portraits of the village leaders from the past, Enzo Boccale, Antonio Sanguinetti, and Vittelio Vasaio, graced the walls of the room.

The meeting that afternoon was quickly called to order by the head of the *Società*, Giorgio Monachino, as he banged his fist on the table, signaling that the meeting was beginning. Giorgio, like his father Turridu before him, had a fiery temperament.

Monsignor Mancini and Giuseppe stood next to each other, and as they were about to sit down at the table, Giuseppe leaned in close to the Monsignor and whispered, "The Jews are already on their way."

"Then, we must make sure this vote goes well."

They took their seats and immediately reported to the other members of their meeting in Rome. They spoke at length about their discussions with Monsignor Costantini and what he had said about the persecution of the Jews all across Europe, and how emigration out of Europe was becoming more and more difficult. The members listened intently as Monsignor Mancini and Giuseppe worked their way through the awful plight of the Jews, beginning with *Kristallnacht* and to the deportations to the camps. They described the weight and severity of the treatment of the Jewish people.

The group listened with great concern when Giuseppe told them that Monsignor Costantini had requested that the village of Bellafortuna accept and hide Jewish refugees. Monsignor Mancini passionately tried to explain why he believed this mission was a request from God himself. He wove his fingers through his hair and added, "We cannot turn our backs on this request." He ended his speech by saying, "Father Biaggio told Monsignor Costantini to put his faith in the villagers of Bellafortuna. We must show Monsignor Costantini that Father Biaggio was correct in believing in the people of our village. Our villagers must be willing to welcome these refugees and, more importantly, protect them and their freedom. This *Società* and all of our villagers know more than most the importance of freedom. What better way to thank God for the miracle that happened here so many years ago that we now do whatever we can to save others."

The members appeared to be greatly moved by his words.

Monsignor Mancini asked, "Does anyone have any questions?"

Giorgio Monachino spoke first. "So, we would allow these refugees, these Jews, to live in Bellafortuna even though Mussolini has passed laws against hiding them?"

Giuseppe quickly answered, "Laws that are not enforced."

Giorgio stood, and with a raised finger, announced, "The laws are sporadically enforced. I will give you that. But if the Nazis were ever to come to Bellafortuna, what then?"

Monsignor Mancini replied without hesitation. "They cannot be discovered here."

Giorgio chuckled. "Exactly. Then they should not be here. I am dumbfounded that the two of you think this is a good idea. You are putting Bellafortuna and all of the villagers in harm's way. Do you not realize this?"

Monsignor Mancini stared directly at Giorgio. "Of course, we are aware of what can happen. But we believe these very same villagers will welcome the opportunity to save these people, even if it means they are in harm's way."

Giorgio stiffened. "What about ration cards? How will these people eat when it's hard for our own villagers to get food?"

Monsignor Mancini answered. "The Vatican will provide them with cards just like the ones you have so that they can get food, the same as you."

"Are they aware of the limited food supply?"

"Yes," replied Monsignor Mancini. "We told Monsignor Costantini that life is a struggle here. The Allied blockade of Sicily is taking its toll on everyone. These people will suffer the same way you are, nothing different."

Enzo Pecorara said, "I'm all for helping these people, and

I agree with Monsignor Mancini that this is what we should and must do. But I fear what will happen if the Germans come here, and these people are discovered . . . Well, all of us know what will happen. So how do we keep them from being discovered if and when that day ever comes?"

Giuseppe said, "We must help the refugees assimilate quickly into the life of our village. Thankfully, the Germans don't care about us. As for the Fascists, they already know us. Most of them are Catholic. They won't bother us. Haven't we been dealing with Mussolini and his gang since 1929?"

Elizabetta Adorno, a young widow, and the only woman in the *Società* asked, "I'm not saying we should not do this but are we certain it will work?"

Giorgio quipped loudly, "No. There is nothing certain here."

Monsignor Mancini stood up and declared, "Elizabetta, Giorgio is correct. I cannot guarantee that this will work." At these words, all the members stared at each other. "We must act with faith in this entire endeavor. Faith is all we have. By letting these people into our lives and our village, we all know what could happen. So be it. Our Lord teaches us there is no greater sacrifice than to lay down one's life for another. With that said, we will take every precaution to protect ourselves while saving the Jews. If and when the Germans come, they will find no strangers here, only the loving villagers of Bellafortuna. Each of these refugees will become one of us."

Santo Vasaio asked, "What do we tell the villagers? How do we get them to agree to accept these people?"

Giuseppe Sanguinetti said, "We tell them God's children are coming to stay with us. Open your hearts and your homes to them, and be prepared to protect them – even to your death. If there is one thing my father taught me, it is this. God put us on this earth for one purpose, to love. By showing love, we conquer the world, and through our faith, we show the existence of God. Now, Giorgio, I think it's time for a vote."

Giorgio said, "As the head of our group, I only get to vote to break a tie. So, although I cannot vote, I would like to make it known that I am opposed. Now, let's get to it. All in favor, raise your hands."

All of the hands around the table shot up.

Giorgio shook his head from side to side. He took a deep breath, and then said, "It is obvious I am in the minority. With this vote, all I can is let them come. Let them live here. We will protect them."

Monsignor Mancini responded with, "Amen. There is nothing more to say."

The meeting came to a close.

<hr>

LATER THAT NIGHT, Giuseppe climbed into bed next to his wife, Maria. He told her about the meeting earlier that day and the vote. He said at one point. "I'm glad the vote went the way it did, as the Jews are already on their way. Monsignor Mancini had faith the vote would go well."

"Where are they going to stay?" asked Maria.

"In the homes of our villagers. We need to teach them our customs, our language, our history."

"If the Germans ever come here, what would happen?"

"The Jews would be arrested."

"I mean to us."

Giuseppe simply nodded. His facial expression gave the answer Maria thought he was going to say. She quickly replied, "Then we must make sure they are not discovered while they are here."

Giuseppe smiled. "That's why I love the beautiful girl I met so long ago in Monreale. You are brave and fearless. Courageous. *Mi hai dato una vita felice.* (You have given me a happy life) *T'amo*, Maria."

"*T'amo*, Giuseppe. I would not have a problem with allowing one of the Jewish families to live with us."

"I was hoping you would say that. Biaggio would be proud of your decision."

"How is my son?"

"Thin. But he is wonderful. Monsignor Mancini says he is moving up in the Church."

"I miss him."

"I was waiting for the right time to surprise you, and I guess that time is now. He's coming home with the Jews."

She rolled over and kissed her husband. "Oh, Giuseppe. I can't wait to see him. *T'amo*," she said as they kissed deeply.

18

THE LONG ROAD HOME

*T*ravel during the war in Fascist Italy was not easy. Whether by car, truck or train, anyone traveling had to have the proper papers when stopped or questioned by the Italian authorities.

Luckily for the Jewish musicians, the papers provided by Monsignor Costantini passed inspection every time. The Jews began their travel by train from Castel Gandolfo. Fathers Biaggio and Dominic, the priests that Monsignor Costantini sent to travel with the group, did most if not all of the talking for the refugees during their journey. The priests did a very credible job when questioned by soldiers or train personnel as they pretended that they were in charge of the small group of Sicilians who were merely on their way home after making a pilgrimage to Rome. The priests carried the papers of all the Jews and would present them as a group, to avoid any interaction between the Jews and the Italian authorities. Kurt

Hofmann and Ludwig Adler helped with their passing knowledge of Italian.

The train traveled down to Reggio di Calabria, where the group then transferred to a ferry, which brought them to the city of Messina on the island of Sicily. Once in Sicily, the weary group of refugees boarded trucks. They carried no belongings, for they owned nothing in the world except for one. On his lap, Heinrich Bergman held his violin case while riding in the back of the truck.

As they traveled deeper into Sicily, the trucks finally reached the *Corsa Calatafimi*, the main road that runs between Palermo and Monreale. Eventually, they came to a small dirt road, the *Via Valle*.

Heavy rainfall over the last two days made it impossible for the trucks to make the trek over the dirt road leading to Bellafortuna. The group excited the trucks where the *Corsa Calatafimi* met the *Via Valle.* The group would have to walk the rest of the way. Heinrich, Alfred and Kurt walked together, while Josef was with the Adlers and their children, as he had been for most of the trip.

The Jews' journey by foot along the *Via Valle* began late in the afternoon. They would have to snake their way up the small, winding dirt road that meandered through the valley toward the beautiful hilltop village of Bellafortuna. The weather was cool, but not too cold when the band of refugees began their long walk through the valley. They admired the landscape. They called the valley, framed in by the Sicilian hills on all sides, majestic.

Mulberry trees, with large, gnarled branches, shimmered in the light of the sun, alongside the grapevines, olive trees, and wheat fields dotting the entire valley. Small farmhouses sat close to the road. The vineyards with their perfectly straight rows were behind most of the homes. This was wine country, the place where the grapes used to make *Vino di Bellafortuna* were grown.

Biaggio spoke warmly about his beloved village to the Jews, and when the road passed the *Via Boccale*, the old winding road that led to the Boccale Winery and *Campanèlla*, he gave them a brief history of his village. He recounted the village's beginnings centuries ago down in the valley when it was originally called *Campanèlla*, after a small chapel located by a pond of sparkling blue water known as the *Stagno Azzurro*. And how, after a devastating earthquake, the village had been moved up the hill to its current location, and the name changed to *Bellafortuna*. (Beautiful Fortune.)

Further up, the *Via Valle* made a slight bend east, past a clump of trees. Once the group had passed the trees, the refugees got their first glimpse of Bellafortuna rising in the distance. Biaggio pointed. "There it is. Bellafortuna."

The Jews stood silent and took in the view before them. The buildings of the village had been constructed with colored brick, which over time, mellowed into a golden hue. The Sicilian sun made the buildings shine like gold. The church bell from the *Chiesa della Madonna* echoed across the entire valley, welcoming the visitors to their new temporary home.

Biaggio said, "Let's go. I believe the villagers are waiting for us."

After reaching the hill, they made their way up to the village. At the top of the hill Biaggio said, "Turn around and view paradise."

With the rest of the Jews, Heinrich, Alfred, and Kurt

turned together and studied the view. The entire valley floor, draped in shadows, lay below. The vineyards dotted the valley floor. Off to the right, one could see a pond with crystal clear blue water, and the remains of old, abandoned structures. The serene scene in front of their eyes made the Jews forget their plight momentarily as they took in the breathtaking views.

Alfred said to the other two, "It's so beautiful and peaceful here."

Heinrich answered, "True. It is beautiful and peaceful." He scratched the back of his head before adding, "I just hope it's safe as well."

The Jews made their way to the main square.

THE *PIAZZA SANTA CROCE* served as the focal point of the entire village. In the middle of the piazza, a large statue of the revered Enzo Boccale, founder of the Boccale Winery centuries before, seemed to guard the village. Enzo Boccale was the person responsible for relocating the village after the earthquake. On the base of the statue was a huge poster of Benito Mussolini, in an attempt by the Fascists on the island to remind the villagers who was in charge. In full military garb and in a triumphant pose, *Il Duce* stared across the piazza with his bald-head and chiseled jaw. The poster was the only vestige of Fascism in the entire village. Years before, the villagers reluctantly caved in and allowed the placement of the portrait on the base of their beloved statue by OVRA, but in doing so, they allowed the OVRA men to believe that the villages were all good little Fascists. They were dead wrong.

On the southern side of the *Piazza Santa Croce* was *Chiesa della Madonna,* the Baroque house of worship. The hotel stood on the eastern side. The Sanguinetti wine store, *Il Paradiso,* was located on the northern side of the square. Other stores and businesses surrounded the piazza.

Horses and carts were still the mode of transportation for the villagers. Although automobiles did make a trip to the village every now and again, and a truck came weekly to transport cases of *Vino di Bellafortuna* and other wines to Palermo and Monreale. None of the villagers owned or drove a truck or a motor vehicle.

A large number of villagers had lined up on all sides of the piazza to welcome the newcomers. The Jews silently moved between them. Monsignor Mancini, along with Giuseppe and Maria Sanguinetti, was waiting outside *Il Paradiso* to greet them. Biaggio, after many kisses from his mother, introduced the families, who were quickly escorted to *Chiesa della Madonna,* where all the members of the *Società* joined them while they took their seats in the pews.

Monsignor Mancini spoke first. Father Dominic translated his words into German. "Welcome. Welcome to our village. This will be your home. Our home is your home." Spreading his arms to indicate the *Società,* he told the refugees, "These are the members of the *Società,* the leaders of our village. They have worked out your living arrangements. We believe it is best to split up your group. A few of you will live with our families up here in the village. Some of you will live down in the valley. Some will become farmers. With some of our boys away at war, your help will be very handy. Others will work at the Boccale Winery for Santo Vasaio."

Santo proudly rose and raised his hand. He wore a friendly smile and his eyes twinkled. "Those who work with me will help create one of the greatest wines Sicily produces."

Monsignor Mancini took over. "For those who live in the village itself, you will work in our various businesses. For all of you, your children will attend school. You will truly become villagers of Bellafortuna."

The Jews, exhausted from their trip and anxious about their future remained silent until Eli Pach stood, and with his shoulders drooping, looked over at his wife and child, and asked, "Are we safe here? That is our main concern." All of the Jews nodded.

After Father Dominic translated the question, Monsignor Mancini replied, "Have no fear. Although there are Germans stationed in Palermo, they do not come to our small, secluded village. You will live freely here. The Italian Army does not bother us either, and we are less concerned with them. They are not interested in rounding up Jews."

Ludwig stood up and said in German, "I am Ludwig Adler from Munich . . ."

Monsignor Mancini quickly cut him off, and with a smile said, "No. You are Franco Giacone. That is your wife, Isabella Giacone." Pointing to the children individually, he added, "And your adorable children: Gianni, Caterina . . .," he paused momentarily before pointing his finger directly at Josef, as he said, "and of course, Vincenzo." Before they left Castel Gandolfo, Monsignor Costantini thought it best to make young Josef a member of the Adler family. Alfred had agreed it was probably the best idea.

Ludwig replied slowly but in perfect Italian, "*Scusi. Mi chiamo Franco Giacone.*"

Momentarily the anxiety was broken as the entire group laughed. Then continuing in Italian, Ludwig said, "*Grazie a tutti per averci accolto. Parlo per tutti noi quando dico, grazie.*" (Thank you all for taking us in. I speak for all of us when I say, thank you.)

The whole group of refugees, including the children, stood and in unison, and said pointedly, "*Grazie.*"

The members of the *Società*, visibly moved, stood and clapped their hands. Monsignor Mancini turned to Biaggio. "Monsignor Costantini's people have done a good job teaching them Italian."

Father Biaggio replied, "Yes, but we have a long way to go."

Monsignor Mancini spoke to the group again, and begged, "Please take your new identities seriously. Your Jewish names can never be mentioned again. You must try hard to avoid speaking German. I know it will be difficult, but you will get better at it with the passage of time. Father Dominic and Father Biaggio will remain with us for a while, to help teach you Italian. The villagers will assist you in acquiring clothing."

Giuseppe entreated, "For this to work, and for your safety, all of you must become like us. Study our habits. Perform your assigned chores or jobs every day as though you have been doing it for many years. Learn our customs. Eat and drink like us. The villagers will help you. You will also come to Mass."

There were worried looks on the faces of the Jews. Finally, Giuseppe, aware of the sudden change, inquired, "What is wrong?"

Kurt Hofmann, after realizing no one was saying anything in return, stood. "I think I speak for all of us when I say we appreciate all that this village is willing to do for us, and agree that we need to become like you. But we are Jews. We cannot go into your Church and sit through a mass."

The Jews all nodded.

Giuseppe turned and looked at Monsignor Mancini who rose and said, "We are not asking you to attend Mass so that you can worship like a Catholic. On the contrary, the sole purpose of this request is your safety."

Giuseppe looked around the room and then said matter-of-factly, "Blending entirely into our village life may one day save your life . . ." He paused and then said, "and ours."

Those words made things very real for the refugees. They looked at each other and collectively shrugged as they realized their life and the life of the villagers were intertwined from this day forward. They all nodded in agreement.

Giuseppe ended the meeting, much like it had started. "So once again, on behalf of the *Società* and all of our villagers, welcome to your home. *Benvenuto a Bellafortuna.*"

19

A NEW LIFE

*H*einrich Bergman, now Matteo Gagliano, moved
into the rectory of the *Chiesa della Madonna* to live
with Monsignor Mancini and Fathers Dominic and Biaggio.

Alfred, who moved into a farmhouse in the valley with a
young family, had the easiest name to remember, Alfredo
Catania.

Kurt was housed with the Sanguinettis, above the wine
store in Mamma Lucia's old bedroom and became known as
Luca Marino.

As for the Adlers and all their children, now known as the
Giacones, they were placed in the *Albergo*. It provided a little
more privacy, and with the addition of Josef, a bit more space
for their suddenly expanded family.

The refugees settled into their new homes and began the
process of getting to know their new housemates. Many tears
were shed that first night in beds throughout Bellafortuna

and the valley, as the experiences of the past few weeks came crashing down upon the Jewish refugees.

———————

THE NEXT DAY, Saturday, the sun rose and brought a spectacular day to Bellafortuna. The sky was crystal clear blue. The villagers began the day as usual with Mass at the *Chiesa della Madonna* at six o'clock in the morning. The Jews accompanied them. They did not understand so much as one word of the Latin Mass. Father Biaggio assisted Monsignor Mancini at the Mass. At communion, the Jews remained seated in the pews.

After distributing communion to the villagers, Monsignor Mancini turned and told the Jews. "Come. Come up." He pointed to the cup holding the hosts and explained, "These are not consecrated. We must fully keep up the charade." Father Dominic, also on the altar with Monsignor Mancini, translated for the refugees.

The Jewish musicians and their families walked up and knelt at the altar rail. The priests taught them how to receive the host on their tongues properly. After Mass, they went to work and began their indoctrination as villagers of Bellafortuna.

———————

LATER THAT MORNING, Kurt was in the Sanguinetti wine store, learning what wines went where, and how to pack some of the wines for shipment to Palermo and other parts of Sicily.

Biaggio was upstairs visiting with his mother, while Giuseppe introduced Kurt to the world of wines.

For many years, the Sanguinetti wine store was known for its inventory. The Sanguinettis traveled all over Italy, purchasing stock for their store. But since the war, the store's inventory was limited. Giuseppe's main product was *Vino di Bellafortuna* that he sold. He sold to locals and also transported the wines to Palermo, and from there, the suppliers would ship out the wine to other parts of Sicily and Italy. He also purchased other wines from those suppliers to sell in his store. Because times were hard, the locals could not afford to buy a lot of wine. Therefore, most of his sales came from the shipments to Palermo, where the Germans stationed there bought them.

While Giuseppe worked with Kurt that morning, talk soon turned to Kurt's background and of his life in Vienna.

At one point, Giuseppe asked, "How did you come to speak Italian so well, Luca?"

"I studied voice."

"Really? Opera?"

"Yes." He moved his head from side to side. "I thought opera was my calling but soon realized a career in opera was not for me."

"Have you heard of Rodolfo Giulini?"

"Sure. He was a very good tenor in the 30s."

"He is my brother-in-law. He is retired now and teaches voice in Monreale. He used to sing a lot in our village."

"I heard about your opera festival. Your son, Father Biaggio, told me about it while we were on our way here. It sounds like a beautiful thing, this festival. He says you are the man single-handedly responsible for it."

"I guess you could say that. I am the director. The festival is spectacular. It's a shame we had to cancel it this year. We were planning on doing *La Bohème*. The tenor, Beniamino Gigli, had agreed to sing. Perhaps when this stupid war is over, we will have our festival once again."

Kurt walked over to the front door. In the corner was an antique Victrola, and hanging on the wall above it were two drawings in a frame. He studied them closely. One was of a man dressed as a clown. It was signed. "To Giuseppe Sanguinetti, *Vesti la giubba*. November 17, 1898, Angelo's *Milano*, Enrico Caruso." Next to that drawing was another one of another clown, and on that drawing, read the words, "*Va, pensiero*, Bellafortuna, July 28, 1908. *Ecco Caruso!*" He pointed to the drawings and asked Giuseppe, "Caruso? Are you a fan of Enrico Caruso?"

"Yes. I met him a long time ago. One drawing is of Caruso. The other is of Rodolfo Giulini drawn to look like him. Let me just say that Caruso played a part in the history of our village."

"How? Did he sing here?"

"He did; once, a very long time ago."

"My God. You heard Caruso. What did he sound like in person?"

"His voice was like liquid gold. His power was immense. His high notes made the hair on your arms stand up. And to top it off, he was a genuine, nice man."

"I would have loved to hear him live."

"I will never forget that sound for the rest of my life."

"Signor Sanguinetti, thanks for allowing me to work with you. It's good to be around someone with a love of music in their heart."

Giuseppe smiled. "Our village is a place where a love of music thrives."

"That's good to hear. That's what I miss most of all about Vienna. Before the Nazis came, music was literally in the air in Vienna. There was a certain Viennese *Lebenskunst*. That is what we called it."

"*Lebenskunst?*"

"It means the 'art of living.' It was a place where culture and art took precedence over everything. It was a place that remembered and celebrated its past and all of those great artists who called Vienna home. For me, as a musician, I had the privilege to play music nightly in concert halls all across Vienna where once Mozart and Beethoven themselves had played. After performances, we would go drink at cafes where the patrons would be audience members, musicians, ballerinas, and opera stars – a great meeting of the artistic world of Vienna, enjoying and celebrating the life and pulse of Vienna. That's what I miss most." He breathed deeply. "God, I love music, Signor Sanguinetti."

"Your descriptions of life in Vienna break my heart for what has happened there. Do you have any family still back in Vienna?"

"My parents and my sisters were all sent away to a camp. My girlfriend was sent to one as well."

"I am so sorry."

"Where they are, or if I will ever see them again, I have no idea. All I have left are my two friends who are here with me. We have been through so much. Yet, somehow, we made it out. I would never have guessed I would have ended up in your beautiful village all the way in Sicily."

"I guess it was in God's plan. In a small way, the people of

Bellafortuna share the importance of what did you call it, *Lebenskunst*? The rhythm of life here is tied to the grapevines, but music is our roots. Has anyone told you what happens here every Saturday at Noon?"

"No, what happens?"

"Well, you will find out shortly. Now, let's get back to work."

20

OPERA ORCHESTRA DI
BELLAFORTUNA

*S*iesta occurred every day in the village of Bellafortuna from 12:00 p.m. to 2:00 p.m., with all work ceasing in Bellafortuna, the valley, the groves and the vineyards. Siesta was a time for the villagers to renew their energy for the rest of the day. During every siesta, the villagers gathered in the *Piazza Santa Croce,* where under the shadow of the Enzo Boccale statue, the villagers would eat light lunches, and discuss different aspects of life; and in particular over the past few years, the war.

At noon on that Saturday, as the church bell of the *Chiesa della Madonna* tolled, the villagers began to arrive in the piazza for siesta. However, today they were not alone, as they brought with them the Jewish refugees now living under their roofs. And being a Saturday, all were in for a special treat. For the *Opera Orchestra di Bellafortuna* performed in the piazza every Saturday during the last hour of siesta, a tradition begun many, many years before by Antonio Sanguinetti, Giuseppe's father.

The *Opera Orchestra di Bellafortuna* had been in continuous existence in the village since the late 1700s and was made up of those villagers with a musical gift. The music they played ranged from classical to opera, and Neapolitan love songs.

Most of the villagers sat on the ground, while a few occupied chairs brought out from the shops located nearby. The Jews sat among them, and the villagers introduced the Jews living with them to the other villagers. Maria Sanguinetti sat near the front, holding tightly to Biaggio's hand. She was so glad to be spending time with her son.

Some of the village children played with a ball off to one side. The Adler children, including Josef, sat with Anikka. When Alfred walked into the piazza, young Josef got up, ran to him and hugged him. Alfred spoke briefly with the boy until the other Adler kids came to get him, and they all ran over to join the ball game now in full swing with the other village children.

Alfred walked over to Anikka and asked, "Did you have a good night?"

"Yes, the hotel is very comfortable. You?"

"Never thought I would be a farmer in my life. But life is strange. The family I am living with is very nice and caring. How is Josef doing?"

"He is doing well. He asks about his mother now and then. My kids love that little boy."

Suddenly, a thunderous eruption of applause rattled the piazza. The conductor of the *Opera Orchestra di Bellafortuna*, Vincenzo Occipinti, took his position in front of the orchestra, and the concert began.

The *Opera Orchestra di Bellafortuna* consisted of fifteen members. They played arias from all of the famous operas beautifully. The entire crowd sat quietly throughout all of the selections, save when they were singing along. The locals loved to sing the arias.

The Jewish musicians, sitting in the sun-splattered piazza, were mesmerized. It was good to hear music again. It was good to live again.

Toward the end of the concert, Monsignor Mancini walked over to the conductor. Monsignor Mancini had taught Vincenzo everything he knew about music, and he took great pride in the fact that his pupil was now such a good conductor. Monsignor Mancini quieted the crowd and then spoke. "Let's give another round of applause to our beloved orchestra." The crowd cheered. "As some of you may know, we are blessed today to have some other musicians with us. I think all of us would agree; it would be an honor to hear you play something." The crowd roared its approval. Monsignor Mancini pointed to Ludwig Adler and said, "Bring them up."

Ludwig led the Jewish musicians to the stage, all except Heinrich, who remained seated on the ground with his back against the statue of Enzo Boccale. The members of the orchestra left their orchestra seats and sat out in the piazza, while the Jewish musicians took their places and picked up the instruments the village musicians had left on their chairs.

Ludwig Adler shook hands with Vincenzo Occipinti, who handed him the baton. Ludwig stood in front of the Jewish musicians. He asked, "Korngold? *Die tote Stadt? Marietta's Lied?*"

With a simple nod, the Jewish musicians assured Ludwig that they knew the wonderful aria, *Glück das mir verblieb* from

Korngold's opera, *Die tote Stadt*. Ludwig raised the baton and brought it down swiftly, as the musicians started playing on cue.

They played the aria by Korngold, an exquisitely crafted piece, with an unabated passion that went right to the heart of every listener. Giuseppe was seated next to his son. "My God, Biaggio. Listen to that sound. They are amazing musicians." There was prayerful sadness to the music, brought more to the forefront by the way Ludwig conducted and the intensity of the musicians playing it.

Hitler had banned this glorious musical piece in Germany, just as Ludwig's music had suffered the same fate. As Kurt and Alfred played, they recalled their dear friend from Vienna, Erich Wolfgang Korngold, who was now living in Hollywood, safe and far away from the Nazis, and writing music for Errol Flynn movies. They understood his comment well. "We always considered ourselves Viennese. Hitler made us Jewish."

When the aria was completed, the villagers clapped widely, yelling *Bravo. Bis. Bis.* Ludwig complied, and they played *Dein ist mein ganzes Herz* from Lehars' *Das Land des Lächelns*. When it was finished, the crowd cheered once again.

The orchestra members from Bellafortuna came back to their spots. Vincenzo changed places with Ludwig, who told the Jewish musicians to remain in place. Giuseppe moved up to the front and told the crowd, "Let's hear it again for our beloved Orchestra as well as for our new friends." The crowd roared. He then said, "So our friends will understand, this next piece is how we end every concert. And it's not Benito Mussolini's *Giovinezza*." The villagers croaked in laughter. "No, you will not hear that Fascist hymn played here in our village. Instead, what we are about to play is what we have always played. This is how it has always been. This is our tradition. A tradition seared into the soul of every village member. This music is the anthem of our village and brought us our freedom."

Vincenzo lifted his baton up swiftly, and the initial notes of Verdi's "Va, pensiero" from his opera *Nabucco* echoed throughout the piazza. The crowd - old, young, male and female – rose as one. Even the orchestra stood. The villagers quickly told the Jews to stand with them.

Verdi's chorus from his opera *Nabucco* is sung by Jewish slaves who are being held captive in Babylon. They sing of their homeland and the hope of ridding themselves of oppression. The opera's theme of freedom borne of oppression resonated with Verdi, just as it did with the villagers of Bellafortuna many years ago, and now for the Jews listening this day.

One by one, the villagers in the crowd grabbed hands and began to sing. The Jews listened in rapture.

Va, pensiero, sull'ali dorate;
Go, thoughts, on wings of gold;

va, ti posa sui clivi, sui colli,
go, and settle upon the mountains and hills,

ove olezzano tepide e molli
where you feel and smell the

l'aure dolci del suolo natal!
sweet breezes of our native soil!

Del Giordano le rive salute,
Greet the banks of the river Jordan

di Sionne le torri atterrate.
and the destroyed towers of Zion.

Right at this point, the villagers sang the next line with great emotion.

Oh, mia patria sì bella e perduta!
Oh, my country so beautiful and lost!

Oh, membranza sì cara e fatal!
Oh, memory so dear and fatal!

The Jewish musicians were moved to tears for they understood more than most the meaning of the words of the song.

Arpa d'oro dei fatidici vati,
Golden harp of our ancestors,

perché muta dal salice pendi?
why do you hang mute upon the willow?

Le memorie nel petto raccendi,
Rekindle the memories in our heart

ci favella del tempo che fu!
and speak to us of times gone by!

O simile di Solima ai fati,
Mindful of the fate of Jerusalem,

traggi un suono di crudo lamento,
either sound a cruel lament,

o t'ispiri il Signore un concentoto
or else allow God inspire with a sound

che ne infonda al patire virtu!
that will give strength to bear our suffering!

When the song ended, the villagers hugged one another and their new friends. Giuseppe Sanguinetti made his way to the musicians, and said, "We have instruments in storage that we keep for the summer opera festival when our orchestra is supplemented by musicians from Palermo and other parts of Sicily. We would love to have our friends join us for our weekly concerts and become members of our *Opera Orchestra di Bellafortuna.*"

The Jewish musicians stood and clapped, while Ludwig shook hands with Giuseppe and thanked him for his offer.

Then as happened every Saturday, the villagers proceeded back to work. But for one hour that day, they had been able to relax and come together as a community, a community that cared for each other.

As the refugees made their way back to assist the villagers with their jobs, they realized that the concerts held by the villagers were not just about entertainment. These concerts renewed their hope and gave them life. The villagers would not be the same people without the concerts. The concerts gave the villagers a soul. The refugees hugged each other and danced in excitement over participating in these concerts.

Santo Vasaio came up to Giuseppe, who stood with Maria and Biaggio. Santo asked Giuseppe, "Do you think it's a good idea to have them perform with the orchestra? I get nervous when I think of how they will be in the public eye so much. What if we ever have unwanted visitors to our concerts?"

Before Giuseppe could respond, Biaggio replied, "Santo, I can't think of a better way for them to blend into our community. Let them work among us, eat with us, and as is the case here, play music with us."

Giuseppe nodded his head in agreement.

"I hope you are right," replied Santo.

Giuseppe kissed his wife and then said to Santo, "I'm on my way to continue to teach the one living with me about wine inventory."

"Great concert," replied Santo. "They sounded really good."

Giuseppe agreed and continued. "Well, our new members are unbelievably talented musicians. I can't wait to see how this orchestra turns out."

Santo extended his hand and said, "We shall see. *Prendere cura, amico.*" (Take care, my friend.)

Meanwhile, Ludwig Adler caught up to Heinrich in the piazza. "You should have joined us and played. Why carry that Stradivarius around if you won't play?"

"I'm just not in the mood, and they sounded great without me."

"Did you see their faces. They were so happy to have music in their life again. Most probably thought they might never play music again."

"I'm sure they were all very pleased to be playing again."

"Heinrich, will you meet me tonight in the *Albergo*? I want to talk to you about something."

"Yes, of course."

"Great. I will see you then. *Buona sera*."

21

A JEWISH PRAYER

That same Saturday evening at sunset, Giuseppe and Biaggio sat at the top of the hill overlooking the entire valley. Biaggio scanned the valley and the Sicilian hills, which framed the valley. He said, "Papa, if you only knew how often I reminisce about this view when I'm at the Vatican. I miss this place so much. This was always my most favorite time of the day."

"It's been great having you here. I know your mother has been beside herself, being able to spend time with you."

"Even with her food being rationed, she still is a fabulous cook. Not as good as Mamma Lucia, but good enough."

Giuseppe laughed. "We are so proud of you. You followed your dream and have done very well. To think, my son works at the Vatican for the Pope."

"Papa, I yearn for the day that I can be nothing more than a parish priest, like Monsignor Mancini. I'm becoming more aware that is the sole reason why I became a priest."

"I think the Lord has bigger plans for you."

"I hate to tell mother this, but I will be leaving shortly to go back to the Vatican. Father Dominic will stay."

"I knew it would happen soon. I hate to see you leave."

Biaggio hung his head down, and when he again looked up, he put his hand on his father's shoulder. "Please be safe. If the Allies land in Sicily, the fighting will be fierce."

"I will be safe and will protect your mother, as well as our new friends. I'm so glad you brought them here."

"What is happening to the Jews all across Europe is terrible."

Giuseppe raised his finger. "My son, you seem to be questioning the purpose of your vocation and your being assigned to the Vatican. And yet, when called upon, you stood up for the persecuted and offered Bellafortuna as a place of protection. There is no greater love. But I would expect nothing less from you. Antonio would be so proud of you. I know me and your mother are both very proud. Perhaps the Lord knew what he was doing when he sent you to Rome. Now let's go home and see what your mother has made for us to eat." Giuseppe paused before saying, "And I'll let you break the news to her that you will be leaving soon."

"Oh, really. You want me to do that. Thanks."

They both laughed.

———————

LATER THAT NIGHT, Heinrich walked into the main room of the *Albergo* and was surprised to see Ludwig standing there with the Vinterberg Stradivarius. Ludwig extended the gorgeous instrument toward Heinrich and simply said, "Play."

"I cannot. Is that why you asked me here?"

"Kurt told me back at Castel Gandolfo why you don't play your violin anymore."

"It's too painful. My memories are too hard, too heart-wrenching."

"Let me ask you this. Do you pray?"

"I used to." Heinrich bowed his head. "I miss praying. We could probably all use prayer now."

Ludwig raised the violin. "Use this to pray. Use your gift of music to bring prayer to your fellow Jews. Play your music to make a prayer."

"What do you mean?"

"Music makes us inhabit another place, just as prayer does. Use your music, your gift, to remember your loved ones. Your music will become your prayer to them." Ludwig handed the violin and bow to Heinrich.

Heinrich reached out and took it, lovingly holding the violin momentarily, fingering the strings before handing it back to Ludwig. "I cannot," he said as his eyes filled with tears.

Ludwig refused to take it back as he put his hands behind his back. He then bore his stare into Heinrich's eyes and said, "Play it for her. Through your music, pray for your mother. Through music, pray *Kaddish* for her. Let your notes flow up to her."

Heinrich again cradled the violin before putting it under his chin. He closed his eyes, reaching deep inside himself. He left his surroundings and entered into the "magic time" of making music. After such a pause, staying in this other dimension, he lifted his bow toward the strings. He began to play the violin solo from Ludwig's *Munich's Tears*, pouring out his heart into the music.

The simple, yet haunting melody of the piece, flowed from the strings of the violin, as the romantic heartbreak and longing of the score passionately came to the forefront. Heinrich played with emotional intensity and with an undeniable depth of musicianship.

Ludwig stood with his mouth open as he was surprised how well Heinrich knew the music from just looking at the score that one-day back at the Castel Gandolfo. He was also much impressed with the richness and individual character of Heinrich's sound. But what stood out above all else was how Heinrich's violin soared. The Vinterberg Stradivarius produced a tone of unmatched clarity and sweetness, producing a perfect brilliance of sound that washed over Ludwig, as Heinrich's bow effortlessly flowed across the strings.

Anikka, who was upstairs in her room in the *Albergo*, heard the music and came down to listen. A smile came across her lips as she saw Heinrich playing. She closed her eyes and listened intently. Heinrich's playing and the soulful music filled her heart.

While playing, Heinrich thought of his mother and the *Kaddish* Jewish memorial prayer. When Heinrich finished, tears were streaming down his face.

"That was beautiful," Anikka said when she could speak.

Heinrich said, "Your husband wrote a great piece of music." He turned to Ludwig and said, "Thank you for urging me to play again." The corners of Heinrich's mouth turned up in a tiny smile. "And you were correct. It is like praying."

Ludwig said with great emotion. "That was stunning. Absolutely stunning. You made my music sound better than it is."

"It's the music, Ludwig. I merely played the notes."

"Well, I never could have imagined those notes sounding like that. And your violin, no doubt that is a Stradivarius."

"The secret to a Stradivarius is to discover the intricacies that Antonio Stradivari's own hands crafted, lovingly and tirelessly building it within his hot workshop in Cremona. Every musician who plays a Stradivarius must discover the secret of the violin and, once discovered, they can unlatch the mystery of the instrument. Each Stradivarius is unique, and every musician who plays one must find how to make that violin sing to its highest potential."

"No question, you discovered how to make your violin sing. Never stop playing, Heinrich, Never. Don't let the Nazis take that away from you. Never."

Heinrich smiled. "You have opened my heart to music again and to life, and you have brought to my mind the memory of my dear mother. For all of that, I am forever grateful."

Ludwig replied softly, "*Zich ro nah Livracha.*" (May her memory be a blessing.)

"*Zich ro nah Livracha,*" repeated Heinrich.

"Play something else, please."

Heinrich lifted the Vinterberg to his chin once again and closed his eyes once again, before he started to play Brahms Violin Sonata No. 1. Ludwig and Anikka sat enraptured. For over two hours, Heinrich played selection after selection.

It was well past midnight by the time Heinrich laid in his

bed to sleep. His Stradivarius, now back once again in its case, was underneath his bed. He fell asleep with the sounds of the Stradivarius in his head from earlier that night. He missed those sounds and was glad they were back. He drifted asleep.

THE NEXT DAY, right after the morning Mass, Alfred, Heinrich, and Kurt remained in the Church and spoke briefly. Alfred asked, "How is everything going?"

Heinrich simply said, "I started playing again."

His two friends smiled. Kurt asked, "So will you join us in the Orchestra?"

"*Si*," he replied in perfect Italian.

They laughed.

Alfred said, "I watched little Josef in Church today. He was having fun with his new family. I sure do miss that little guy. I often wonder about his mother. Is she still alive? If she is, can you imagine her pain? She has no idea what happened to her son in that forest. It reminds me of my own parents. Deep down, I know that they are dead. What I find weird is that part of me hopes that they are dead instead of suffering. I mean, how horrible is that?"

"It's not horrible at all," Kurt said. "It's understandable. I often think of Gina and my family and wonder if they are alive or dead. I have come to believe that all we can do is try to survive. We must just keep living. True, we can't pray publicly. But you can bet I pray every night and morning. I pray that all of our loved ones still alive come back to us. I pray that we all survive. I pray for these villagers that they are protected for taking us in. And I pray that this damn war ends so that we can all go home one day."

Alfred replied, "I pray for little Josef. I wish I could have forced his mother off that damn train."

Heinrich replied, "You saved him, Alfred. That is what she wanted. If she died, then at least she died thinking that she gave her son a chance at life."

"Yes, but what will become of him?"

Kurt shrugged. "What will become of all of us?"

Heinrich replied, "We were saved from that train for a reason. So many were not. You have to believe that God has a plan for us. Look where he brought us. Could we have come to a better spot? The villagers have a passion and love for music. Monsignor Costantini did a good thing by sending us here."

Alfred pursed his lips. "Do you think we are safe here?"

Heinrich laughed. "We are in Fascist Sicily, in a village where, other than Kurt, none of us speak the language. On top of that, we are surrounded by Germans just a few miles away who want to kill us for the sole reason that we are Jews."

Kurt said, "That sounds perfectly safe to me; even more, the reason why we need to go to our Italian lesson, which begins in fifteen minutes." He rose and motioned them forward.

The three friends departed and made their way to the *Albergo*.

22

A GOODBYE

A few days later, Giuseppe, Biaggio, Santo, and Father Dominic enjoyed lunch around a table in the rectory located next to the *Chiesa della Madonna*. Monsignor Mancini sat at the head of the table.

Just as lunch ended, Monsignor Mancini raised his wine glass. The others followed suit. Monsignor Mancini said, "Here's to Father Biaggio. As he prepares to return to Rome tomorrow, we thank him for entrusting these people to us. We also thank our villagers. They have welcomed the refugees with open arms."

Santo interjected, "Even Giorgio, I think, has come to embrace having them here."

They all laughed before Monsignor Mancini ended his toast with, "I thank each one of you for your leadership and your courage."

They all raised their glasses higher and said *salute*, before draining their glasses.

Father Dominic asked, "Are they safe?"

Giuseppe responded, "Safe for now. We must continue to bring them closer and closer into our community. Language will always be an issue though."

Monsignor Mancini replied, "Agreed. The language barrier is a problem."

Biaggio cleared his throat loudly, such that they all turned and looked at him. He said with emotion, "Trust me when I tell you they are safer here than the places from where they come. The treatment of the Jews has been abysmal in the countries where Nazism has flourished. So, you ask if they are safe. It is safer here than there. That's all I can say."

Father Dominic said, "For my part, I will continue working with all of the refugees with learning our language. As for our friends, rest assured they will have the perfect advocate in Biaggio at the Vatican." Dominic paused and stared right at Biaggio. "I know you will be mad at me for saying this, but I will anyway. Take my word on it; he is fearless. In meetings on liturgical and music reforms, even when the Pope is present, he has no fear in raising his voice and taking on some of the older members of the Curia, who are usually entrenched in their beliefs. The Cardinals usually are surprised that Biaggio, a simple clerk, has the fortitude to point out why a Cardinal's reasoning is wrong on a certain matter. Their surprise does not lessen the respect they have for him nor in ultimately changing their positions occasionally." Father Dominic smiled at Biaggio. "The Pope seems much impressed with your courage."

Biaggio leaned in. "Thank you. But you are more courageous than I. Please keep teaching our friends Italian."

"I will."

Giuseppe said, "Good. And all of us will continue to teach them our customs and ways."

Monsignor Mancini looked down at the table and then, slightly raising his head, asked, "And if the Germans ever visit our little village?"

There was dead silence in the room until finally, Giuseppe said, "We do what we can. And for the things that are out of our control, we put it all in the hands of God."

"Amen," they all replied.

"*FANTASTICO*. THIS PLACE IS AMAZING," Ludwig Adler said to Father Biaggio as they walked on the stage of the *Anfiteatro di Bellafortuna* down in the valley later that day. The *Anfiteatro* sat on the edge of the *Stagno Azzurro*, the beautiful pond located in the valley.

"This is where my father produces all of his magical opera performances every summer. I know how much you love music and thought you would like to see it."

Standing on the stage, Ludwig looked all around, taking in the view down in the valley and then said, "I love how the Sicilian hills surround the entire area. It must be quite a sight to take in a performance in this valley. You must be very proud of what your father has accomplished here."

"This place means the world to my family and me."

"I think all of us refugees have fallen in love with your village. We are so happy Monsignor Costantini sent us here. Your father and Monsignor Mancini are so kind."

"Thank you. The Monsignor is the reason I became a priest. The way he always lived his life impressed me from a very young age, and I wanted to be just like him. I know I am biased when I say it, but both Monsignor Mancini and my father are special people."

Ludwig feared it might not be appropriate to ask the next question, but he did anyway. "Were your parents supportive? I mean of you becoming a priest."

"Very. They are very proud."

"As they should be. Did your father think you would take over the wine business one day?"

"Yes, but he understands my vocation." He chuckled. "Besides, it's every Italian mother's dream for their son to become a priest." Then he whispered, "My father would never admit that my mother rules the roost."

A broad smile briefly brightened Ludwig's face at Biaggio's last statement. But his smile quickly turned to a frown. "My vocation was music; to make music so that I could bring joy to people. But the Nazis outlawed my music. Both my music and I are enemies of the Reich."

"I'm so sorry for everything happening to you and your family."

"The hardest part for me was when people that I considered close friends of mine turned their backs on me just because a lunatic told them that they should. They abandoned my family and me. We try not to dwell on it. We just keep moving forward as we try to survive. We were blessed to escape Munich. So many were not."

"I pray for all of the persecuted every day, as does our Holy Father."

"And I thank you for that. Since fleeing Munich, we have been assisted by the Pope's children. Perhaps through the Pope's prudence, those avenues to save Jews will remain open."

Father Biaggio smiled. "I am leaving tomorrow for Rome, as I must get back. I will continue to do whatever I can to assure that the Vatican continues assisting the Jews."

"You're leaving?" he moaned. "I know we will all miss you. Thanks for all you have done. When you have no hope in your life, finding decent, caring people, does help bring a sense of security and hope back."

"To be honest, Ludwig, we did nothing more than any other Sicilian or Italian family would do. We always look to help others. That's what people do."

"Not all, Biaggio. Trust me, not all. There have been some people who stood up for us and helped. While others have betrayed us. Yet, the ones who helped have blessed my family, and some have suffered the absolute sacrifice for doing so. I think about them every day, as I know we owe our very lives to them. Individual people. But here, in Bellafortuna, it is unbelievable how the entire community has accepted us. Why we may never know."

"I will tell you why. *Siamo tutti figli d'Adamo.* (We are all sons of Adam.) That is why. Before I leave, I want to show you *Antica Campanèlla* and the ruins of the old village. But let's first go across the *Stagno Azzurro* to the ruins of the *Cappella di Campanèlla*, an abandoned chapel located at the water's edge. And then we can proceed to *Antica Campanèlla* where we can wonder around the old village. All of the ruins are such a great place to visit.

"I would love to see it all."

The two made their way to the other side of the *Stagno Azzurro.*

THE NEXT MORNING, Biaggio stood in the piazza, waiting for his father to bring the horse-drawn cart from the Pandolfini stables behind *Il Paradiso*. All of the Jews were in the piazza to bid their friend and protector, Father Biaggio Sanguinetti, goodbye.

When Giuseppe arrived with the cart, he climbed down and joined Maria, Santo Vasaio, Father Dominic, and Monsignor Mancini, who were all with Biaggio. Maria stood right next to Biaggio, holding his hand.

Ludwig Adler spoke first. "We all know the reason we are here is because you brought Bellafortuna to the attention of Monsignor Costantini. And for that, we are eternally grateful."

The crowd cheered.

Ludwig continued, "We wanted to give you a token of our esteem, something to remember us by. We took a vote, and this is what we decided upon." He pulled a yellow Jewish star from his pocket. He handed it to Biaggio. Across the entire Jewish star were the signatures of all the refugees. And in the middle, in Italian, were the words: *La speranza ci dà la vita.* (Hope gives us life.) Biaggio cried while reading the inscription.

Heinrich interjected. "This star represents our persecution. Our signatures represent hope. Hope that we only have because of you. We shall overcome our persecution, thanks to you and to all of these wonderful people from Bellafortuna."

The Jews clapped wildly, as Biaggio accepted the star from Ludwig. Wiping away his tears, he said, "Whenever I look at this star, my thoughts and prayers will be with you all. I will pray for your safety and for the day that you can return home, home to your own communities and your families. Now, I must leave. My work in the Vatican beckons me. Rest assured that I will dedicate myself to assisting the Pope in all of the Church's endeavors to save as many Jews as we can."

Applause broke out again as Biaggio hugged Monsignor Mancini and Father Dominic, and then he embraced his mother, who was crying uncontrollably. Biaggio then stood before Ludwig Adler. Biaggio smiled at the composer to whom he had quickly grown so close. The two embraced as Biaggio whispered into his ear, "Stay safe."

Ludwig replied, "Don't forget about us."

"Not one day will pass where I will not think and pray for all of you."

Then, Biaggio and his father climbed into the cart. Biaggio bent down from the cart to kiss his mother goodbye one last time. The cart slowly began to leave the village. The Jews followed it until it reached the road leading down into the valley.

The Jews remained at the top of the hill for quite some time, watching the cart roll along the valley road, wondering if they would ever see Biaggio again.

23

AN ORDINARY MOMENT

*T*he days and weeks since the Jewish musicians had come to the village of Bellafortuna passed quickly. They settled into the daily routine of their new lives. They continued to study the customs of their neighbors as well as their language. With the help of Kurt, Ludwig and Father Dominic, the Jews slowly learned to communicate better and better with their fellow villagers.

A sense of excitement filled the Jewish musicians when they joined the village performers in the *Opera Orchestra di Bellafortuna.* Heinrich was readily granted the first violinist spot. Music was back in his life. The orchestra continued to play its Saturday concerts and on Sundays, rehearsed at the *Anfiteatro di Bellafortuna.*

Ludwig continued to compose again. He finished *Munich's Tears* and presented it to Vincenzo, who said it would be an honor for the orchestra to play it at one of the concerts.

While living and working among the villagers, friendships between the refugees and the villagers began to grow. The Jewish refugees fell more and more in love with Bellafortuna, its surroundings, and its people. And of course, more than friendships blossomed.

One day in March, Elizabetta Adorno, the female member of the *Società*, came into *Il Paradiso* to buy a bottle of wine. Giuseppe and his wife had gone out but had left Kurt inside checking the inventory.

Elizabetta, upon entering, said, "Oh, I was expecting to see *Signor* Sanguinetti. I am looking to purchase a very cheap bottle of wine."

Kurt looked directly into Elizabetta's cornflower-blue eyes and was immediately captivated. *"Buon giorno, fanciulla. Mi chiamo..."* He stopped himself and then proceeded to say pensively, "Luca Marino."

Elizabetta spoke slowly in Italian and replied, "Very nice to meet you, *Signor* Marino. You speak Italian well."

"Parlo un po 'di Italiano." (I speak a little Italian.) His heart raced inside his chest.

"Just a little? You know more than that. How did you learn it?"

"Opera. I studied opera."

"I have seen you in the orchestra. Do you sing too?"

"Not in a very long time."

"Where are you from?"

"Bellafortuna," he said with a nervous smile.

She laughed. "No, really. Where?"

He shrugged his shoulders and said not a word.

Elizabetta smiled. "Tell me. I won't tell anyone."

"Vienna," he whispered.

"Vienna. I bet that's a beautiful place."

"A magical place."

"Do you have a recommendation for wine?"

"*Signor* Sanguinetti just got this Spanish wine. It's cheap. He says it's cheap because it's Spanish wine. I think it tastes good."

"That would be great. *Grazie.*"

"*Prego.*" Kurt walked over to grab the bottle, and upon handing it to her, said, "Pay me over there."

As they walked to the counter, Elizabetta asked, "Would you mind if I asked you your real name?"

He leaned forward and said quietly, "Kurt. Kurt Hofmann."

"Kurt. It's a pleasure to meet you."

"And you as well. What is your name?"

"Elizabetta. Elizabetta Adorno."

"Is there a *Signor* Adorno?"

"No. My husband was killed in the war. He was fighting with the Resistance in Milan."

"The Resistance in Austria saved my friends and me. Your husband was a brave man."

"*Grazie.*"

"I am sorry for your loss."

Elizabetta asked, "Do you have a wife?"

"No. I am not married. I had someone close to me, but I have not seen her for a long time now."

"Where is she?"

Kurt was quiet for a moment before adding, "*Lontano.* She is far, far away." His mind was awash with images of Gina. Her dark hair; her brown, beautiful big eyes, and her red, full lips. What am I doing, he thought to himself.? Kurt hung his head down and was silent.

Elizabetta thought the conversation was getting uncomfortable for Kurt. "Well, I'll let you go. It was a pleasure speaking with you."

Kurt gathered himself, and without even thinking about it he said, "Could we talk again sometime?"

A smile crossed her lips as she quickly replied, "*Si.*"

After she had left, Kurt began to cry. He missed Gina so much. Not a day had gone by without thinking of her. Yet today, for this first time in a very long time, life felt normal, if just for one moment. No fears. No running. No thought of death or Nazis. For one moment, all of his thoughts were on a beautiful woman. He wept hard.

24

PRESSURE MOUNTS ON THE POPE

*I*n April 1943, a train carrying wounded Italian soldiers back from the front arrived in Rome. Onboard was Pirro Scavizzi, an Italian priest, who acted as the army chaplain on the hospital train that was sent by the Order of Malta to pick up Italian soldiers wounded all across Europe. Father Scavizzi was a good friend of Pope Pius XII. After all of the wounded soldiers had been taken from the train, Father Scavizzi hurried to the Vatican to secretly meet with the Pope. As he had done on numerous occasions, he brought to the Pontiff his personal testimony – that which he had witnessed with his own eyes as well as what he learned from conscience stricken Italian officers - from the front lines of Nazi occupation as he traversed all across Europe on the train.

Sister Pascalina immediately allowed him into the Vatican apartments, where he met the Pope in his private study. Monsignor Costantini sat off to the side of the Pope, listening intently to what Father Scavizzi said. The priest told the Pope of the gruesome treatment of the Jews by the Nazis, of the horrific conditions of the concentration camps, and that murder of the Jews had reached a whole new level without any judicial process. "Holy Father," he said, "even the elderly and the infants are being killed without mercy."

The Pope walked to a window, and with his back turned, continued to listen to the report by Father Scavizzi. While Father Scavizzi kept talking, Monsignor Costantini scrutinized the Pontiff. His friend looked weary and burdened. He appeared bent, not standing to his full height. His gaunt body made him look sick and unhealthy.

Father Scavizzi said, "The suffering of the Jews and all of those being persecuted is immense."

Toward the end of the report, the Pope turned back around. Both Monsignor Costantini and Father Scavizzi were caught off guard by the tears that flowed freely from the Pope's eyes. The Pope raised his hands to heaven and said, "Please. Please let them know they are all in my prayers. I am in anguish for them and with them. But I am burdened to silence as the results of my words would only lead to horrific consequences."

The Pope then dropped to his knees and wept even harder. Both priests joined him on their knees as the Pope led them in prayer. Monsignor Costantini himself was moved to tears at the emotion demonstrated by his friend. As he would relate to acquaintances long after, on that day, the Pope cried like an infant and prayed like a saint.

After the prayers, Father Scavizzi conversed with the Pope a little longer. As the meeting came to an end, Father Scavizzi said, "The local Bishops plead with you, Holy Father, to not speak out, as they fear even greater retaliation both against those being oppressed and against their own priests."

"I will write to Bishop von Preysing in Berlin," the Pope said. "I will explain that based on our experiences with the Dutch in 1942, the Vatican must tread carefully. But I will give to the local pastors the authority to speak out on behalf of the persecuted, as they alone can judge if and to what degree their actions and words will result in reprisals and retaliation. Please continue to bring me updates from Europe."

Once Father Scavizzi had departed, the Pope told Monsignor Costantini, "I trust very few people. Father Scavizzi is one of those, like you and Sister Pascalina. To hear about these atrocities, brings me to tears. Call a meeting with the Curia at once. I will meet with them in an hour. Let Father Lieber know and ask him to attend."

"Your Holiness, I am hearing that some members of the Curia have voiced their belief that you should consider excommunication of the leadership of Nazis, including Hitler himself. That way, you would open the eyes of the world to what the Germans are doing."

In a thoughtful manner, the Pope responded, "There is no doubt that such an action would gain me the praise and respect of the whole world, but I would unwittingly submit the Jews to possibly even worse persecution and to those who are protecting them. On top of that, Hitler does not practice his Catholic faith, so what would be the purpose. Keep him from the Sacraments that he does not partake in. It's not worth the horror such action would bring upon the Jews."

Monsignor Costantini replied, "All of those poor people. I will let the Curia know about the meeting. You look exhausted. You need to take care of yourself."

The Pope smiled at his dear friend before responding. "You are correct. I will relax before the meeting with the Curia. Now go, let everyone know about the meeting."

The Pope walked back toward the window and stared out.

Sister Pascalina walked into the study carrying a cup of tea for the Pontiff. As Monsignor Costantini began to leave, he looked one more time at the Pope and thought he looked like an old man with the weight of the world on his shoulders. He quickly departed to arrange the meeting with the Curia.

Sister Pascalina put the tea down but said not a word. Pope Pius stood staring out the window, silent. Sister Pascalina remained quiet watching as the Pope continued staring out the window.

With his back to her, he finally said, "If I speak out, I sign the death certificate for so many Jews and Catholics. Yet how can I remain silent? I am constantly questioned and vilified by many for not doing so. It would be so easy to answer them all and just take the Nazis to task for what they are doing. But I am convinced I would only cause more suffering."

"Your Holiness, you have done so much for them."

He turned and faced his faithful friend as he bore his gaze into her piercing, luminous, blue-gray eyes, which were exaggerated by her white coif and black veil. He said, "Not enough. I tried to keep Italy out of this war. I failed. I tried to facilitate the end of Hitler's reign, but that failed as well. Father Scavizzi has confirmed the horror of the Nazi persecutions of the Jews. He has seen it with his own eyes. Yet, I can say nothing. His descriptions of those persecutions and the treatment of the Jews has put my silence on trial, with myself and with God."

Sister Pascalina interjected. "But you have suffered so much and agonized over this for so long. You did not come to this strategy overnight."

"It is true that after many tears and prayerful reflections, I concluded that it was best that I remain silent. But I still have doubts if this is correct."

"You're tired, your Holiness."

"That is true. However, that is not the reason for my doubts. What if my fears are unrealized? What if the fears of the German clergy, or Müller, or others who have advised me to remain quiet are unfounded? What then?"

Sister Pascalina was quiet momentarily. She then placed her fist over her left breast. "What does your heart tell you, your Holiness?"

Pius turned back toward the window; his head bowed low. With his back still turned, he quietly responded. "One miscalculated word by me could lead to the deaths of countless thousands of innocent people. Just by my mere words alone. That's what I am faced with day in and day out. Moral grandstanding would allow the Vatican to look great to the outside world but would do nothing for the persecuted. This pontificate of mine is like my own crown of thorns." He then turned and faced her again. "What does my heart tell me? My heart tells me that I must follow my duty, my duty to remain silent, and do what I can to save all human lives, all the while knowing that my silence will be misunderstood."

"Your Holiness, to remain silent in order to save lives, is not a silence of fear or indifference, but instead is a silence of prudence, a silence of the utmost love for those you are trying to protect and save."

Pope Pius smiled for the first time since their conversation had begun. "Thank you, Sister. I'm going to feed my canaries before I attend a meeting with some members of the Curia. I'll take my tea with me."

She picked up the cup and handed it to him. He started to leave the room, but stopped before turning back toward her. He said, "I will always bless God for convincing you to come with me from Germany and remaining with me all these years."

She blushed and silently bowed her head as the Pontiff slowly left the room.

25

AN UNWANTED VISITOR

*E*ither by pure luck or perhaps by design, Kurt and Elizabetta ran into each other more and more. During the Saturday concerts, she could not keep her eyes off of him as she tried to pick out the sound of his instrument among the rest of the Orchestra.

She came daily to *Il Paradiso* to pick out a bottle of wine for the day. As they met on different occasions, Kurt slowly opened up more about his life in Vienna and what happened once the Nazis had come to power.

As their talks grew in-depth, Elizabetta was confident a bond was growing between them. Yet, it seemed to her that there was something holding him back from showing her if he had the same feelings that she had for him. There was one thing she was certain. She was convinced that her interest in him would have to remain hidden from the other villagers. She truly believed it was one thing for the villagers to help the Jews; it was something entirely different for a villager to fall in love with a Jew.

Then one day, it happened. It was a Saturday morning in early May. She had come into *Il Paradiso*, as usual to get her wine before the concert that day. As she walked in, Kurt was walking out, heading toward the winery down in the valley to deliver some paperwork to Santo for Giuseppe. She asked to join him on his walk. He nodded his approval.

During that walk, they shared their hopes and fears between them. She spoke about losing her husband, and what a dark time that had been. He spoke about Gina as well as his family. He dropped off the paperwork at the winery and while making their way back to the village, they stopped and sat on the slope of the hill overlooking the entire valley.

The sky was punctuated with white, billowy clouds. The sun was bright, and there was a slight breeze blowing across the valley that brought the smells of oleander and rosemary up to the village.

While they sat on the slope, Kurt related to her the entire story of how he and his friends had been dismissed from the Vienna Philharmonic, and what occurred to them during the following months. He told her how he went into hiding and how his family was deported, along with Gina. Tears began to flow from his eyes. He then described how they had escaped from the train.

She grabbed his hand. "You are here now. Safe in Bellafortuna."

"I know. Yet my Gina and my family are all gone. I have no idea if they are alive or dead."

"You must live. That is what they would want. I know that is what my husband would have wanted."

Elizabetta then pulled him close, and he laid his head upon her shoulder. She gently stroked his hair. As he lifted his head off her shoulder, their mouths were right next to each other.

She whispered, "It's all right." She leaned in, and they kissed before he pulled away and laid his head back upon her shoulder. Her face warmed in embarrassment. Surely, he would think her too forward. How humiliating!

She tried to cover up the shame of her actions. "I'm sorry for all that happened to you."

Elizabetta was fairly certain that her kiss had surprised him. Suddenly, he lifted his head again, put his hand against her cheek, and ran his fingers gently down her face until his arm settled around her neck. He pulled her toward him, and he kissed her harder this time. Encouraged by his move, she slightly opened her mouth, which allowed him to enter her mouth with his tongue. Her heart pounded inside her chest with excitement; excitement that she had not felt in a long time. With his return kiss, she didn't feel so ashamed. He held on to her before they returned to the village for the Saturday concert.

ON THAT SATURDAY, in May 1943, the piazza was filled with the villagers ready for the concert. After the first few selections, Vincenzo turned to the crowd. "It is with great joy that today we present you with a new piece by the talented composer, Franco Giacone."

Ludwig stood and took a bow as the crowd cheered.

Vincenzo continued, "The title of this piece is *Munich's*

Tears." Vincenzo called Ludwig up. When Ludwig reached him, Vincenzo bowed low with the baton raised toward Ludwig. "It's your piece and your orchestra," Vincenzo said from his bent position.

Ludwig grabbed the baton and took his place in front of the musicians. He raised it and brought it down swiftly as the music commenced. From the start, the faces of the audience showed they were in awe at the majestic sweep of the music and the lush orchestrations.

When the orchestra reached the solo violin part, Heinrich rose from his seat and began playing. The villagers felt the sadness and beauty of the emotional music coming from his violin.

Suddenly, Heinrich stopped playing.

Ludwig turned toward him and raised his eyes to question why he had stopped. Heinrich did not look toward him, but instead was staring across the piazza. Finally, Ludwig turned to see what he was looking at across the piazza. A grayish, black vehicle had entered the piazza. The rest of the *Opera Orchestra di Bellafortuna* stared across the piazza. This caused the villagers to turn and see the vehicle as well

Seeing a vehicle in the horse and cart world of Bellafortuna always drew attention, but it was the occupants of that vehicle that made them take notice today. In the front seat, a young German soldier was seated in a full military uniform. Two men were in the backseat of the open Mercedes – one, a German officer, the other an Italian officer. The car pulled right in front of *Il Paradiso* and stopped.

The Jewish refugees were immediately seized with fear, a feeling that had been absent since their arrival in

Bellafortuna. It was a feeling they all remembered but had hoped to never feel again. Maria Sanguinetti, sitting next to Anikka, put her arm around her shoulder, and said, "Everything will be ok. You will be all right."

The young German soldier opened the door and allowed the officers out the back. Giuseppe Sanguinetti and Monsignor Mancini sprinted across the piazza and made their way over to the officers.

The German officer was a huge man with a big belly that hung over his belt. The Italian was a thin man with little spectacles that hung off the end of his nose. In ungrammatically correct Italian, the German officer said to Giuseppe and Monsignor Mancini as they quickly approached, "Please. Please. Continue your concert. I am *Standartenführer Hans-Jurgen Fromm.*"

The Italian said, "*Il mio amico qui ama la musica.* (My friend here loves music.) I am *Capitano Massimo Gabadono.*"

Monsignor Mancini extended his hand. "I am Monsignor Mancini and this is *Signor* Giuseppe Sanguinetti."

"Nice to meet the both of you," said the Italian. He shook their hands.

The German officer extended his hand and said, "Monsignor, it's good to see you. I am a Catholic from Waldshut, Germany. I am in charge of the Germans stationed in Palermo. Some of the locals told me about your wine here, *Vino di Bellafortuna.* I am hosting some Generals tonight in Monreale, along with Captain Gabadono. We are beginning to plan for the potential Allied invasion of Sicily, although we are promised Greece will be the spot where they will land. Still, we must be ready. Captain Gabadono said we had to stop here and pick up the wine on the way instead of looking for the wine in some of the local wine stores in Monreale. We want to purchase three cases."

"*Signor* Sanguinetti is the man you need to deal with," replied Monsignor Mancini.

Giuseppe, trying to think of a way to get them out of his village quickly, said, "That should be no problem. It's on the house. Can I load your car?"

"My orderly will assist you," said the German. "Now, while I wait, I want to hear this music." He made his way toward the concert.

WHILE GIUSEPPE WENT into the wine store with the young German soldier, the two officers walked with Monsignor Mancini and took a stood near the Boccale statue. The refugees, both in the crowd and in the orchestra, desperately tried to avoid eye contact. The German officer bellowed, "Play. Please, play. Continue with what you were playing."

Ludwig raised his baton, and they picked up from the solo violin portion. Colonel Fromm listened intently. His facial expression indicated he was more than pleased. He clapped loudly at the conclusion and told Monsignor Mancini how moving the piece was and how beautiful it was played. He then asked, "Do they know any Wagner?"

Monsignor Mancini said, "Oh, I'm sure they do."

"Great. Ask them to play something."

Monsignor Mancini made his way to Vincenzo and told him to play some Wagner. He reluctantly agreed while he quickly changed places with Ludwig, who went to take a seat in the orchestra to play his oboe. They began with the opening to Wagner's *Lohengrin*. The Jewish musicians knew this piece well, as it was often played in Germany and Austria. The German officer sat on the edge of his seat, blown away by the power and perfection of the playing. "My God, they are terrific," he whispered to the Italian.

When the orchestra finished playing the piece, the German officer abruptly yelled, *"Wunderbar. Bravo."* He ran up to Vincenzo and shook his hand. He then turned his gaze toward the orchestra. "That was stunning. Beautifully played." He turned to Monsignor Mancini. "Are some of these musicians professionals? I mean, you hear playing like that in Berlin or Vienna."

"No, they are all locals. They are all from Bellafortuna."

"What a sound. How many members?"

"About thirty."

"They sound like a full orchestra."

"Thank you, sir," Monsignor Mancini said, as he looked to *Il Paradiso*, hoping to see Giuseppe, but he was not out yet.

"Play me another. Please play something else for me."

Vincenzo turned to the orchestra again and played a musical selection of Puccini's *Madama Butterfly*. When the piece was completed, the Italian officer joined the German on his feet, clapping wildly. The Italian said to the German, "You can keep your Wagner. Just listen to our Puccini."

Just then, Giuseppe came out of the store. Monsignor Mancini tried to escort the officers back to their car, but Colonel Fromm just had to hear one more, the *Overture* from *Tannhäuser*.

Colonel Fromm was brought to tears when the orchestra played the powerful Wagner melody. This was the music of his youth. This was the music from a time before he joined the *Wehrmacht*; for a cause and a leader, he did not completely believe in.

When the piece was finished, Monsignor Mancini finally got the two officers to make their way to the vehicle. The orderly had already placed the three cases of wine in the trunk. The German officer turned to Giuseppe and said, "Thank you once again for the wine. I have heard nothing but good reports about it."

"You're welcome."

He then turned to Monsignor Mancini. "Please, tell your conductor how moving his orchestra plays. I would love to bring them to Berlin to play for our soldiers back home."

Monsignor Mancini bit his lip. "They barely have enough time to play for this one hour on Saturdays."

"I bet. We are all very busy. We noticed the beauty of your village on the way driving in. Your village offers a commanding view of the entire valley."

Monsignor Mancini replied, "Thank you." The officers climbed back into the car and began to depart.

As the vehicle left the piazza, the *Opera Orchestra di Bellafortuna* played Verdi's chorus, *Va, pensiero*. The villagers, particularly the refugees, sang the song at the top of their lungs.

WHEN THE SONG WAS DONE, Monsignor Mancini asked Giuseppe, "What took so long?"

"That damn German soldier wanted to taste some wines. Hopefully, he gets in a wreck on his way to Monreale and kills them all."

Monsignor Mancini said matter-of-factly, "The German officer loved the music."

Giuseppe voiced his concern to Monsignor Mancini. "You know they will be back. He may bring more friends."

"I know."

"They are making plans for the invasion. If they are wrong about Greece, and Sicily is invaded, I fear Bellafortuna may finally get a taste of the horrors of war."

"We need to pray that if it happens, Bellafortuna avoids the conflict. I also think we need to talk with our musicians. I am sure they are quite shaken up by our visitors."

"I agree. They all must have been terrified and are wondering why they were here," replied Giuseppe.

"We should also discuss our visitors with the *Società*."

"Yes. We must be prepared and have a plan for the next time we get a visitor. But, to be truthful, I have no idea what that plan should be. I was so nervous that Colonel Fromm or Captain Gabadono would speak with our friends. I know they have been working on their Italian, but I just don't know how it would have gone."

"Let's go settle their nerves with some wine."

A SPECIAL PLACE

*D*ays turned to weeks after the German officer's visit. Life, as best it could returned to normal for the Jewish refugees. They continued living and working among the villagers. As the weeks progressed, most of them could have a brief conversation in perfect Italian. The assimilation of the Jews was almost complete.

For Heinrich, Alfred, Kurt, Ludwig, and all of the refugees, life in Bellafortuna provided them a normalcy that had long been missing in their life. The fact was that what they considered normal in wartime Sicily showed the absolute hell they had lived through before coming here. Those memories were never far from their thoughts.

One day, Heinrich found himself walking along the *Stagno Azzurro*, the beautiful, quiet pond down in the valley, close to the *Anfiteatro*. As he walked along the edge and passed the *Cappella di Campanèlla*, he noticed a man in the distance sitting under a tree on the knoll of a hill. He walked over that way and made his way up the knoll and finally recognized Giuseppe Sanguinetti. Off to his left were two crosses.

"*Buon giorno, Matteo,*" Giuseppe said when Heinrich approached. "Enjoying a long walk today?"

"*Si, Signor* Sanguinetti. It's so beautiful down here. I love this valley."

"Indeed. It's a special place."

"Whose graves are those?"

"That one is my father, Antonio, and the other one is my friend, Biaggio."

"Biaggio? Was your son named after him?"

"He was. He was my closest friend when I was a boy. He was young when he died and was instrumental in saving our village from the Vasaios, the family who once ruled this village."

"This is such a beautiful spot."

"It is. I often come here to meditate and draw inspiration from these two men, who meant so much to me and to our village."

"*Signor* Sanguinetti, your son, Father Biaggio, has been so kind to us and has done so much for us. There is no doubt that's because of how he was raised."

"He is a good person. He has dedicated his life to others. I am glad he brought all of you to us. I can't even imagine the hell you have lived through."

"It was all very painful. The Nazis robbed us of everything. I often think back to my time in Vienna before the Nazis came to power. Have you ever been to Vienna?"

"No."

"Before the war, it was an enchanted place. However, it was at night when its true charm came alive. Music was everywhere, in the concert halls, in the pubs, and in the piazzas. Music gave Vienna its soul, much like your orchestra does here. Haydn, Mozart, Beethoven, and Schubert all drew from the inspiration of living and composing in Vienna. It's easy to see why. After a performance with the Philharmonic, I loved walking around the city at night, taking in the old buildings and the life of the city filled with wonder and excitement.

"Then the Nazis moved in. Their flags came to dominate the landscape. I was no longer considered a gifted musician. Instead, I became nothing more than a worthless Jew. The things I saw still haunt me. The way those Nazis treated people shocked me. So many of us tried to hide but were easily betrayed by other Austrians, ready to turn us into the authorities. Most of us feared the same would occur here. It's hard to feel safe – to trust others. Slowly, we have overcome those fears, and now we do feel safe here in Bellafortuna."

Giuseppe, thinking back to the unwanted visitors to the village, replied, "Of course, there is no guarantee of what will happen. But you can rest assured that I will do whatever I need to do to protect you and your friends."

"Why? Why do you feel such an obligation to us?"

Giuseppe turned and pointed to the graves. "Because they are watching. Because that is what they would have done, and because that is what they want and expect me to do."

"We are truly blessed to be here. I need to go back to the village. Coming?"

"*Si*. Let's walk together. Tell me more about Vienna before the Nazis came."

"I will, as we walk."

They made their way back to the village talking the whole

time. Heinrich loved talking about old Vienna, and more importantly, he realized how safe he felt in Bellafortuna, far away from the hatred and fear.

But, as is the case, life does not always continue along the path we think it should.

ON TUESDAY, during the second week of June, Kurt and Elizabetta were sitting in their favorite spot overlooking the valley. Although hidden from the other villagers, their friendship had grown into a deep love for each other.

Kurt pulled her close and covered her lips with his. He desperately wanted this woman, more than he'd ever desired Gina. With that move to pull Elizabetta closer, her dress rose and exposed her thigh. When he gently traced his fingertips up her thigh, she pressed harder against his body. Then she suddenly jerked away.

Kurt said, "*Scusi me.*"

She quickly replied, "No. No. I want to, but listen."

Then Kurt heard it too, the sound of vehicles on the valley road.

She said emphatically, "Oh my God. It's the Germans. Look, two cars. They are making their way up the valley road again."

They quickly stood up and sprinted to the piazza to find Giuseppe Sanguinetti.

Giuseppe was in *Il Paradiso*. When they informed him, he said with haste, "Luca, you go to the *Albergo*. Wait in there. Anyone you see in the piazza, tell them to go with you. Go now. *Andiamo*. Hide in the bedrooms. Make Luca and his family stay in there with you. If you are found, remember you are all villagers. Elizabetta, quickly go find Monsignor Mancini and tell him to come here immediately. Tell him to bring Father Dominic as well."

Kurt and Elizabetta ran out of the store as Giuseppe called for his wife. "Maria! Maria!"

She ran down the stairs. "What is the matter?"

"The Germans are back. Two cars are headed this way."

"Oh, my Jesus. Do you think they know?"

"I surely hope not."

"Oh, those poor people. What are you going to do?"

"Hide who I can. For those we can't, we shall now see if we were successful in teaching them our ways. I need you to go down to the valley and tell any Jews you find to stay away from the village."

"I will," Maria replied.

She ran out. As she did so, Monsignor Mancini came running into the store with Father Dominic, both out of breath. Monsignor Mancini exclaimed, "Elizabetta found us out in the piazza. She took Alfredo, who was with us to the *Albergo*. The Giacones are inside as well. I think two or three more families who were in the piazza made it inside the *Albergo*. The rest are down in the valley or in the winery at work. They will have to make do. Hopefully, these bastards will leave them alone. What do you think they want?"

"I hope they've come for more wine," replied Giuseppe.

Giuseppe, Monsignor Mancini, and Father Dominic stood in the doorway and waited. They gulped hard when the two grayish, black vehicles pulled into the piazza. In the driver's seat of each vehicle sat a soldier, while in the backseat of the first car sat two officers of the German Third Reich.

27

LIFE CHANGES FOR THE JEWS

Standartenführer Hans-Jurgen Fromm exited the vehicle. He noticed Monsignor Mancini and the others in the doorway. "Monsignor. Good to see you again," he said in his broken Italian.

While he said this, the other officer made his way over to them.

Colonel Fromm said, "May I introduce to you *Stadtkommissar* Eric von Jeschonnek."

A tall, thin, thirty-six-year-old German officer stood at attention before them. His close-cropped, blonde hair and bright, gleaming blue eyes left no doubt of his German heritage. He clicked his heels and said to the group now standing outside the wine store, "*Heil Hitler.*"

There was no response from the group.

Colonel Fromm said, "*Stadtkommissar Jeschonnek* is the man now in charge of Palermo for the Third Reich. Your village falls under his jurisdiction."

Giuseppe asked, "Colonel, I guess you liked the wine. Need two more cases?"

The officer laughed. "You can bet that I will leave with two more cases, but that is not the reason for our visit. *Stadtkommissar* Jeschonnek wanted to take a look at your village."

Monsignor Mancini said, "Giuseppe would love to show you around."

Stadtkommisar Jeschonnek said out loud, *"Nein."* He moved alone to the middle of the piazza and allowed his gaze to peruse everything for a couple of minutes. Colonel Fromm stood silently back with the group outside of *Il Paradiso* before the *Stadtkommisar* walked back to where they were all standing.

He spoke to Colonel Fromm in German. Father Dominic strained to hear their conversation. At one point, the *Stadtkommisar* pointed to the *Albergo*. Colonel Fromm turned to Mancini. "Monsignor, what is that building?"

Before Monsignor Mancini could respond, Giuseppe blurted out, "It's a convent. The nuns who live there are a cloistered order."

Monsignor Mancini, although he was caught momentarily off guard, responded, "Yes. The Poor Clares live there. Cloistered nuns."

Colonel Fromm smiled. "I love those nuns. They are true friends of St. Francis."

"They spend all of their time in prayer and silence," Monsignor Mancini said. "They do all the manual work on the grounds of the convent."

Colonel Fromm's conversation with the Monsignor was interrupted when the *Stadtkommisar* asked about the building.

Fromm began speaking in German to him once again. The *Stadtkommisar* nodded his head a few times to what the Colonel was telling him. He also pointed to the Church across the piazza. The conversation continued for a few more minutes until the *Stadtkommissar* turned to the group and asked a simple question.

"Wie viele Juden leben hier?"

Colonel Fromm translated, "He would like to know how many Jews live here."

Monsignor Mancini responded without hesitation. "None. No Jews have ever lived here. We are a Catholic community."

The *Stadtkommisar* began speaking with Colonel Fromm in German once again. When they finished, the *Stadtkommisar* turned to the group and clicked his heels. *"Heil Hitler."*

He climbed back into the first vehicle. He called Colonel Fromm over, and they spoke again in German. Meanwhile, Monsignor Mancini asked Father Dominic, "What were they talking about?"

"It was hard to hear, but it has to do with a proposal and something about a *hospitalstadt*."

"A hospital city?" replied Monsignor Mancini.

As the engine started, Colonel Fromm and the soldier standing next to him outside the first vehicle raised their arms and said to the *Stadtkommisar*, "Heil Hitler." The car with the *Stadtkommisar* drove off.

Colonel Fromm turned and said to the group. "It would be wise for all of you to salute the *Stadtkommisar* with 'Heil Hitler.' He can make your life hell if you so desire. Now, I would like to speak privately with Monsignor Mancini and Signor Sanguinetti."

Monsignor Mancini said, "Sure, let's go into the wine store."

As the German walked into the store, Monsignor Mancini whispered to Giuseppe, "Really? A convent?"

Giuseppe shrugged.

THE MEETING TOOK place inside *Il Paradiso* at a table by the window that looked out upon the piazza. Colonel Fromm said, "The *Stadtkommisar* is a man of few words. But I am not lying when I tell you he is very powerful. You will soon realize how lucky you were that I came to get your wine and heard your wonderful orchestra that last time I was here. The *Stadtkommisar* has a... proposal... for the villagers of Bellafortuna."

Giuseppe asked, "What is your proposal?"

Colonel Fromm said, "As I told you, I loved your village. I spoke to the *Stadtkommisar* about it. It's too beautiful to be destroyed. I convinced him to declare Bellafortuna a hospital city."

Monsignor Mancini and Giuseppe listened in disbelief. They knew well what having their village declared a hospital city would mean, yet it was a two-edged sword. On the one hand, the village would be spared from Allied bombing; on the other, Germans would be living among their Jewish refugees as the wounded German soldiers would be treated in the village.

Colonel Fromm responded, "Your village will be saved from all destruction. We know the invasion will come soon. If it comes here, there will be fighting all over this island. We will drive the Allies off this island, and the cities and villages of Sicily will suffer. In return, our wounded soldiers will have a place to heal." Then in German, Colonel Fromm asked, "*Es ist gut?*" (Is that good?) He asked it in such a way that he was only expecting an affirmative answer.

Monsignor Mancini responded, "Yes, it is good. Our beloved village will be safe."

Giuseppe asked, "Colonel Fromm, what does the *Stadtkommisar* want in return?"

"Only your orchestra."

Both Giuseppe and Monsignor Mancini wore confused frowns.

Colonel Fromm laughed. "We really only want to borrow them. We would like to send them to Rome to play for the soldiers stationed there. We want them to bring a slice of Sicilian life to our troops in Italy."

Giuseppe and Monsignor Mancini's faces went from a look of confusion to absolute panic as the impact of Colonel Fromm's words settled in. Monsignor Mancini said, "The orchestra members are part-time musicians only. They work down in the valley among the vineyards and olive trees or in the Boccale Winery, making *Vino di Bellafortuna*. They cannot be spared from their work."

Colonel Fromm smiled. "You don't have a choice. The *Stadtkommisar* desires this. And he gets whatever he wants."

Giuseppe asked, "Why? They have orchestras in Rome."

"They don't sound like the *Opera Orchestra di Bellafortuna*. Besides, the *Stadtkommisar* is hoping to make an impression with the powers that be to get him an assignment back in

Germany once this invasion is repelled. It would be a feather in my cap to assist in this endeavor. We really would rather not end up somewhere on the Eastern front. The man in charge of Rome, SS *Obersturmbannführer* Herbert Kappler, loves music. This will assure our being held in a good light in his eyes."

Monsignor Mancini rubbed his chin in thought. "We cannot refuse, can we?"

"No, Monsignor. But, on the bright side, your village will be saved all unnecessary suffering. You will become a hospital city while your orchestra will go to Rome. In two days, two trucks will come to pick up the musicians. That should fit the thirty members along with their instruments. Once in Italy, they will travel to their destination by train. I would guess they will return home within two weeks. That is not too bad of a payment for your village to be declared a hospital city in return."

Giuseppe asked, "When will the wounded soldiers arrive?"

"If and when the invasion comes, our wounded will be brought here. In the meantime, we will begin the process of preparing your village for them."

"Preparing the village? Where do you plan on putting them?" asked Monsignor Mancini.

"The *Stadtkommissar* thought the building across the way was perfect, but when you told me that it was a convent, I convinced him to look elsewhere. We will not make those Sisters move. Instead, we will make the Church a hospital. When the invasion comes, the Church will be filled with cots, so our doctors and nurses can save our soldiers."

Monsignor Mancini responded with bulging eyes trying to hold back his temper. "The Church? It's a house of God."

"What better place to care for our sons of Germany? Now, I would love to have two more cases of that wine. But please, let me pay you this time."

The car soon was loaded with the wine.

Monsignor Mancini and Giuseppe stood by the Mercedes. Colonel Fromm said, "I will be back in two days. *Auf Wiedersehen*. Until I see you again."

The car pulled away.

WHEN THE CAR left the village, Father Dominic and Maria, who had returned from the valley, quickly came to the wine store. Giuseppe and Monsignor Mancini were talking excitedly to each other. Giuseppe quickly related the events by saying, "Bellafortuna will be declared a hospital city. This means if the invasion comes to Sicily, we will be inundated with German wounded. And in two days, Colonel Fromm is taking the orchestra to play for the Germans."

Maria said, "Oh my God. The Jews."

Father Dominic exclaimed, "In two days! Where are they going?"

Giuseppe said, "To Rome."

Father Dominic stomped his foot. "To Rome! To their deaths, more than likely."

"And the ones who stay here," Maria said. "What will happen to them when the Germans move in?"

No one said a word until finally, Giuseppe raised his

voice. "I think we have to do two things right away. First, we need to call a meeting of the *Società*."

"And the second?" asked Monsignor Mancini.

"We better find a way to somehow turn the *Albergo* into a convent."

28

HIDING THE JEWS

*P*anic set in quickly during the meeting of the
Società. All of the members of the *Società* were
seated at the table inside the *Albergo*. Elizabetta Adorno sat at
the table in tears. Giorgio Monachino stood at one point and
said, "Can't we just send all of the Jews to the camp at
Ferramonti? I hear they treat their prisoners well."

"We cannot, Giorgio," Giuseppe said. "These people are
our friends. Besides, if the invasion occurs, more and more
Germans will pour into Italy. Who knows what will become
of those people at Ferramonti. I will not allow these people to
be put into a camp where they could easily be shipped off to
somewhere even worse."

Giorgio quickly retorted, "Who knows what will happen
to us. We are hiding Jews with Germans on our doorstep. You
do know the punishment for hiding Jews, don't you?"

Giuseppe frowned but remained silent.

Monsignor Mancini rested his face in his left hand and

rolled his bottom lip between his teeth. "Look, there is really nothing to debate at this point. Colonel Fromm is coming to pick up thirty musicians, and thirty musicians must go with him. He has seen our orchestra. He has seen our musicians. They must all go. Besides, Monsignor Costantini instructed me to protect the Jews here in the village, not send them to a camp. So I agree with Giuseppe about not sending them to a camp."

"I don't think your Monsignor would want you to send them back to Rome to play music for the Nazis," Giorgio angrily replied.

Monsignor Mancini said, "I know that Giorgio. Anger will not solve anything. It is what it is. Now we need to make do."

Santo Vasaio said, "So what is the plan?"

Giuseppe stood and said, "The nine Jewish women, along with their children, will move into the *Albergo*. We will hide them in here. It will now be known as the *Casa Santa Croce*, a convent of the Poor Clare Nuns. We will protect them and care for them. We will provide them with supplies late at night once or twice a week. We will bring items over from the Church for the foyer inside the *Albergo*, to make it look like a convent in case someone stands at the front door. Elizabetta has agreed to move in and act as the Abbess. She will now be known as *Madre Elizabetta*. She will be the one to answer the door if need be."

Giorgio asked, "But if she answers the door, she doesn't look like a nun."

Giuseppe looked at Elizabetta and then replied, "She will. Santo, tonight you and my wife will go to Monreale to see *Suor Dorotee*. Ask her to give us at least two complete nun habits. More if she can provide more. Father Dominic and I will begin moving the ladies and children into the Albergo. Depending on how many habits we get, we will begin making a plan on dressing the others as nuns."

Elizabetta Adorno fought back her tears and asked, "And what about the fifteen Jewish musicians?"

Giuseppe shot a glance toward Monsignor Mancini before responding matter-of-factly, "They go to Rome."

RIGHT AFTER THE MEETING, Giuseppe, Monsignor Mancini, Father Dominic, and Santo met with the Jewish refugees in the Church. Elizabetta also attended, after asking that she be allowed to participate. The Jews sat in the pews as they listened intently to the villagers standing on the altar.

Anikka was the first to cry when the news was broken to her about Fromm's proposal, as well as having to hide out in the convent. She hated to be separated from Ludwig. She held tightly to her husband while seated in the pew.

Heinrich, with a look of fear, asked, "Rome? We are going with the orchestra to play for the Germans in Rome?"

All of the other Jewish musicians voiced concerns. The Church echoed with their questions and comments, often with the refugees speaking over one another. "How could you agree to this? We will be discovered. Why did you agree to this proposal?"

At one point, Monsignor Mancini said, "There were no other options."

Ludwig Adler rose from his pew, and all attention turned to him. He said, "Listen, we appreciate all that this village has done for us. But now you are asking us to rely on faith that it will all work out. Well, most of us relied on faith in the past, either in hiding, or trying to live our lives without being molested by the Germans. Needless to say, our faith did not save us from that suffering. So now you want us to go into the belly of the beast, stand before German soldiers and play for them, while our wives will be living here as nuns surrounded by German soldiers."

Giuseppe looked kindly at the little composer who he had quickly become close to. With a compassionate tone, he responded to Ludwig. "There is nothing else for us to do. Simply put, the Germans are coming to take you to Rome whether we like it or not."

Kurt asked, "And what of the women left behind? Will the Germans not search the *Albergo*?"

Monsignor Mancini replied, "I think not. I believe that they will respect the cloister. Our sisters must stay out of sight. All of you ladies will have to play the part. You will say your Latin prayers in the meeting room every day. The meeting room will be converted tonight into a little chapel. It is imperative that if the Germans ever do come into the building, they will find only the Poor Clares."

Anikka said, "I'm not Catholic, but I don't think nuns have kids. What about the children?"

Giuseppe said, "If the kids are discovered, we will say that they are all orphans and that you have a mandate from the Pope himself to care for them. But that will only be said if they are discovered. We believe having the children with you is worth the chance. It's better to have your children with you, instead of splitting them up among the villagers."

Some of the Jewish musicians started to talk loudly

among themselves. A few of the wives sobbed as they thought of what lay ahead.

Isaac Schoenberg, a trombonist from Hamburg, said, "I agree with Ludwig and what a lot of us are saying. We are all scared. Very scared."

Giuseppe nodded his head in agreement. "I know you are scared. We are scared. All I can tell you is that I trust my villagers with my whole heart. They will protect the women and children here to their death. As for the musicians, Father Dominic and I will go with you to Rome. Father Dominic is returning to Rome and will not come back. The other village musicians who come with us will do whatever is necessary to protect you. I understand your unwillingness to trust. But you must. That is all we have. We must trust each other, and we must trust God."

There was more murmuring between the Jews until Kurt rose. He looked directly at Elizabetta and smiled. He then turned to all of the Jews and said, "We all have loved our time living in Bellafortuna. The villagers have been kind to all of us. These people stood up and accepted us at a time when many others hate us. We indeed have no other option. But not just for our sake. If we do not agree to this, imagine what it would mean to the people of this village; the very people who took us in and made us one of them. We owe it to all of them to protect them, just as they have taken it upon themselves to protect us."

The other Jews slowly studied his words. Slowly they all nodded their heads in agreement.

Ludwig rose and extended his hand to Kurt, who shook it emphatically. Ludwig then turned to the group on the altar and said, "I'm sure I speak for all of us when I say we will go to Rome. If by doing so, we can protect the ones we leave behind as well as the ones protecting us, so be it. The ladies will stay here with the children under your protection."

The Jews stood as one in solidarity but said not a word.

Kurt added, "We ask for your help in pulling this off."

Monsignor Mancini responded, "Not our help, but God's. Tonight, if you want to, you can say your evening prayers."

The Jews smiled as they had not publicly practiced their religion in a long time and would come together, creating a minyan and offer evening prayers and petitions.

Monsignor Mancini said, "Pray tonight as Jews, but tomorrow, you are Bellafortunians once again."

When the meeting ended, Santo Vasaio pulled Giuseppe aside. He asked Giuseppe, "Do you think this can work?"

"Caruso came to our village against all odds a long time ago. We need faith. That's probably all we have in reality."

ELIZABETTA FOLLOWED Kurt out of the *Albergo*. They walked across the piazza and disappeared down one of the offshoots from the piazza towards her small home. She was still weeping.

"Your speech was great tonight," she said. "But I don't want you to go."

"I have to. If the Germans ever discovered that this village hid Jews, the members of the *Società* would be killed first. I cannot let that happen to you. I must go to Rome with my friends. It is a good thing you are moving into the convent to help with the women."

"You have brought me so much happiness the little time

we have gotten to spend together. I am so afraid. Please be safe. Return to me."

"I will."

They reached her home. Kurt walked her to the door, and after she had opened the door, he leaned over and gave her a quick kiss.

"*T'amo*, Kurt Hofmann," she said, as she wrapped her arms around him and pulled him closer. Kurt pressed his body against hers. Her eyes drew his lips to hers. Lost in the moment, he embraced her lips fully with his. Her body shook as she became excited in his kiss. She pulled away, grabbed his hand, and said quietly, "*Vieni*. Come inside."

"Are you sure?"

"I have never been more certain of anything in my life."

They walked inside, holding hands and closed the door.

TWO DAYS LATER, June 10, 1943, two brown canvas-covered trucks pulled into the *Piazza Santa Croce* led by a black Mercedes. They parked in front of the *Casa Santa Croce*, a cloistered convent of Poor Clare nuns.

Colonel Fromm exited from the back of the black Mercedes. He had come to the village to pick up his musicians and take them to Rome.

PART IV

ROME, ITALY
June 1943

29

ARRIVAL IN ROME

*F*ather Biaggio Sanguinetti walked briskly across the *Piazza di Spagna*, the most famous piazza in all of Rome. He crossed between the awe-inspiring 135-step Spanish Steps and the Fountain of *La Barcaccia* (the ugly boat), which is one of Rome's most beautiful fountains. He continued to the very southern end of the piazza until he came to the *Palazzo di Propaganda Fide* (Palace of the Propagation of the Faith). Biaggio entered the building and made his way down a short hallway that led to an office. He knocked on the oak door, and a voice from inside said, *"Venga."*

Biaggio opened the door and stepped inside. The office was small. A desk sat across the room, with a window located behind it. Floor to ceiling bookcases were on every wall. Seated behind the desk was Monsignor Costantini. The palazzo was where the Monsignor lived and worked, right in the heart of Italy, away from the politics of the Vatican. Biaggio approached and did the obeisance.

Biaggio stood. "They arrived in Rome two days ago. They are staying at the Hotel Quirinale. They are performing in the Piazza Navona tomorrow night."

"*Oh, gran Dio* (Oh, great God)," exclaimed Monsignor Costantini, as he made the sign of the cross. He motioned for Biaggio to sit and pressed him for more information. "Any problems on the trip?"

"None. My father and Father Dominic traveled with them and have both confirmed there were no issues at all."

Monsignor Costantini smiled briefly. "I arrived from Castel Gandolfo this morning. I am meeting with the Holy Father at the Vatican this afternoon. I will advise him of their presence here."

"I also wanted to make you aware of something," Biaggio said. "My father told me that Bellafortuna had been declared a hospital city by the *Stadtkommissar*."

Monsignor Costantini folded his hands, closed his eyes, and sat thoughtfully. He then opened his eyes and smiled. He said, "As long as the Germans don't move in, I'm glad the *Stadtkommissar* did that. But don't trust that man. He is dangerous. I met him several times in Rome. He hates the Jews with a passion."

"I know the villagers are scared of him."

Monsignor Costantini walked to a window overlooking the piazza. He stared at the Roman citizens sitting on the Spanish Steps, enjoying a moment from the weariness of war. With his back to Biaggio, he asked, "Where are the women refugees?"

"In a convent."

Monsignor Costantini spun around quickly. "In Bellafortuna? What convent?" His thick brows almost met over his nose. "There is no convent in Bellafortuna!"

"There is now. The *Casa Santa Croce*. It was a hotel a week ago. It's now a cloistered convent."

"*Oh, gran Dio,*" Monsignor Costantini replied again, more emphatically this time, as he crossed himself once again.

"My father and Monsignor Mancini believed it was best to hide them in the hotel and turn it into a so-called convent."

"Do you think they are safe?"

With assurance, Biaggio replied, "I would trust both of those men with my own life."

"Then, I will trust them as well. Are you going to attend the concert tomorrow night?"

"Yes. Are you planning to attend?"

Monsignor Costantini replied, "Yes. I need to be there for these people. I sent them to Bellafortuna. I feel a great responsibility for them. Let us say the *Pater Noster* for those people as well as for all of your villagers."

They grabbed hands and began to pray.

THE HOTEL QUIRINALE sat in the heart of Rome, right near the Rome Opera House. The night before their performance, the non-Jewish members of the orchestra had left the hotel to see parts of Rome. The Jews stayed in the hotel.

Heinrich, Alfred, Kurt and Ludwig all shared a room. While sitting on their beds, they discussed music, mostly as a way to forget their fears in playing for the Germans tomorrow night.

At one point, Kurt said, "I just want to get back home to Bellafortuna."

Heinrich said, "I guess you do, and it's not because you miss the little portion of food you get."

The others all laughed, as Kurt said, "What are you getting at?"

"We all know. We are not idiots. I bet most of the villagers know about you and Elizabetta. We see you sneaking off with her down to the valley and the way you look at each other."

"You could have told me you suspected something. I miss her."

"I miss my Anikka," chimed in Ludwig.

Heinrich said, "Let's play our music tomorrow night and get back to Bellafortuna."

"We have been truly blessed having been sent to Bellafortuna," Ludwig said. "The people are just wonderful."

"Each and every one of those villagers has a sense of decency about them. That attribute does not exist in many today."

Alfred replied, "Very well stated. They really do. They are good-hearted people. I'm sure they will do everything they can to protect the ones still there, including my little Josef."

Ludwig said, "I pray no harm comes to these villagers for their actions on our behalf."

Kurt replied, "Let's just get back home, home to Bellafortuna."

THE GERMANS MOVE IN

he day of the performance brought clear skies above Rome. That night the *Opera Orchestra di Bellafortuna* was scheduled to play in the Piazza Navona to a large crowd of German and Italian officers and soldiers. Meanwhile, back in Bellafortuna, all the weeks and months of planning to protect the Jews were about to be put to the test.

Around ten o'clock that morning, four trucks rolled along the valley road headed to Bellafortuna. The trucks carried cots, medical supplies, and equipment. The village was about to become a hospital city officially.

Monsignor Mancini met the trucks as they pulled in front of the *Chiesa della Madonna*. The piazza was empty. Each truck had two soldiers in the back riding with the supplies. One of the Germans walked up to Monsignor Mancini. *"Heil Hitler,"* said the young, blonde German. Monsignor Mancini nodded in return.

Then in very well-spoken Italian, the German said, "I am

Gefreiter Karl Frenzel of the 65th German Army Medical Corps. The *Stadtkommissar* has given me orders to convert this Church into a hospital. My men have supplies in the trucks to unload. Can we get some help from your fellow villagers?"

"Yes. I will find some to lend a hand. Are you leaving once you set everything up?"

"No. We will be here for a while."

"Where will you be sleeping?"

"We will sleep in the Church."

"Are there more coming?"

"No. For now, it's just the twelve of us. If the invasion comes, then nurses, doctors and more support staff will arrive."

Monsignor Mancini pointed to the Church. "Please keep in mind that this is God's house."

"Monsignor, all of us are Catholic. We will be respectful of the Church."

"Thank you. Can we still have Mass in there?"

"Of course. We will set it up so that you can still have Mass."

"*Grazie*. Let me get some villagers to assist with the unloading."

As Monsignor Mancini began to walk away, the young German said, "Monsignor, what is that large building across the way?"

Mancini gulped hard. "It's a convent of the Poor Clares. They are cloistered nuns who only live within the confines of their convent behind the "papal enclosure." Of course, being cloistered, they receive no visitors, and no one can ever go inside. This convent has been here for centuries. Now, let me go get you some help."

Monsignor Mancini quickly cut across the piazza. As he did so, he passed in front of the *Casa Santa Croce.* He looked at the building and murmured a quick prayer. The "nuns" inside would need it.

The German occupation of Bellafortuna had begun.

THE CONCERT

*G*iuseppe and Biaggio met all of the members of the *Opera Orchestra di Bellafortuna* in the small room located inside the Hotel Quirinale. A few of the Jewish musicians fiddled nervously with their instruments, some bit their nails, while others sat in complete silence. Each handled the fear of the unknown differently.

When Biaggio walked into the room, a few smiles broke out across their faces as they ran up to say their hellos and welcome their friend.

Biaggio said, "It's so good to see all of you again. I just wish it was back in Bellafortuna. Colonel Fromm is on his way over to wish all of you luck. I will be quick. The Holy Father knows you are here in Rome. He sends his prayers to all of you, and, in particular, to our special friends. I know I also speak for Monsignor Costantini when I say all of you are in our prayers. He will be out in the piazza listening tonight. Now my father has a few words."

Giuseppe took his place before the group. He said nothing at first but drilled his gaze into the eyes of each and every member of the orchestra. Finally, he spoke. "Play your hearts out tonight. Your passion for music will save you. Make everyone in the audience get lost in the music, so that tomorrow we are all on the road back to Bellafortuna and to your ladies and children. Remember that you are playing for yourselves and for those back home." He walked away with tears running down his cheeks.

Shortly after that, Colonel Fromm entered. "The Piazza Navona is packed. They are ready to hear a great orchestra. I wish each and every one of you luck. Do not let us down. The *Stadtkommissar* is expecting great things. Now, it is time. Let's go."

The members of the *Opera Orchestra di Bellafortuna* filed out of the room and boarded the trucks for the Piazza Navona and the concert.

―――――――――

THREE FOUNTAINS DOMINATE the Piazza Navona. On the northern end is the *Fontana del Neptune;* on the southern end, is the *Fontana del Moro;* and located directly in the middle of the piazza, is the largest of all the fountains – the *Fontana dei Quattro Fiumi.* The piazza, both magnificent and elegant, was alight with excitement as the soldiers talked loudly, awaiting the start of the concert.

A small stage had been set up between the *Fontana dei Quattro Fiumi* and *Sant'Agnese in Agone,* the church that sat directly across from the fountain. Chairs had been set up all over the piazza and were already filled as the trucks unloaded the musicians on the northern side of the piazza. Led by Colonel Fromm, they climbed out of the trucks and made their way toward the stage. The Jews walked behind the other orchestra members, with Giuseppe and Biaggio taking up the rear. Ludwig Adler turned and caught the eye of Biaggio. Biaggio nodded his head with a smile. Ludwig smiled back, which did nothing to quell his sense of dread and fear that all of the Jewish musicians were feeling.

As the musicians got closer to the stage, the *Stadtkommissar* rushed over to greet them. He shook hands with Colonel Fromm, asking, "Are they ready? Look at this crowd already."

"Yes, let them set up, and we will get started right away."

"Please note the stars out in the audience. We need to impress them – everyone one them. There must be ten generals."

"We will."

The orchestra members climbed the stairs and began taking their places on the stage. The Jews swallowed hard as they looked around the piazza filled with Nazi and Italian soldiers. Giuseppe and Biaggio stood next to Colonel Fromm. Alfred nudged Kurt and whispered, "Second row. Look."

There sat Monsignor Costantini. His presence brought a feeling of relief to all the Jews as they all became aware of his appearance. They knew he would not speak with them, but it meant so much to see him offering his support and encouragement.

Once they were set up, the *Stadtkommissar* stepped to the front of the stage. The crowd quieted. "It is my pleasure to bring to you the *Opera Orchestra di Bellafortuna*. They come from Bellafortuna, Sicily, a beautiful hilltop village. Here is the conductor, Vincenzo Occipinti."

Vincenzo stepped out in front and shook hands with the *Stadtkommisar*. He then turned to the orchestra, who rose as one and accepted the applause of the audience. Vincenzo then raised his baton, and the musicians sat down. When his baton came down, they began playing Puccini's gorgeous aria, *O mio babbino caro* (Oh my dear father.)

The soldiers were immediately transfixed as the passionate sound of the music resonated all over the piazza. This continued as they played aria after aria. They even played some Wagner, including the *Liebestod* (Love-death) from *Tristan und Isolde*, which sent some of the German generals into ecstasy.

For the finale, the Orchestra played *Va, pensiero*. It felt wonderful to play this song in front of the Nazis. Giuseppe and Biaggio both sang the words under their breath.

At the conclusion, the crowd cheered, which did bring a smile to the Jews' faces.

Colonel Fromm and the *Stadtkommissar* came up on the stage to a large round of applause. They asked the Orchestra to stand, and once they did, the greatest ovation of the night occurred. The *Stadtkommissar* leaned over to Colonel Fromm and said, "The generals are standing. We are assured Russia will not be our destination."

Colonel Fromm said, "We have one more piece I want them to hear." He motioned for Vincenzo, and said, "Play that violin piece."

Vincenzo turned to the Orchestra and said, "*Münchner Tränen.*"

Heinrich grabbed his violin tightly and waited to play.

Under a blanket of stars that lit the entire Piazza Navona, the crowd sat in amazement at the beauty of the music. Ludwig Adler played his oboe with passion, while at the same time, he could not get the feeling of redemption out of his very soul as his outlawed music was being played to the very people who rejected it. When Heinrich played the solo part, many tears were shed out in the audience, as the longing in the music made the soldiers think of their own homes, their families, and loved ones so far away. When the piece was completed, the audience rose in a tremendous ovation.

The *Opera Orchestra di Bellafortuna* bowed to accept the applause as the concert came to a welcome end.

As the crowd continued to applaud, the talk among the musicians was to pack their instruments hurriedly and return to the trucks as quickly as possible. As they departed the stage, the Germans swarmed over them and congratulated them. The village musicians made sure they were the ones responding, while the Jewish musicians nodded or simply replied, "*Grazie, grazie,*" over and over again, as they made their way through the crowd toward the trucks.

Heinrich held his violin close to his chest. What a night of music. They had actually pulled it off, he thought, as the trucks came into view. Alfred and Kurt came up on the side of him. As they walked, a group of Germans yelled toward them, "*Danke. Wunderbar.*" (Thank you. Beautiful.)

"*Grazie,*" was their quick response.

Ludwig Adler walked with Vincenzo Occipinti. They

were the last two on their way to the trucks. Vincenzo put his arm around Ludwig. *"Bellissimo.* Your friends played wonderful. And what an outstanding composition you wrote."

"Your orchestra sounded magical, Vincenzo."

"It was indeed a glorious night."

As they took a few more steps, a German soldier hastened behind the two. As he got closer, he called out, "Ludwig? Ludwig Adler?"

Ludwig turned around and saw the German officer. He froze as he immediately recognized Otto Steiner from his days attending the dinner parties at the Stolzs' home in Munich. Ludwig's face went ashen white, as the German made his way toward him.

LEFT BEHIND

*L*udwig Adler said nothing to Vincenzo, but quickly handed his oboe case and gave him a push forward trying to make him continue on to the trucks. But Vincenzo stopped.

"My God, Ludwig. What are you doing here?" Otto then noticed Vincenzo, whom he recognized as the conductor. He looked back at Ludwig and asked him, "Are you with the orchestra?"

"No. No. I live in Rome now. I just had to come hear this orchestra. Weren't they fabulous? That is what I was just telling their conductor."

"Indeed. The orchestra sounded great." Otto then turned to Vincenzo and, in Italian, said, "You are speaking to one of Germany's most gifted composers."

Vincenzo nodded his head without saying a word. Otto, still speaking in Italian, then asked Ludwig, "How long have you been living in Rome? Where is Anikka?"

"I have been living in Rome for a few months now." He was quiet momentarily, before he said, "As for Anikka, she is dead, along with my entire family."

Vincenzo shot a quickly startled glance at Ludwig.

Almost in a whisper, Otto said, "Dead. How?"

"They were sent away."

"I am so sorry, Ludwig. I miss our days at the Stolzs' home listening to your compositions. Come walk with me." Otto turned to Vincenzo. "It was a pleasure meeting you. Congratulations on the concert. Now, excuse us."

Ludwig extended his hand to Vincenzo. "It was a pleasure meeting you as well. I must be going home." Then Ludwig and Otto walked in the opposite direction.

Vincenzo stood there dumbfounded, not knowing what to do, as he watched the German and Ludwig walk together across the piazza. Ludwig's words, "I must be going home," resonated in his head. His thoughts were interrupted when some Germans came up to offer their congratulations. Not knowing what else to do, he began quickly making his way to the trucks so that he could alert the others.

Now speaking German, Otto, while walking across the piazza, asked Ludwig, "Where do you live in Rome – the Jewish Quarter?"

"Yes, the Jewish Quarter"

"You could be arrested, you know. It is past curfew. If you are discovered out of the Quarter."

"I just wanted to hear some music. I heard some of the Italian guards speaking about it."

"Have no fear. You are with me. I will take you back to the Quarter tonight. Nothing will happen to you that way."

"No need. I will get back in the way I got out."

"You are crazy. Come, I will walk with you back and speak with the guards. I will tell them you were with me."

"No. It is fine."

"I insist and will not take no for an answer."

They began making their way toward the Jewish Quarter. Along the way, Otto said, "Ludwig, I am very sorry about Anikka and your family. You must be very careful here."

Ludwig closed his eyes and simply replied, "*Danke.*"

VINCENZO MADE it back to the trucks and found Giuseppe as quickly as he could. "They took Ludwig," he exclaimed.

"Who?" replied Giuseppe.

"A German soldier."

Giuseppe's voice showed great concern as he said, "Where did he take him?"

"I'm not sure. The German knew him. He knew his name. He knew he was a composer from Munich. Ludwig acted like he did not know me. He told the German he was not in the orchestra. He said he lives in Rome."

Anxiety rose in Giuseppe's voice. "My God, if the German knows him, he must know that he is a Jew. Where did they go?"

"He walked with him across the piazza. I have no idea. He definitely knew him. He told the German his entire family was dead."

Giuseppe shook his head. "He lied to protect his family, the other Jews . . . and us."

"What should we do?" asked Vincenzo.

"I will speak with Biaggio. Perhaps Monsignor Costantini will be able to assist. It is far beyond anything that we can do for him."

"Here comes Colonel Fromm with Biaggio. You best speak with him quickly."

Colonel Fromm walked up to the trucks with Biaggio. The Colonel clapped loudly. *"Wunderbar.* The *Stadtkommisar* is thrilled. Now let's load up. We will go back to the hotel and then head out for Bellafortuna first thing in the morning."

Giuseppe walked over to Biaggio and quickly related the story Vincenzo had just told him. Biaggio, overcoming the shock, asked, "Should we go look for him?"

"This German must know he is a Jew. We can't arouse suspicion. Lord, if they discovered that he was in the orchestra from Bellafortuna, all of us, including the villagers and the women, would be in trouble. I am sure that is why he lied. You need to get Monsignor Costantini involved. Let him find out where he is and see what he can do to help."

"I will. Look, the trucks are loaded. You must go. I will pray for him."

"And his poor family," Giuseppe said. "They will be devastated."

"I will find him, Papa. I will find him."

"Grazie," replied Giuseppe as he kissed his son, and then climbed aboard the truck, sitting next to Alfred, Heinrich, and Kurt.

Colonel Fromm passed the truck and looked up at Giuseppe. "All onboard."

Giuseppe hesitated. "Yes. Counted them myself."

"Good. Let's go."

As the engine turned on, Kurt asked, "Giuseppe, you looked distressed. Is anything the matter?"

The story related by Giuseppe brought tears to the eyes of the three friends as the trucks began pulling out of the piazza.

33

THE RABBI

*K*urt, Alfred and Heinrich sat on the beds inside the Hotel Quirinale, unable to sleep. They wanted to look for Ludwig and would have, but for Giuseppe, reiterating to them what would happen if they allowed the Germans to know that Ludwig was one of them.

As they grappled with how they would break the news to Anikka once back in Bellafortuna, the door to their room opened, and Giuseppe walked in.

"What have you heard?" Alfred asked.

"Yes, tell us," added the other two.

Giuseppe took a deep breath. "Biaggio spoke with Monsignor Costantini immediately after it happened. He assures us the Vatican's spies will track him down."

Heinrich asked, "No idea where he is?"

"None."

Kurt asked, "So what now?"

Giuseppe shrugged.

Heinrich said solemnly, "We will be leaving without him."

"Yes," replied Giuseppe. "Hopefully, he will be returned to us."

Kurt replied, "We all have so many family members and loved ones that have been taken from us, and we have no idea where they are or if they are still alive. Hope is all we have. Faith that everything will be fine is long dead."

Giuseppe replied, "Hope comes first. Hope breeds faith. Together they bring love. With hope, over time, you will have faith. Let me tell you a quick story. You asked about the Caruso drawings in *Il Paradiso*. My village, many, many years ago, was under the power of the Vasaio family, Santo's family. They ruled the village, and our villagers suffered because of crushing debt owed to them. We hoped for freedom for a long time. My father and I came to believe, through faith, that we could achieve freedom. And we did, thanks to Enrico Caruso, who came to our village and saved us. Have hope for now, and eventually, you will have faith; that wonderful belief that lets you know deep down that all will be well. For now, rest assured that Biaggio will continue working with Monsignor Costantini to bring Ludwig home."

"We know, Giuseppe," Kurt said. "We are all just scared."

"Get some rest. We return to Bellafortuna tomorrow. Believe that Biaggio and Monsignor Costantini will bring him home."

LUDWIG ADLER KNEW there was no other option. He was Ludwig Adler once again, a Jewish composer from Munich.

By becoming a Jew again, he would protect his family as well as those protecting them.

Otto Steiner had walked him right to the Italian soldiers at the front of the Jewish Quarter and then left him alone once Ludwig entered the Jewish Quarter to make his way to his non-existent apartment. It was dark, and the streets were quiet as he walked along the cobblestones of the ancient Roman Jewish ghetto.

More than 2000 years before, Jews had settled here along the banks of the Tiber and across the Ponte Garibaldi in Trastevere, on the small island on the bend of the river. The Jewish Quarter, as it became known, was the oldest Jewish community in the Western world. Over many centuries, the Jews squeezed into this tiny corner of Rome and against all odds continued to survive. Over those centuries, the Jews living here had witnessed the fall of the Roman Empire, many wars, and countless persecutions. In 1555, those persecutions reached a whole new level when Pope Paul IV confined all Roman Jews to the area to make life miserable for them and in an attempt to convert them eventually. A wall was built surrounding the entire ghetto. The end result did not provide the outcome envisioned by the Pope. By forcing the Jews to live so close together, the Jewish culture and customs flourished. Life was harsh, but the Jewish spirit survived and grew.

Finally, in 1870, the persecutions came to an end, and all ghetto restrictions were removed, the walls were torn down, and the residents of the ghetto granted Italian citizenship. The entire area was rebuilt, and construction began on the *Tempio Maggiore*, Rome's largest synagogue. The hospital on Tiber Island, the *Fatebenefratelli*, began to allow Jews to seek care. For the first time, life improved for the Jews. It was short-lived. With the rise of fascism and Italy's marriage to Nazism, persecutions began once again. Racial laws were introduced that prevented Jews from doing any work for non-Jews. A curfew was instituted. And non-Jews were no longer allowed to enter the Jewish Quarter.

The 8,000 Jews who lived in these cramped quarters continued to try to scratch out a life just as their ancestors had done generations before. The inhabitants worked hard, peddling their wares in carts through the streets of Rome before returning at night to the ghetto before curfew. The entire cramped area of the Jewish Quarter ran for four blocks, wedged between the Tiber, the *Fontane delle Tartarughe*, the *Teatro di Marcello* and the *Palazzo Cenci*. The Jews here had always lived with a strong sense of spirituality that thrived even amongst poverty and persecution. One all-encompassing thing bound the residents together, and that was their faith, which centered on the *tempio maggiore*, the large synagogue that sat close to the Tiber.

As the war in Europe raged, some Jewish refugees were smuggled out of Europe and found their way to the Roman ghetto. These refugees soon would spread the word to the residents of the Jewish Quarter of the atrocities going on in parts of Europe under the control of the Third Reich. But the Roman Jews still felt safe. The president of the Jewish community in Rome, Ugo Foa, had assured them that the Pope would never allow anything to happen to them. The Chief Rabbi, Israel Zolli, felt differently and had grave concerns for the Roman Jews. He knew the Pope was powerless to stand up to Nazi aggression.

As Ludwig walked along the narrow street that night, he

passed kosher butcher shops, shabby tailor stores, and other shops and stores, all closed for the evening. He found a young man walking along the street and asked for directions to the synagogue.

Ludwig thanked the man for the directions and continued walking until he came to the *Portico d'Ottavia*, in the very heart of the Jewish Quarter. He stared at the ancient ruins of the massive 2,000-year-old portico and then made his way into the piazza. He continued across the piazza and made his way to the *Tempio Maggiore di Roma*.

The building, framed by palm trees, towered over all of the other buildings in the Jewish Quarter. But what caught Ludwig's attention was the square roof. The only one of its kind in all of Rome. He made his way to the side and found a door. He knocked, and an elderly woman answered.

In his simple Italian, he asked, "Can I see the Rabbi, please?"

"It is late," she replied.

"I know. I just arrived."

"He is not taking visitors now." She began to close the door.

Before she closed the door, Ludwig said, "I am Ludwig Adler from Munich. The Vatican is hiding me in Italy, but a German soldier recognized me tonight here in Rome."

She flung the door open and said in German, "*Komm herein.*" (Come in.)

He entered a small foyer. "I am Adina, the Rabbi's assistant. Wait here," she said, before slipping off down a hallway.

A few minutes had passed before Ludwig heard someone

coming down the hallway. A man dressed in his pajamas walked in.

Speaking German, the man said, "I apologize for how I am dressed. I am the Chief Rabbi of Rome, Israel Zolli."

"I need help."

"How can I be of assistance? If the Vatican is assisting you, I will do whatever you need me to do."

"I need a place to live. I need to become a Roman Jew."

"Your family?"

"Hiding in Sicily."

"Are you trying to get back to Sicily?"

"No, Rabbi. The Vatican provided me with a new identity, and I was living in a peaceful village in Sicily. Tonight, in Rome, an old acquaintance from Munich recognized me. He knows I am a Jew. He brought me to the Jewish Quarter. I need to stay here to protect my family."

"How are you here, my son?"

"Music, Rabbi. I am here because of music."

"Music? What do you mean? What brought you here? What happened to you?"

Tears welled up in Ludwig's eyes. "I lost my family tonight. But I lose them to save them."

"Tell me how you found your way to Sicily. Give me every detail. What did the Vatican do for you?"

"It all started in Munich. Just a few months ago."

Rabbi Zolli and Ludwig spoke late into the night. Ludwig related the entire story of his journey. Rabbi Zolli stopped him numerous times with questions.

When they finished, Rabbi Zolli said, "You can sleep here tonight. Tomorrow, I will put you in an apartment where you can live. It is very small."

"Rabbi, since this nightmare began, I have slept in all sorts of places. I'm sure it will be fine."

"Good. Get some sleep. We will continue our discussion tomorrow morning. Adina will show you to your room."

THE NEXT MORNING, Ludwig found himself sitting in a small apartment overlooking the *Fontane delle Tartarughe*.

Rabbi Zolli sat at an old table in the dingy, tiny kitchen. "I hope you find these accommodations suitable. You will be safe living here, for now. The Italians leave us alone. The Germans do not bother us, as they leave the persecution to our fellow Italians. But the Italians do us no harm. My wife, Emma, and I have a friend who works in a tailor shop. He will assist you in getting some clothes. I will also speak to a few friends and find you a job. I need to submit your name and address as a resident of the Jewish Quarter. That is required. But don't worry. The Italians just keep the list to track who lives here."

"My only papers are these," Ludwig said, as he pulled out his Italian identity card showing him as Franco Giacone.

"I will take that card from you and hold it for safekeeping. There is a printing press here in the Quarter. I think it best if you use the name Franco Giacone, a Jew from Rome. You will have your papers later today."

"Thank you, Rabbi. And thank God the Italians leave you undisturbed here. They are unbelievable in the way they treated us."

"Don't get me wrong. Life is not easy in the Jewish

Quarter. It is hard. Just mind your business, stay in the Quarter, stick to your job, and all will be well."

"I will do just that. I will once again be Franco Giacone, but now a Roman Jew," replied Ludwig. He then was silent before saying, "A Jew whose family is dead."

"I understand. I reiterate again; stay inside the ghetto. It's too dangerous in Rome. However, if you ever do leave, make sure you come back before curfew. Now let me find you a job."

34

A RETURN TO THE VILLAGE

From the time the Germans arrived in Bellafortuna, they quickly settled into their routine and began to make Bellafortuna their home away from home. They would sit in the piazza day in and day out, talking to each other and watching the ladies of the village as they walked across the piazza. They continued their preparations inside the Church and made it ready for its first wounded soldier. But most of their time was spent sitting out in the piazza.

The villagers, for their part, ignored them and tried not to speak with them at all, unless they were spoken to. And when they were spoken to, the conversations were kept quick and to the point.

As for the Jewish women living in the convent, they were prisoners in the few rooms where they spent their time. They cared for their children and tried to support each other as much as possible. But having the children inside with them and unable to go outside, quickly brought nerves already on edge to a whole new level.

Anikka had her hands full with her own two children and Josef. She tried to keep them active. She knew they had to be taught not to make a lot of noise so that the Germans would not hear them. And, of course, she was concerned for her husband. She waited with great anticipation to hear that the orchestra had made it back to Bellafortuna.

Elizabetta missed her home, but she knew how important being inside the convent with these women and children was, and what her presence might mean one day if a German came to the door.

The ladies spent the days sewing habits for each and every one of them. And right on time, they went to the first-floor meeting room that was now converted to the chapel, where they chanted the Divine Office, learning it as they went along.

Life went on in a way that was normal yet different. It was about to get even stranger.

IT WAS midday on a beautiful but hot day in Bellafortuna. The Germans were sitting in the piazza in the shadow of the Enzo Boccale statue to avoid some of the heat of the day when the sound of trucks coming up the valley road was heard inside the village.

The *Opera Orchestra di Bellafortuna* had returned.

Colonel Fromm's car led the trucks into the piazza. He exited first. The soldiers in the piazza jumped to attention and yelled, "Heil Hitler."

Colonel Fromm replied, "I hope you are enjoying the sites. Music has returned to the village." He pointed to the trucks and the members of the orchestra who were climbing out the back.

Monsignor Mancini came out of the rectory and was met by Colonel Fromm before he could get to the orchestra.

"You should be very proud, Monsignor. They were a sensation."

"I would expect nothing less."

Colonel Fromm then said to the soldiers, "Before I leave, let me see the hospital." He turned to his driver. "And you go to the wine store and get me two cases."

As Fromm left with the soldiers, Monsignor Mancini told the members, "We are so glad you are back."

As more and more of the villagers flooded into the piazza to welcome their loved ones back home, Kurt said to Monsignor Mancini, "Not all of us, Monsignor. Not all of us."

"What do you mean?"

Giuseppe Sanguinetti walked up and said in a whisper, "Franco Giacone stayed behind. He ran into a German who knew him. We have no idea where he is."

Slowly, Monsignor Mancini made the sign of the cross and said, "Oh my God. Anikka and the children."

Giuseppe asked, "Can you go to the convent?"

"I can. The soldiers think I go there to say Mass or hear their confessions."

Let me tell you the whole story of what we know, and then you can go speak with her."

Alfred walked over. "We wanted to tell her, but it's best if the Monsignor does it. Monsignor, when you go inside, please let Elizabetta know has happened. She will help Anikka get through her pain tonight."

"I will." Monsignor Mancini then spoke to everyone out in the piazza. "Before our friends come back from the Church, go home. All of you. Take our musicians home. If you live around the piazza, make sure you go to your new location. Trust me; you do not want to live close to the piazza with the Germans in it every day. Go now."

They began to file out of the piazza. Soon, Colonel Fromm returned with his driver. He said to Giuseppe and Monsignor Mancini, "You really should be proud of that group. They were spectacular."

"They work hard," Giuseppe said. "It's good to have them all home."

"Well, till I see you again. I will have a drink with the *Stadtkommisar* tonight as we celebrate all that happened in Rome. Take care." With that, he departed.

Monsignor Mancini turned and said, "Giuseppe, let's go to *Il Paradiso* to talk. You need to tell me what happened."

As the duo began to walk to the wine store, Giuseppe looked toward the convent. Through the windows, he thought he saw the faces of Ludwig's family peeking out to catch a glimpse of their father returning from Rome.

THE RETURNING Jewish men from Rome quickly returned to their life in Bellafortuna. But with the absence of Ludwig, the women and children being confined to the convent, and the German soldiers living in the village, the past few months of their feeling safe was now gone. They continued working at their jobs and lived among the villagers. They loved those Sicilians and trusted them with their lives.

Anikka put up a brave face and understood that Biaggio and Monsignor Costantini were doing everything possible to find Ludwig. But deep down, she feared the worst. She believed that Monsignor Mancini was probably correct that her husband had lied to protect her and their family as well as all of the other villagers and Jews. She spent many a late night discussing her pain with Elizabetta, who quickly became her closest friend and ally.

One such night, Anikka, with tears in her eyes, came into Elizabetta's room. Elizabetta, still in her full habit opened her arms, and pulled Anikka close. Anikka buried her head into her shoulder and muttered, "I miss him so much. I just keep having this premonition that I will never see him again."

Elizabetta picked Anikka's head up and stared into her eyes. "You cannot believe that."

"I can't shake this feeling. He's such a good father to our children. I love him so much. What will happen to us? Why is this happening to us?"

Elizabetta said, "I cannot answer those questions. All I know is you must continue on and put all your trust in God – for you and for your children."

"But how can you say that when you lost your own husband to this terrible war?"

Elizabetta sat on the edge of the bed and pulled Anikka downward, inviting her to sit next to her. Holding both of Anikka's hands tightly, she said, "My soul has been to the darkest place imaginable, yet I clawed my way back to the light. And now, I have found happiness once again. In your thoughts and dreams, think of the day Ludwig will return to you, his touch, his smell, and his love. Make that take over all of your thoughts, your entire being."

Anikka smiled. "I will try. I will. I do cherish our friendship."

"I do too."

"What you Sicilians are doing to save us is quite unexplainable."

"No, Anikka. Not helping is more unexplainable."

Anikka leaned in and hugged her. "Thank you. That's all I can say. Now, let me go and make sure my children are sleeping."

After Anikka left the room, Elizabetta could no longer hold in check her emotions, and her tears shed freely.

THE FIRST SATURDAY since the orchestra's return brought back the concert. The German soldiers sat in the piazza like they normally did to listen intently to the concert. They were mesmerized by the sound. The village children played games across from *Il Paradiso*, while their mothers watched over them.

After the concert, everyone returned to work. June turned into July, and everyone settled into the new way of life.

A NEW LIFE

*R*abbi Zolli had called upon his good friend, Isaac Nola, to provide a job for Franco Giacone in his bakery on the eastern side of the Jewish Quarter. Ludwig knew nothing about baking bread but was assured that under Isaac's tutelage, he would soon know all he needed to know. After all, he was being taught the craft by Isaac Nola, one of the best bakers in all of the Jewish Quarter. The Nola family had lived in the Jewish Quarter for centuries, and the little bakery shop had been founded by Isaac's great-great-grandfather.

Ludwig was a quick study learning how to bake the goods Isaac sold. He also enjoyed the friendship that blossomed between them. Ludwig's days began early at the bakery. Isaac noticed that his new employee did not talk much about himself while learning his new skill. As the days passed, the two men slowly formed a friendship.

Isaac's bakery shop also served as a meeting spot for the

Jews to congregate after the Sabbath service in the synagogue and discuss Rabbi Zolli's sermon of the day, as well as other pressing matters in the ghetto. Although the *giunta*, the Jewish council, were the representative leaders of the Jews and had their own meeting room in the synagogue, the Jewish congregation felt like their life was better served and protected among their friends holding court at weekly at Isaac's shop.

The Jews in the Quarter over time had grown to love and respect Israel Zolli, a man who was born in Austria-Hungary, had become a Jewish Scholar in Italy, and who had been the Chief Rabbi of Rome since 1939. He was often at odds with the Jewish leadership, and in particular, with Ugo Foa. As for the Roman Jews, they had complete trust that Zolli would see them through the gathering storm.

AS THE FRIENDSHIP grew between Isaac and Ludwig, Isaac questioned in his own mind who Ludwig was and where he came from. He desired to find out more. One late afternoon, Isaac finally asked, "You don't have to tell me if you don't want to, but where are you from?"

"Munich, but I moved to Rome a few years ago."

"What brought you to Rome?"

"I fled the Nazis."

"Were you married?"

"I was." His eyes watered. "But my wife and children were all killed. I have no family."

"I'm sorry for your loss, Franco. Rabbi Zolli said you were a musician."

"Yes. A composer."

"Were you famous?"

Ludwig laughed and shrugged his shoulders before answering Isaac, "I guess so. People liked my compositions."

"If you composed music as well as you bake bread, you must have been quite good."

"I was. But now I bake bread."

"Let's finish this batch so we can call it a day. The Shabbat is coming. Would you like to come over to my home and celebrate the Sabbath with me?"

"I would love to."

"Great. Rabbi Zolli may join us."

Ludwig stood close to the oven, as his mind raced to Anikka and his children. Thoughts of many Shabbats back in Munich with his own family sitting around the table in celebration bombarded his mind causing his heart to ache like it might burst. He missed Anikka so much. He longed to see her beautiful face again. He imagined his hand caressing her soft skin. He ached to feel her body next to his and make love to her until they could hardly breathe.

The harder he tried to erase her from his memory, the more he was haunted by memories. Part of him would never let her slip completely away. He picked up the dough, placed it onto the board, and began kneading it.

Like the Jews in Bellafortuna, life went on for Ludwig as he settled into his new life. With the passage of time, he got to know Isaac better as he spent more and more time with him at the bakery. He also began to get to know the other Jews well from their meetings in the shop after the Sabbath services.

Isaac also began spending time at Ludwig's apartment,

talking late into the night about their fears, religion, and music. Rabbi Zolli often joined them for their late-night talks.

Life was harsh in the Jewish Quarter, but at least the Jews were left alone. The sun rose over the Jewish Quarter on July 10, 1943. Little did the Jews in Rome know that as they went about their morning activities that Saturday morning, down in Sicily, Operation Husky had begun.

OPERATION HUSKY

On Saturday, July 10, 1943, the Allied Forces, under General George Patton for the Americans and Field Marshal Bernard Montgomery for the British, invaded Sicily. The invasion combined air and sea landings, involving 150,000 troops, 3,000 ships and 4,000 aircraft, all directed at the southern shores of the island. The offensive caught the Axis powers unprepared, as Greece was the spot where Hitler had expected the invasion to occur.

The villagers of Bellafortuna first became aware of the landing on Monday when the first convoy of trucks arrived carrying the wounded, doctors and more supplies. The trucks pulled into Bellafortuna, and ten wounded soldiers were rushed into the Church, followed closely by two doctors and a small support staff. There were no nurses, as they had been deployed to Greece.

While the doctors began working on their patients, Monsignor Mancini came into the Church and found Karl

Friedrich furiously working on a young German, who had been shot in the neck. The injured German soldier cried out, "The Americans are coming. We can't stop them."

Monsignor Mancini asked Karl, "Anything I can do?"

Karl, with bloodied hands, stood and whispered to Monsignor Mancini, "He's not going to make it. Can you pray over him?"

Karl moved away as Monsignor Mancini sat on the edge of the bed, and comforted the dying soldier, preparing his soul for its final journey.

THAT NIGHT, the *Società* met in the Boccale Winery, far away from the piazza and the Germans. Monsignor Mancini addressed them. "I have gotten to know the medical corps soldiers assigned at the Church. I glean lots of information that way. This invasion caught the Germans off guard, and they offered little resistance to the Americans and British when they landed. Hitler now realizes the direness of the situation. He is sending more German troops from Italy and Russia to defend Sicily.

"It seems our Sicilian sons are not putting up much of fight and are gladly laying down their weapons. I fear Bellafortuna will be in the crosshairs because Palermo is the place the Americans are trying to reach."

Santo Vasaio asked, "And our friends? What should we do with them?"

Giuseppe stood. "Hide them. Keep them hidden in the valley. The women are safe in the convent. But the men need to stay in the valley."

Vincenzo asked, "And the concerts?"

"It breaks my heart to say it, but we will have to stop the concerts."

Monsignor Mancini said, "I agree with Giuseppe. It is too dangerous. I know there has been heavy fighting with some American paratroopers and Germans. They are expecting a lot of casualties to arrive in our village tomorrow. The Germans are pouring forces into Sicily. Our friends must be protected at all costs."

Giuseppe suggested, "When you go home tonight, please warn the ones who are staying with you to remain in the valley. I think they'll take heed once you tell them what we know. Assure them that they will be safe."

Santo Vasaio said, "That's probably the hardest part."

IT WAS AROUND NOON the next day when the first truck of a steady convoy arrived in Bellafortuna. Wounded soldier after wounded soldier was carried into the *Chiesa della Madonna*.

By 3 p.m., sixty-five soldiers were lying on cots in different parts of the Church. The two doctors worked non-stop. All operations were performed on the altar.

The *Stadtkommissar* arrived just about then. An additional three trucks arrived carrying more soldiers. Karl Friedrich rushed outside to meet the *Stadtkommissar*, clicked his heels, and said, "*Heil Hitler.*"

"*Heil Hitler,*" he responded. "How is it in there?"

"Busy. The doctors need help. They need nurses. We are completely overwhelmed."

The *Stadtkommissar's* eyes were hard and angry. "The

invasion is not going well. You can expect a lot more wounded. They caught us by surprise. Let me go and speak with the doctors."

He entered the Church. The coppery smell of blood and death invaded his nostrils. He assessed the scene before him.

Both doctors were covered in blood. They spoke to him briefly, reiterating what Karl had said about the absolute need for additional help. Monsignor Mancini prayed at the foot of a German soldier's bed. The *Stadtkommissar* moved toward him. "Thank you for your work with my men, Monsignor."

"You are welcome. Many have been lost."

"And we will lose many more. My doctors are exhausted and need help."

"There are no doctors in the village. We go to Palermo when we need a doctor."

"I want you to get the nuns from the convent and bring them to the church. They will work as nurses."

Mancini's eyes widened. "They are cloistered, *Stadtkommissar*. And they are not nurses."

"I don't care. Get them here now! They will remain here until there is not one man left here."

"They took a monastic vow," pleaded Monsignor Mancini. "They cannot do it."

"Bring them here!"

"I will not. They are under papal enclosure."

The *Stadtkommissar* stiffened as though his back was made of iron. He then brought his face to not more than two inches away from Monsignor Mancini's and punctuated each word with a jab of his finger into Mancini's chest. "Have you any idea of how many priests have been shot in Europe? Don't be another one. You either bring the nuns to this Church now, or all of you will be shot. You and the nuns."

"I will get some ladies from the village. They will work hard to care for your men."

"I want the nuns! When I was in Africa, I watched the nuns care for our wounded. They were excellent in that role." The *Stadtkommissar* then looked passed the Monsignor and called Karl over. "I want you to get the nuns and bring all of them here to assist."

Before he could respond, Monsignor Mancini declared, "No need. I will fetch them."

"Good. And Monsignor, due to the current situation, I will be in Bellafortuna for quite some time. As such, I will take over your office." He waved the fingers on his right hand toward the convent. "Now, get my nuns."

Monsignor Mancini turned and ran toward the convent.

After he had left, the *Stadtkommissar* told Karl, "Follow him. Make sure all the nuns come to lend a hand. Old, young – every one of them."

"Yes, sir. Every single one of them. *Heil Hitler.*"

THE LIST

*L*udwig was hard at work in the bakery early in the morning when Isaac came rushing in. "It has begun," Isaac said. "The Americans and British have invaded Sicily."

Ludwig went to his knees and wept. "God be praised," he said.

"They landed yesterday. They are fighting their way to Palermo."

"Palermo?" asked Ludwig as his thoughts raced to the nearby village of Bellafortuna.

"I was told the Nazis have been leaving Rome in force to defend Sicily. There was little resistance at first, but now the fighting is getting intense."

Shivers of excitement raced up and down Ludwig's spine, and he smiled. "If the Americans and British can take Sicily, they will march to Rome."

Isaac headed for the door. "When that happens, I would

be the first person on the street to welcome them. We will give them loaves of bread when they walk down the street. I will tell my neighbors the good news. I won't be long."

Isaac Nola left quickly. Intense fighting near Palermo was all Ludwig could think about. His mind was frantic, and his heart raced with fear. But being so far from his family, all he could do was pray for their safety.

LATER THAT SAME MORNING, Monsignor Hugh O'Flaherty made his way across St. Peter's Square on his way to attend a hastily called meeting with Monsignor Costantini at a small office near the Apostolic library. With his strong, wide-brimmed hat, large glasses, flowing black and red cassock, and bright red sash, Monsignor O'Flaherty made quite the figure.

He was a proud Irishman and a member of the Curia. O'Flaherty held the position of Secretary and Notary in Monsignor Alfredo Ottaviani's Holy Office, one of the most important groups in the Vatican. Being with the Holy Office gave him access to the Pope. Counting Sister Pascalina as a friend helped with that access. Always with a funny story, the younger priests admired O'Flaherty while the older members of the Curia thought he was too close to the Pope – particularly for a non-Italian.

He reached the office and went in.

Monsignor Costantini was seated behind a desk. Standing on the other side of the desk was Father Biaggio Sanguinetti.

Monsignor Costantini stood up from his chair. "Ah, here

he is. Monsignor Hugh O'Flaherty, I don't know if you have met Father Sanguinetti."

In a large booming voice, punctuated with a strong Irish accent, Monsignor O'Flaherty extended his hand, and said, "Of course I know *Il piccolo Siciliano*."

Father Biaggio shook hands and said to Monsignor Costantini, "I brought him wine one day from my village. That's the only reason he knows me."

Monsignor Costantini laughed and said, "I asked Monsignor O'Flaherty to be here. He is aware of our friends in Bellafortuna."

"Thanks for coming, Monsignor," Biaggio said.

"Please call me Hugh."

Monsignor Costantini settled back into his chair. "Biaggio, have you heard the invasion of Sicily has begun?"

"Yes. I am greatly concerned for my village and for all of its people."

"Me too. The Nazis know if they lose Sicily, Italy will be next."

"Is this why you wanted to see me, Monsignor Costantini?"

"No. I have some news that I wanted to tell you personally with Monsignor O'Flaherty present." Monsignor Costantini paused and smiled. "Monsignor O'Flaherty has been working tirelessly and at great personal peril to himself in saving the lives of Allied POWs as well as Jewish refugees here in Italy. He has set up an entire network of safe houses with our brother priests and nuns to assist him in this endeavor. While he has been doing this, I asked him through his network to look into a pressing matter for me. He was successful."

"What was this pressing matter?" asked Biaggio.

"We have found him," interjected Monsignor O'Flaherty.

Father Biaggio's eyes grew large. "Ludwig Adler? How? Where is he?"

"We found his name, well his Italian name, on a list of Jews living in the Jewish Quarter," Monsignor O'Flaherty said. "The Chief Rabbi of Rome, Israel Zolli, must submit a list every week with the current addresses, names, and occupations of all the inhabitants of the Jewish Quarter. Franco Giacone was on that latest list. He is at *Via dei Funari*, 8. And his occupation is a baker."

Father Biaggio laughed and asked, "A baker?"

Monsignor Costantini said, "It seems our composer friend has tried to make a life for himself in the Jewish Quarter. I can't even imagine his pain being that far from his family."

Biaggio asked, "What can we do? Can we get him out?"

Monsignor Costantini shook his head. "I don't think we can, but at least we know he is safe. We know where he is. The Jewish Quarter may be the safest place for him. The Italians don't bother those Jews. The Nazis leave the Jewish Quarter for the Italians to handle. For now, I think it's best for him to stay there. I am afraid if he knows we know, he may try to flee to protect his family in Bellafortuna."

"Can we let his wife know?" asked Father Biaggio.

Monsignor Costantini stood up from the desk. "I think not. He made the decision to hide in order to protect them. It's not our place. That's what I believe. If and when Sicily is liberated, then I would think we could tell her."

Father Biaggio leaned forward in his chair and said emphatically, "Monsignor Costantini, may I disagree. I don't understand why we don't tell her. That poor woman has no idea if her husband is alive or dead."

Monsignor Costantini came over by Biaggio and patted his shoulder. "My son, there has been so much death. What do you think is more important to her? Becoming aware that he is alive or the day when they can be reunited? I would think the latter." He stood quietly for a second and then said with great emotion, *"Non farò nulla per jeapordize quella riunione* (I will do nothing to jeopardize that reunion)."

"I will pray for that reunion, your Excellency."

"We can only hope that there will be many reunions for all our Jewish brethren when this horrible war is ended. Let us pray for that. Let us pray for them."

Father Biaggio turned to Monsignor O'Flaherty. "Thank you for finding him."

"Glad to help."

Father Biaggio said, "Hugh, I'm aware of your activities in helping the POWs and the Jews. Is the Pope aware of all that you are doing?"

"Of course," replied Monsignor O'Flaherty. "He told me not to get caught."

They all laughed before Monsignor Costantini brought the meeting to a close by saying. "Ludwig Adler is safe. Safe for now."

38

THE NURSES

*M*onsignor Mancini left the Church and ran to the convent. He banged on the door. Elizabetta, the Mother Superior, quickly opened it and stood in the doorway in her full habit. The look on Monsignor Mancini's face frightened her.

"What's wrong?" she asked.

"The *Stadtkommissar* wants all the nuns to report to the *Chiesa della Madonna* at once to act as nurses."

"Nurses?"

"Are they dressed?"

"Of course. We sleep in our habits and have always been prepared for the day we would hear a knock on the door. But they can't ..." She stopped in mid-sentence.

Monsignor Mancini happened to look back toward the Church and saw Karl walking that way. The Monsignor quickly ordered, "Get them out now. Hide the children upstairs. I will get Giuseppe and Maria to come for the kids later. We will place them with villagers. Now go. Hurry."

She shut the door, just as Karl walked up.

Monsignor Mancini said to him, "They are coming."

"All of them," asked Karl.

"Yes, all of them. They should be just a moment."

Karl said, "I'm glad you said you would do this. I thought for sure he was going to shoot you."

Just then, the door opened, and Elizabetta walked out, followed by the nine other women. Elizabetta and Anikka wore the habits that Santo and Maria had retrieved from Palermo. The other nuns wore simple black dresses and a black veil.

Monsignor Mancini said to Karl as he introduced Elizabetta, "This is *Suor Elizabetta*. And these are her nuns."

Karl clicked his heels. "*Heil Hitler*. The Third Reich needs your assistance to take care of its wounded sons."

Elizabetta responded, "We will offer our support and our prayers."

"Good. Let's go," responded Karl as the group made its way to the Church.

THE JEWISH WOMEN had never seen so much blood in their entire lifetime. They spoke very little, just a few words in Italian here or there, and followed orders.

Elizabetta and Anikka were sent to work with the doctors and would assist them while they performed operations. The other ladies cared for the wounded. As the Jewish women comforted the wounded and dying young Germans, the women quickly came to think of the soldiers, not as Nazis. Instead, they thought of them as scared boys who wanted nothing more than to go home to their mothers.

What the women did not know about nursing they made up for in compassion. Monsignor Mancini, for his part, kept a watchful eye on his nurses. Even the *Stadtkommissar* was impressed with the care they provided.

At midnight after that first day, the exhausted nuns retreated to the convent. The irony that they had spent the last few hours working on the very soldiers who were fighting for a cause that resulted in their own persecution was not lost on them. But what made them more upset than anything else was the fact that the children had been removed upon their return. They would be lonely tonight and for many nights to come.

They stayed up late into the night washing the blood from their clothes, so that they could wear the same outfit again the next day.

39

AN OLD FRIEND

O ver the course of the next two days, more and more wounded troops came into Bellafortuna. The nuns continued to work tirelessly, caring for them. The Jewish men remained hidden in the valley along with the children, who were living with different villagers.

The Adler children, including Josef, had been split up between various families. Josef no longer asked when he would see his mother again. Instead, he asked when he would see Anikka and Ludwig again.

Around this time, Colonel Fromm returned to Bellafortuna. He arrived in the piazza and made his way to the Church. He was amazed at all the wounded soldiers.

He saw Monsignor Mancini and asked, "Monsignor, have you seen the *Stadtkommissar*."

"Yes, he took over my office in the rectory."

As he looked around the Church, he asked, "Are those the nuns from the convent?"

"Yes, he demanded that they work as nurses. There are so many wounded. He made them break cloister."

"I'm sorry for that. My God, look at all of the wounded. And this is a small hospital compared to the ones I saw yesterday in Corleone. It is going badly. The Americans are pushing to Palermo, and our forces are dropping back to defend it. I'm here to speak with the *Stadtkommissar*." As he began to walk away, he turned back to Monsignor Mancini and said, "Please thank the nuns for me." He walked out of the Church toward the office the *Stadtkommissar* had taken as his own.

COLONEL FROMM WALKED into the office in the rectory and found the *Stadtkommissar* seated behind the Monsignor's desk. When he arrived, the *Stadtkommissar* stood stiffly and said, "*Heil Hitler.*"

Colonel Fromm returned the salute, and then in a very personal tone, said, "Eric, it is not going well. The Allies have begun the push inland. The Americans have already taken Niscemi, and the British have taken Vizzini. General Patton is driving toward Palermo."

"What would you expect, Hans. The defenders of this island are mostly Sicilians fighting for Italy. They are dropping their weapons and surrendering at an alarming rate. They will not fight. But don't worry. Our sons of the Third Reich stand ready for a fight. We will defeat the Allies in Palermo."

Colonel Fromm said, "While that might be true, the Americans are close to Bellafortuna. They will more than likely be here by tomorrow night. We need to move our wounded. I have trucks coming in the morning to bring the wounded to Palermo. The critical ones will remain here. I will ask Karl Friedrich, along with another medical person, to stay with them. The nuns will assist with the care of them until the Americans arrive. Karl will be in charge of the evacuation, as I must get to Palermo."

"I am coming with you," the *Stadtkommissar* replied. "I will meet you in the Church to speak with Karl."

Colonel Fromm began to walk away, but he stopped. "Eric, you do know we are going to lose Sicily."

"If the damn Italians would stand and fight, we would have a chance. Our forces will be strong in Palermo. We will crush them there. *Heil Hitler.*"

Colonel Fromm left the office and made his way back to the Church.

———

COLONEL FROMM FOUND KARL FRIEDRICH. "The Americans are coming to Bellafortuna. We are pulling out tomorrow. You are in charge of the evacuation of the wounded. Those who can survive the journey will depart on trucks in the morning."

"Many will not survive the journey."

"I need you to remain behind with the critical ones. Find one more medical person to stay with you."

"I will talk with the doctors so they can advise who they think cannot make the trip," Kurt said. "I know we just received five more wounded soldiers from Rome, who are all critical. They were riding in a truck and got shot up pretty bad. Most of them probably won't make it through the night."

"I will speak with Monsignor Mancini to give them the last rites."

"Colonel, what will happen to me when the Americans come?"

"Your war is over. They will inter you. You will survive this war. I'm off to find Monsignor Mancini, so he will know what is going on. The *Stadtkommisar* and I are leaving for Palermo tonight. The evacuation of our sons is on you."

THE FIVE NEWLY ARRIVED CRITICAL patients lay on the floor under a window in the far corner of the Church. Monsignor Mancini was already standing by them when Colonel Fromm approached. A doctor was looking at all five.

Colonel Fromm asked the doctor, "How are they?"

The doctor was working on one with a massive chest wound. "This one will not survive for more than an hour. The others are critical and will die soon." The doctor motioned to Anikka, who was on the altar cleaning up after an operation. He yelled to her in German, as he did not know Italian, "*Suor Agatha,* we need morphine for these five. Now." As he did so, he pretended to give himself a shot, to make sure the nun understood what he needed.

Anikka nodded her head and quickly readied the morphine while the doctor told Monsignor Mancini, "There is nothing more I can do for these boys. They are under your care . . . and God's." He went to help other soldiers.

Colonel Fromm stood next to Monsignor Mancini and

said, "Monsignor, we are evacuating the wounded tomorrow. The Americans are coming. The critical ones are staying here with Karl."

"We will take care of them, Colonel Fromm," replied Monsignor Mancini.

"I thank you for the care of our men."

At that point, Anikka came over with the morphine. The first soldier she came to was the one with the chest wound whom the doctor had been working on. The soldier was still conscious, moaning in pain. She leaned down and said to the soldier, "*Medicina.*"

The soldier opened his eyes and tried to focus on the nun, until he finally said, "Anikka Adler."

Monsignor Mancini stopped speaking with Colonel Fromm the moment he heard the soldier say her name. The soldier, speaking German, said, "It's Otto. Otto Steiner. Your husband told me you were dead."

Anikka gasped, and without thinking, replied in German, "*Sie sah meinen mann?*" (You saw my husband?)

"*Ja, in Rom.* (Yes, in Rome.) He lives in Rome in the Jewish Quarter. He thinks you are dead. Help Me, Anikka. I am in so much pain. Please help me. Make the pain stop." Anikka buried her head in her hands before composing herself and administering the morphine.

While Annika worked on Otto Steiner, Colonel Fromm stood there in disbelief. Finally, looking down at Anikka, he said to Monsignor Mancini. "The Jewish Quarter in Rome? Is she a Jew?"

Monsignor Mancini said not a word.

Colonel Fromm then looked around the Church at all of the other nuns. He then asked, "Are they all Jews?"

Monsignor Mancini looked directly into the eyes of Colonel Fromm and simply replied, "*Si.*"

"Damn you. I trusted you. And this is how you repay me. The *Stadtkommissar* will have you killed. Your villagers will be shot. The Jews will be arrested and sent away to their death."

"Colonel, the Americans are coming. Sicily is lost. Think about your future. Don't lose your soul for them. Let these people live."

"They are Jews!"

"They are human beings. They are God's creatures, just like you and me. You are leaving Bellafortuna. Just leave. You are a good man. You're not one of them. Leave, and one day, you will remember the goodness that you did here. Amid all the darkness, you will remember this light, this goodness. Please let them go. I beg you."

Anikka sat next to the now unconscious Otto Steiner. She was on her knees, with her head again buried in her hands in tears.

Colonel Fromm replied, "I am a soldier and an officer of the Third Reich."

"You are a man first, a Catholic man at that. Look deep inside yourself. I know there is still goodness in your soul. Don't give in to the evil."

The *Stadtkommissar* walked up at that moment. He looked at Anikka, weeping on the ground. Then he turned to Colonel Fromm and asked, "Is anything wrong?"

Colonel Fromm, with his head, bowed down, was silent.

Monsignor Mancini responded quickly, "These men are dying. She is upset."

"It's war. More will die," the *Stadtkommissar* coldly responded.

Colonel Fromm lifted his head and stared at the *Stadtkommissar*. He bent down and lifted Anikka up with both of his arms. Her face showed absolute fear. Colonel Fromm smiled broadly and framed her face with both of his hands. He said, "Sister, thank you for taking care of my men. Thank you for your compassion. Please thank the other sisters for me."

She burst into tears as she pressed her body tightly to his. Colonel Fromm then let her go and said to the *Stadtkommissar*, "*Gefreiter* Karl Friedrich is over there if you want to talk with him. We will leave for Palermo shortly."

When they walked away, Monsignor Mancini hugged Anikka, who was still in tears. "You are all right," he assured her.

"Monsignor, your words to him saved me. Your words saved all of us."

"No, my dear. God saved us. He was at work here. Finish giving your morphine and then go about your business. Don't let the others know that Fromm knows you are all Jews. Just thank God that your husband is alive. I will get Giuseppe to let the men in the valley know this glorious news."

As she looked down at the unconscious Otto Steiner, she asked, "What about him?"

"I will stay with him until he dies. Leave me with some morphine, just in case."

An hour later, Otto Steiner died amid the prayers of Monsignor Mancini.

40

THE LIBERATION OF BELLAFORTUNA

*T*he next day, Alfred was at work in the vineyard down in the valley, helping Enzo Adarato prune his grapevines. Alfred was still relishing the words he had heard last night when Giuseppe Sanguinetti had come to the home and informed him of the fate of Ludwig Adler as well as the pending evacuation of the Nazis.

All morning long, he and Enzo had seen the convoy of trucks leaving the village carrying the wounded soldiers. By noon, the trucks had stopped. Alfred knew there were still a few wounded Germans in the village, but for the first time in a long time, his heart lightened inside his chest, and he was encouraged.

Heinrich and Kurt were cleaning the vats in the Boccale Winery. That had been their duty since returning from Rome. They, too, relished Giuseppe Sanguinetti's words from the night before. They thought of poor Anikka, and Giuseppe assured them she was aware of Ludwig's fate.

Around four o'clock that afternoon, Alfred heard a rumble on the valley road. He stepped outside with Enzo and made his way to the road. Soon other villagers, including Heinrich and Kurt, heard the sounds and rushed to the side of the road.

As Enzo's vineyard was the furthest from the village, Alfred saw it first. Four tanks, with helmeted soldiers peering out of the turrets, moved up the valley road. The first tank stopped by Alfred and Enzo. The white star on the side of the tank provided all the information they needed.

The Americans had come.

MONSIGNOR MANCINI, Giuseppe Sanguinetti, and Santo Vasaio all stood by the statue of Enzo Boccale. The four tanks were parked all around the piazza. The villagers of Bellafortuna were flocking to the piazza to celebrate this momentous day. The bell of the *Chiesa della Madonna* rang out across the village and the valley. The women carried flowers and were handing them out to the young American GIs. The men carried wine bottles and were handing them to the American soldiers, who took more interest in the wine than the flowers. A young, good-looking American stood speaking with Monsignor Mancini and the others, his helmet held at his hip. He spoke in Italian with the group.

"I am Captain Vincent Castanza. The American Army officially liberates you."

"*Grazie,*" replied Monsignor Mancini as he introduced the group to him. He then said, "Castanza? Where is your family from?"

"I am from Chicago. But my family is originally from Cefalù. I am hoping that soon I will get to liberate my own ancestors' hometown."

Giuseppe said, "We are glad you came here first. Welcome to Bellafortuna. And now for our first act as a liberated village." Giuseppe walked over to the base of the statue of Enzo Boccale. He reached up and tore down the poster of Benito Mussolini. The villagers cheered emphatically, as Giuseppe, while tearing the poster, said loudly, "*Un uomo fallito e un ideology del male.*" (A failed man and an evil ideology.)

The crowd cheered even louder. Captain Vincent Castanza, with a huge smile, extended his hand to Giuseppe and said, "*Si. Il tuo villaggio è ora libero.* (Your village is now free.)"

Santo Vasaio gave him an open bottle of *Vino di Bellafortuna.* The American took a swig and rolled his eyes. "That's some good stuff."

Monsignor Mancini said, "Captain, there are critically wounded German soldiers in the Church with two German medical personnel. May I put in a good word for those two Germans?"

"We will take good care of them," responded the American. "The wounded are in the Church? Let's go see." He called another soldier over to come in with him. Monsignor Mancini, Giuseppe and Santo joined them.

The group walked over to the Church. The critically wounded soldiers were lying in cots. The nuns were walking amid the beds caring for each and every one of them. When Karl saw the group, he walked over.

"I am *Gefreiter* Karl Friedrich of the 65th German Army Medical Corps."

"I am Captain Vincent Castanza of the 2nd Armored Division of the United States Army. I will radio for medical assistance at once. Please continue your work in caring for them."

"Thank you. These men need help."

Captain Castanza turned to the soldier with him and gave him instructions to radio for medical help. The soldier left.

Captain Castanza asked, "How many Germans were here?"

Karl replied, "About 70 wounded left this morning. There must have been a staff of about 25 medical personnel."

The American turned and asked Giuseppe, "And these nuns are from your village?"

"Yes," replied Giuseppe.

Monsignor Mancini was thoughtful for a moment. "There is one other thing we need to tell you."

"What is it?"

Monsignor Mancini turned and looked at the nuns, and then turned back to the young American and said, "They are not nuns. They are Jews."

"Jews," Castanza repeated.

Karl's mouth dropped open as he turned and looked at the nuns.

"Yes. We have Jewish refugees hiding in the village."

"Jewish Italians?" asked the American.

Monsignor Mancini replied, "No. They are from Munich, Austria, even Germany itself."

Castanza chuckled. "You're kidding?"

Santo spoke up. "Not at all."

"How did they end up here?"

Monsignor Mancini said, "They were in need of a place to live. We took them in."

"I will need to let my superiors know about this. Good God, Jewish nuns. I've seen it all."

The group returned to the celebration out in the piazza.

41

THE ITALIAN COLLAPSE

hroughout the summer of 1943, Pope Pius XII had used Vatican Radio as his weapon against Nazism. His strategy of silence with regard to direct protests did not preclude him from using his most powerful weapon he possessed, his words, as he continued to bring to the people's attention the fate of the Jews all across Europe who "because of their race are condemned to die." He often quoted St. Paul stating that "there is neither Gentile or Jew," and reminded the faithful that "every man has the stamp of God." He reminded all that his love "embraces all peoples, whatever their nationality or race." He took on Hitler directly, reminding the dictator that he "was not the master over life and death," and went further stating that "he who makes a distinction between Jews and other men is being unfaithful to God and is in conflict with God's commands." The German response was to attempt to jam the radio broadcasts, which was unsuccessful.

As the Allied forces pushed further and further into Sicily during the summer of 1943, any remaining public support for the war and Mussolini quickly disappeared. The invasion of Sicily quickly led to events that would affect all of Italy.

On July 19, 1943, the Allies launched a massive bombing campaign around train stations near Rome as a means to disrupt Axis troop movement to assist Sicily. On that very day, Monsignor Costantini and Monsignor Giuseppe Caprio, economic secretary of the propaganda, were at the *Bagni di Tivoli* station boarding a train to make the short trek back to Rome after a day of meetings. The forward cars were too crowded, so they made their way to the last car. Just as the train began its journey, Allied B-17 bombers attacked the railroad yard. The sky was quickly filled with smoke as thuds and crashes repeated in all directions. Sirens wailed, and people screamed. The front cars of the train took a direct hit, instantly killing many. Costantini and Caprio jumped from their railcar and took shelter behind a low wall. It was against that wall that Costantini prayed for his life. A packed railcar forcing him to the back of the train had saved his life.

Harold Tittmann was attending a meeting on the top floor of the Apostolic Palace that day with Monsignor Montini and Minister Osborne. Suddenly the sound of anti-aircraft fire could be heard across Rome. Biaggio, who had been sitting outside the office, rushed in and said to the group that Rome was being bombed.

They all ran to the *Loggia di Raffello*, an open-air gallery in the Papal Palace, where other clergy stood in shocked silence. From that location, they could see smoke rising above Rome. A young Italian priest, a member of the secretary of state's clerical staff, shouted: "Damn the Americans. Damn the

British. They bring this down upon Rome. To hell with all of them."

Biaggio said loudly. "My God, they are bombing Rome. How can they?"

Minister Osborne interjected, "The same way Italian planes flew over London and dropped their bombs."

Tittmann, the Great War fighter pilot, stood on the gallery amazed at the precision of the formation of the hundreds of bombers, three abreast, all gleaming in the bright sunlight. At the same time, he was fully aware that those planes were bringing the horrors of war to the people of Rome.

Pope Pius XII stood by the window inside his office. Sister Pascalina stood silently next to him. From the window, they could see the smoke billowing above the Basilica of San Lorenzo.

Pius's eyes flashed with anger as he glared across his city. "They have done it. They have bombed the citizens of Rome. They have bombed my city. All my pleading and they ignored me. Call Stoppa, tell him to get my car."

Sister Pascalina was caught off guard. "Your car? Where are you going?"

"To the citizens of Rome. They need me."

"For God's sake, Holy Father, you can't go out now."

"My car, please."

Sister Pascalina quickly left to find the Pope's chauffeur, but along the way, she ran into Monsignor Montini and told him of the Pope's request for a car. She told Montini that objecting was a waste of time, as the Holy Father was determined that he was going and that he would probably walk there if no car was brought to him. She asked Montini to go with the Pope, which he agreed to do.

Pope Pius XII, utterly distraught, waited outside in the courtyard as the Cadillac pulled in, adorned with the papal flags on the front fender. Mario Stoppa thought it strange that with Rome being bombed, the Holy Father would be going out to the Vatican Gardens, which was the only place he drove him during the war years. He was surprised when he was told that the destination was outside the Vatican. Along with Monsignor Montini, the Pope left the Vatican without any security escort. This was the first time since the war began that he left the confines of the Vatican.

Rome Radio began broadcasting urgent appeals for all able-bodied men to quickly go to the San Lorenzo district to help with the injured and dying. In the Jewish Ghetto, Ugo Foa heard the appeal on the radio and quickly organized some of the Jewish residents of the ghetto to go help. They confiscated trucks, and, loaded with picks and shovels, they departed the ghetto. Isaac Nola and Ludwig Adler were among the Jews on board the trucks.

Many parts of Rome were bombed that day, with at least 1000 citizens being killed around San Lorenzo. Upon arriving at the scene, Ludwig and Isaac immediately began digging, pulling wounded and dead Italians out of the rubble. Fires raged in many buildings. The wounded were carried to ambulances that began to arrive.

Just as Ludwig Adler carried a young girl to an awaiting ambulance, he heard the sound of an approaching vehicle. Isaac, standing next to him, was the first to see the car and its occupant. "It's the Pope," Isaac said emphatically.

The Pope immediately exited the car and kneeled on the ruins. The distraught residents of San Lorenzo flocked around him. Ludwig and Isaac stood back, taking in the very moving scene. The Pope stood up as the residents reached out to touch him. Standing amidst his fellow Romans, the Pope extended both arms as Christ on the cross. The people kneeled down all around him, and they prayed for the victims. Overtaken by the scene, Ludwig went to his knees.

After this, the Pope began distributing his own money to assist the survivors. Ludwig noticed that the Pope's white cassock was stained red with blood. The memory of the Pope, with his blood-stained cassock surrounded by the Italians, would be forged in the minds of the people who witnessed the scene for the rest of their lives.

As the Pope overlooked the death and destruction, he vowed it would never happen again. The Pope also walked to the cemetery behind the Church. The tomb of his parents was located there. He stared in silence as he realized that their tomb had been completely destroyed by the bombing.

After the Pope left, Ludwig and Isaac stayed late into the night digging for survivors. They were both there at midnight when Mussolini came to visit the area. His reception by the Italians stood in stark contrast to the Pope's earlier that day.

Once back at the Vatican, the Pope wrote an angry letter to President Franklin Delano Roosevelt demanding that Allied bombing of the Eternal City cease at once. As the Bishop of Rome, he believed it was his sacred duty to spare Rome and its citizens from destruction by the Axis as well as the Allies.

A few days later, on July 22, 1943, Palermo fell to the Allies.

On July 24, 1943, Victor Emmanuel II, the King of Italy, deposed Benito Mussolini. Even though the King had been a longtime supporter of *Il Duce*, he ordered him arrested and sent to a penal colony on the island of Ponza – one of many locations over the next few weeks the Italians would move him to while under arrest – as they feared Hitler would try to free the Italian dictator. A new government was set up under Marshal Pietro Badoglio, who, from the start, had opposed Italy's alliance with Nazi Germany.

General Badoglio kept up the appearance of loyalty to the Axis, yet at the same time, he dissolved the Fascist Party two days after taking over and immediately began secret discussions with the Allies about an armistice.

With the fall of Palermo, Hitler began to order the evacuation of his army out of Sicily. The race was on to Messina. The Nazis took defensive positions, trying to provide cover for their troops fleeing out of Sicily.

Meanwhile, since the liberation of Bellafortuna, the villagers were trying to return to normal. Two days after the arrival of the Americans, the wounded had been removed from the village. Karl Friedrich and the other medical person became POWs, but Monsignor Mancini was assured that they would be well cared for.

The next day, word reached Bellafortuna that Palermo had fallen, and Mussolini had been deposed. The villagers, overcome with relief and joy, openly wept. For Bellafortuna, the war was over.

WITHIN AN HOUR of receiving the news, Monsignor Mancini and Giuseppe Sanguinetti met in *Il Paradiso*. They waited with great anticipation for the others to arrive. When the door was opened, Maria, Alfred, Kurt, Heinrich, and all of the other Jewish male refugees along with all the Jewish children entered. Alfred held Josef.

Giuseppe asked, "Is everyone ready? Let's go."

They all walked across the piazza. Monsignor Mancini knocked on the door of the *Casa Santa Croce*. *Suor Elizabetta* opened the door. Tears poured out of her eyes when she saw the Jewish fathers and all the children.

Monsignor Mancini said, "Call them out, Elizabetta. Tell the ladies to come see their families."

She turned back inside and yelled loudly, "Ladies. Hurry. Come outside. Come outside now."

The women, still dressed in their habits, came into the foyer and burst into tears as they were reunited with their husbands and children. The children ran to hug their mothers. Alfred put Josef down. He ran to see Anikka, whose arms were around her own children. She picked up young Josef and kissed him.

Kurt made his way to Elizabetta. He pulled off her coif and veil and kissed her as they fell into each other's arms.

Monsignor Mancini called the entire group all over to the Boccale statue. They gathered all around, clinging to each other.

"Your nightmare is ended. You can once again be called by your Jewish names, and you will all be able to live as a family once again. We will put you up in houses around the village, but you will live together with your family. The Americans are sending envoys in to help relocate you. They will discuss different options with you."

"Where will we go?" asked one of the Jews.

"I'm not sure."

"What about our other family members? What of their fate?" asked another.

Monsignor Mancini chose his words carefully and said, "Until the war is over, their fate will remain unknown. Pray for them. After the war, you will have to search for them and hopefully be reunited with them."

"When will we be going?" asked someone else.

"Soon," replied Monsignor Mancini.

Kurt asked, "What about Anikka?"

"She can stay with us until she is reunited with her husband. She and her children can remain here if she so desires."

Crying, she nodded.

"I will meet with each of you to give you your new sleeping arrangements. I would expect the Americans to arrive within the next few days to discuss the options with you. Until then, enjoy each other and your freedom."

Heinrich walked up to the statue and turned to the crowd. "What this village and these villagers have done for us will never be forgotten." The crowd erupted in applause.

Anikka made her way up to the front, her children in tow with Josef. "I, too, want to thank all of the villagers for caring for my children. I also would like to offer my sincerest praise for Monsignor Mancini." The crowd roared again. "You should know, the German officer who was here, Colonel Fromm, discovered that we were Jews." The crowd gasped. "But Monsignor Mancini stood up for all of us. And God be praised, that officer walked away."

The people clapped wildly.

"God indeed be praised," Monsignor Mancini said. "I know

you still have many unanswered questions. We will work on finding those answers. For now, tomorrow at noon, music will once again return to Bellafortuna. We will have a concert."

The Jewish musicians smiled as they had missed music in their life and looked forward to playing once again.

Giuseppe stood in the front of the crowd and said, "Our first piece will be *Munich's Tears*, in honor of those not with us."

Anikka smiled toward Giuseppe. Giuseppe continued, "We all deserve a celebration. Tonight, we will have a Jewish service."

The Jews clapped loudly as Monsignor Mancini asked the refugees to come up and learn of their new sleeping arrangements. They stood in line to receive the information.

As the last person in line received their information, Monsignor Mancini turned to Alfred and said, "I gave out all the sleeping arrangements to all of the refugees, save one. Where did Kurt Hofmann go?"

Alfred pointed across the piazza where Kurt and Elizabetta could be seen walking hand in hand toward the street that led to her home off the piazza. Alfred whispered, "I think he found a place to live, Monsignor."

Monsignor Mancini smiled.

WHEN THE AMERICAN envoys arrived three days later, they arranged for the Jewish refugees to be relocated to Syracuse, Sicily. There was a large Jewish community there. The ultimate goal was to eventually send the refugees to Palestine or America, if America would take them. When Monsignor

Mancini inquired about the fate of the German POWs, he was advised that they would be put on a troop ship with wounded GIs bound for New Orleans. One of the POWs was *Gefreiter* Karl Friedrich.

Heinrich, Kurt and Alfred asked to remain behind in Bellafortuna with Anikka until her husband came back to her. She begged them to go establish their new life and leave Bellafortuna, although deep down she hoped they would stay with her. The three friends refused to abandon her.

As the calendar changed to August, and with the war over for Bellafortuna, Heinrich, Kurt, Alfred and Anikka settled into their new life, hoping for the day Ludwig would return.

The villagers of Bellafortuna began to pick up the pieces, and the rhythm of life returned. As the weeks passed, their Jewish friends who had left for Syracuse were not far from their minds.

Meanwhile, the drastic events of the summer of 1943 in Sicily made the Italians believe that the war would be shortly coming to an end. In reality, it only brought the war closer to them.

————————

EVER SINCE COMING TO POWER, General Badoglio had been negotiating with Eisenhower for an armistice. Finally, on September 8, 1943, Badoglio approved the surrender of Italy to the Allies. This action allowed the Allies to land in southern Italy and begin beating the Germans back up the peninsula.

The Italians felt relief. In their minds, this meant the end of the war. The Jews in the Jewish Quarter in Rome, for the first time in what seemed to be ages, breathed a sigh of relief. They believed their nightmare was over. Sadly, the celebrations did not last long.

Hitler, already prepared for this act by the Italians, snapped into action and invaded Rome. The German's marched unimpeded down the streets of Rome, directly toward the Vatican.

Sister Pascalina nervously looked out the window from the Pope's Vatican office. Pius stood across the room, conversing with his secretary of state, Cardinal Maglione. Pius had his head down deep in thought.

Cardinal Maglione said, "Pontiff, we have received word that with Hitler's invasion of Rome, Badoglio, as well as the King and the entire Royal family, have all fled Rome for Southeastern Italy. You must consider leaving yourself."

Pius picked his head up. "No," was his simple reply.

Sister Pascalina suddenly gasped. "I see German soldiers marching toward St. Peter's. Look, they are far away, but they are coming this way."

Pius moved quickly to the window and peered out. He quickly turned toward Cardinal Maglione. "You must go at once to the Swiss Guard. Tell them if the Germans break Vatican neutrality and come into St. Peter's Square, the Swiss Guard, must stand down. They must take no action."

"But your Holiness, that would mean the Vatican will become occupied."

"That is my order. Now go."

When Cardinal Maglione left, Pope Pius turned back to look out the window. He and Sister Pascalina watched with dread as the troops got closer. But when the Germans reached St. Peter's Square, they stopped.

"Look, they will not come into St. Peter's Square," Sister Pascalina exclaimed.

"Indeed. Come with me to my chapel. We must pray for Rome and for all of its citizens."

They slowly departed the office together.

THE CITIZENS of Rome now lived under German occupation. As the days since the occupation passed, Pius watched the events unfold all around him with great trepidation.

On September 12th, German commandos raided the location where Mussolini was being held and freed him. They brought him to the Wolf's Lair to meet with Hitler. Hitler immediately established a new government in Northern Italy known as the *Repubblica Sociale Italiana* and placed Mussolini as the head. It was nothing more than a puppet government for the Nazis.

With the invasion and occupation, the Nazis were now in complete control of Rome. The German army entrusted the internal security matters of Rome to the dreaded Waffen-SS, under the direction of SS *Obersturmbannführer* Herbert Kappler, an imposing figure of a man, with piercing, deep, gray eyes and a long dueling scar down his left cheek. He was ready for his new assignment. He thought it would be easy as all of Italy's leaders had fled Rome – all but one.

Pope Pius XII remained at the Vatican.

PART V

JEWISH QUARTER
Rome, Italy
September 1943

THE RANSOM

*W*ith the SS now in control of Rome, life changed quickly for the Jews in Rome and Northern Italy. Almost overnight, the Jews were stripped of their Italian citizenship. The SS and the Gestapo began enforcing the racial laws that the Italians had long ignored.

The Gestapo begin offering a bounty to Italians who turned in Jews, as well as providing information on fellow Italians who were harboring Jews. Italian Jews were beginning to be forced from their homes and either sent to ghettos or to camps. The DELASEM organization, which had helped so many Jews, was forced to go underground. It quickly became known that any Italian hiding or assisting Jews would be either killed or sent to a camp.

Meanwhile, the talk at Isaac's bakery shop during their weekly meetings after the Sabbath service became most concerned with the German occupation of Rome. At one such meeting, Isaac stood up in front of the large crowd crammed inside his shop. "Since the occupation, food is scarce. Franco and I can't even get supplies to make even a dozen loaves of bread."

Ludwig replied, "That's true. Supplies of food throughout the Jewish Quarter is very limited."

Amos Festus, a cobbler, stood. "More concerning to me than the lack of food is my belief that the Germans are going to deport us, all of us Jews living in the Jewish Quarter."

Augustus Pavo came to the front of the crowd. He was a friend and confidant of Ugo Foa. "The Germans have stated that we will not be touched. They have stated that fact over and over again to our leaders. Ugo Foa has stated to me personally his belief that we will be untouched. He even told me that the Pope had been promised by the Nazi leadership that we would be untouched."

A debate started with about half of the Jews present arguing their belief that they would be safe. The other half had grave concern that the Nazis would take action against them.

While the debate raged in the bakery shop, Israel Zolli and Ugo Foa had their own meeting with the entire Jewish leadership. Zolli believed that there was a strong possibility for the deportment of the Roman Jews by the Nazis. Having spoken to many refugees from Europe hiding in the ghetto, he had learned what had happened to other Jewish communities throughout Europe. He questioned in his own mind how long Rome could be spared. He argued that the Jewish community of Rome should disperse, infuriating some of the Jewish leadership, including Ugo Foa, who repeated over and over again his belief that the Roman Jews would remain safe.

Both meetings ended with no conclusive answer. While it was true the vast majority of the leadership and inhabitants of the Jewish Quarter still believed they were safe in the ghetto, there was definitely a growing murmur of fear among some of the Jews.

On September 27, 1943, all doubt was removed.

On that day, *SS Obersturmbannführer* Herbert Kappler placed a ransom on the Jews of Rome. The Nazi commander demanded 50 kilograms of gold in exchange for the safety of the Jewish community of Rome. If the Jewish leadership did not pay the ransom within thirty-six hours, 300 Jews would be arrested and deported from Rome.

Israel Zolli was in his office inside the synagogue, staring at a list of names. As Chief Rabbi, he had been given the list of the 300 Jews to be arrested. As he sat at his desk, he read every name. He knew each and everyone on the list.

That afternoon, he changed his clothes and put on a pair of khaki pants and a light blue shirt he had borrowed from a friend. He rolled up his sleeves and left the synagogue. He knew he had a job to do, but he would make one stop along the way. He made his way to Ludwig Adler's apartment.

Ludwig Adler met him at the door. "Rabbi, it's good to see you. Is it true? Is there a ransom?"

"Yes. We have 36 hours to raise the gold."

"How much gold?"

"About 50 kilograms. The Jewish Community Council has raised some, but we are well short."

Ludwig's eyebrows rose, and he sucked in a breath. "That is an awful lot of gold to raise in a short amount of time."

"There is something else, the reason why I am here."

A thick blanket of worry covered Ludwig. "What is it, Rabbi?"

"The SS confiscated the list of Jews living here. They have everyone's names and addresses. From that list, they have identified 300 Jews in the ghetto who will be arrested if the ransom is not met." Then with a look of compassion, Rabbi Zolli said, "You are on that list."

Ripples of fear raced up and down Ludwig's spine.

The Rabbi said, "Ludwig, don't be too discouraged. My name is first on the list."

Ludwig tried to smile but was unsuccessful. "What are we to do?"

"If you are in Rome and need 50 kilos of gold and need it quick, I can only think of one place where to go."

Ludwig's eyes widened. "You're going to the Pope? You are going to the Vatican?"

"I am."

Ludwig said, "The SS will stop you."

"Do I look like an engineer? The SS is expecting an engineer to come to Vatican City today to look at a construction problem. I'm that guy."

"Do you think the Vatican will help?"

"I will tell them the New Testament cannot abandon the Old. They will help."

Ludwig said, "Be safe."

"I will. Hopefully, I will come back with the ransom payment. However, I fear even this payment is just a momentary respite for the Jews. My hope is that it may provide the time needed for action. No matter what happens, you must prepare yourself to flee in the coming days. I am advising all of the Jews to flee the ghetto. Some members of the *giunta* disagree with me. I had a friend, a Jew in Lodz, who lived in a ghetto there. He said to me on many occasions what a relief it was to live in the ghetto, a place where you could live your Jewish life and not have people spit on you or threaten you." Zolli was quiet as he lowered his eyes. When he raised them up again, they bore deep into Ludwig's, as he said, "That ghetto is no more. The Nazis took its people, including my friend, and sent them to their death. I used to believe we would be safe here, but no longer. The Nazis are coming. Promise me you will leave."

Ludwig simply nodded.

"Good. Take Isaac with you. He will not want to go but make him. Now let me go take care of this ransom."

Ludwig saw Rabbi Israel Zolli to the door as he left for his meeting at the Vatican.

LUDWIG ADLER SAT in his apartment the whole day, unable to stop thinking about his earlier conversation with Israel Zolli. His thoughts were interrupted when Isaac Nola came running into the apartment. "You need to see this. Right now."

Isaac took off running with Ludwig following closely behind. Isaac led him to the synagogue where there was a long line of people waiting to get in.

"Who are these people?" Ludwig asked.

"Roman citizens. People from all over Rome. They came to bring gold."

"Gold."

"Yes. They are helping us with the ransom."

They ran to a side door and entered the synagogue.

The line of Romans snaked to the front where a table and a bin were set up. The people in line carried gold jewelry, watches and cigarette cases with them to help with the ransom.

Israel Zolli saw Isaac and Ludwig and came quickly over to them. "Can you believe it?" he asked. "This is happening all over Rome. Our Roman brothers and sisters are turning their gold over to us to help us meet the ransom."

Ludwig asked, "What happened with the Vatican?"

"The Pope agreed to loan us any amount of gold that we need, with no interest and no timeline to pay it back. But with what is happening all over Rome today, we will not need to use the Vatican's gold. The Italian people will save us."

Ludwig beamed, and his heart seemed to swell inside his chest. And for the first time since being in the ghetto, he thought reuniting with his family might be a reality.

Isaac said, "God be praised. We are safe." He hugged Ludwig as they, along with the Rabbi, walked toward the line of Romans to thank them all.

By the next day, the ransom was paid to the Nazis. The Roman Jews were saved, or so they thought.

Just days after the ransom was paid, a cable from Germany was sent to SS *Obersturmbannführer* Herbert Kappler in Rome. It simply read: *"Fahren Sie mit den geplanten Deportationen und der Ausrottung der römischen Juden fort."* (Proceed with the deportations as planned and the eradication of the Roman Jews.)

THE SECRET ORDER

*W*ith the invasion and occupation of Rome, Pope Pius XII and Vatican City were surrounded. The Pope controlled no divisions and had no way to defend the Vatican. His only army defending him consisted of white-gloved soldiers, in colorful uniforms, carrying a halberd as their weapon. The concern that the Pope would be arrested or kidnapped was a real threat.

The Pope sat at his desk inside his Papal office. Across the desk from him sat Luigi Cardinal Maglione and Father Robert Lieber, his secretary, along with the four most powerful members of the Curia, as well as Monsignor Costantini, who, as usual, was off to the side and close to the Pope. Rain ran down the windowpane. The weather outside matched the gloom inside the office.

The Pope said, "I believe there is a plan in place for me to be arrested. Hitler desires to have me removed from power."

Elia Cardinal Della Costa from Florence asked, "Your

Holiness, do you think that might happen? Do you really believe that they will try to have you arrested?"

"Hitler would love to have someone he designates to take my place, one who would support him and his terrible, deathly agenda. That cannot happen. The Curia must ensure that the legitimate Papacy continues."

Pietro Cardinal Boetto of Genoa said, "Then you must depart Rome at once."

The Pope wagged his head slowly from side to side. "I will never leave Rome. I am the Bishop of Rome, and I will not abandon my people. I am obliged to do everything in my power to save Rome from any and all destruction. This is my city. I grew up just a twenty-minute walk away from here. I will not leave Rome."

Luigi Cardinal Lavitrano from Palermo said, "But they will arrest you."

The Pope leaned forward and placed his elbows on the desk. "Now listen closely. If the Nazis should arrest me, my resignation will take place immediately. The Nazis must only arrest Cardinal Pacelli, not the pope. Have the Curia move the Holy See to another country, perhaps Spain. There the College of Cardinals will quickly elect a new pope."

Alfredo Ildefonso Cardinal Schuster of Milan stood. "I agree with your plan, your Holiness. But I am troubled for the Jews living in Rome. They are in danger. I fear the Nazis will still try to deport them, even though the payment of this ransom was accomplished."

Cardinal Lavitrano said, "What are we to do? We have to tread very carefully."

A small debate took place among the Cardinals until the Pope straightened in his chair. They all quieted down. "Now we come to it, and the real reason for this meeting. The Nazis are here in Rome. They control most of Northern Italy. We must act now. We must hide all of the Jews. With the Germans all across Northern Italy, and fighting going on below Rome, we must prepare to hide the Jews in and around the Vatican. We must do what we can to save as many as we can."

"But how?" asked Cardinal Maglione.

The Pope said emphatically, "All of you will let it be known to our clergy that all religious buildings are to give refuge to the Jews. I hereby release all monasteries and convents from the cloister rule so that they can be used as hiding places for all refugees, regardless of political leanings, gender, religion or race."

The Cardinals sat in shock as they listened to the Pope. Monsignor Schuster said, "The monks and nuns' own families are not allowed to break cloister."

Cardinal Boetto said, "By doing this, you are opening the Church up to direct conflict with Hitler. You are putting our clergy and perhaps our very Church in danger. To provide such assistance is dangerous as the Germans will regard it as a breach of the Lateran Treaty. They will enter and possibly confiscate our properties. They will arrest you."

The Pope's face was filled with intensity, as he said, "I am fully aware of that, Cardinal Boetto. But this is a risk that we must take. These properties are protected by the Lateran Treaty. We must pray that the Nazis will respect these properties and not enter them. I do this even at the price of great personal sacrifice on the part of my clergy. Yet, I am driven by the absolute belief that my clerical brothers and sisters want to do this." He added with great authority, "It is my wish and my command for Italy's Catholic clergy to save human lives by all possible means. Go spread the word. Have our priests go to every parish, church, convent, monastery, rectory, friary, university, and seminary. Tell them to open their doors and take in anyone they can. Now go."

"Your Holiness," they replied as they bowed and left the room, leaving Monsignor Costantini in the room.

When they left, the Pope said, "I agree with Cardinal Schuster, and I, too, am gravely concerned for the Jews here in Rome. The Chief Rabbi, Israel Zolli, has already spoken to me about his fear that the Nazis will round up the Jews in the ghetto and deport them, even though they made the ransom payment. We need to begin the process of thinking about how we will hide them as well. I want you to speak with Monsignor Hugh O'Flaherty. Relieve him of all duties in the Vatican Holy Office and put him in charge of putting a plan together. He is doing such good work with the Allied prisoners-of-war, hiding them since the fall of Mussolini."

"Monsignor O'Flaherty has been fearless. Since the capitulation of the Italians and the release of the Allied POWs, thousands upon thousands, with nowhere else to go, have made their way to Rome. All the while, *SS Obersturmbannführer* Kappler has viciously hunted them down, recaptured them, and put them in Nazi camps. O'Flaherty has hidden thousands of them."

"I would expect nothing less from him in this endeavor with regard to the Jews," Pope Pius replied. "Tell him to act quickly. He must use his network, his secret network of priests and nuns, to assist the Jews, all the Jews. And in particular, the Jews here in Rome."

"Your Holiness, there are over 8,000 Jews living in the

ghetto under the very noses of the Nazis. I don't know how we can get them all out."

"Hide them at the Castel Gandolfo. Hide them in the Gregorian University. Hide them here in the Vatican. Recruit some of them into the Swiss Guard. Hide them where anyone will assist and protect them."

"But how?"

With a smile, the Pope said, "You took care of the musicians. I have faith you will figure it out."

"Don't put too much trust in me. One of those musicians is stuck in the ghetto here in Rome."

"You are all I have, *amico*. You are all I have."

THE SCARLET PIMPERNEL

*M*onsignor O'Flaherty had been in a daring cat and mouse game with the head of the SS in Rome, Herbert Kappler. It was a game that Kappler was currently losing, as he was always a step behind his unknown nemesis, although he finally had come to believe that it was a priest that was rescuing and hiding the enemies of the Third Reich. O'Flaherty had resorted to wearing different disguises to avoid detection as he went across Rome reaching out to convents, monasteries and churches, recruiting priests and nuns to care for and hide Allied POWs and some Jewish refugees. Wearing those disguises and being able to slip away down secret Roman alleys at night gave O'Flaherty the nickname of the 'Scarlet Pimpernel of the Vatican.'

But now that game was even more dangerous. O'Flaherty was using his very same underground network to save more and more Jews, all under the nose of Kappler. He had carefully studied the list of Vatican properties protected under the Lateran Treaty. O'Flaherty made notes as to the mother superiors of the convents, heads of colleges, and priests in charge of any of these properties. He knew if the Germans discovered that the Holy See's extra-territorial proprieties protected under the Lateran Treaty were housing and hiding Jews and Allied Prisoners of War, it would mean not only capture and death for those in hiding, but death for the protectors as well, and grave problems for the Pope. Yet not one head of any of these properties turned down his request to hide Jews.

Monsignor O'Flaherty met with Monsignor Costantini in the small office near the Apostolic library inside the Vatican. Monsignor O'Flaherty advised him that all was going according to plan. Monsignor Costantini leaned back in his chair, taking in the conversation, and when Monsignor O'Flaherty paused to catch his breath, he said, "Well done, Hugh. Well done. Your network has begun saving the Jews. There are so many Jewish refugees already here staying at the Vatican. Pope Pius has been speaking with the families when he takes his daily walks. He particularly loves watching the children play. How did you get this together so quickly?"

In his Irish baritone voice, he said, "I called upon my fellow brother Irish priests. They answered the call and got the word out. Most of it had already been established through my work with the POWs."

"Please be careful. Kappler suspects that it is a Vatican priest is who is behind hiding the Allied prisoners in Rome. He is desperate to find out who that priest is, and he will use everything in his power to do so."

"I am being very careful. I make my contact with the monasteries and convents in secret and in disguise."

Monsignor Costantini smiled. "What type of disguises?"

He laughed. "One night a street sweeper, one night a cobbler, and one night a nun."

"Little tall there for a nun, don't you think?"

"It worked," Monsignor O'Flaherty replied with a laugh.

"Sister Pascalina has made a few calls on the convents you have spoken to. All of them were thrilled to be called upon by the Holy Father to open their doors to save the lives of people in danger, even at great risk to themselves. She is constantly checking to see if the Jews staying with them need anything. The Pontiff has given his approval to allow her access to the Vatican Bank to help with all their needs. The Pope is even using his own money to help."

O'Flaherty rubbed his cheek with his left hand. "Even ordinary, everyday Italians have opened their homes, apartments and farms to the Jews and allies all across Italy. You realize the courage it must take to do so, under the control of the Nazis as they are now. I have even heard that the *Fatebenefratelli* Hospital on Tiber Island has taken in Jews, and that the doctors there have even invented a 'deadly' and highly contagious illness they have dubbed '*Il Morbo di K*' to keep out the Gestapo."

"*Il Morbo di K*?" asked Monsignor Costantini quizzically.

"Yes. The K stands for Kappler."

Costantini laughed, as the Monsignor continued, "Even our nuns who work there have taught the patients to cough correctly, like a contagious illness. The Gestapo won't go near the place."

Monsignor Costantini sat quietly, taking it all in.

Monsignor O'Flaherty wrapped up his report with "I will be visiting the Roman ghetto today, to meet with Zolli and

Foa and all of the leadership, to let them know of the Pope's plans for the Jews. To let them know that there are places for them to seek refuge."

Monsignor Costantini stood and extended his hand. "I will let the Pontiff know. He will be pleased. Sister Pascalina visited the ghetto yesterday. The Jewish mothers told her of their need for milk for the children. The Pontiff, at her request, will be sending milk from the Vatican farm at Castel Gandolfo."

Just then, the door flew open, and Father Biaggio rushed in. "Monsignor Costantini. Monsignor O'Flaherty, you as well. Please. The both of you must come to St. Peter's Square immediately," Biaggio said excitedly.

Monsignor Costantini, Monsignor O' Flaherty and Father Sanguinetti rushed to St. Peter's Square. Directly outside the front of the square, German trucks had stopped and set up positions with soldiers armed with machine guns. A young soldier was on the ground, with a paint can and a brush painting a white line on the cobblestones directly at the entrance.

Alfredo Cardinal Ottaviani, for whom Monsignor O'Flaherty worked for at the Holy Office, stood nearby as the three priests came out into St. Peter's Square. He turned toward the three priests. "Well, Kappler is at war with the Vatican, or at least one of the Vatican's priest who is giving him fits. We have gotten word that he has finally discovered the name of his nemesis."

Monsignor Costantini and Biaggio turned and looked at Monsignor O'Flaherty, who merely folded his hands in front of him.

Cardinal Ottaviani continued, "Kappler has decided to lay

down the law. He has ordered that a white line be painted, separating the Vatican from Rome. The boundaries are set, assuring the inhabitants of Vatican City that the Vatican's jurisdiction ends at that line and that Germany now controls all of Rome."

"My God," said Biaggio.

Monsignor Costantini, almost in a whisper, said, "The Vatican is isolated."

Monsignor O'Flaherty put his arm around the shoulders of Monsignor Costantini. "I do believe that line is meant for me."

"What will you do?"

O'Flaherty smirked. "Guess I will need to get better disguises. "

Costantini frowned.

O'Flaherty smiled at him reassuringly. "Of course, I know that this changes things. That line means I am safe inside the Vatican. The refugees will have to come to me. I will stand on the steps of St. Peter's every day after morning and evening Mass, reading my Breviary. That's where members of my network, as well as refugees looking for assistance, will meet with me, provide me news, and where I can give them instructions. But for the Germans, I will be nothing more than a penitent priest saying his prayers and speaking with pilgrims going in and out of the Basilica."

"You do know the risk you are subjecting yourself to? Kappler would have you killed."

"I know the risk, but it's a risk I must take. The Nazis will not break Vatican neutrality."

All of the priests turned and stared as the soldier completed painting the white line. Monsignor O'Flaherty noticed a German officer standing outside a limousine parked close to the trucks watching as the line was being painted. It was *SS Obersturmbannführer* Herbert Kappler. While the line was setting a boundary, it was also sending a message. A message heard loud and clear. If O'Flaherty crossed that white line, he would face certain death. Kappler was now at war with the Scarlet Pimpernel.

45

THE GUILT

*S*ince the liberation, life slowly became easier in Bellafortuna. The Allies sent food supplies to Monreale and Palermo, which allowed the villagers to travel down to those cities and stock up.

Alfred, Heinrich, and Kurt went on with their new way of life. They missed the Jews who had emigrated but were happy they stayed behind to support Anikka and her children.

One day, Kurt wandered into the *Chiesa della Madonna* looking for Monsignor Mancini. He found him still cleaning parts of the Church from its days as a hospital.

"Monsignor, may I speak with you a moment?"

"Sure. Let's sit in the pew. How is work at the wine store?"

"Signor Sanguinetti is a wonderful host. He knows his wine and the wine business."

"That he certainly does."

"Monsignor, I was wondering if I could speak to you about my faith?"

"Of course. What do you mean, your faith?"

"I would like to become a Catholic."

Monsignor Mancini smiled. "Is it because of your relationship with Elizabetta?"

"Yes. Well, I mean, I want to."

"Have you discussed this with her?"

"No."

"I think you should do that first. But remember, you should only convert if you truly believe and have faith. Otherwise, it's not a true conversion."

"Monsignor, one of my favorite operas, is *Madama Butterfly*. There is that beautiful line in the opera when she tells her American sailor that she changed her religion. She says, '*È mio destino; nella stessa chiesetta in ginocchio con voi pregherò lo stesso Dio.*' (It is my destiny that in the same little church, beside you on my knees, I will pray to the same God.) I want to be with Elizabetta, Monsignor."

"You can, my son. You can be with her. But don't tie your being with her to your conversion. Again, convert only if you truly believe. Enjoy your time with her. And enjoy your time with us. Study our religion. Talk with me whenever you desire. Ultimately, if you decide this is what you want, then so be it."

"Thank you, Father. Can I ask you one more question?"

"Of course."

"I was in love with a girl back in Vienna. She was sent to a camp far away. I have no idea where she is. When I am with Elizabetta, I feel I am unfaithful. It's as though I walked away from her. I watch Anikka as she awaits her husband's return, and I feel like I abandoned my Gina."

"These are terrible times. We all must live and continue to live. Unlike Anikka, you do not have a spouse. You do not have children with that person. You have no covenant or commitment to her. Pray for her safe return, but you must live your life. You must go on."

Kurt smiled and said, "Thank you, Monsignor. Thank you."

"You're welcome. Come talk anytime."

46

THE ROMAN RAZZIA

*L*udwig stood over the dough in front of him in the bakery but did not touch it. He was stunned at the news a customer had just told him. Rabbi Israel Zolli had disappeared overnight. When Isaac Nola arrived later, Isaac told Ludwig the rumor going around the Jewish Quarter was that Rabbi Zolli had gone into hiding in the home of some wealthy Romans.

Some of the Jews in the Jewish Quarter, Isaac included, felt abandoned by their leader. Others thought it was a signal to save themselves and that they should try to get out of the ghetto.

For Ludwig, after the initial shock settled in, he felt a sense of relief for his friend, Rabbi Zolli. After all, the Chief Rabbi of Rome was at the top of the list of the Jews who were to be arrested. Of course, it was unsettling to Ludwig that he had been on that same list.

Slowly and quietly, some of the Jews of the Roman Jewish

Quarter began to leave and seek safety among non-Jewish Roman friends as well as inside some of the Church's institutions. Many Jews sought refuge at the Vatican, where they were given new identities and allowed to join the Pope's Palatine Guard.

Ludwig, not knowing anyone in Rome, and still scared from his run-in with Otto Steiner, decided that he would remain in the Jewish Quarter. Isaac Nola would not even consider leaving. His life was the Jewish Quarter. He truly believed that he and the other Jews who stayed would be safe here. After all, they were Roman Jews. The Nazis would not disturb them. They would not dare do anything to the Jews who were living right under the Pope's very nose.

Ludwig remembered the promise he had made to Rabbi Zolli that he would flee and make Isaac come with him, but there was nowhere for him to go and no way to get Isaac to change his mind. Ludwig's only option was to remain where he was in the Jewish Quarter, protecting his family back in Sicily.

ON THE NIGHT of October 15, 1943, Monsignor Costantini summoned Biaggio Sanguinetti to his office near the Spanish Steps. It was late as Biaggio hurried across the *Piazza di Spagna*.

Before Biaggio could even sit down, Monsignor Costantini got right to the point. "Biaggio, Jews all over Italy are seeking asylum in our institutions across the country. Even the Roman Jews are going into hiding as well. Our network is in full swing, and it is working. We have placed hundreds of

Jews in the Palatine Guard. The Italian people are also taking them in."

Biaggio said, pointedly, "God be praised."

"I need a favor. I would have asked O'Flaherty, but he is so involved with his network. That man is fearless. I need you to do something."

"Anything, Monsignor Costantini."

He pulled out a sheet of paper and handed it to Biaggio. "This is the address for Franco Giacone in the Jewish Quarter," Monsignor Costantini said. "Tomorrow morning, you need to go get him out and bring him here."

Biaggio smiled and simply replied, "Actions more than words." Ludwig Adler would be saved.

LATE THAT NIGHT, *Haupsturmführer* Theodor Dannecker sat in his apartment at *Via Tasso 145*, very near the Jewish Quarter. He had arrived in Rome back on October 6, dispatched personally by *SS Obersturmbannführer* Adolf Eichmann, one of Hitler's most trusted commanders, to supervise the *razzia*, the roundup of the Roman Jews. He was sent to relieve Kappler of the matter. Dannecker had seen this before. Eichmann was convinced Kappler had become too soft, living in Rome all these years. Some members of the German military leadership were pressuring Kappler to not allow the deportations to take place. Eichmann had direct orders from Adolf Hitler to bring the Final Solution to Rome. Eichmann knew the *Judenaktion* required a person who exuded fear and hatred and one who would act with unquestioning malice. In Theodor Dannecker, Eichmann found his perfect man.

Dannecker had proven his mettle in Paris, and the deportations he had handled there. But this time, Dannecker was resolved not to make the same mistakes he had made in Paris. Here, in Rome, he would deport every last Jew, all eight thousand of them.

Dannecker quickly developed a plan for Jewish deportation. He had taken 44 SS veterans of the dreaded Death's Head Corps with him to Italy. Since his arrival in Rome, Dannecker had done nothing but develop his plan. He went over the operation in his mind over and over again, until every last detail was engraved into his brain. The operation would last two days.

Dannecker, a tall, gangly, awkward man with a facial tic that shook his head violently from side to side, sat at the table in his charmless, dark apartment. The building where the apartment was located was now the Gestapo headquarters, a place of confinement and torture. A place feared by all Italians. Dannecker picked up the list sitting on the table one more time. Here was the list of every name and address of all the Jews in Rome. At least Kappler had been useful enough to somehow obtain this list, thought Dannecker. He had studied the Jews' residential patterns, their work habits, leisure times, and religious customs. He also made sure that the perception put forth was that the Nazis were only here to round up the Jews for forced labor purposes. He knew he could never let it be known that the sole purpose for the deportations was the unequivocal and complete liquidation of the Roman Jews. He would not let Eichmann down.

Tomorrow morning would be the *razzia*. Tomorrow morning would begin the roundup. Tomorrow morning, he would unleash hell upon the eight thousand Roman Jews.

THE NEXT MORNING, Ludwig Adler got up and was ready to head to the bakery. He peered out the window of his third-story apartment and noticed the rain. It was a heavy, steady rain. He dressed, then put on his jacket in the hopes he would avoid getting too wet during his walk to work. As he was about to leave, the sound of barking dogs caught his attention. He opened the window and peered out.

SS soldiers, with dogs and machine guns, were walking down the side of the street, while cars loaded with soldiers drove past on their way to seal off the entire Jewish Quarter. He watched as four SS soldiers went inside an apartment across the street. One of the SS soldiers had a whistle he kept blowing. Ludwig could hear the yelling from the apartment across the street as the SS soldiers screamed at the occupants.

One soldier in the middle of the street screamed out instructions to the entire neighborhood. "You are being transferred out of the ghetto. Take along enough food for eight days, blankets, money, and jewelry. Close the apartment and bring the key. The sick cannot stay behind. There is a hospital in the camp where you are being sent. You have twenty minutes to get ready." He yelled it over and over again.

Suddenly, from the door of the apartment across the street, two soldiers came out carrying two children still in their nightgowns. They were crying. A woman was being dragged out by her hair by an SS soldier. Behind her was a man, bent over and bloodied from the butt of the SS soldiers' rifles. The Goldman family had been rounded up. "To the trucks," barked a soldier as the family was led off down the street.

Ludwig watched in horror as the Goldmans were led down the street, and as the SS soldiers began to enter apartment after apartment. All across the Jewish Quarter that morning the same scene took place.

Suddenly, Ludwig noticed people on the rooftops across the way. Some of the Jews were running along the rooftops, trying to escape. One of the last escapees he saw was Isaac Nola, who was almost running at a full sprint across the rooftop. Ludwig knew the time to leave was now. He made his way to his apartment door, opened it, and was about to proceed to the small stairway at the end of the hall that led directly to the roof when the door below leading to the street was kicked in, and four SS soldiers stormed into the building.

Ludwig quickly retreated into his small apartment. He heard the SS soldiers coming up the stairs. He looked around and made a dash for the fireplace. He quickly stepped in and pulled himself up the chimney. His feet were only about an inch from the opening of the fireplace. He wedged his body against the bricks and waited. The wait was not long.

Within seconds, Ludwig heard them by the door and then the pounding sound of a fist on the door. "Franco Giacone. Get dressed and come with us." After a few more seconds, the door was kicked in, and the four SS soldiers came into the room. They opened a closet door and went through it. They also turned the bed over and went into the bathroom. "*Er ist nicht hier!*" said one of the soldiers.

"Well, of course, I can see he is not here," said one of the other soldiers. "Let's go," said the first, as they left the apartment.

Ludwig tried to climb up the chimney, but he could not get a good footing to make his way up. Far above, he could see the sky out of the top of the chimney. He knew that was the way to freedom, but he was unable to move. He tried rearranging himself to make it more comfortable inside the chimney but failed at that too. He wedged himself in tighter and waited. The muffled sounds of whistles, SS soldiers' yelling, dogs, and tears took his very soul to a very deep, lonely place.

FATHER BIAGGIO SANGUINETTI had gotten up early that morning and began walking toward the Jewish Quarter. Over his clerical garb, he wore a dark overcoat, protecting him from the steady rainfall. He knew something was wrong when German soldiers blocked the *Lungotevere*, a street leading into the ghetto. He walked over to one of the soldiers and asked what was going on.

The soldier looked at the man in front of him and noticed the Roman Collar. "Go home, Father. There is nothing for you to do here."

"But I have friends in there. What is happening?"

"Father, the Jews are being relocated. Now go, before you get caught up in all this mess."

Biaggio walked a little way before he noticed an open door in a building. He entered the door, walked through the building, and found a back door, which led to a street inside the Jewish Quarter. He went out the door and into the streets of the Jewish Quarter.

Biaggio unbuttoned his coat to show his clerical garb as he

walked unmolested down the streets. Groups of soldiers were leading families at gunpoint down the street. Raids were still going on with more and more Jews being forced from their homes. Biaggio could see Jews running down alleys, trying to get away.

He was startled when a door opened from an apartment building, and a Nazi SS soldier stepped out and was face to face with him.

The German spoke a little Italian. "Padre, this is not the place for you. Leave. Leave now."

"Where are they taking the Jews?"

"Moving."

"But where?"

"Padre, please leave."

"In the name of God, where are they taking the Jews?"

"The Military College, Padre. Now go before you get put on a truck."

The German soldier ran off down the street, as Biaggio continued to Ludwig's apartment. When he arrived, he made his way up the stairs to the third floor.

Ludwig, still crammed inside the chimney, could hear the sound of footsteps on the stairway. He pushed harder against the walls to ensure he would not slip down the chimney. The door to the apartment was already open from being kicked in. Biaggio entered and quickly realized that the room was empty. The bed was overturned. Ludwig Adler was gone.

Ludwig struggled to keep himself still. He knew someone was still in the apartment. His face was covered with soot from the chimney. He bit his lip to stop the unstoppable urge to sneeze. His brow moistened with sweat as he tried holding it in, but could not. He sneezed, trying to muffle the sound as best he could. The echo in the chimney made it only worse.

He closed his eyes and said a brief prayer when he heard, "Ludwig? Ludwig Adler?"

Ludwig slowly made his way out of the chimney.

When he came out, he stood face to face with Father Biaggio Sanguinetti. Tears rolled down his soot-blackened face. Biaggio extended his hands and hugged the German composer.

"Biaggio, why are you here?"

"To get you out. Your family needs you."

"The Germans, they are everywhere."

"I know." Biaggio walked across the room and stood by the overturned bed. He quickly took off his overcoat, his Roman Collar and all-black cassock and laid them on the underbelly of the bed. He picked up the Cossack and Roman Collar and said, "Put this on," as he stood there in his white undershirt and a black pair of pants.

"Why?"

"They will leave you alone."

"No. I cannot."

"Take it and put it on. Here are my papers. Use them. Leave your face covered in soot. They will never know it's not me with your dirty face."

The sounds of more trucks and cars coming down the street could be heard, as Ludwig donned the cassock. "What will you do?"

Biaggio put his overcoat back on. "I will get out. I will be fine. Now you must go. Make your way to the Vatican. Go."

"I can't, and I won't."

"You will, if not for me, then for Anikka and your children."

Ludwig finished dressing and then turned to Biaggio and simply said, "*Grazie.*"

"*Va!*"

Ludwig Adler left the apartment and made his way to the street. He turned and began walking toward the street that led out of the ghetto. Before doing so, he looked up and saw Father Biaggio Sanguinetti at the window. With his right hand, the priest blessed him by making the sign of the cross.

Ludwig Adler walked briskly down the street to freedom. Biaggio lost sight of him. He put his hand in his pocket. He felt the Jewish star the refugees had given him so many months ago. He always carried it with him in remembrance of every single one of them.

UNDER THE POPE'S WINDOW

*M*onsignor Costantini sat in a small private office alone inside the papal residence after leaving a hastily called meeting with the Pope. Word had been received in the Vatican very early that morning that the *razzia* was underway. The first thing that morning, Princess Enza Pignatelli Aragona Cortes, a friend of the Pope, had seen canvas topped trucks carrying men, women and children leaving from the Jewish Quarter. As she drove to the Vatican, more and more trucks passed her. She immediately went to the Pope and was quickly ushered in by Sister Pascalina. She was in a hurry to see him to relate what was happening. The Pope listened in silence as she described what she had seen. When she finished her report, the Pope was furious and immediately called for a meeting with Monsignor Maglione, Monsignor Costantini, Sister Pascalina, and Father Lieber.

At that meeting, Pope Pius XII was distraught but gave

specific directions regarding what he wanted to be done. "We must mobilize our network at once. I will advise Monsignor O'Flaherty to send his priests out in the streets to see what is going on. The Vatican switchboard has been advised to give all calls related to saving the Jews priority. We must contact all of the religious houses who are hiding Jews to advise them of this tragedy going on in Rome. Sister Pascalina, can you pass along the news to all the Jews hiding in the Vatican?"

"I can."

"Also, can you check on the Jews arriving en masse at the Vatican, fleeing from the Jewish Quarter. The reports I have received are that so far, at least 200 have come into the Vatican this morning, crossing right over the white line surrounding the Vatican as they made their way into St. Peter's Square. Do so now, please."

Sister Pascalina hurriedly left the room.

"Robert, I want you to contact Osborne and Tittmann. Ask them if their respective governments of Britain and the US will lodge a protest to Berlin. Please do so now."

Father Lieber quickly left the room.

"I need to speak to the German Ambassador at once," continued the Pope. "Luigi, get him here within the hour."

"I will," replied Monsignor Maglione.

"You can use that phone." He pointed across the room.

Monsignor Costantini stayed close to the Pope while Monsignor Maglione walked over to the phone across the room. He picked it up and dialed.

"Pronto," Monsignor Lucado sleepily replied when he answered Monsignor Maglione's call.

With no introduction, Monsignor Maglione forcefully

said, "The Holy Father wants to meet with Ernst von Weizsäcker immediately."

"Now?" Monsignor Lucado asked.

"Now. The *razzia* is underway. His Holiness is not pleased. He wants to issue a public protest. He wants the German Ambassador at the Vatican within an hour."

"A protest?" replied Monsignor Lucado. "The Church should not get involved."

"Well, he is. They are deporting Jews right under his window. Have Weizsäcker here in an hour." Monsignor Maglione hung up the phone, and then turned to the Pope and nodded his head.

Monsignor Costantini stared at the Pope, who put his head down deep in thought. After a few moments, the Pope lifted his head and looked directly at Costantini. "I want you to do something for me. You can use the office down the hall."

"Certainly. Tell me what you want me to do."

"Hudal."

"Hudal?" Costantini questioned, as he turned and looked toward Monsignor Maglione. Costantini turned back toward the Pope. "Why Hudal?"

Cardinal Maglione walked back to where the Pope was seated. "Hudal's in bed with the Nazis," stated Cardinal Maglione forcefully.

The Pope replied, "Exactly. We all know that he is a Nazi sympathizer, but his German contacts may help. We must act and act now. We will be careful in our dealings with him. We will use my nephew, Carlo, to make the contact. Let me tell you exactly what I want you to do."

After leaving the Pope, Monsignor Costantini quickly

went to the private office nearby. He sat alone behind a small desk and gathered his thoughts. He then placed his call to the Pope's nephew, Carlo Pacelli. Costantini explained what was happening in the Jewish Quarter. Monsignor Costantini said, "Carlo, the Pope wants you to contact Bishop Alois Hudal and ask him to immediately reach out to General Rainer Stahel. Hudal should tell Stahel that the Pope wants the deportations to stop immediately. As the German Military Commander of Rome, Stahel has the power to stop this. If they are not stopped, then the Pope shall issue a public protest." Monsignor Costantini hung up.

Costantini then begin calling some of the religious houses where the Jews were hiding to advise them of what was going on in Rome and to do what was necessary to protect the Jews.

He hung up the phone and hung his head low. He wondered if Ludwig Adler and Father Sanguinetti would be among the refugees arriving at the Vatican.

He then got up and made his way back to the Pope, where he would sit with his friend awaiting the arrival of Ernst von Weizsäcker.

BIAGGIO COULD SEE the SS soldiers heading back to the apartment across the street, rechecking each apartment for any Jews left behind. They had dogs with them. Biaggio quickly slipped out of the apartment to the door that led to the roof. He took the stairs and came out on the roof. The rain had stopped, and now, with more light, he knew it would be dangerous. He began making his way across the rooftops.

He could see Nazi trucks down below, loaded with mostly women and children. He could also Jews running up and down the alleys, making a break for freedom out of the ghetto. He jumped from roof to roof until he finally came to a ladder, and with no other roof to jump too, took the ladder down to the street.

He quickly walked down the street until two Germans turned the corner and headed his way. He was about to run in the opposite direction, when a voice whispered from an open door leading to an apartment, "In here."

Biaggio went inside. The man inside put his finger to his mouth, motioning him to remain silent.

The Germans passed the opened door and continued on. Once they passed, the man said, "That was a close one."

"Indeed," replied Biaggio.

"My name is Isaac Nola."

"I am Father Biaggio Sanguinetti."

"You are a priest?"

"Yes."

"What are you doing here?"

"Helping a friend."

"Well, you picked a fine time for a visit."

Biaggio explained, "We need to make our way to the Vatican. You will be safe there."

Isaac answered, "We are close to getting out of the Jewish Quarter. Follow me."

Biaggio followed closely behind Isaac.

They came to an alley, and Isaac turned. "This alley right here is the quickest way to the Vatican. The Germans should not be watching it. This is the best way out."

As they turned into the alley, they heard a voice yell out from the street behind them, *"Halt."*

Biaggio said to Isaac, "Look. Get to that ladder down the alley. Get to the roof."

Isaac ran down the alley toward the ladder. Biaggio turned and walked out of the alley and met the SS soldier on the sidewalk. "I'm here. I'm not going anywhere."

Isaac quickly made his way up the ladder to the roof. He came back around and peered down, where he saw the soldier questioning Biaggio.

The soldier held his Luger pointed directly at Biaggio.

"Papers. I want to see your papers," the soldier demanded.

"I lost my papers," Biaggio answered.

Isaac stared down from the rooftop as the young soldier said again, "Where are your papers? Why were you running?"

Before Biaggio could answer, the German squeezed his trigger. Blood splattered on the brick wall, as Biaggio crumbled immediately to the ground, having taken the round directly in the middle of his forehead. Isaac covered his mouth with his hand as the German walked away, leaving the dead priest on the street, mumbling, "Damn Jews."

Isaac gathered himself and began making his way across the rooftops until he finally got to another ladder, which would come down on the street outside of the ghetto. The Dome of St. Peter was in the distance. He descended the ladder and hurried toward the Vatican.

———————

LUDWIG ADLER SAT along a wall in a hallway deep within Vatican City alongside numerous other Jewish refugees who had all fled from the Jewish Quarter and other parts of Rome that morning. Ludwig was still wearing the black cassock of Father Sanguinetti. There were hundreds of refugees lined up and down the long hallway. More and more kept arriving. Nuns and priests were running back and forth, offering care, including Sister Pascalina.

Ludwig was lost in his thoughts when he heard a voice say, "My, oh my, look who it is."

Ludwig stared into the face of Rabbi Israel Zolli. "What are you doing here?" Ludwig asked.

"I've been living here in the Vatican. The Pope took my family and me in many weeks ago. I'm so glad you made it out."

"The gold, Rabbi. The gold was a lie."

Rabbi Zolli nodded. "This was their intention all along. I believe Kappler used the gold as a means to allow the Roman Jews to feel safe so they wouldn't leave. With the Vatican's assistance, thankfully, many did not stay. They got out well before today."

Just then, a priest yelled from the hallway, "Rabbi, you are needed down here."

Rabbi Zolli patted Ludwig on his head. "You will be safe here. The Pope will protect us." Rabbi Zolli went to see the Jewish group down the hall.

Ludwig sat dumbfounded. Everything had happened so fast that morning: it was all a blur. Somehow, he had made it out. He began thinking about Father Sanguinetti and what he had done for him and began praying for his safe return.

As he was sitting there, he spotted Isaac Nola entering the

336 | SAVING THE MUSIC

hallway. Ludwig quickly got up and ran to the baker. The two
embraced tightly.

Isaac said, "It's so good to see you."

"You too. You made it out."

Pointing, Isaac asked, "Is that Rabbi Zolli down there? I
thought I saw him walk by when I walked in."

"Yes. He has been living here at the Vatican."

"Really. So this is where he has been."

Ludwig said, "I saw you on the rooftop. Is that how you
escaped?"

"Yes, the roofs and alleys. But why are you wearing a
priest's outfit?"

Ludwig said, "That is how I got out. A priest gave it
to me."

Isaac asked, "A young priest?"

"Yes."

"Was his name Father Sanguinetti?"

"Yes, how did you know that?"

The story that Isaac Nola told Ludwig Adler that day
would forever be etched in Ludwig's memory. He would
honor the name of Father Biaggio Antonio Sanguinetti for the
rest of his days.

———————

LATE THAT NIGHT, Pope Pius XII was seated at his desk. Sister
Pasqualina sat opposite the Pontiff. Their conversation was
interrupted when Monsignor Costantini came into the study.

Monsignor Costantini said, "It seems your threat of
protest has stopped the *razzia*. They have called off the roundup tomorrow."

Sister Pasqualina rose and clasped her hands together. "God be praised. I will go tell the Jews who fled here the good news." She retired from the room.

With his head bowed, the Pope asked, "How many?"

Monsignor Costantini replied, "We believe a thousand Roman Jews were loaded onto trucks. For now, they are being held at the Military College. We don't know where they are being sent."

"A thousand of them," the Pope remarked as he crossed himself. "Men, women and children?"

"Yes. We saved 7,000 Jews. 400 are with us hiding in the Vatican. Over 4000 are hiding in other religious institutions throughout Rome, including Castel Gandolfo and the Gregorian University. The rest are hiding with everyday Italians."

"But a thousand have been taken."

"I went and met with the Jews who made their way to the Vatican. I spoke at length with one of the Jews as well as with our composer friend from Munich. It has been confirmed that Father Biaggio Sanguinetti was murdered inside the ghetto."

The Pope said nothing but closed his eyes.

Monsignor Costantini continued, "It seems he saved the composer's life. He died without letting the Nazis know he was a priest. The Jewish Committee was called in by the Nazis to identify the body. They told the Nazis it was indeed the remains of Franco Giacone. We now have the body. We found this inside his pocket."

Monsignor Costantini pulled out the Jewish star with the signatures of all the refugees. He said, "I would like to send his body back to his parents along with this star."

The Pope replied, "Agreed. I will speak to the German

Ambassador, and I will tell him that a priest, Father Sanguinetti, died in the Vatican of a heart attack and that he be allowed to be sent back home for burial. I will get papers issued, allowing this to happen."

"Your Holiness, advise them that two priests from the Vatican will accompany the body of Father Sanguinetti back to Sicily."

"Sure," replied Pius. He then asked. "Which two priests?"

"Father Dominic will go back again and a Father Vincenzo Taormina."

"I will. But who is Father Vincenzo Taormina?"

"Ludwig Adler. At least once I complete his paperwork. Let's send him back to his family. He will wear clerical garb on his trip back home so that he can be safely reunited with his family."

"Reunited with his family. I fear so many will not have families to return to."

"You stopped the *razzia*. Over the next few days, more and more of the Jews throughout Italy will be able to hide. They will seek shelter in the Church's institutions and with the Italian people."

"I will speak with the Ambassador tomorrow morning about Father Sanguinetti. Go get some rest. We are meeting with the Curia first thing in the morning. We need to discuss at once what we can do to save the thousand Jews the Germans took from us and find out what the Nazis are planning to do with them."

As Monsignor Costantini left the office, he turned and peered one more time inside as the Pontiff stood looking out by the window. He knew his friend would not sleep at all tonight.

THE POPE WAS unsuccessful in having the Jews who had been arrested during the *razzia* released. Two days later, Monsignor Costantini entered the Pope's office. The look on his face informed the Pope that the news he carried was not good.

"We have just learned that twenty railcars left Tiburtina Station in Rome with the Jews that were rounded up."

The Pope clasped his hands behind his back and asked. "Where is that train going?"

"It is believed that the final destination of the train is Auschwitz."

The Pope wept openly. "I want nothing more than to condemn this action publicly and speak out in support of our Jewish brethren, but we are hiding so many."

"Prudence is understandable. Particularly in this situation."

"Not for those who have been taken. Not for those. I will reach out to Ambassador Weizsäcker and see about sending supplies for the Jews. Keep me informed as to what you hear about our Roman Jews."

A WEEK LATER, that train reached Auschwitz. Dr. Joseph Mengele, nicknamed the Angel of Death, met the Roman Jews on the platform. It was there that he quickly performed his sick and twisted selection process. Death to the right. Life to the left. The entry in the Auschwitz log on Saturday, October 23, 1943 read as follows:

*OSHA -Transport, 1007 Jews from Rome. After the selection, 149
men registered with numbers 158451-158639, and 47 women
registered with numbers 66172-66218 have been admitted to the
detention camp. The rest have been gassed.*

When the Pope inquired about the fate of the Jews and if a
shipment of warm clothes and blankets could be sent,
Ambassador Weizsäcker informed him that it was not
necessary and that the Jews would not be coming home.

A FEW DAYS LATER, the Pope stood on a balcony inside the
Vatican, overlooking an inner courtyard. Down below, some
Jewish children hiding at the Vatican were playing ball. The
Pope looked on, watching the children at play. Monsignor
Costantini walked over to him, but before he could say
anything, the Pope said, "Some members of the Curia believe
that I should make the Jews leave the Vatican, as they are a
danger to our Church."

"What do you think?"

He continued staring at the children. "I say that they can
stay here. For now, this is their home. While watching these
children at play, I wondered if we have done enough. I am
convinced that had we spoken out unequivocally against
Hitler, my words would have brought me great praise and
respect from across the globe, while it would have done
nothing to save the Jews. How many more would have died
because of my words?"

"I came to let you know what we have learned."

The Pope turned toward Monsignor Costantini. "What is it?"

Monsignor Costantini smiled. "We have become aware that everyday Italians – peasants, doctors, lawyers, housewives, nuns, and priests – are opening their hearts and their doors to the oppressed. The Italians are welcoming Jews in large numbers into their homes and buildings and hiding them. They are following the Holy See's example. Monsignor O'Flaherty's network has blossomed."

The Pope turned once again and watched the children. He said, "I have tried to alleviate the suffering of all people in whatever form it may be. With so much evil present today, we must turn to the Christian world and pray that their universal charity becomes more active. Charity should know neither boundaries nor nationality. It should make absolutely no distinction between religion, sex and race. Charity is for all. After all, for those who have the capacity to offer charity and mercy, the Lord will judge us on the fulfillment thereof, and not by our piety or faithfulness alone. That is the Lord's plan for salvation. God bless all of those who are suffering."

"Amen."

"Now, I am going for my walk. I will see you later." He began to walk away, but turned back and said quietly, "I do thank you for being my friend."

Monsignor Costantini nodded his head, as he watched the Pope walk alone as usual, across the balcony headed toward his car to take him down to the Vatican Gardens. Although Monsignor Costantini had known Eugenio Pacelli since childhood, he still was in awe of the man and was proud to serve him and call him a friend.

THE NEXT DAY, a train left Rome headed south. Onboard were Father Dominic and Ludwig Adler, dressed as a priest. They sat in the luggage car, next to a coffin that carried the remains of Biaggio Antonio Sanguinetti, a Vatican priest on his last journey back to Bellafortuna.

FINDING A PURPOSE

A few days later, at midnight, a small, horse-drawn cart traveled along the *Via Valle*. It carried the casket of Father Biaggio Sanguinetti. Father Dominic, holding tightly to the reins, and Ludwig Adler, both sat quietly next to each other as the cart continued up the road toward Bellafortuna. Ludwig still wore Biaggio's clerical garb. When the cart reached the village, Father Dominic drove directly to the *Piazza Santa Croce* and stopped outside the *Chiesa della Madonna*. The piazza was deserted.

Ludwig said, "Why don't you tell the Monsignor what has occurred and get help to carry Father Biaggio into the Church. I will go tell Giuseppe and Maria about their son."

"Are you sure you don't want me and the Monsignor to come with you?"

"No. This is something I must do alone."

AFTER A FEW KNOCKS on the door of *Il Paradiso*, Ludwig heard footsteps from inside. He heard Giuseppe say, "I'm coming. We were sleeping. Who is it at this late hour?"

"Giuseppe, it is Ludwig. Ludwig Adler."

The door quickly opened, and Giuseppe stood face to face with Ludwig Adler. Giuseppe stared at him for a second. "Ludwig Adler. Good God. It is so good to see you."

Giuseppe wrapped his arms around Ludwig. He then asked, "Why are you dressed like a priest?"

"May I come in? I need to discuss something with you."

"Sure."

As he entered, Maria came into the store in her nightgown and robe. "It's Ludwig," Giuseppe excitedly told her.

As Ludwig entered, Maria ran over and hugged him. She asked, "Oh my God. It's a blessing to see you. Have you seen Anikka yet?"

"No. I just arrived. But I wanted to see both of you first."

Maria replied, "Come in. Please. Sit down by the window."

He walked to the chair by the table while Giuseppe shut the door to *Il Paradiso*. Maria joined him at the table.

Giuseppe, making his way over to the table, asked, "What is it, Ludwig?"

Ludwig sat with his head bowed. He lifted it up and stared into the eyes of Maria. He began telling his story.

ABOUT TWO HOURS LATER, Ludwig was standing in the back of the *Chiesa della Madonna* with Monsignor Mancini. The Sanguinettis, still both in tears after being told of what had happened, were seated in the Church next to the body of their son. They would remain there for the rest of the night.

Monsignor Mancini said to Ludwig, "I will walk with you to the *Albergo*. I am sure there is a young woman who has waited and prayed for your return for a very long time."

Ludwig smiled and then turned one more time toward the Sanguinettis, who were holding tightly to each other in the pew. He said, "Those poor people."

"Ludwig, I know what you are feeling, but it is good that you are alive. Biaggio is smiling tonight. We will ring the church bell at five in the morning to let the villagers know of his passing. Go to Anikka. She is a wonderful woman, strong and intelligent. As we walk to the *Albergo*, I will tell you briefly what she has been through."

They walked across the piazza, speaking the whole time. When they reached the *Albergo*, Monsignor Mancini unlocked the door, and then turned and hugged Ludwig, who was still in his priest outfit.

"It's so good to see you. Go to her. She deserves your return so much."

"*Grazie*, Monsignor Mancini."

Ludwig entered the *Albergo* and went to his wife.

LUDWIG ENTERED the room where Anikka was sleeping. She was lying on her left side. He climbed into bed on the opposite side and, leaning on his elbow, gently touched her hair and lightly rubbed her face with his fingertips. She woke and rolled over. Opening her eyes, she gasped and threw her arms around his neck.

"My Ludwig. My Ludwig. You came back to me," as tears began to pour from her eyes.

He softly said, "*Ich liebe dich, Annika.* (I love you, Annika.) I love you more than anything in this world. I'm so sorry for putting you through this. All I wanted was for you to be safe, and one day to hopefully see you again."

"I'm here, my love. I'm safe and here. And you made it back to us." She reached her hand up to his head and pulled him close, and they kissed. "You came back," she said, as they fell back onto the pillow, all the while kissing. She pressed her body against him and felt his excitement.

He stopped and pulled away for a moment and said, "How are the children? How is Josef?"

"They are great. They will be overjoyed to see you."

"Should we go wake them?"

"No. We will tell them in the morning. Right now, I want you for myself."

"I need to tell you something. Something that happened in Rome."

She took his hand and placed it on her breast. "*Sag mir morgen.*" (Tell me tomorrow.)

He slipped her nightgown off her right shoulder and buried his head between her breasts. He wanted to bury himself inside her and remain there forever. Her skin was soft and supple. He had missed being with her.

She lifted his head again to remove his shirt when she realized what he was wearing. She smiled and, pulling his shirt off, said, "Tell me about your outfit tomorrow as well," as she then took his hand and kissed it. He lifted her nightgown, and when she was nude, he gently rubbed her thigh. She spread her legs and pressed her head deeper into the pillow.

"Tell me everything tomorrow," Anikka said. She put her mouth close to his ear and whispered, "For now, make love to me, Ludwig. I love you so."

"I love you too."

Later, when they were spent from lovemaking, they finally fell asleep, wrapped in each other's arms. The tolling of the church bell, announcing the death of a villager, awakened them.

LATER THAT DAY, Father Biaggio Antonio Sanguinetti was laid to rest on the knoll of the hill overlooking the *Stagno Azzurro*. Biaggio was buried next to the graves of his grandfather, Antonio Sanguinetti, and Biaggio Spatalanata, his father's good friend, and his namesake.

Monsignor Mancini presided over the funeral mass. At the burial, the entire village of Bellafortuna stood on the hill, along with the Ludwig and Anikka, and Henrich, Alfred and Kurt.

Anikka held tightly to Ludwig, both with tears in their eyes. Giuseppe and Maria Sanguinetti stood close to the grave. Their eyes were red from crying for so long. They had been like that since yesterday when Ludwig had returned with Biaggio's body and informed them of the death.

After a few brief prayers, Monsignor Mancini announced, "Ludwig Adler has asked to say a few words."

Ludwig made his way to the front, and after wiping away tears, he began to speak. "I owe my life to this man, to this good and holy priest. My family and I also owe our lives to all of you as well, this entire village. All of us Jews who came here are alive today because of you. Your Sicilian spirit showed that love conquers hate, compassion conquers indifference, and kindness and generosity conquer evil.

"There is no way on earth we can ever repay you for what you did. When the world was at it darkest, you provided the light. This long war is not over. Our people are still suffering; yet, it is through acts of decency that there is a stirring in our very souls that leads us to a belief that all will be well; that there is indeed hope for us; that there is life and happiness and perhaps, one day, a place for us in this world once again. I stand here today over the burial place of my friend, and the only word that comes to mind is: *Grazie*. I will never forget him and what he did for me." He turned to Giuseppe and Maria, "Your son is a hero."

Ludwig walked over to Giuseppe and Maria and hugged them both, as the tears flowed freely from all of their eyes. Ludwig then pulled from his pocket the little Jewish star and handed it to them.

"He would want you to have this." He pointed to the three Jewish musicians and said, "We want you to have it in memory of what he did for us. He saved us by bringing us to your village. As our *Talmud* teaches, 'Whoever saves a life, it is considered as if he saved the entire world.'" He hugged them both.

Then the Adler family, including Josef, Heinrich, Alfred, and Kurt, individually walked to the grave and placed a stone on top of the grave in accordance with Jewish tradition, just as biblical Jacob had placed a stone on the grave of his beloved Rachel. The legacy of Father Biaggio Antonio

Sanguinetti would never be forgotten. Then the Jews sang Verdi's *Va, pensiero*. All of the villagers of Bellafortuna joined in.

After the service, the mourners began leaving the gravesite. Giuseppe, after getting a hug from Santo Vasaio, remained standing by the grave. Monsignor Mancini stood nearby.

Giuseppe said to his good friend, "It seems like it was only yesterday when we buried my best friend right here. But that was over forty years ago. I still remember the words you told me so long ago now. 'Giuseppe, the pain of your loss will subside, and so will your anger. However, your love of your friend will grow, and he will never be forgotten in your heart. And by living, you will find a purpose in your loss. It will take time, but you will. And perhaps, that purpose was why God acted.' Those words sustained me at that time and for my entire life. But now, with my son's death, I am lost once again. I hope I find a purpose soon, Pietro. Very soon. The pain I feel right now is so intense."

"Giuseppe, your son laid down his life for another. Even Jesus says there is no greater love. Your son dedicated his life to the service of others and to God. It's one thing to say you will live your life and strive to follow the teachings of our Lord. It's another to actually do it. Your son did it. When he was needed most, he showed his true mettle. So, what was God's purpose? One day you will find it. For now, let your entire body and soul be filled with pride. Jesus will meet your son today and tell him – welcome good and faithful servant. Welcome to Paradise."

"Life is hard, Pietro. Life is too hard."

"Giuseppe, that is why we have each other; to lean upon

each other for support; to help each other when times are tough; to help each other. Perhaps that is the purpose in his death. To show the world how we should act toward each other. When the world turned its back on the Jews, your son stood up and said no. He rebelled. He acted. He stood to be counted. He brought them to Bellafortuna. He allowed us to be touched by God's grace. He died for them. He died for a Jew. Jew, Christian, Catholic, Muslim, or atheist – it doesn't matter. Live life with a heroic passion for decency. Live for others. After all, isn't that what Jesus did and what He demands of all of us? Come. Let's go have a drink with the others in remembrance and in celebration of a life well-lived."

Giuseppe and Monsignor Mancini headed back toward Bellafortuna. Beautiful Bellafortuna, a tiny village, tucked among the Sicilian hills, but one whose villagers, when called upon, were willing to stand as one and accept people who were being persecuted, and protect them no matter what the cost.

In a time of unmitigated horror and death, betrayal and brutality, and inhumanity to man, let what they did never be forgotten.

EPILOGUE

*T*he war would last another year and a half. In the end, six million Jews were killed as a result of Hitler's hatred. While approximately 80 percent of European Jews perished during World War II, remarkably 80 percent of Italy's Jews were saved.

Colonel Hans-Jurgen Fromm was eventually named a General in the *Wehrmacht* Army. He served with distinction and was loved by his men. He became more and more disenchanted with Hitler, although he rejected the opportunity to get involved with the July 20, 1944 plot to kill him. After the war, he moved his family to Salzburg, where he ran a hotel for the remainder of his life. He kept up a correspondence with Monsignor Mancini for many years until the Monsignor's death.

Stadtkommissar Eric von Jeschonnek, after the liberation of Sicily, was sent back to Berlin. He was appointed as an officer at the Dachau Concentration Camp, where he became known for his brutal treatment of the Jewish prisoners. When the Americans liberated the camp, he fled but was eventually found while on a train to Switzerland. He stood trial at Nuremberg and was sentenced to be hanged for his war crimes. But the hanging never took place as he took a cyanide pill and died on July 16, 1946. His final words were *"Heil Hitler."*

Gefreiter Karl Friedrich, after his arrest in Bellafortuna, was sent to America, where he was interred in a POW Camp in Lockport, Louisiana. While there, he worked at Felicia Plantation, a sugarcane farm, with other German and Italian POWs. He fell in love with the daughter of the owner of the plantation, and after the war married the girl and lived the rest of his life in Louisiana as a sugarcane farmer.

SS *Obersturmbannführer* Herbert Kappler remained in Rome after the *razzia* and turned his attention to tracking down Allied prisoners of war in Rome who were liberated once Italy switched sides. He publicly accused the Vatican of harboring fugitives. At the end of the war, Kappler was arrested by the Allies and sentenced to life imprisonment for his role in demanding the ransom for the Roman Jews and for committing numerous atrocities against the Jews and the Roman civilian population.

Haupsturmführer Theodor Dannecker, a lawyer by training, was one of Adolf Eichmann's most trusted henchmen and one of the SS's most ruthless and experienced experts on the Final Solution. It is thought that he was responsible for the death of over seven hundred thousand Jews. He remained loyal to Eichmann to the end and was arrested in Germany by the United States Army when he attempted to flee. Before he could go to trial, he committed suicide in his prison cell.

Father Alfred Delp, the Jesuit priest who helped the Adlers escape Munich, continually spoke out against Nazism and Hitler. He was implicated in Claus von Stauffenberg's 1944 plot to kill Hitler. He was arrested and severely tortured, as the Nazis tried to get him to implicate the Vatican in the same plot, which he refused to do. He was sentenced to death for high treason but was given the opportunity for a reprieve provided that he would renounce the Jesuits and leave the order. He refused, writing to his fellow priests, "The real reason for my conviction is that I am and have remained a Jesuit." The Nazis hanged him on a meat hook on February 2, 1945.

On June 5, 1944, the day after the liberation of Rome, while the United States Army marched through the streets of Rome amid the residents cheering, singing, drinking and celebrating the end of the German occupation, more than 100,000 people flocked to St. Peter's Square where they called upon *Papa Pacelli* to come to the window in his Apostolic apartment and receive their accolades. They were certain that this was the man who had saved the Eternal City from destruction. Not only had he stopped the Allied bombing of Rome, but he had also kept the Germans from turning Rome into a battlefield.

Among the crowd that day were thousands of Jews who were there in support of the Pope for a wholly different reason. That very day, the Jews had come out of the shadows from the numerous Vatican properties where they had been hiding all across Rome. They came to St. Peter's and wanted to show personally their support for the man they knew was most responsible for saving their lives. As the crowd reached a fever pitch, the Pope appeared on the *loggia*. He outstretched his hands to heaven, accepting the applause. He then said to the crowd, "Yesterday, Rome feared for her children. Today, she rejoices in their liberation. You come to thank me, but it is God we must thank for saving Rome." At his words, the crowd cheered even louder. The Pope, with tears in his eyes, blessed everyone. The Jews silently stood with their heads bowed in honor of the man they believed was most responsible for their life. As the days passed after the liberation of Rome, the Roman Jews began to tell the entire world all that the Vatican had done in saving them.

Eugenio Pacelli – Pope Pius XII - was looked upon with great favor after the war and as a friend of the Jews. Immediately after the war, countless Jewish leaders thanked him for the number of Jews he saved, which some put in the neighborhood of eight hundred and fifty thousand. Pope Pius XII died in 1958. He was buried in the Vatican Grottos, below the altar in St. Peter's Basilica, and above the tomb of the Fisherman. The first official dignitary to react to his death was Golda Meir, the future prime minister of Israel. She said in her public message:

> *"We share in the grief of humanity at the passing away of His Holiness, Pope Pius XII. In a generation afflicted by wars and discords, he upheld the highest ideals of peace and compassion. When fearful martyrdom came to our people in the decade of Nazi terror, the voice of the Pope was raised for its victims."*

Soon after his death, the canonization process began. However, thanks in part to Soviet antagonism towards the Vatican and a 1963 German play by Rolf Hochhuth called *The*

Deputy, which vilified the Pope, accusing him of silence and inaction over the Jews, the tide turned, and the canonization process came to a halt. It became fashionable to criticize Pius as being indifferent to the suffering of the Jews, or worse, as a collaborator with the Nazis. The debate intensified much later with the 1999 publication of *Hitler's Pope*, a book by John Cornwell, which took the stance that Pius was guilty of anti-Semitism. Also, *Under His Very Windows: The Vatican and the Holocaust in Italy*, a book by Susan Zuccotti and released in the year 2000, was extremely critical of the Pope's actions regarding the Roman Jews.

As the years have progressed, the pendulum seems to be changing yet again. As proof of the changing attitude, Pope Benedict XVI declared Pius XII Venerable on December 19, 2009. And once again, the discussion of his canonization has been raised. The debate continues today. A major shift in the argument occurred with the release of *Church of Spies* by Mark Riebling, which provided details of the Pope's involvement in the plots to assassinate Hitler and the development of a new government for shattered Germany. It's hard to accuse someone of being "Hitler's Pope" when behind the scenes that same man is trying to have Hitler killed.

As more and more documents from the Vatican Archives are released, the poor perception of Pope Pius XII by some may continue to swing the other way. Time will tell. Perhaps now that the wartime files are finally open in the Vatican Archives, the answer will be provided once and for all.

Mother Pascalina Lehnert, a Sister of the Holy Cross, Menzingen order, served Eugenio Pacelli tirelessly from 1917, when she first met him when he was *Apostolic Nuncio* in Germany, until his death as Pope in 1958. At a time when women had no role in the Vatican, Mother Pascalina is recognized as the most powerful woman in Vatican history. She was one of the Pope's closest confidants and protectors. Some clergy despairingly called her *La Popessa* (The Lady Pope) as they viewed her as the Pope's gatekeeper and the person through which you had to navigate to get an audience. She was with the Pope when he died at the Castel Gandolfo. Within two hours of his death, some of the powerful members of the *Curia*, who did not like her, evicted her from the Papal apartments. She left with only one small suitcase and the Pope's two pet canaries. That night she wrote in her diary, "The world is on the eve of a new era. Let us not forget all his Holiness has done to help so many people."

She was sent to live at the North American College, where she was given a small room and was once again a simple housekeeper. While there, she worked on her memoirs entitled *His Humble Servant*, which was not published until 1982 thanks to the express wish and desire of Pope John Paul II, who wanted it in print. Published in German, it became a bestselling book. Later, she founded and became Mother Superior of *Casa Pastor Angelicus*, a home for elderly women located outside of Rome. In 1983, at the age of 89, Mother Pascalina died in Vienna while she was there to commemorate the twenty-fifth anniversary of Pius XII's death. Her body was brought back to Rome where she was buried in the Vatican cemetery. Several bishops and Monsignors attended her funeral, including Monsignor Joseph Ratzinger, the future Pope Benedict XVI.

Monsignor Celso Costantini remained in Rome for the rest of his life. His friend, Pope Pius XII, named him a Cardinal in 1953. He soon began readying for publication of his diary, which he had kept all during the events of World War II. The diary provides a great insight into life in Rome and the Vatican during World War II. After the war, he became a staunch defender of the Pope's record against the Nazi atrocities. He was with Pope Pius XII when he died on October 9, 1958. There was strong talk that Cardinal Costantini was in line to be the next Pope. However, during the *sede vacante*, Costantini fell ill and went into the hospital. Two days before the Conclave to elect the new Pope convened, Angelo Cardinal Roncalli, his good friend, visited him in the hospital. Costantini thanked Roncalli for his own wartime effort to save the Jews. He replied, "In all these painful matters, I have referred to the Holy See and simply carried out Pius XII's orders - first and foremost to save human lives." The next night, October 17, 1958, Cardinal Costantini passed away just eight days after the death of his beloved friend, Eugenio Pacelli. Two days later, Cardinal Roncalli was elected Pope and became known as Pope John XXIII. Cardinal Costantini was buried next to his brother in his hometown of Zoppola. His cause for sainthood is presently under investigation.

Israel Zolli remained at the Vatican until late 1944, at which time he was reinstated as the Chief Rabbi of Rome. However, in 1945, he converted to Catholicism, causing a tremendous scandal. He took the baptismal name of Eugenio in homage to Pope Pius XII and all that he had done for the Jewish people. His answer to all of his critics who felt that he had abandoned his Jewish roots, was that he was still a Jew; he was just a Jew who came to believe in the Jewish Messiah. He died on March 2, 1956, ostracized and forgotten.

Monsignor Hugh O'Flaherty, the Scarlett Pimpernel of the

Vatican, hid Jews and Allied POWs in monasteries and convents, at Castel Gandolfo, colleges, and in his network of apartments all across Rome and Italy. Daily he stood on the porch of St. Peter's, in plain view both of the German soldiers across the piazza and the windows of the Pope's apartments. Escaped POWs and Jews would meet him there, and he would offer them protection. Sometimes he would disguise them in the robes of a monsignor or the uniform of a Swiss Guard. His real-life game of hide and seek with Herbert Kappler was legendary. So much so, that O'Flaherty was played by none other than Gregory Peck in the movie about his episodes, *The Scarlet and Black*. The SS commander had tried to kidnap or kill him on many occasions, but O'Flaherty continued to outwit him. After the war, it became known that he and his network had saved over 6,500 Jews and POWs. For many years, it was believed that Monsignor O'Flaherty worked without the support of the Vatican. However, recently the Pope's role in establishing and supporting this network has begun to come forth. After the war, O'Flaherty, every month, visited his old nemesis, Colonel Herbert Kappler in prison and a sort of friendship was born between the two. In 1959, Kappler converted to Catholicism and was baptized by O'Flaherty. O'Flaherty died in Ireland on October 30, 1963. A monument to his memory was erected in Killarney.

Isaac Nola lived at the Vatican for a short period. When the Vatican-run Cinematographic Center commissioned one of Italy's greatest moviemakers, Vittorio de Sica, to make *La Porta del Cielo* (The Gate of Heaven), Isaac was hired as an extra, along with 300 other Jews. The movie was shot inside the Basilica of St. Paul's in Rome and came under the protection of the Vatican. The Jewish extras were allowed to live within the Basilica. Filming was only supposed to last for a few weeks, but De Sica purposely delayed and delayed as a means to protect the Jews while waiting for the Americans to liberate Rome. In the end, De Sica was only pretending to be filming as he had run out of film. With the arrival of the Americans and the ending of filming, Isaac Nola left the Basilica and returned to his beloved Jewish Quarter. After the war, he left Rome and settled in Palestine, and eventually was one of the first residents of the newly formed State of Israel. He married and, with his wife, ran a successful bakery until they both died in a bombing by the PLO of their store in 1969.

Harold Tittmann remained at the Vatican until the liberation of Rome. While at the Vatican, he was the only link between President Franklin D. Roosevelt and Pope Pius XII, as his boss, Myron Taylor, only came to Rome three times during the war years. After the war, Tittmann rose to the rank of Career Ambassador. He died in 1981. In 2004, his remarkable memoirs, which were edited by his son, were released. Tittmann was in a position more than most to evaluate the Pope's actions during the war. While at times he was frustrated with the Pope, in the end, he concluded that the Pope chose the better path and saved many Jewish lives.

Ludwig and Annika Adler lived in Bellafortuna for a year after the war. His composition of *Munich's Tears* brought his composing skills back to the forefront. The piece became so popular that it was used as background music in an Italian film, with Heinrich Bergman recording the solo violin part. With the success of his foray into movie music, Ludwig received an offer to move to Los Angeles and compose movie music for Hollywood. He and Anikka moved and lived in

Los Angeles with their children, which included Josef Adler, whom they formally adopted, as well as another son that was born in the 50s. That child was named Biaggio Sanguinetti Adler. Some of the most famous movie music in the 60s and 70s was scored by the little Jewish composer from Munich.

Heinrich Bergman and his violin moved to New York after the war. He became a violinist at the Metropolitan Opera and married a New York schoolteacher. He had three children, and when he retired from the Met, he became a beloved teacher at The Juilliard School until his death in 1990. His violin was donated by his family to Julliard, where it is still prominently displayed to this day.

Alfred Keller lived in Bellafortuna for a year and was a godfather to little Josef Adler. He spent months after the war trying to determine the fate of Josef's mother, but nothing ever turned up. When the Adlers moved to Hollywood, Alfred decided to move back to Vienna. He opened a bookstore and joined a small orchestra that played out in the piazza for both the locals and the tourists. He never married and lived out the remainder of his life quietly and peacefully in Vienna. He died at the age of 78.

Kurt Hofmann and Elizabetta Adorno remained in Bellafortuna their entire life and were wed, without Kurt becoming a Catholic. They had three children together. Kurt continued working at *Il Paradiso* and eventually became the conductor of the *Opera Orchestra di Bellafortuna*. He became like a son to Giuseppe and Maria Sanguinetti, and upon their death, *Il Paradiso* was turned over to him, which is still in his family today.

Monsignor Mancini remained in Bellafortuna his entire life, caring for his fellow villagers and providing them with moral guidance. He rejected the overtures of the Vatican, through the encouragement of Monsignor Costantini, to come to Rome and become a part of the Holy See. He died at the age of 93 years old, respected and loved by all.

Santo Vasaio picked up production of *Vino di Bellafortuna* after the war at the Boccale Winery. He brought prosperity and pride to all of the villagers of Bellafortuna. Of course, in the 1950s, that prosperity brought in an interest by the Mafia, but that is another story.

Giuseppe and Maria Sanguinetti remained in Bellafortuna all their lives. Giuseppe continued his work at *Il Paradiso* and as the head of the summer Opera Festival, which grew in strength and popularity after the war. He remained a leader in the village and was beloved by all. Maria died at the age of eighty. He would join her only six months later. He was buried on the knoll of the hill overlooking the *Stagno Azzurro* and the amphitheater next to his wife, his friend, his father, his mother, and his son, Father Biaggio Antonio Sanguinetti.

———

IN 1965, twenty years after the end of the war, the Jews, or as they called themselves, the *Juden von Bellafortuna*, arranged a reunion in the village. Every one of them returned with their children and grandchildren. They stayed in the renovated *Albergo di Bellafortuna* and reminisced of a time when the building served as a convent. Monsignor Mancini convinced Colonel Hans-Jurgen Fromm to attend, which he did. Fromm personally shook hands with all of the Jewish refugees. When he met with Anikka, he hugged her for quite a long time, remembering the day that he learned that she was a Jew.

In a ceremony held at the gravesite of Father Biaggio Antonio Sanguinetti, Monsignor Mancini, who had just turned ninety, and Rabbi Josef Adler, who was now a leading Rabbi in New York, said prayers of Thanksgiving. Heinrich, Alfred, and Kurt all stood together. Their friendship, although now separated by a great distance, was still as strong as ever. Their faces beamed with joy as Josef led the people in prayers. Their thoughts drifted back to the train ride and their leap of faith with him so many years ago.

After the prayers had been finished, Ludwig Adler announced that the Yad Vashem Museum of Jerusalem had posthumously recognized Father Sanguinetti as one of the Righteous Gentiles of the Nations, which is the way non-Jews are honored who risked their lives during the Holocaust to save Jews from extermination by the Nazis, and advised that a tree had been planted in his honor along the Avenue of the Righteous. Ludwig Adler handed the award to Giuseppe and Maria Sanguinetti, the parents of the man who had saved his life.

Giuseppe thanked Ludwig. "I accept this award on behalf of my son, but more so in the name of all of the villagers of Bellafortuna, who, when the time came to be counted, stood up for what they knew was right."

A single newspaper reporter from Palermo covered the event. As the event came to a close, the reporter walked up to Heinrich Bergman and asked, "How did you survive? How did you avoid the camps?"

Without hesitation, he responded, "We are alive today because of the generosity and love of Pope Pius XII and the Italian people. *Viva il Papa! Viva l'Italia!*"

The reporter seemed puzzled and asked Heinrich, "The Pope? Wasn't he silent on the whole matter?"

Heinrich smiled broadly. "His actions were more important than mere words. His love of his fellow man unlocked the hearts of the Italian people, who welcomed us with open arms. That is not silence. The constant drumbeat from the Vatican about a world based on a love of God and a love of man was better than an obvious statement that persecuting Jews was wrong. If the German people really needed the Pope to tell them that what was going on was wrong, then his words would not have mattered anyway."

TODAY, the actions of the inhabitants of Bellafortuna concerning the Jews during the war, and all of Italy for that matter, are mostly forgotten and unheralded, while the actions of the Pope are questioned and vilified.

After the war, the Italians who took the Jews in and protected them went on with their lives without shouting to the rooftops of what they had done. They did not look for recognition. Perhaps because deep down, they felt they did nothing out of the ordinary. Not acting would have been inconceivable to the Italian spirit.

Every now and then, one does come across a historian talking about the Italian treatment of the Jews during World War II. Or one may discover a small plaque buried in a museum dedicated to the Italian response to the Holocaust. Or one may hear about specific individuals, such as Gino Bartali, Father Rufino Niccacci, Giorgio Perlasca, and Monsignor Hugh O'Flaherty, as well as others who greatly assisted and protected the Jews. But, for the most part, what the everyday, ordinary Italians and communities did on behalf of the Jews has been Italy's hidden gift.

As for Bellafortuna, there is no plaque, memorial or remembrance for what they did in any museum around the world. However, if one visits *Il Paradiso* today, the wine store in the village of Bellafortuna, there is, located above an antique Victrola and by the drawings of Enrico Caruso, a simple, brown frame. Inside the frame, there is a small yellow Jewish Star with the words *La speranza ci dà la vita* (Hope gives us life) written across the middle, surrounded by signatures. Visitors to the wine store pass by daily without giving the star a single thought. There is no explanation about the item, but for a small card located below the star in the frame that simply says:

Thank you to the villagers of Bellafortuna, Sicily.

AUTHOR'S NOTE

I was always fascinated by how a writer derives his/her inspiration for the story that is being told. I always love reading the author's note and seeing if the author provided to the reader a clue as to what triggered the inspiration for the story. However, how an inspired flame of an idea eventually turns into a full-blown novel is a mystery that, even as a writer, is hard to understand how it happens or explain.

As for my story, I can pinpoint how this story came to be. *A Song for Bellafortuna* is my second novel. One day, I received a review from a reader who loved the novel and the characters. The reader mentioned that she wished the story would continue, as she so much desired to know what happened to the characters as they got older.

A week later, I found myself in Washington D.C. with my wife and our friends on our annual trip to an away New Orleans Saints football game. It is a great way to recharge the batteries, enjoy extended date nights, all the while enjoying sightseeing, great food and drinks with friends. While in D.C, we visited the Holocaust Museum. The Museum does a great job in the way it tells the story of the Holocaust with respect. But there was one display that greatly affected me. It was a room filled with shoes, shoes from the victims of the Holocaust. Not far from this display was a plaque thanking the Italian people for what they had done in saving the Jews during the Holocaust.

Upon my return to New Orleans, and since I am a proud 3rd generation Sicilian-American, I began researching the Italian response to the Holocaust. My research blossomed into this book as I began to contemplate even more that reader's comment wanting to know what happened to the characters that she loved from *A Song for Bellafortuna*. Those characters would only be in their 60s during World War II. I wondered what would have happened to them, and the idea of this novel came blasting into my head. It is a historical fact that Italians hid the Jews. Bellafortuna would be such a location where they would be hidden.

As I began my research, the controversial subject of Pope Pius XII came to the forefront. The deeper and deeper I got into the history, the more and more I became fascinated by the whole controversy. I knew some of the history of Pope Pius XII, but had never studied it like this before. My earliest memories of the Pope come from my father.

Upon graduating from Jesuit High School in New Orleans, my father entered the seminary. He attended Notre Dame Seminary in New Orleans and St. Benedict Seminary in Covington, Louisiana. In 1956, he was sent by Archbishop Rummel of New Orleans to Rome, to study at the North

American College on the Juniculum Hill and at the Pontifical Gregorian University.

While he was in the seminary in Rome, Pope Pius XII died. My father was selected as one of the seminarians to sit vigil with the body at Castel Gandolfo the night before the funeral at St. Peter's. That was quite an honor for the son of Mustache and Sugar LoCoco, his middle-class, first-generation Sicilian-American parents of New Orleans.

Thankfully, for my sisters and me, my father shortly thereafter left the seminary prior to ordination as he heard the pull of another vocation, and he heeded that call - a call to marriage and fatherhood. This novel is dedicated to him – a wonderful man, husband, father, grandfather, friend, and lawyer.

With my research complete, I began writing the story. The inspiration was there, and the story developed.

I will state here for the record that this is a fictional novel, historical fiction, but fiction none the less. After researching and writing this story, I did come away with a few things that a lot of historians are now coming to consensus on. Did the Pope help the Jews? I believe that there is little doubt that he did. Pinchas Lapide, a Jewish theologian and Israeli diplomat to Milan in the 1960s, wrote in *Three Popes and the Jews* the Pope was instrumental in saving close to a million Jews from certain death at Nazi hands. Was he Hitler's Pope? No. That theory has now been completed debunked. Did he participate in plots to remove Hitler from power? Yes. Was he aware that the Jews were being hidden in various religious institutions? He certainly knew. Did the Pope release monasteries and convents from the cloister rule to house Jews? I believe the evidence is strong to back this claim.

As for the controversy of Pope Pius XII, I have attempted to leave open the arguments that he did not do enough. The story is told from his standpoint, from his thought process. But historians or readers can look at it and say yes, but he did not do x, or he did not do y.

Of course, now with the facts of history present, overhanging any discussion of Pius and support for his actions, is the sobering fact that 6 million Jews died at the hands of Hitler and the Nazis. Perhaps an in-depth study of Pius makes us uncomfortable for another reason. We, as human beings, always put trust in this world that evil can be reckoned with; that evil can be overcome. To put it simply, good always triumphs over evil. The study of Pius XII and his response to the Holocaust works against that axiom. I believe it leads to the uneasy conclusion that no matter what the Pope said or did, the only way that Hitler and the Nazis were going to be stopped was with the absolute destruction of the Third Reich. The people who knew that best were the men inside Germany who plotted to remove Hitler by killing him.

The other idea I came away with during the writing of this novel was a sense of pride and awe at the courageous actions of the Italian people in welcoming and hiding so many Jews. The story of what this country did needs to be remembered and told for future generations.

Humility is a concept that has become void in today's world of trumpeting one's actions. Yet, humility, I believe, is the reason why the story of what the Italian people did has gone unnoticed for so long. And perhaps, humility has played into the criticism of Pope Pius' actions. I quote the person who knew him best, Sister Pascalina Lehnert, who stated that "Pius XII, who for the sake of honor and reputation of the Church was forced to do much in public that would otherwise certainly have been done behind the scenes, was always happy when he was able to do good quietly without making a fuss about it. There would be so much to tell if I did not know that this would be contrary to the great Pope's wishes." Quoting from her book, *His Humble Servant – Sister M. Pascalina Lehnert's Memoirs of Her Years of Service to Eugenio Pacelli, Pope Pius XII.*

Now for some insights into the story.

The story of the Jews hiding in the village of Bellafortuna is loosely based on the town of Assisi during the war, where the Assisi Network flourished, an underground network established by the clergy to help and hide the Jews in their community. Bishop Giuseppe Placido Nicolini and Father Rufino Nicacci led this effort. Giuseppe Nicolini, Bishop of Assisi, under orders from Monsignor Giovanni Montini (future Pope Paul VI) of the Vatican, ordered Father Aldo Brunacci to hide the Jews in twenty-six monasteries and convents around Assisi, and provided them with false papers. After the war, both Bishop Giuseppe Placido Nicolini and Father Rufino Nicacci were named Righteous among the Nations by Yad Vashem. When Israel approached Monsignor Montini about an award for his efforts, his simple reply was that he was merely working under the orders of Pope Pius XII.

Any study into the Vatican's response to the Holocaust, one will find time and again the comment by the person being praised that they were merely following the directions of the supreme Pontiff, Pope Pius XII. It's quite curious that the praise is heaped on the rescuer, yet the person they praise as the inspiration for their actions is vilified.

As for the hiding of the 15 Jewish musicians and their families, this is a fictional account. However, there are many, many instances where the Pope was personally involved in the rescue of Jewish refugees, either by issuing fake baptismal certificates, assisting with emigration to America or Palestine, bringing them to work at the Vatican, or hiding them at Castel Gandolfo or at the Vatican and monasteries around Rome. Who in the world at that time did more? It's a fair question.

The escape from the Nazi death train is loosely based on the attack on Convoy XX by three resistance fighters in Brussels. On April 19, 1943, a train carrying 1,631 Jews set off from a Nazi detention camp in Belgium for the gas chambers of Auschwitz. But those three heroic resistance fighters stopped the train, which allowed a large number of the detainees to escape.

All during the war years, Pius XII lead the way to excavate under St. Peter's. The discovery of St. Peter's tomb was announced to the world by Pope Pius XII in December 1950, but he advised at that time that the bones of St. Peter could not be confirmed with certainty. It was finally thorough the expertise of Professor Margherita Guarducci, that the bones of the first Pope were finally discovered and confirmed to be those of St. Peter. On June 26, 1968, Pope Paul VI announced that the relics of Saint Peter had been discovered. And on November 24, 2013, these relics were held by Pope Francis and displayed publicly for the first time.

I have so many people to thank in assisting me with this novel, and I will do so now in no particular order.

Ronald Rychalk: Professor of Law at the University of Mississippi School of Law, and known for his published works on the role of Pope Pius XII in World War II and his critical work against John Cromwell's book, *Hitler's Pope*. His expertise on the subject of Pope Pius XII served me immensely as he was never too busy to answer a question. It has been a pleasure getting to know him. I will always remember fondly our lunch at Mandina's Restaurant in New Orleans and the stories he related to me that day.

Fr. Peter Gumpel, S.J.: He is a Jesuit German priest and a Church Historian. Born in 1923, he had to flee Germany due to his anti-Nazi views, first to France and then to the Netherlands, where during the war he went underground and helped Jews flee. After the war, he became a professor emeritus at the Gregorian University (Rome) and the relator in Pius XII's cause for beatification. Imagine my surprise when he provided to me six beautifully handwritten notes of changes to the manuscript, tweaking a word or adding an anecdote from his vast knowledge on the subject matter.

Barclay Tittmann: The son of Harold Tittmann, Jr., who was chief assistant to Myron Taylor, Franklin Roosevelt's personal representative to the Vatican, between 1940 and 1946. Barclay was of great assistance to me in providing insights into his father's dealings with Pope Pius XII as well what life was like living inside the Vatican during WWII where he resided with his brother and his parents. I thank you for sharing your experiences with me.

Bislan Babatov: Reference Historian at the United States Holocaust Memorial Museum. Bislan provided great details to me concerning the Nazi trains and what transportation was like for the poor Jewish detainees inside.

Johannes Eichhorn: A teacher at Stiftsgymnasium Melk, at the Melk Abbey. His discussion with me about the school and the abbey at Melk was invaluable.

Gary Krupp: A retired Jewish businessman from Long Island, he is the founder of Pave the Way Foundation, who has spent years defending Pope Pius XII in what he describes as "the worst character assassination of the 20th century." He provided to me his book, which shows the actual documents and speeches of Pope Pius XII issued during the War, which was an invaluable asset in my research.

Professor Vincent Lapomarda, S.J.: Author of *The Jesuits and the Third Reich*. Vincent not only suggested that I use Monsignor Celso Costantini as a basis for one of the characters in the novel, but he provided to me the book that was most useful in all of my research; *The Secrets of a Vatican Cardinal: Celso Costantini's Wartime Diaries, 1938-1947*, edited by Bruno Fabio Pighin. His many comments and recommendations on the manuscript were very helpful.

Brian Morgan: A former cloistered monk, former Artistic Director of Opera Quotannis (New York) and former Programme Annotator of the New Orleans Opera, his writings on æsthetics have appeared in various publications, including Opera News and he is the author of the definitive book on the life of Norman Treigle. Brian, who resides in our hometown of New Orleans, has an undying love for Pope Pius XII. His expertise on his life and his exuberance for the man provided me with a great deal of excitement in taking on this endeavor.

Ana Grigoriu-Voicu: Ana lives in Stuggart, Germany, and designed the cover for *Saving the Music*. She is so talented, and the way she takes the concept in my head and converts it into the finished cover is amazing. I thank her for all of her assistance.

Kathy Schott: Every author needs that one reader – that one poor person who has to endlessly read the same paragraphs again and again as slight changes are made. Kathy Schott is that person for me. With degrees in philosophy and secondary education, she, without a doubt, has made this a better book, and for that, I am eternally grateful to her.

Janet LoCoco: An author in her own right whose layout designs and proofreading skills made this the book it is. For that, I am indebted to you as always.

Amazon Reviewer: I would be remiss if I did not thank the Amazon Reviewer who wanted to know more about the characters from my novel, *A Song for Bellafortuna*, as she was the true inspiration for the novel before you.

My Family: I have been blessed to be surrounded by the love of family. To my wife, Wendy, and my children, Matthew and Ellie; to my mom, Lynda, and my sisters Pam and Beth, I thank all of you for your support and love on this writing journey of mine. My wife, Wendy, read a very early version of the novel, and her support for this work never wavered.

I write to tell stories. Stories about the love between people, between communities, and with God. I truly believe that people have an overwhelming desire to live a life of decency, grace and love, in the way that God wants us to live.

As a person who has a passion for music, but with no musical talent, I have been blessed that writing my novels has provided to me an outlet to show my love of music to the world, and hopefully, in some small way, allow a reader to seek out a love and passion for music in their own life. This story about the Jewish musicians was close to my heart. The musicians in my story survived the Holocaust. So many did not. Their music was forever silenced by hatred and madness. There are wonderful organizations around the world that are attempting to bring their music to light. Please offer them support if you are able.

Lastly, a few words about my father, Vincent T. LoCoco, and to whom this book is dedicated. He finally has all the answers. In heaven, he can debate the great philosophers in the morning; in the afternoon, he can play baseball with all of his childhood heroes, like Ted Williams and Joe Dimaggio; and at night, he can attend an opera concert with Enrico Caruso, Jussi Bjoring and Giuseppe di Stefano. That's quite the Three Tenors Concert. He raised my two sisters and me teaching and showing us that the most important thing in life is Love. Love of your fellow man. Love for your spouse. Love for your children. And Love of your God. He was a man who did not even attempt to live a life conformed to our present society. Instead, he lived unashamed of living a life of love and unwavering dedication to God. He showed everyone in the World through the way he lived his life that God was in his soul.

It has been a honor to bring this story to you. I hope it leads you to do your own research and draw your own conclusions, and when the Vatican Archives are opened, to listen with an open mind as to what discoveries are found.

I end this Author's Note with a wonderful quote I came across while in the very early stages of researching that really highlighted the mostly untold actions of the Italian people: It read:

"The Holocaust is to a considerable extent a study in the

potentialities of human evil and inhumanity. However, within all the horror, there were still sparks of good and hope. Italy was one of these sparks, which illuminated human good, compassion, and tolerance. While the evil of the Holocaust cannot be forgotten, its darkness all the more serves to contrast with the light of the Italian response." - Paul Bookbinder: *The Italian refuge: Italy in the overall context of the Holocaust*

It is my hope, in some small way, that this novel will lead the reader to discover for themselves the stories of many courageous Italian men and women who stood up for an entire people, even with the threat of death hanging over them. It truly is a testament to the human spirit. It truly is a testament to the Italian spirit.

Viva Italia!

Chip LoCoco, New Orleans, Louisiana.

ABOUT THE AUTHOR

Vincent B. "Chip" LoCoco has previously written *Tempesta's Dream - A Story of Love, Friendship and Opera* and *A Song For Bellafortuna*. *Saving the Music* is his 2nd book in his Bellafortuna Series. He is an estate planning attorney in New Orleans, where he lives with his wife and two children. Chip is a member of the Italian American Writers Association. For more information, visit him at www.vincentlococo.com.

f facebook.com/Authorchiplococo

🐦 twitter.com/VincentBLoCoco

a amazon.com/author/vincentlococo

MORE INFORMATION

Be sure to check out

A Song For Bellafortuna

Book 1 of Vincent LoCoco's Bellafortuna Series.

If you would like to let others know about this novel, please consider leaving a review on Amazon.

If your group or book club is interested in inviting Mr. LoCoco to discuss his novels or the writing process in person or by Skype, please use the contact form on his website at www.vincentlococo.com.

Made in the USA
Monee, IL
19 July 2020